A Modest Independence

"Matthews immerses readers in the intricate descriptions of exotic locales...Fans of the series will enjoy exploring secondary characters' lives and the truly heroic compromises Tom makes to be with the woman he loves."

-Library Journal

"As always, Matthews' attention to historical accuracy is impeccable...Strong, smart characters and a daring quest result in a Victorian love story with a charmingly modern sensibility."

-Kirkus Reviews

"For fans of sweeping romances with exotic vistas...Jenny Holloway is a powerful female heroine that Jane Austen would be proud of, setting off with an inquisitive mind and a superb sense of exploration...A very excellent and entertaining read."

-Readers Favorite

The Matrimonial Advertisement

"For this impressive Victorian romance, Matthews (*The Viscount and the Vicar's Daughter*) crafts a tale that sparkles with chemistry and impresses with strong character development... an excellent series launch..."

-Publishers Weekly

"Matthews (*The Viscount and the Vicar's Daughter*) has a knack for creating slow-building chemistry and an intriguing plot with a social history twist."

-Library Journal

"Matthews' (*The Pug Who Bit Napoleon*, 2018, etc.) series opener is a guilty pleasure, brimming with beautiful people, damsels in distress, and an abundance of testosterone…A well-written and engaging story that's more than just a romance."

-Kirkus Reviews

A Holiday By Gaslight

"Matthews (*The Matrimonial Advertisement*) pays homage to Elizabeth Gaskell's *North and South* with her admirable portrayal of the Victorian era's historic advancements…Readers will easily fall for Sophie and Ned in their gaslit surroundings."

-Library Journal, starred review

"Matthews' novella is full of comfort and joy—a sweet treat for romance readers that's just in time for Christmas."

-Kirkus Reviews

"A graceful love story…and an authentic presentation of the 1860s that reads with the simplicity and visual gusto of a period movie."

-Readers' Favorite

The Viscount and the Vicar's Daughter

"Matthews' tale hits all the high notes of a great romance novel...Cue the satisfied sighs of romance readers everywhere."
-Kirkus Reviews

"Matthews pens a heartfelt romance that culminates into a sweet ending that will leave readers happy. A wonderfully romantic read."
-RT Book Reviews

The Lost Letter

"The perfect quick read for fans of Regency romances as well as Victorian happily-ever-afters, with shades of Austen and the Brontës that create an entertaining blend of drama and romance."
-RT Book Reviews

"A fast and emotionally satisfying read, with two characters finding the happily-ever-after they had understandably given up on. A promising debut."
-Library Journal

MIMI MATTHEWS

A Modest Independence

PARISH ORPHANS of DEVON

A MODEST INDEPENDENCE
Parish Orphans of Devon, Book 2
Copyright © 2019 by Mimi Matthews

Edited by Deborah Nemeth
Cover Design by James T. Egan of Bookfly Design
Cover Photo by Ildiko Neer / Trevillion Images
Design and Typesetting by Ampersand Book Interiors

E-Book: 978-0-9990364-8-8
Paperback: 978-0-9990364-9-5

www.PerfectlyProperPress.com

# Dedication

In memory of Sapphire
December 24, 2001–February 1, 2019

Author's Note

Colonial India has always been a source of great fascination to me. My paternal grandfather lived there before partition, when it was still under British rule. For nonwhites, like him, there was nothing romantic about the British Raj and I had no intention of romanticizing it in my novel. When writing *A Modest Independence*, I attempted to portray Victorian-era India as it truly was, in all its good and bad. In doing so, I may have inadvertently used period words or descriptions that some might find offensive by modern standards. For this, I humbly apologize.

To that end, a word on nomenclature: In my novel, the residents of various countries are often referred to as "native Indians," "native Egyptians," or just plain "natives." This is a reference to their status as native-born citizens of a particular country—as opposed to colonial occupants of said country. It is not meant as a pejorative.

Chapter One

London, England
February, 1860

Jenny Holloway raised the hood of her wool cloak up over her head. It was snowing in London. Little flurries that fell to the ground, disappearing in the icy black slush that was soaking through the hem of her sensible skirts as she stood outside the Fleet Street law offices of Mr. Thomas Finchley, Esquire.

She'd visited the unassuming building several times before and had no good reason to hesitate. It wasn't as if she was paying a call on a former beau, nor even on an estranged friend. Mr. Finchley was neither of those—not to her, at least. He was only a solicitor.

More to the point, he was *her* solicitor. Which made this a business matter.

She stiffened her spine and made her way up the steps to the front door. A brass plaque fixed beside it bore the names of both Mr. Finchley and Mr. Keane, the solicitor who shared his offices. It was the latter who greeted her when she rang the bell.

"Miss Finchley!" Mr. Keane's thin face lit up in recognition.

Miss Finchley?

Jenny blinked. Had Mr. Finchley told Mr. Keane that she was his sister?

"Do come in out of the cold." Mr. Keane opened the door wide, standing back for her to enter before shutting it behind her. He assisted her out of her wet cloak. "Finchley is occupied with a client. I daren't disturb him. But allow me to offer you a cup of tea." He turned to address a weedy-looking young clerk hovering nearby. "Tea, Mr. Poole! And here. Put the lady's cloak by the fender to dry."

Jenny removed her bonnet and gloves, permitting the young man to take those as well.

"Is your brother expecting you, ma'am?" Mr. Keane asked.

Her brother. How absurd. The two of them looked nothing at all alike. She was tempted to correct Mr. Keane, but common sense kept her silent. There was no good reason to destroy whatever fiction Mr. Finchley had woven on her behalf, especially if it had been spun to protect her reputation. Besides, she wasn't likely to see Mr. Keane again after today. By this time tomorrow, she'd be on board a steamer bound for Calais.

Providing Mr. Finchley cooperated, that is.

"He was aware I'd be arriving in London this week," she said, "but we hadn't yet fixed upon a day for me to call. I daresay I should have made an appointment."

"It mightn't have done you any good." Mr. Keane ushered her up a narrow staircase and down an equally narrow hall to a small anteroom. It was warm and snug, equipped with a set of comfortable-looking chairs and a low wooden table. "Do have a seat. Your brother shouldn't be too much longer." His head tilted slightly at the sound of a raised voice drifting through the closed door of Mr. Finchley's office. "I'd give it another ten minutes."

Jenny lifted her brows. She couldn't make out the words being exchanged behind the door, but the raised voice was definitely female. She reminded herself again that Mr. Finchley's affairs were none of her business. Even so…

But she didn't have time to ponder, for at that very moment the door to Mr. Finchley's office burst open. Shrill words, no longer muffled, spilled out into the anteroom.

"You're ever cruel to me. Trying to punish me. To deny me the things I want most in life. It's your way of getting revenge on me. Don't say it isn't." The woman gave a dramatic sniffle. "If you cared for me at all, you'd increase my allowance. It's the least you owe me."

"I don't owe you anything." Mr. Finchley's deep voice was quiet, his words hardly audible.

"*You ruined my life!*" The woman's voice elevated to as-yet-unreached heights as she at last emerged through the open door of Mr. Finchley's office. She was garbed in a fashionable silk and velvet afternoon gown, a velvet-trimmed hat perched atop a head of impressively coiffed mahogany curls.

Jenny stared at her. She'd half expected a cheaply clad young tart. Instead, Mrs. Culpepper was a mature woman. A beauty, to be sure, but not one in her first bloom.

"And what are you looking at, madam?" She seared Jenny with a poisonous glare. "I'll thank you to keep your eyes in your head." She sniffled again, though Jenny could see no evidence of tears, and with a swish of starched petticoats, marched from the room.

Jenny waited for Mr. Finchley to storm from his office and follow after her, but there was no sign of him. Perhaps he didn't care enough about his relationship with Mrs. Culpepper to try and salvage it.

He certainly hadn't cared when their own friendship had fallen apart last October.

"I say," Mr. Keane muttered in embarrassment. "Where has Poole got to?"

"Here, sir!" Mr. Keane's clerk trotted down the hall, a silver tray in his hands.

"Is that tea?" Mr. Finchley at last emerged from his office. He was dressed in a well-tailored black suit, his frock coat worn open to reveal a single-breasted waistcoat draped by the gold chain of his pocket watch. He looked calm and composed. Perfectly at his ease. One would never know he'd just been engaged in a heated altercation with a woman.

Well…perhaps his dark brown hair was a little mussed. As if he'd lately run his hands through it. Other than that, he looked as ordinary as ever.

If one could ever call Thomas Finchley ordinary.

Jenny clasped her hands tight in front of her. She'd hoped that when they met again, she'd be indifferent to him. That she'd feel nothing at the sight of his handsome face and figure.

Not that most people would have described Mr. Finchley as handsome. Bookish, maybe. Or scholarly. A gentleman with a weight of responsibility on his shoulders. Someone to confide in. To solve one's problems, for a fee. Not a man to make a woman's heart beat faster.

Jenny's heart didn't seem to understand that, the treacherous thing. It was thumping quite madly. As if it were only yesterday he'd laughed with her and danced her around the parlor in Half Moon Street. As if he'd never lied to her. Had never played her for a fool.

It was those eyes of his that caused her such alarming palpitations. So worn and wise—and so much older than all the rest of him. As if they'd seen everything, experienced everything. They weren't the eyes of an overworked solicitor. Not any that she'd ever seen. No. Thomas Finchley had the eyes of a weary angel.

All he need do was look at her and her pulse lost its rhythm.

But he wasn't looking at her now. He didn't seem to notice her at all. His attention was entirely fixed on the dratted tea tray. A typically selfish male, only bestirring himself at the prospect of food and drink. But then he turned his head and those light blue eyes met hers. His gaze was solemn behind the lenses of his silver-framed spectacles and…not at all surprised.

He'd been aware of her the whole time. He'd known she was there, even as Mrs. Culpepper stormed from his office. Possibly even from the moment Jenny had first crossed the threshold.

Was there anything Thomas Finchley didn't know?

She moistened her lips. Her mouth was dry as the Sahara. She couldn't summon the barest croak. Not that there was any need for speech. The silence between them spoke volumes. Indeed, the very air seemed to echo with the last words she'd uttered to him. Words to which he'd offered no response.

What sort of man are you?

"Put the tray down in my office, Poole," Mr. Finchley said. And then: "Miss Holloway? Will you join me?"

"Miss Holloway?" Mr. Keane's eyes darted from her to Mr. Finchley and back again. "Oh dear, and to think I've been addressing you as Miss Finchley."

"One name's as good as the other." Mr. Finchley motioned toward his office door, a hint of impatience in the gesture. "Ma'am?"

Jenny smoothed her skirts. This was business. Strictly business. "Yes, of course." She walked past him to enter his office, careful that her gown didn't brush his legs as she went by. She wanted no illusion of intimacy between them. They might have met before—might have dined together and danced together—but they were as good as strangers. The Mr. Finchley she'd known last year had been an illusion. A convenient mask behind which the real Thomas Finchley hid himself to achieve his ends.

Who the real man was, she neither knew nor cared.

He shut the door behind her. "For what it's worth, I never claimed you were my sister. I simply refrained from correcting Keane's assumption."

"Would it have been so scandalous for an unrelated female to call on you as I did last October?" Jenny hadn't had much choice at the time. There had been no one else to turn to after the Earl of Castleton had dismissed her from her position as lady's companion to his niece, Lady Helena.

"Not scandalous, no. Only out of the ordinary."

"And, therefore, worthy of remark."

"Precisely."

She cast a cursory look round his office. It was large and fairly well organized. A monstrous barrister's desk formed the heart of it, its surface covered in neat stacks of papers and rolled documents tied with ribbon. The walls were lined with bookcases filled with row upon row of leather-bound books, their gold-stamped spines unreadable behind closed glass doors.

"You arrived in London only this morning," he said.

It wasn't a question. She answered it nonetheless. "I caught the early train from Abbot's Holcombe."

She'd spent the past three months living with Mr. Thornhill and Lady Helena at Greyfriar's Abbey, their isolated estate on the North Devon coast. Neither had expected her to remain on in her role as Helena's companion. Certainly not after Helena had settled a generous sum of money on her.

Five thousand pounds, to be precise.

Helena called it a modest independence. To Jenny it was an absolute fortune. "I saw no reason to delay," she said.

"Quite." Mr. Finchley went to the tea tray. "Will you sit down?"

Jenny took a seat in one of the upholstered chairs opposite his desk. She arranged her skirts about her legs, ignoring the brief twinge of self-consciousness about the age—and relative plainness—of her woolen gown. It didn't matter one jot whether or not it was as stylish as that worn by his last client. She hadn't come to London to engage in a fashion contest with a highflyer.

Mr. Finchley poured them each a cup of tea, not bothering to ask how she took hers. There was no need. They'd shared countless cups of tea during their brief acquaintance.

"Thank you," she said.

Mr. Finchley inclined his head. "I trust Thornhill and Lady Helena are well?"

"They were in excellent health when I left them."

He sat down behind his desk. "And Mr. Cross? How is he adjusting to the new mistress of Greyfriar's Abbey?"

Neville Cross was yet another resident of the Abbey. A childhood friend of both Mr. Finchley and Mr. Thornhill, he'd suffered a head injury as a boy that still affected his speech—though not, Jenny suspected, his reasoning.

"Mr. Cross is quite well." Jenny took a delicate sip of her tea. "He and Helena get on famously." She hesitated before adding, "But it can be a bit trying to live with a newlywed couple. The pair of them are in their own world much of the time. One feels like an intruder."

A vast understatement.

What one felt was inadequate.

She'd never been the sort to pine after love and affection. She was too sensible. Too pragmatic. But being in Helena and Mr. Thornhill's company day in and day out—seeing the little touches they shared, the whispered confidences and private glances—had begun to make her feel a certain emptiness. A lack of something in her life.

No doubt Mr. Cross felt the same.

"Is that why you left in such haste?" Mr. Finchley asked.

"You think my decision to come to London was hasty?"

"Wasn't it? You might have stayed at the Abbey through the winter. Lady Helena has made it quite comfortable, I understand."

"Indeed, she has. It's filled with fine furnishings now, and there are new draperies, paint, and paper on the walls. You could have seen the improvements yourself if you'd come for Christmas."

His expression was unreadable. It registered neither embarrassment, nor regret. "Business has been unrelenting of late. I made my excuses to Thornhill."

"Is that all that kept you away? Business?"

"What else?"

She shrugged one shoulder. "I don't know. I thought, perhaps, you may have some other reason for avoiding a visit to Devon."

"I'm not Thornhill, Miss Holloway. I don't enjoy tormenting myself with the past. To me, North Devon is no different from Sussex or Cornwall."

Jenny's conscience twinged. In all the many hours she'd fretted over Mr. Finchley's failure to join them for Christmas, she'd never once given a thought to his childhood connection to the region. She'd assumed that *she* was the reason he hadn't come to Devon.

Only now, seated across from him at his desk and surrounded by all the manifestations of his profession, did she comprehend the inherent selfishness of such an assumption. She wasn't the center of Thomas Finchley's world. Far from it. She was just an unremarkable female he'd known for a brief moment in time. Neither rich, nor beautiful, nor even particularly sweet-tempered. Merely a friend of a friend of a friend. A connection so tenuous it hardly merited thought.

"I have no good reason to avoid visiting Thornhill and Lady Helena," Mr. Finchley continued, "save the demands of my clients."

"Your clients appear to be excessively demanding."

Another gentleman might have flushed at her words. Mr. Finchley only looked at her, his countenance solemn and possibly a little tired. "You're alluding to Mrs. Culpepper."

"Do you have many other clients who accuse you of ruining their lives? It doesn't seem a good business practice."

"Mrs. Culpepper is a special case."

Jenny raised her teacup back to her lips. "She's very handsome."

And there it was. The slightest hint of red on Mr. Finchley's neck, just above the line of his black cravat and starched white linen collar. A blush so faint she might have missed it if she wasn't looking. "Miss Holloway—" He started and stopped. "I wouldn't read too much into what you overheard."

"I'm simply making conversation."

He shook his head. "Why are you here?"

"For my money, naturally. I thought that was plain."

"Yes, but…it's snowing out. Not ideal weather for making the journey to London. You'd have been better off delaying. Whatever you wish to do with the money Lady Helena has given you can surely wait until spring."

She lowered her teacup back to its saucer. "It's not winter everywhere in the world, sir."

"Ah." He leaned back in his chair. "You wish to travel."

"Yes. I wish to…that is…I *intend* to leave for India without delay."

If he was surprised by her revelation, he didn't show it.

She pressed on. "I've already obtained my travel documents. The only difficulty lies in my need for ready funds. Since Helena has appointed you guardian over my money, it seems I must apply to you for my needs. Though I must say I find it rather an inconvenience."

Mr. Finchley continued to look at her, his regard never wavering. "Why India?"

"Am I obliged to explain myself to you? Is that how this works?"

"You owe me no explanations. I'm neither your father, nor your brother to command one. However, Lady Helena has reposed certain obligations in me as trustee—"

"Not because of any concerns about my capacity for managing my own money. You realize that, don't you? It's only because I'm her closest friend and you're Mr. Thornhill's. She wishes us to get along together."

"I wish the same," he said.

"Do you?" After the antics of his last client, she supposed he must expect her to rage at him. To lose her temper and storm about his office. As if she would ever make herself so ridiculous.

"Yes, I do. But you're obviously still angry with me."

Jenny's temper flared. He was so calm. So infuriatingly steady and reasonable. Did nothing in the world rattle his resolve?

Well, he'd soon learn that her resolve was just as unshakable as his own.

"Not any longer," she said. "Not even then, really."

"No?"

"If I was angry with anyone, it was with myself. I trusted you too easily."

"And I breached that trust, did I? Simply by counseling Thornhill on how he might annul his marriage? He was my client, Miss Holloway. He still is."

"Yes, yes, I understand. The solicitor-client relationship is sacrosanct. But it doesn't follow that you needed to squire me about town as if you were enjoying my company. To talk with me and dance with me as if you were my friend, when all the while you—"

"I *am* your friend."

Jenny was horrified to feel her lips tremble. She told herself to turn the subject. There was no point in confronting any of this head-on. It surely didn't matter anymore. And yet…

She was incapable of holding her tongue.

"I thought you were," she said. "But when I looked into your eyes that day outside the house in Half Moon Street, I didn't see a friend looking back at me. I saw a stranger. A man who would do anything to achieve his ends—and those of his client."

"I won't dispute the latter. It's who I am. My clients must always come first. Before friends and family. Even before myself." He paused. "I apologize if I hurt you in the process. It wasn't my intention."

Her gaze dropped to the contents of her teacup. She didn't know what to do with his apology. She wasn't certain he meant it. For all she knew it was nothing more than a gentlemanly platitude uttered to placate her. "It doesn't matter." Good lord, now her voice was trembling as well. She cleared her throat, striving to make her next words as brisk and businesslike as possible. "It isn't as if there's a need for us to cry friends. Indeed, once you've released my funds, I don't expect we'll have any cause to see each other again."

Mr. Finchley was silent for a long moment.

And then another.

Jenny's stomach tightened with apprehension. "Is there a difficulty with you giving me my money? I don't require the entire balance. I only need enough for travel expenses."

"Are these travel expenses for you alone?"

"Who else would they be for?"

"You're a young lady. Surely you'll wish to hire a companion or a—"

"Hire a companion?" She failed to contain a laugh. "I *am* a companion. Or, rather, I *was*. And as for being young, I'll have you know, sir, that I've just passed my twenty-eighth birthday. I'm what society charitably refers to as a dyed-in-the wool spinster. A veritable artifact collecting dust on the shelf."

"I hardly think——"

"Do you imagine I mind such labels? Not a bit of it. I embrace them. I've longed for spinsterhood these many years. And now I've been given an independence, I intend to take full advantage of the state."

"I beg your pardon, but…" Mr. Finchley's eyes betrayed a hint of exasperation. "You're no gray-haired grandmother. Unless you mean to announce your age to every person you meet——"

"Perhaps I shall."

"Miss Holloway——"

"A spinster isn't so different from a widow, you know. We're afforded a great deal of freedom in the world. Society will think nothing of my traveling alone."

"Society may be disposed to accept it, but there are men—— I'll not call them gentlemen——for whom your advanced years won't act as a repellent. Without a companion or a maidservant, you'll be fair game for all sorts of mistreatment."

"I can take care of myself, thank you."

"I don't doubt it. But as a lady, there's only so much you're capable of defending against. You simply haven't the strength. Now, if you were to take a maid and a footman on your travels, then——"

"I'm not hiring a companion," she said firmly. "Nor am I surrounding myself with a legion of stuffy British servants. I mean to experience the world. To have an adventure. Not to recreate the same tedious environment I've been hostage to here in England."

His brows lowered. "You feel as if you've been a hostage? It was my impression that Lady Helena treated you as a sister. A friend."

"She has. Always. But Helena doesn't exist in isolation. To everyone else in society, I was only her companion. Not her sister, as you say. Certainly not her friend. When her uncle ascended to the title, he had no qualms about tossing me into the street."

"Lord Castleton was a blackguard, I won't dispute that."

Jenny didn't know many who would. When Helena's elder brother, Giles Reynolds, 6th Earl of Castleton, had been reported dead in India, her uncle had not only taken his title, he'd also attempted to take the vast fortune Giles had left to his sister. The means he'd employed to do so had been brutal, indeed.

"But he's well out of the picture now," Mr. Finchley said. "Unless something has changed?"

"No," she admitted. "He's still cooling his heels at the family seat in Hampshire. He's made no more threats to any of us."

"Then you have no legitimate reason to abandon your life with Thornhill and Lady Helena."

"No legitimate reason?" Jenny was incredulous. "Do you have any idea what it's like to exist in the background of other people's lives? To be an afterthought? A nonentity, neither proper lady, nor proper servant? I can count on one hand the number of people who've actually seen me, who've paid me any attention. It's no life for anyone, least of all for a woman like me."

"A woman like you," he repeated. "Are you so different from every other lady in your position?"

"Look at me." She gestured at herself with her teacup, causing the contents to slosh against the rim. "I wasn't created to shrink into the shadows. I'm strong and stubborn and opinionated. I need more from life than a half existence. I need the sand and the sea and the baking sun of distant lands." She stilled her hand before her tea spilled over and soiled her skirts. "But you're a man. You couldn't possibly understand."

Mr. Finchley leaned forward. For the first time, his face betrayed a flicker of emotion. It was gone before she could grasp it. "I understand more than you know."

She exhaled, feeling somewhat deflated. Of course he understood. He'd grown up in an orphanage in Abbott's Holcombe along with Mr. Thornhill, Mr. Cross, and another boy. Helena hadn't confided the particulars, but Jenny knew enough to appreciate that the experience had been rather traumatic for all of them.

"Yes, well, then you must see why I want to leave this place. I need to experience the world as a whole person. To live among people who never knew me as a lady's companion."

"Must you go as far away as India to do so?"

"As to that…" She fidgeted with her teacup. "You did say that your clients always come first, didn't you? Before your friends or even yourself."

"It's the truth, I'm afraid."

She met his eyes. Her heart gave another traitorous thump. "Am I your client now?"

His regarded her steadily from behind his spectacles. "You are."

"And whatever I tell you—"

"Anything you say to me will be kept in strict confidence."

Jenny nodded. She'd thought as much. "You asked me why I wished to travel to India. It's because I want adventure. To see the world and to live in far-off places. But I have another, far more compelling reason." She bit her lip, fully aware of the folly of what she was about to confess. "I want to find Giles Reynolds, the missing Earl of Castleton."

Mr. Finchley didn't even blink. He knew as well as she that Giles's body had never been recovered. To this day, Helena still clung to the hope that her brother was alive out there somewhere. "You and the private inquiry agent that Thornhill has already employed."

"Oh, him."

"Yes, him. What makes you think you'll succeed where he hasn't?"

"Because, unlike that unassuming fellow, I'll actually be traveling to India forthwith. I won't be delaying on every pretext, dithering here and there in England to absolutely no avail. Besides, I know Giles. And, if what I suspect is true, that agent will never be able to run him to ground."

"If the inquiry agent can't find him, Miss Holloway, it's surely because he's dead."

"No," Jenny said. "If he can't find him, it's because Giles doesn't want to be found."

Chapter Two

Tom removed his spectacles so that he could massage the bridge of his nose. It was a reflexive action, one he performed multiple times per day without giving it a thought.

Only now did it occur to him how he must look without them.

He wasn't an insecure man, merely a realistic one. He understood full well that his spectacles were more than an aid to his poor vision. They were a barrier between him and the rest of the world. A scholarly prop behind which he hid the plainness of his person.

And he *was* plain. If he ever had any doubt on that score, he need only consult the evidence of his shaving mirror. He was tall but not too tall. Broad-shouldered but lanky. His hair was a commonplace shade of brown, and his lean face was possessed of two nondescript blue eyes, a once broken nose, and bowed lips that were slightly thin.

None of which would matter if Jenny Holloway wasn't sitting across from him.

He settled his spectacles back onto his nose. Miss Holloway's face and figure once again shifted into focus. "Are you suggesting that the 6th Earl of Castleton has chosen to hide himself away somewhere in India?"

"It has occurred to me, yes." She placed her teacup and saucer down on his desk. His gaze flicked to her hands. They were slim, with elegant, tapered fingers. He recalled how well they had fit in his when he'd danced with her. "You must understand something about Giles. He was ever moody and quiet. Never more so than after his and Helena's mother died."

Tom listened in silence. He knew of the tragic fate of the late Countess of Castleton. She'd suffered from acute melancholia after the birth of her children. Her husband had committed her to a private asylum, where she'd remained until her death some years later.

"Giles was never happy in England," Miss Holloway said. "There are too many bad memories here. Too many reminders of what happened to his mother. Why do you think he didn't return home and assume the title after his father passed away?"

"Happy or no, I hardly think he'd remain in India knowing that his sister was in peril."

"How could he know? No one else did. Not until that editorial was printed last October. And if the inhabitants of London didn't know, how was Giles to learn of it all the way in India?"

Tom opened his mouth to respond only to shut it again. She had a fair point. The editorial in the *London Courant* that revealed how Lady Helena's uncle had tried to have her put away had only gone to press in October. How long before news of it reached India? A month? Two months? Longer?

"As far as he knew," Miss Holloway continued, "Helena was safe and well. He'd arranged it so, don't you see? He left her all of his fortune. Perhaps he never intended to come home at all."

"This is so much conjecture."

"I have reason to think it more than that." She opened the little cloth reticule at her side and withdrew what appeared to be a crumpled piece of paper.

No. Not a paper.

A letter.

She held it tight in her hands. "Giles wrote to me a month before the siege of Jhansi."

A surge of jealousy took Tom unaware. "You exchanged letters with him?"

"There's nothing out of the ordinary in that."

He schooled his features. She was right. He had no reason at all to be jealous. She wasn't his sweetheart. He had no claim on her at all. She was only a friend.

An exceptionally lovely friend, the sight of whom made his heart beat faster. Made his palms damp and his mouth dry.

It was that dratted auburn hair of hers. Thick and gleaming, coiled up in plaits at the base of her neck. The strands were more red than brown. Almost flaming in their vibrancy.

He wondered what it looked like unbound.

"I assure you," she said, "it's quite unexceptionable."

What?

It took him a moment to regain the thread of their conversation. He cleared his throat. "No. I suppose not. You're related, aren't you?"

"After a fashion." She paused before explaining, "My maternal grandmother was a very distant cousin of Helena and Giles's grandmother. It's not much in the way of aristocratic pedigrees. Barely enough to persuade Helena's father to take me on as her companion. But he did. I was with her for a very long while and, consequently, I—"

"You came to know her brother."

A flush of color rose in her cheeks. "Yes."

Tom's senses flickered a warning. "How well did you know him?"

"Well enough." She extended the letter to him. "This was the last time he ever wrote to me."

He took it from her hand. "May I?"

"Please do."

He smoothed out the creases of the letter on his desk. It looked as if it had been balled up at some point. Crumpled and thrown into a dustbin, perhaps. It wasn't the first such letter Tom had encountered in this condition. The sort rescued from a fireplace grate before the secrets within could be incinerated.

"I apologize for the state of it," Miss Holloway said.

He glanced up at her from behind his spectacles. The blush in her cheeks had darkened. The sight of it made his chest tighten. Had there been something between Miss Holloway and Lady Helena's brother? "I've seen worse," he said.

At that, he bent his head and began to read.

My Dear Jenny,

I trust you're keeping yourself out of trouble. I've had a letter from Helena lately, but nothing from you since Michaelmas. You're not still angry with me, are you? There's only so many times a fellow can apologize.

If you were anyone else, I suppose you would have written by now, pleading with me to come home and propose or some such rot. But you've always been more sensible than that. You know I have no desire to marry and set up my nursery. I never have. Besides, it didn't mean anything. You and I are friends, that's all.

It's beastly hot here at the moment. The lads and I have taken to swimming in the river in the evenings. Afterward, we lie out on the bank and look up at the stars. You never saw so many. They make one feel quite small and unimportant. A man could lose himself amongst so much nature and humanity.

There was a fellow at the bazaar last week selling Kashmiri shawls. I bought one for you. It's the exact colors of the spices they use to season our food. Orange and yellow and brown. They look quite dull until you taste them, and then they fair burn the roof of your mouth off.

I shan't be able to replicate any of this at home. Only a fool would try. And despite my past behavior (for which I again most humbly beg your pardon), you know I'm no fool.

Quelling this rebellion is brutal and bloody, yet there are days I pray my duties will never end. I don't miss the rain and fog one jot. A man can breathe here. Can really feel alive. It's all colors and flavors and heat. The natives are quite good chaps, as well. One can't help but sympathize.

I must sign off now. Please take care of my sister. And take care of yourself. You deserve better than a fellow like me.

Fond regards,
  Giles

Tom lifted his gaze back to Miss Holloway's face. He felt slightly queasy. "What is it that he was apologizing for?"

Miss Holloway's chin lifted a notch, even as her blush deepened to scarlet. "He kissed me."

"When?"

"When he was last home on leave."

"I see." He slowly folded the letter. "Did he make you any promises?"

"None at all. It was simply a kiss. I daresay Giles kissed a great many girls. It meant absolutely nothing to him."

Tom's jaw hardened. The late earl was beginning to sound like a scoundrel of the first order. He searched Miss Holloway's face. It was no less arresting than her hair. Dark brows and equally dark lashes framed eyes that were neither blue nor green. They were the exact color of the sea that raged beneath the cliffs of Abbot's Holcombe. A shade which provoked a bitter longing in his chest. "What about you?" he asked.

"What about me?"

"Did it mean anything to you?"

She plucked the letter from his desk and returned it to her reticule. "Such events loom large in the life of a young woman."

"Undoubtedly."

"When his letter arrived, I crumpled it up and pitched it into the coal scuttle. It took me a good half day to regain my composure."

"At which point you retrieved it."

"And thank goodness I did. We received news of his disappearance a month later. Had I destroyed his final letter, I'd never have been able to forgive myself." She shut the silk-corded drawstrings of her reticule with a snap. "But all that's beside the point."

"Which is?"

She gave a huff of impatience. "Didn't you notice all the times he mentioned how happy he was in India?"

"I don't believe he used those exact words."

"No, but…he spoke highly of the weather and the stars and the spiced foods. He said a man could get lost there. He even said he sympathized with the natives and their cause."

"That's not unheard of. Thornhill is a great sympathizer of the natives' cause as well. He believes we have no right to be there."

"Giles never went that far. Not that I can remember. But you must see that he had an affinity for the place. Taken as a whole, it's only logical to conclude—"

"That he preferred India to England? It's certainly possible. However, a gentleman of his class would prize duty above all else. He could hardly have remained there in good conscience. He would have known—would have accepted—that he was needed at home. Not only to take up his position as head of the family, but to take his seat in the House of Lords."

"What if he didn't wish to come home? Not only because of his mother and all the bad associations he had, but because of me? Perhaps he thought I would make a clamor about his having kissed me. Appeal to Helena or something of that nature. He feared being forced into marriage above all things."

"Miss Holloway…I appreciate what you're proposing, but it's still only conjecture."

Her face fell. "I know it isn't enough to justify much hope."

"There's always reason to hope," he said. "But…"

"But?"

"It isn't enough to justify a journey to India."

"It needn't. I'll already be there. What would it hurt if, during my visit, I did a little investigating of my own?"

"Aside from the fact that you're not a professional inquiry agent?"

"One doesn't have to be a professional to ask basic questions. All one need do is employ a bit of logic. A bit of common sense. And I'm more than equipped to do that, whatever you might think."

"What I think is that you would be a vulnerable female in a foreign land. Lest you forget, India hasn't shown itself to be very kind to vulnerable British females of late."

"The uprising ended two years ago. Things have settled down now. It isn't as if I'll be walking into a battleground."

"There are some injustices people don't forget. Not in two years. Not ever."

She gave him a long look. For a moment, he felt as if she could see straight into his soul. "You and I are never going to see eye to eye on this, are we?"

"Probably not."

"Does that mean you're refusing to give me the necessary funds?"

Tom ran a hand over his hair. It would have been easy to play the villain. To bully and condescend to her, or to tie her up with confusing legal jargon. He spent most of his days doing just that. But he hadn't the heart to thwart Miss Holloway. He understood only too well what it was like to thirst for freedom, to dream of starting one's life anew.

No. He didn't intend to refuse her. What he intended to do was to offer her an alternative.

If she was dead set on traveling to India—and equally set on refusing to take along any proper English servants—he'd employ Indian servants to accompany her. He could think of two likely candidates off the top of his head, a brawny man-servant and his kinswoman, who were presently working in a disreputable establishment in London's East End. Tom had met them on a case last year and had found them to be both trustworthy and resourceful.

It would take him a day—possibly two—to arrange it. And then...

He'd simply present Miss Holloway with a fait accompli.

"It's an easy enough question," she said.

He exhaled heavily. "Miss Holloway...this requires a longer conversation than I presently have time for."

She stiffened. "Are you dismissing me?"

"No," he said. And then again, more forcefully, "*No*. It's only that, had I known you were calling today, I could have blocked out the afternoon for you. As it is, I'm required elsewhere."

"By Mrs. Culpepper?"

He scowled. "She has nothing to do with it. Whatever you're thinking—"

"I wouldn't presume—"

"I have other clients who make demands on my time. One rather specifically at the moment. I can't ignore an appointment I've made with him just because you happen to turn up. You'll have to call again tomorrow." He glanced at his diary. "At one o'clock, perhaps?"

"I'm not calling again tomorrow. I'm here now. And I don't see what the difficulty is in authorizing a withdrawal at the bank—"

"Miss Holloway—"

"I want this settled today."

"Impossible. I'm not free again until well past seven."

She folded her arms. "I'll wait."

"Don't be ridiculous."

"Well? What do you propose I do?"

He leaned back in his chair. He knew what he'd like to propose. But it wasn't a good idea. He was barely hanging on to his professionalism as it was. To be alone with her would be absolute folly. Nevertheless... "I could stop by Half Moon Street this evening."

He'd leased an elegant little house there for her last year. She'd lived in it for a short time after the present Earl of Castleton had cast her off without a penny. Tom had visited her on occasion. It had all been completely aboveboard. Indeed, within days, Justin Thornhill had taken over the lease himself.

"She's my wife's relation," he'd said. "It's only right that I see to her lodging."

Later, when Justin and Helena had come to London, the four of them had spent a great deal of time together in Half Moon Street. They'd dined together. Danced together. Faced down newspaper reporters and society busybodies.

Tom had many fond memories of those days—most of which prominently featured Miss Holloway.

"I'm not staying at the house in Half Moon Street," she said.

His brows snapped together. "*What?*"

"I've taken a room at a ladies' hotel near Hyde Park."

"Why? The house is in perfect order. Surely Thornhill and Lady Helena—"

"They offered for me to stay there. Of course they did. It was my own decision to stay elsewhere. I'll only be in town for a short time."

"What has that to do with it?"

"It needn't have anything to do with anything. Where I stay is my own choice, and I choose to stay at a hotel."

"Don't be stubborn merely for the sake of it. The house in Half Moon Street is far more comfortable than any hotel. It's safer for you as well. Not to mention more convenient for me."

"As if that would be any concern of mine," she retorted.

"No, I don't suppose it would be. However, as your solicitor, it would be easier—and far more discreet—to meet with you this evening if you were at the house." He hesitated, feeling more than a little out of his element. "We could…we could have dinner together."

Her brows lifted almost to her hairline. "You wish to *dine* with me?"

Tom inwardly winced. Good lord, did she have to make the prospect sound so appalling? "It would be a business dinner. A chance for us to speak candidly with one another."

"If all you want to do is make excuses for why you're not giving me my money—"

"Give me some credit. I solve things. That's what I do. When I see you tonight, I'll bring a solution to this dilemma. All I require is a few hours to settle affairs with my other client. Will you grant me that much?"

Miss Holloway looked thoroughly put out. For several seconds, he was convinced she would say no. That she would storm from his office just as Mrs. Culpepper had before her—and to much more devastating effect. His breath stopped in his chest.

"Will you?" he asked again.

She frowned, her gaze fixed on the edge of his desk. As if she were weighing the assets and liabilities on either side of a business proposal. And then her eyes met his. "Very well."

Some of the tension seeped from Tom's muscles. "Thank you."

Within minutes, she was gone. Bundled into a hansom cab bound for her hotel. She promised to gather her things and remove to Half Moon Street. Tom would join her there at eight.

Or so he hoped.

He glanced at the clock on the mantelshelf as he shoved a sheaf of papers into his leather attaché case. It was already half three. He'd have to walk fast.

It was snowing as Tom exited Viscount Atwater's mausoleum-like mansion in Grosvenor Square. His hat, coat, and gloves provided little protection against the chill. This wasn't the sort of weather for striding through Mayfair. This was the sort of weather in which a fellow should be at home in front of the fire, surrounded by his family.

But Tom had neither home, nor family.

By choice, he reminded himself.

Had he wished to settle down, plenty of women would have been happy to oblige him. He was fit and intelligent and possessed of a comfortable income. So what if he was a little plain? He had all of his hair and teeth, didn't he? That was more than most men of his age could boast.

Would it be so bad to marry?

The situation had seemed to work out well enough for Justin. He and Lady Helena were happy together. Ridiculously so. But theirs was a love match. They relied on each other. Trusted each other. While Tom... Well. He relied on no one. Trusted no one.

Even Justin, his best friend and the closest thing he had to a brother, was not privy to all of his secrets. Tom didn't wish to burden him—or disappoint him.

How would Justin Thornhill react if he learned some of the secrets Tom had been keeping? Dark secrets uncovered during their time together in the orphanage. Dangerous secrets gleaned during the course of his employment as Mr. Fothergill's clerk. Secrets built upon secrets, each one mounting upon the other until Tom felt as if he bore the weight of the world on his shoulders.

The day that Josiah Fothergill had first visited the orphanage in Abbot's Holcombe, Tom had thought him an odd-looking fellow. Though not much above forty, the gimlet-eyed solicitor had already had the look of an old man. His head had been bent, his back slightly slumped. Had it been the weight of all those secrets? The unrelenting burden of so many confidences—so many crimes?

Fothergill had been looking for a boy to take on as his clerk. Someone he could raise in his likeness. Someone to help him to bear the burden.

His shrewd gaze had settled on Tom. An underfed wisp of a twelve-year-old with a pair of bent spectacles perched on his still-swollen nose.

"Who did this to you?" Fothergill had asked him, examining the poorly set break.

"No one," Tom had said.

He'd thought his expression bland. But Fothergill had seen something in his face. Something Tom used to think was hidden from view.

"It was rage," Fothergill had told him many years later. "Raw, unmitigated rage." He'd looked at Tom with an expression of grim approval. "You hide it better now."

Fothergill had officially retired from practice two years ago. Or so he claimed. But Tom felt himself just as much under the old solicitor's power as he'd been as a child. There was no end to his apprenticeship, it seemed. No point at which he'd be free to go his own way.

He stepped down from the pavement and crossed the busy street. Carriages rattled by, driven by coachmen swathed in greatcoats and mufflers, their heads tipped down against the fresh-falling snow.

"What-ho, Finchley!" the driver of a hansom cab called out as Tom weaved through the oncoming traffic.

Tom raised a gloved hand in greeting. If he'd learned anything from Fothergill, it was to remain on good terms with the working and criminal classes. As a consequence, he had friends everywhere. At least, he supposed one might call them friends. He knew about their lives; about their jobs, their wives, and their children. They, in turn, knew nothing about him.

What was there to know?

He was a solicitor. It was the sum total of his existence.

As for the past, he'd long ago learned to compartmentalize it. To lock it away somewhere in his head behind a series of bolted doors. It was there, always, if he wished to revisit it. But it no longer controlled him. It had no influence at all on the man he'd become.

"Need a lift, do you?" the jarvey asked. "Where to?"

"Belgrave Square," Tom said as he climbed into the hansom. "And double quick."

Mere minutes later, he was deposited at the front steps of an all-too-familiar townhouse. A stone-faced butler greeted him at the door, granting him entry without a word.

Tom swiftly disposed of his hat, coat, and gloves. "Is he in his study, Palgrave?"

"He's been waiting for you, sir."

A frisson of apprehension skated its way down Tom's spine. Attaché case in hand, he crossed the Italian marble entry hall and made his way to the set of dark wood-paneled doors that led to the study.

Josiah Fothergill was within, seated in a leather chair near the fire. "You're late."

"I'm well aware." Tom shut the doors behind him before joining Fothergill at the hearth. The room smelled heavily of pipe smoke, with an underlying fragrance of alcohol and turpentine—chief ingredients in the liniment Fothergill used for his rheumatism.

"Sit down," Fothergill said.

Tom took a seat opposite his aging mentor. He lifted his attaché case onto his lap and withdrew the sheaf of papers he'd brought from his office. Fothergill took them. "Warren signed them this morning," Tom said. "Under duress."

Fothergill snorted. "Am I expected to sympathize with the man?"

"By no means."

"And Atwater?"

"I've just come from seeing him. He claims he's pleased with the terms. Not that his word has ever carried much weight."

Fothergill gave Tom a brief measuring look before dropping his gaze back to the documents. He proceeded to go over them page by page, his gnarled fingers tracing the words as he read.

He was plainly ill. His coat and trousers were loose and his skin was waxen, stretched tight over the bones of his face. He had the look of a well-heeled cadaver. A man too stubborn and willful to die.

Tom straightened his waistcoat. Good God, was this to be his future as well? Alone in a fine house, wasting away by bits, with nothing to warm him save the occasional news of a vanquished adversary?

"The doctor's been," Fothergill said, as if he could read his mind. "I'm not at death's door yet."

"I wouldn't presume to think you were."

"I'm fit as can be expected. Fitter than most, I'll wager. Why, I could return to practice tomorrow."

"You may take over the reins whenever you please."

Fothergill gave another snort. "Conceited pup. You know you're the better solicitor. You've known it for ten years and more." He turned to the next page of the contract. "I credit myself."

"Naturally."

"That's not to say you don't have a God-given talent for legal maneuvering. Take this phrasing here." He pointed at a line. "Ingenious, Finchley. Utterly ingenious."

"I thought it was rather clever myself."

"Indeed. You've bound the villain up good and proper for the foreseeable future. He won't even realize it until it's too late."

"The villain," Tom repeated. "In this case, it's difficult to tell which one of them that is."

Fothergill's head jerked up. "Difficult, you say? What's so difficult about it?"

"Both parties have behaved abominably. Blackmail. Corruption. Kidnapping. Between them, they've done it all. Were they anyone else, they'd have been brought up on charges."

"The difference being that Viscount Atwater and the Earl of Warren are not anyone else. Neither are they both villains. If you don't understand that, my boy, you understand nothing."

Tom's expression tightened. "I wrote the contract, didn't I?"

"So you did." Fothergill folded the papers in half. "I'm pleased to see your personal views haven't affected your ethical obligations."

"If you're questioning my loyalty to my client—"

"You as good as said Atwater was a villain."

"And so he is. When has that ever made a difference? I don't need to like my clients. I don't even need to believe them. As long as they pay for the services I render, my loyalty is theirs."

Fothergill's mouth twisted. "One of the first lessons I taught you."

"You may rest assured it has been well learned." The edge of bitterness in his voice surprised him.

It surprised Fothergill as well. The old solicitor's wiry brows lowered in disapproval. "You're not yourself, Finchley. First late to our appointment, and now voicing these erratic opinions. What the devil is wrong with you?"

"Nothing."

"Nonsense. You're distracted. Restless."

Tom exhaled. He *was* distracted. And restless, too. He needed to pay a visit to the East End. And he needed to stop by his rooms. With any luck, he'd have just enough time to shave and change before he was due in Half Moon Street. "If I'm anything, it's exhausted. Lest you forget, I worked straight through Christmas."

Fothergill waved the folded papers. "Then take some time off, by all means. Now that you've executed an agreement on that cursed plot of land—"

"There's no guarantee they'll abide by it."

"Of course they'll abide by it. They'll have to. It's a signed contract, enforceable by law."

"For common men, perhaps. Men of little money and less learning. But Warren and Atwater are a different breed."

"They're gentlemen."

Tom gave a short, humorless laugh. "They're no gentlemen, Fothergill. Maybe in breeding, but certainly not in practice. The pair of them have no honor that I can see." He retrieved the papers and thrust them back into his attaché case. "They've signed this, yes. But the law is meaningless in these cases. What power does it have if no one obeys it? If no one enforces it?"

Fothergill's features settled into grim lines. "You're tired, my boy."

"I *am* tired," Tom said. "Tired of helping evil men to prosper."

"You call your clients evil?"

"No, I... That is..." He ran a hand over his hair. "I shouldn't have said that."

Fothergill was quiet for a long moment. And then he said, "Ring the bell for Palgrave."

Tom rose and went to the tasseled cord by the fireplace. Within seconds of tugging it, the butler materialized at the doors of the study. "You rang, sir?"

"Go down to the cellar, Palgrave," Fothergill commanded. "Fetch that bottle of port I've been saving."

Tom opened his mouth to protest, but Fothergill forestalled him. "Sit down, Finchley. You and I have much to discuss."

A sinking feeling in his stomach, Tom lowered back into his chair. He cast a glance at the gilded clock on the mantelshelf.

"Do you have somewhere else to be?" Fothergill asked. "Another client to call on?"

"No. No other clients."

Fothergill gave him a sharp look. He disapproved of entanglements with women. Females affected a man's focus. Made him weak in the head. Prone to taking foolish risks and making equally foolish decisions. "The law is a demanding mistress, my boy. She must come first, last, and always. Take care that you don't forget it."

As if Tom ever could.

Chapter Three

"You're over an hour late." Jenny closed and bolted the front door behind Mr. Finchley. The clip-clop of horses' hooves and the clatter of carriage wheels echoed in the street as the hansom cab that had delivered him to Half Moon Street rolled away into the darkness.

Mr. Finchley looked around the empty hall. It was lit by a low-hanging gasolier, which illuminated a wide circle beneath it, leaving the edges of the hall steeped in shadows. "Why are you opening the door? Where's Mr. Jarrow?"

"Assisting Mrs. Jarrow in the kitchen." Jenny helped him off with his coat.

The Jarrows were former clients of his. A stern-faced married couple who, between themselves, represented the entirety of the household staff. Mr. Jarrow acted as a combination butler and footman, and Mrs. Jarrow fulfilled the dual roles of housekeeper and cook. They were fiercely loyal to

Mr. Finchley. He'd saved their son from being hanged, or so Mrs. Jarrow claimed.

"He should be opening the door, not you," Mr. Finchley said. "It's past nine o'clock."

"I know very well what time it is." Jenny draped his coat over her arm, and then, on impulse, leaned close to him—so close that her nose brushed lightly against his collar—and inhaled.

He drew back from her with a start.

"Have you been at your club?" she asked.

"My club? What club?"

"You smell of cigars." She sniffed him again. "And liquor."

Mr. Finchley stared at her. His mouth opened, but nothing came out. The dim glow of the gaslight revealed the beginnings of a blush on his neck.

At least, Jenny thought it was a blush. She supposed it could be yet another aftereffect of a night of overindulgence. Her lips compressed. She had no tolerance for men who couldn't control their vices. "Have you been drinking, sir? Is that why you're late?"

"Miss Holloway…"

She stepped back and took his measure, her gaze raking him from the top of his head to the toes of his leather boots. He was wearing the same suit he'd worn when she'd called on him in Fleet Street. But the fabric of his clothing was no longer starched and pressed. His black waistcoat and trousers were rumpled. His hair was rumpled, too. Brushed carelessly to the side in soft waves that flopped down over his forehead.

Her fingers itched to smooth it back from his face. To straighten and soothe him. As if he were her husband, returning home after a difficult day.

A ridiculous thought. And one that sent a pang of longing through her vitals.

"Well?" Mr. Finchley's brows lifted. The red flush on his neck darkened, creeping up to burn in his lean cheeks. "Do I pass muster?"

"You look dreadful," Jenny said frankly. "Have you eaten?"

He ran a hand over his face.

"Have you?" she asked again.

He shook his head. He looked weary. Wearier than he had at his office. And older, too, if that was possible. His light blue eyes had creases around them. Matching brackets framed the corners of his mouth.

Jenny's heart squeezed with sympathy. She ignored it. He didn't deserve any sympathy. He'd persuaded her to dine with him at eight, against her better judgment. And she'd agreed. She'd put on a silk dinner dress and arranged her hair in fresh rolls and plaits secured with nearly two dozen headache-inducing pins. She'd seen that the table was beautifully set and the chicken cooked just so. All had been in readiness for him. *She* had been in readiness for him.

And here he was, an hour late and smelling of liquor, with his clothes un-pressed and not a drop of pomade in his hair. As if she weren't worthy of a second's consideration.

"Come on, then," she said crossly. "Mrs. Jarrow will warm something up for you."

Mr. Finchley trailed after her up the stairs. Thirty minutes later, after consuming a plate of reheated chicken and downing a glass of watered wine, he put his head in his hands and groaned. "I've bungled this badly."

Jenny regarded him from her place across the dining table. A branch of half-melted beeswax candles stood between them, the flickering flames casting a pattern of shadows over the linen tablecloth, china plates, and glassware. "This? There is no this. There's only my travel plans and my money. I trust you've remembered that much."

He made a hoarse sound. "How could I forget?"

"Men forget any number of things when they're in their cups."

"I'm not in my cups, Miss Holloway. I'm just..." He shook his head. "I was obliged to visit another solicitor this evening. My former partner. The gentleman under whom I studied before I was called to the Bar. He kept me later than I'd anticipated."

"Didn't you tell him you had a prior engagement?"

"God, no."

She hadn't thought it possible to feel any worse. "Why in the world not?"

"That's not the sort of thing one shares with a man like Fothergill. Not unless one wants him to involve himself. To interfere. He can't help it, you see. He enjoys knowing things. It's how he accumulates power."

Jenny frowned. She cast her mind back to conversations she'd had with Helena. Secrets they'd shared during the endless rainy afternoons spent shut up indoors at the Abbey. "Is he the solicitor who took you out of the orphanage?"

Mr. Finchley's gaze sharpened behind his spectacles. "You know about that?"

"Only what Helena's told me."

"Which is?"

"She said there were four of you. Four friends in the orphanage. And that, for a time, you'd all gone your separate ways. That Mr. Cross had his accident, Mr. Thornhill joined the army, and that you were apprenticed to a London solicitor. The other boy—"

"Alex Archer."

"She said he'd disappeared long ago. That he'd broken his apprenticeship and…vanished."

Mr. Finchley's eyes dropped to his plate. He appeared to hesitate. As if he were preoccupied by a sudden thought or feeling. A memory, perhaps. It was the space of seconds. A mere instant. No time at all, really. But when he looked at her again, the change in his countenance was marked. "It's true," he said. "Every word of it."

Jenny fingered the stem of her wineglass. So, the fate of Alex Archer was not a topic that Mr. Finchley cared to pursue. She supposed she could understand that. If someone she'd loved like a brother had simply disappeared from the face of the earth, she might be rather sensitive about the subject as well.

"It seemed to me," she said, "that, among the four of you, it was your situation that ended most happily."

"You believe so, do you?"

"To be articled to a solicitor, and then to become a solicitor yourself? It's quite distinguished. Unless…" A terrible thought struck her. "He didn't mistreat you, did he?"

Mr. Finchley appeared surprised by her question. "Fothergill? No. He was a good mentor, in his way. He taught me everything he knew."

"I expect you feel you owe him."

"I do."

"Do you often drink and smoke with him of an evening?"

He grimaced. "Hardly ever. Had I known he'd keep me so long, I wouldn't have promised to meet you for dinner. I apologize for that, by the way. You appear to have gone to a great deal of trouble."

"No trouble at all." She raised a self-conscious hand to adjust one of the pins in her hair. She was going to have a throbbing megrim in the morning and she'd have no one to blame but herself. What had she been thinking to try such an elaborate coiffure? Her hair was far too heavy to arrange in rolls at the sides and back. It needed plaits or twisted coils to hold the weight of it.

She'd been much more sensible when it came to her dinner dress. The plain brown silk had nary a flounce or a frill. Its only attributes were a bodice that fit snug to her figure and a scooped neckline that showed off the barest hint of her modest décolletage. It made her feel daringly feminine.

Mr. Finchley's gaze drifted over her. "You look very well."

Her heart thumped hard. "Thank you."

She didn't receive many compliments from gentlemen. She was too opinionated. Too sharp and self-reliant. Helena said it intimidated some men. Which was stupid, really. Jenny appreciated a bit of gallantry just as much as the next female. More so, perhaps, since she'd experienced so little of it in her life.

"I, on the other hand, look somewhat the worse for wear." Mr. Finchley gave his wrinkled waistcoat a brief, rueful glance. "I'm terribly sorry. I'd thought there would be time to stop by my rooms and change."

"It doesn't matter."

"No, but still…I'd like you to understand." When she said nothing in response, he continued, somewhat haltingly. "You see…there's a case of mine—of mine and Fothergill's—that's of some duration. A dispute over a parcel of land. It's been going on for more years than I can count. This morning there was a positive development. At least, it's positive on its face. It may yet prove to be another legal quagmire. I was obliged to visit Fothergill to give him the news."

"And he wished to celebrate?"

"What he wished to do was read me a lecture. One that lasted through an entire bottle of port—drunk mostly by him—and two cigars. If he hadn't dozed off, I'd be there still." Mr. Finchley sighed. "Today has been an unmitigated disaster. Absolutely awful, from start to finish."

"I visited you. I suppose that was awful, too."

His mouth hitched in a fleeting half smile. "Nonsense. Your visit was the finest part of my day."

"Was it?" She was mortified to hear a soft thread of hope in her words. A trace of—oh lord, was it neediness? Desperation? As if she were some dried-up old spinster, heart gone aflutter at the barest praise from a gentleman.

She reached for her glass of wine and downed a hasty swallow. "I expect any visit would seem pleasant when compared to the one you received from Mrs. Culpepper."

"True." Mr. Finchley rested his head in his hand. His expression sobered. "I hadn't seen her in months. Not since the summer."

Jenny's pulse ceased fluttering. She lowered her glass back to the table. A sense of the reality of the situation settled low and sour in her stomach. Mr. Finchley had a mistress. A beautiful—if somewhat long in the tooth—mistress.

She shouldn't permit him to speak on the subject. Oh, but she was so terribly curious. "Have you been acquainted with her long?"

"Since I was one and twenty. It was only after I'd been called to the Bar that I could afford her. Prior to that, she wouldn't give me the time of day."

"Do you mean…you'd met her before?"

He nodded. "I first made her acquaintance when I was just a lad. She was performing with a theatrical troupe in a coastal town about five miles south of Abbott's Holcombe. She was young and pretty—and desperately in need of funds. Her husband was out of work and she'd just given birth to her second child."

"Her second child!"

"Her third, if we're being precise." His mouth quirked again, but there was no trace of humor in his expression. "She's my mother, Miss Holloway."

Jenny's mouth fell open. "*Mrs. Culpepper?*"

"Her name was Finchley before she married. Myra Finchley."

She continued to gape at him. "But she looks so young! Why, she must have been just a girl when she—"

"She was thirteen when she bore me."

"Good gracious. I mean to say…heavens." Jenny gave a slightly breathless laugh. It was born more of discomfort that amusement. "I thought she was someone else entirely."

"I know you did."

"I assumed she was your—"

"I don't have one of those," he said. "I never have."

"Oh." Warmth flooded her face. "I see. That's… Well, that's splendid."

Splendid?

Oh, God.

Mr. Finchley smiled. A quiet smile that shone more in his eyes than on his lips. "I've never seen you at a loss for words before."

"I have words. Plenty of them. Just none of the right ones, apparently."

"Have I shocked you?"

"You have, rather."

He fell silent a moment before asking, "Was it the confession about Mrs. Culpepper? Or was it the fact that I don't keep a mistress?"

Her cheeks burned. "They're neither of them fit subjects to discuss with a lady."

"No, they most certainly aren't." He paused. "I beg your pardon for having offended you."

"You haven't offended me." It was the truth, much to her dismay. He'd surprised her. Shocked her, even. But she wasn't offended. Rather the opposite. She felt honored that he'd confided in her. A little greedy, as well. She wanted more of his secrets. More of *him*. "You may tell me anything you like."

"Because you're a jaded spinster who's seen and heard every manner of thing."

"No," she said. "Because I'm your friend."

A spasm of emotion crossed over Mr. Finchley's face. For the barest instant he looked young. Almost vulnerable. "Does that mean I'm forgiven?"

Guilt gnawed at Jenny's conscience. She hadn't realized that it mattered so much to him. After all, he'd only been using her last October, hadn't he? Her opinion of him—for good or ill—surely didn't make one bit of difference. That's what she'd believed, anyway.

But the expression in his eyes told another story.

Those dratted blue eyes of his, so careworn and weary behind his spectacles.

Her heart softened toward him in spite of herself. "Yes," she said. "Yes, I suppose it does."

The parlor in Half Moon Street was one of the coziest rooms Tom had ever encountered. It was furnished with a plump chintz sofa and chairs, a tufted ottoman with tassel-trim, and an abundance of dried flowers and stuffed birds displayed under glass domes.

In the far corner sat the little pianoforte on which Lady Helena had played the night he and Miss Holloway first danced together.

"So many memories," he said.

Miss Holloway took a seat on the sofa. The tea tray was arrayed before her on a low walnut table with delicately carved legs. "There are," she agreed as she poured out their tea. "Not all of them good."

Tom sat down beside her. The sofa cushions dipped under his weight.

Miss Holloway's hands stilled briefly on the handle of the teapot.

The tension between them was palpable. Electric. It crackled in the air all about them.

He was sitting too close to her, that was the problem. He should have taken the chair or—even better—remained standing. It would have been easier to effect an exit. To make his excuses and leave before he said or did something stupid.

As if he hadn't been stupid enough already.

But there seemed to be no end to his idiocy where Miss Holloway was concerned, especially on a day like today.

First had been that despicable business with the Earl of Warren. And then Myra Culpepper had arrived unannounced. By the time she'd stormed from his office, Tom was in no frame of mind to be dealing with anyone—least of all Jenny Holloway.

And yet, here he was. Not only calling on her after dark and without the presence of a chaperone, but sitting beside her on the sofa, so close that her skirts pressed against his leg.

It wasn't very polite. Indeed, it was rather presumptuous of him.

But she was his friend, she'd said.

She was also beautiful and vibrant and unlike any female he'd ever known.

They had only this one night together. Tomorrow she'd be gone, both from England and from his life. Perhaps that was why he felt such an uncommon urge to confide in her. To share something of himself that he'd never yet shared with anyone. "I give her an allowance," he said abruptly.

Miss Holloway's eyes met his as she handed him his tea. "Mrs. Culpepper?"

He balanced the porcelain cup and saucer on his knee. "It's more in the way of a quarterly bribe."

"What in heaven for?"

"Initially? It was because I wanted to see her. To know her."

"And she wouldn't allow that unless you paid her? How very mercenary."

"Can you blame her? She has no education. No breeding. No opportunity for ready coin in her pocket. Her life has been nothing but hardship."

"She looked quite well when I saw her."

"Yes, well…since I entered her life, she's developed a taste for fine things." To put it mildly. Myra Culpepper ran through her quarterly allowance like water. Whether she spent any of it on her husband and children, Tom had no notion. All he knew was that her demands for money were increasing of late—as was her vitriol when he refused them.

"How did you find out she was your mother?" Miss Holloway asked.

Tom raised his cup to his lips. The tea within was piping hot and brewed just as he preferred it. Was it happenstance? Or did Miss Holloway remember?

He certainly hadn't forgotten the afternoons she'd had him to tea while in residence at Half Moon Street last October. Their visits hadn't been particularly intimate. They'd talked mostly of Justin and Lady Helena. But Tom had looked forward to them. He'd dressed for them, too, making certain that his suits were pressed and his hair combed into meticulous order.

It was the closest he'd ever come to properly courting a girl.

Except that he and Miss Holloway weren't courting. And she was—by her own admission—many years past girlhood.

"There was an office in the orphanage," he said. "The fellow who ran the place—a creature by the name of Cheevers—had a sort of filing system there. The door was always locked, but I was a small lad. The smallest among us. One afternoon, Thornhill boosted me in through a crack in the window so that I could rifle through the orphanage records."

"Your mother was listed there?"

"The admittance records weren't very meticulous, but yes. Her name was there. Thornhill's mother as well. They were scullery maids up at the Abbey, back when it was owned by

Sir Oswald Bannister." He hesitated. "Are you familiar with the local history?"

"Only what Helena's told me."

Tom wondered how candid Lady Helena had been with her former companion. Had she told Miss Holloway that the late baronet regularly debauched his female servants? That the orphanage had not only been under his patronage but populated with several of his bastards?

"Was Sir Oswald your father, too?" she asked.

Ah. So she did know something of Sir Oswald's relationship with the orphanage. "No. He's Thornhill's father but not mine."

"Thank goodness for that. I should hate to think—" She broke off. "That is to say, with her being only thirteen."

"Quite." Tom refrained from pointing out that such concerns had never stopped Sir Oswald before. "Though I can't say I'd have minded having Thornhill for a brother."

"He thinks of you as a brother, regardless."

"And I him."

"He never said anything about you having found your mother. Nor Helena. At least, not in my hearing."

"They don't know about her. No one does except for me. And now you, of course."

"Is it a secret?"

"It's been one of mine for a long while." He didn't think she would press him on it, but he nevertheless felt obliged to try and explain. "In the orphanage, I learned rather quickly that there was strength in knowledge. The whole place was built on shameful secrets. The more of them I knew, the more power I had. I developed the habit of keeping things to myself. Of sharing as little as possible. Sometimes there was reason. Other times, not. It's been a difficult habit to break."

She gave him a thoughtful look. "Do you know the identity of your father?"

He rubbed the side of his face. The rasp of his whiskers abraded his palm. There'd been no time to shave after leaving Fothergill's house. No time for anything, really, save a hasty trip to the East End. Good lord, but he must look an absolute disgrace.

"Do you?" she prompted.

Tom cleared his throat. "Mrs. Culpepper believes my father to have been either one of the footmen or one of the stable lads. She's not entirely certain."

Miss Holloway's eyes went wide.

"She's a survivor. She's always done what she needed to do to get by. In that time and in that place, life was easier with the protection of a man. I don't judge her for it."

"You don't seem to judge her for much of anything."

"She was an ignorant girl of thirteen. Younger than thirteen when she started her employment. I won't condemn her for the choices she was obliged to make."

"Not for her actions as a girl, no. But what about how she's behaved as an adult? The way she treated you at your office today. I thought her ungrateful before I knew she was your mother. But now—"

"I'm the least of Myra Culpepper's concerns. She has a life of her own. A family of her own. Not only a husband, but two daughters as well."

"And a son."

"Ah, but she doesn't consider me her son. Her family doesn't even know I exist."

"You've never met them?" She sounded astonished.

"I wanted to, in the beginning," he admitted. "I was just a lad. It seemed a fine thing to have a family out there somewhere. Foolish of me, really. They're not my family. Not in any sense of the word. She made that clear from the beginning."

Miss Holloway's face tightened with something very like anger. "She doesn't deserve you."

Tom's chest constricted. He tried to smile but found he could not.

"You know that, don't you?" She reached out to him, covering his hand with hers. "You're a good man, Mr. Finchley. One of the very best, if my opinion counts for anything."

His gaze fell to her hand. Her skin was silky soft, her fingers closing over his in a grasp that was both strong and tender. He swallowed hard. "It does. More than you know."

She gave him a reassuring squeeze before letting go. "Not all women are cut out to be mothers. They haven't the sensibility for it."

He flexed his hand. It tingled with an indelible warmth. As if she'd branded his skin with hers. Was she even aware of how she affected him? The way her slightest touch—her slightest look—altered the rhythm of his heart and breath? He doubted it. She sounded as crisp and no nonsense as she always did, her apple-tart voice tripping along.

"My own mother was such a creature," she said. "She should never have had children. Though one can hardly blame her. Women haven't many choices, have they? We must all either marry and consent to being perpetually confined to childbed or end our days as a spinster, despised by all." An unreadable emotion briefly clouded her brow. "That's no excuse for Mrs. Culpepper, of course."

"Of course, but..." He tried to wrap his mind around what she was saying. "Surely life holds more choices for females than spinster or broodmare."

Miss Holloway's cheeks flushed scarlet.

Tom inwardly groaned. Hellfire and damnation. Had he truly just referred to married women as broodmares? And in the company of an unmarried lady? "Miss Holloway, I—"

But she answered before he could make his apologies, responding—despite her blushes—as if he'd said nothing untoward at all. "For poor women, perhaps. But not for ladies of good breeding. For us, our very gentility acts as our prison."

He blinked. "Good lord. You sound like a reformer."

"I wouldn't go that far." A wry smile edged her mouth. "I'm not quite ready to exchange my petticoats for bloomers."

He nearly choked on his tea. "Thank God for that."

"You disapprove of reform dress?"

"Only insofar as the women wearing it look deranged."

She flicked a glance at her skirts. "It's far more functional than all of these petticoats and crinoline wires."

"You seem to function well enough."

She shrugged, smiling. "Needs must."

He found himself smiling, too. It was short-lived. Their discussion didn't lend itself much to humor. "Is your mother still living?"

Miss Holloway's own smile faded. "She's been dead these many years." She sipped her tea. "My father is still alive."

"Does he live near to town?"

"No. My father resides in Dorset. He has the distinction of being the longest-serving vicar in Chipping St. Mary— and the one most likely to deliver a sermon while under the influence of elderberry wine. He's a drunkard, bless him, and a sad trial on my two older brothers. I count myself lucky to have escaped before he made me his drudge."

"A drunken vicar?" Tom emitted a short laugh. He didn't know whether he should be amused or appalled. "I didn't realize."

"How could you? It isn't something I shout from the rooftops."

"I'm sorry. I didn't mean to make light of it."

"You needn't apologize. I make light of it myself on occasion. One must, you know. Without humor, one could easily fall into a black melancholy."

"Well, at least you can console yourself with the fact that you're not alone. There are many among us who originate from unhappy families—or no families at all."

"A sad fact." She took another sip of her tea, her expression pensive. "In truth, I don't believe there's any such thing as a happy family. I've encountered only two in my lifetime. And for all I know, their happiness was merely a façade to fool their neighbors."

"You're a pessimist."

"Not a pessimist. A realist. In my experience, human beings are inherently disappointing. It only follows that marriage and family would be as well."

"Perhaps you merely haven't met the right human beings. That is to say, the right gentleman."

She gave him a speaking glance.

Tom's lips quirked. "Come. You can't expect me to believe that you've never dreamed of marrying and having a family."

"And giving up all of my rights? Not only over my money and property, but over my body? No thank you." She lowered her teacup. "That's not to say that I haven't had the odd longing."

"For marriage?"

"Marriage. Romance. Whatever you wish to call it." Her voice dropped. "It comes on as a pang in my chest."

Tom's expression sobered. His own voice lowered to match hers. "I've felt it on occasion myself."

Her brows lifted. "Have you?"

"I expect it's natural in unmarried people of a certain age."

"I blame society. The pressure put to bear on ladies to marry is unrelenting."

"On gentlemen as well."

"It's not the same, though, is it? A gentleman has all the power."

"In theory."

"In reality, sir. You must admit."

Tom privately agreed with her. Even so, her insistence on the rightness of her position left him feeling oddly frustrated. Defensive, even. Could she not admit that there was some benefit to the marital state? "Thornhill and Lady Helena seem happy enough."

"Ah, but their marriage is a rarity. For every relationship such as theirs, there are hundreds—nay, thousands—of couples in misery. And it's worse for the women. Exponentially worse. The sober fellow who courts a girl may well end his days as a violent brute or a drunkard. And what is a married lady with a half dozen children to do then? She's trapped. Her future beyond all hope."

His brow furrowed. "You disapprove of men who drink."

"To put it mildly."

"Was your father violent toward you when he was drinking?" The very thought made Tom's muscles tense with outrage. "Did he ever—"

"No, he wasn't violent. He was unreliable." She briefly fingered the fine gold chain she wore round her neck. It was her only piece of jewelry. A simple necklace, absent the adornment of a locket, pendant, or charm. "He spent the housekeeping money and left the tradesman's accounts unpaid. He was careless and sloppy and said things that he shouldn't. Had I remained there, I'd have been forever making excuses for him. Forever cleaning up his messes. I can think of nothing more repugnant."

"Is that why you were so distressed at the idea of my having been out drinking?"

"I wasn't distressed. I was…disappointed. I never took you for a gentleman who was a slave to his vices."

"I'm not, generally."

She regarded him over the edge of her teacup, her blue-green eyes sharply assessing. "No. I don't believe you are. Indeed, I don't believe you permit anything—or anyone— to gain mastery over you."

"And you do?"

"I haven't had much choice, have I? I was first my father's daughter, and then Lady Helena's companion. But you're right, Mr. Finchley. Now I'm at last myself, a whole person responsible to no one, I shan't let anyone gain mastery over me ever again."

There was a thread of steel in her voice.

"We're all beholden to someone, Miss Holloway," he said quietly. "Like it or not."

She placed her teacup and saucer down on the tea tray. Her posture was stiff. Formal. Unless he was very much mistaken, she was on the verge of saying something sharp to him. Something that would dispel the fabric of intimacy they'd woven around each other with their shared confidences.

It wasn't an ideal time to press such intimacy further. But Tom had learned to always keep his adversaries off balance. It was a useful tactic in law. One that came as naturally to him as breathing.

"Mr. Finchley," she began. "You—"

"May I call you Jenny?" he asked.

Miss Holloway stared at him, lips half parted. "I beg your pardon?"

"I'd very much like to, if I may. And you must make free to call me Tom, if it pleases you."

She didn't answer right away. He'd flustered her—as was his intention. But true to form, Miss Holloway rallied. "Very well. Though I don't see there's much need for excessive familiarity between us. I'll be leaving for India soon. We're not likely to meet again."

"Probably not."

"Once you release my funds, I—" Her eyes narrowed. "You *are* going to release my funds, aren't you?"

"I am."

A profound look of relief came into her face. "When?"

"Tomorrow."

"Thank heaven. I was afraid you were going to be difficult."

"Not difficult. Merely cautious. I have only your best interest at heart, you know."

"Said every man to every woman since the beginning of time."

Tom's mouth curled into a smile. "If that's your idea of men, I'd as soon you think of me as a solicitor first."

"Worse and worse." She leaned back against the sofa cushions, one arm draped over her midsection. Her skirts billowed out in a sea of starched petticoats and mink-brown silk. "How shall we arrange it? Shall I come to Fleet Street in the morning? If we meet early enough, I'll still have time to book passage on the next steamer ship."

"I shall tell you all," he promised. "But first…"

"Yes?"

"Will you play something for me, Jenny?"

She gave him an odd look. "How strange it is to hear you call me that."

"It's what your friends call you, isn't it?"

"Yes, but not you. Never you."

"If you don't like it—"

"I like it," she said. "Tom."

His pulse throbbed. It was only his name, just as Jenny was only hers, but hearing it uttered increased the intimacy between them tenfold. "Play something for me," he said again.

She sighed. "Oh, very well. What would you like to hear?"

"Anything you please."

She rose, crossed the room to the pianoforte, and sat down at the bench, settling her voluminous skirts all about her. Her hands lifted, fingers poised over the keys.

And then she began to play.

It was Chopin. A lullaby of all things.

Tom sank back onto the sofa to listen, his legs stretched out in front of him and his arms crossed. The parlor was toasty warm, a coal fire glowing cheerfully in the grate. This must be what it was like to be a happily married gentleman. To come home in the evenings, to dine with one's wife, and to talk with her. To listen in appreciative silence as she played Chopin on the pianoforte.

He imagined a lifetime of such evenings. A lifetime of stimulating conversation with Jenny Holloway. A lifetime of intimacy. Of affection. Of family.

His eyelids grew heavy.

The next thing he knew, the music had stopped. His eyes were closed, his chest rising and falling as he drifted into sleep.

He felt the brush of skirts against his legs. Smelled the sweet, clean fragrance of herbal soap. And then his glasses were lifted carefully from his face and slim, feminine fingers smoothed his hair from his brow. It was the most delicious feeling. Soft as a caress. Comforting beyond measure.

And a dream. Surely, just a dream.

Chapter Four

When Jenny woke in the morning, Tom Finchley was gone.

"The blanket Mr. Jarrow put over him last night was folded on the sofa, nice as you please," Mrs. Jarrow said as she served Jenny breakfast. "He's off on a case, I expect."

Jenny bit her tongue. She was furious, but she wasn't about to malign Tom in front of Mrs. Jarrow. The woman idolized him. "He didn't leave a note?"

"No, ma'am. Not that I saw." Mrs. Jarrow wiped her hands on her apron.

Alone in the small breakfast room, Jenny made short work of her eggs, toast, sausage, porridge, and tea. She was a hearty eater at the best of times—and even heartier at the worst. At the moment, she felt as though she could lay waste to a seven-course meal.

Drat Tom Finchley! Who did he think he was to slink off before dawn without a word to the servants? She had been too soft-hearted toward him last night, that was the problem. She'd felt dreadful that he was so tired and had tried to make him comfortable—even going so far as to summon Mr. Jarrow to loosen Tom's collar and drape him with a knitted blanket.

What she should have done was wake him up, the devious scoundrel, and force him to explain what he meant to do about her money.

She passed the remainder of the morning writing letters, repacking her trunks, and trying to read a book. It was impossible to focus. When the gilt-trimmed clock in the parlor chimed the hour, she cast her book aside and got to her feet. It was foolish to continue waiting for him to return. Who knew if he even would? Only one thing was certain. If she wished to corner Tom Finchley, the place to do so was at his office. And if he continued to fob her off with his legal tricks and excuses, why...she'd simply send a telegraph to Helena.

Having reached a decision, Jenny returned to her room and changed into a green striped silk traveling dress. She plaited her hair, securing it into a roll at her nape, and tugged on her gloves. Bonnet in hand, she descended the stairs. "Mr. Jarrow?"

The weathered manservant was heading toward the kitchens. At the sound of her voice, he doubled back. "Yes, ma'am?"

"Summon a hansom for me, if you please. I'm going to Fleet Street."

Mr. Jarrow acknowledged her request with a bob of his head; however, before he could act on it, the heavy brass door knocker sounded.

Jenny stilled on the stairs, watching as Mr. Jarrow answered the summons. The locks scraped as he unbolted them and drew open the door.

Tom Finchley's quiet baritone voice filled the hall. "Apologies, Jarrow. I seem to have misplaced my key." He strolled in, his tall beaver hat in his hand. When he saw her on the stairs, he stopped. A faint smile touched his lips. "Good morning."

With an effort, Jenny swallowed down her anger—and her relief—and descended the final two steps into the hall.

Mr. Jarrow shut the door. "Will you still be needing that hansom, ma'am?"

"No, thank you, Jarrow. It's quite unnecessary now."

Tom gave her a questioning look. "Were you going somewhere?"

"Yes." She met him halfway across the floor. He wasn't a great deal taller than her—four or five inches at most—but she still had to tilt her head back in order to look him in the eye. It was maddening, really. She disliked being loomed over. "I was going to call on you in Fleet Street."

"That would have been a wasted journey."

"Well, I didn't know that, did I? We thought you'd gone."

"Ah. I see. Forgive me. I had some business matters to take care of. I'd hoped to be back sooner."

"Business?" Jenny's gaze flickered over his face and his figure. He'd shaved. And he'd changed his clothes as well. Gone was the severe black suit he'd worn yesterday. In its place was a loose-fitting sack coat, vest, and trousers made of light gray cloth. His dark wool overcoat was worn open over it, the shoulders and sleeves dusted with new-fallen snow. "What sort of business?"

"Business I've been conducting on your behalf." Tom stared down at her, his blue eyes searching hers.

Her stomach performed a queer little somersault. "What is it? What's wrong?"

"Nothing," he said. "Are you still determined to leave England today?"

"Yes. It's why I was going to Fleet Street. To make you release my funds so I could book passage—"

"It's done," he said.

Her brows knit. "What?"

"I've done it. Last night and this morning. Everything is arranged. All that's left is to fetch your trunk. The train leaves from London Bridge Station at half one."

"The train? What train?"

"The train to Dover."

Her heart beat heavily in her chest. She had a sense she was rapidly losing control of the situation. "I don't see any reason I must go all the way to Dover."

"No? How did you intend to get to Calais?"

"From London, of course. *Bradshaw's* mentions steamer ships departing from St. Katharine's Wharf."

"You *could* do it that way," he acknowledged. "If you don't mind spending hours longer on the water."

"I don't see that it makes much difference whether I spend those hours on a train or on a ship."

"Have you ever crossed the Channel before?"

"No, but I—"

"You're bound to be seasick. Most people are. The less time spent on the water the better, especially at this time of year." He withdrew his pocket watch from his waistcoat and checked the time. "We should leave within the next quarter of an hour. Do you need assistance with your trunks?"

"I only have one trunk. It's already packed. Mr. Jarrow can—" She broke off, eyes narrowing. "Wait. What do you mean *we*?"

"I'm accompanying you to Dover."

She took a step back from him. "That's not at all necessary."

"On the contrary. You're an attractive lady traveling alone. It will be safer for you if you have an escort."

Attractive?

Good gracious.

Warmth suffused Jenny's veins. She prayed it didn't make its way to her face. She had enough to worry about without adding maidenly blushes to the mix. "Surely you have more important things to do."

"Not a one," he said. "And that's the honest truth."

"Tom…"

His expression softened infinitesimally. "Jenny."

She exhaled. "Very well. If you must."

Riding on the train to Dover with Tom was no great hardship. He was ever attentive, offering her his arm when she required it, and seeing that she was made comfortable and kept well entertained.

He'd booked a first-class compartment for them. It was paneled in dark wood and boasted carpeted floors, upholstered seats, and brass parcel racks.

Jenny was not unaccustomed to traveling in such luxury. She'd often enjoyed first-class accommodations while companion to Lady Helena. With Tom, however, the experience felt fresh and new.

She expected it had less to do with him and more to do with her own independence. Everything seemed finer somehow. It scarcely mattered that Tom handled the tickets or that the porters deferred to him as if he were the one in charge. Indeed, sitting across from him in their compartment as the train left the station, she had a profound sense of the rightness of it all.

Perhaps this was what it would be like to be the wife of a considerate husband. This feeling of being taken care of, but not stifled. Looked after, but not suffocated or made to feel a burden.

The thought sent a pang through her midsection. It wasn't longing. Not exactly. It was something else. A bleak sort of hollow feeling. Regret, she suspected. She'd never know what the future might hold for the pair of them. At Dover, they'd part ways, probably forever.

She turned her head to stare out the window. The sash was open, the scenery whipping by at an accelerated rate.

"Is anything the matter?" he asked.

"No. Nothing. Just thinking."

"About anything in particular?"

She slowly turned back to face him. "I'd better take my tickets. And whatever else I'll need for the rest of the journey."

Tom looked at her for a long moment. "Of course." He withdrew the relevant documents from his pocket book, along with a great many British banknotes. "You'll want to change some of it for foreign currency when you arrive on the continent. You'll get a better rate there."

"Will it be enough?"

"You also have a letter of credit drawn on your bank."

"Yes, I see." She rifled through her documents. "And have you directed them to honor it, down to the last penny?"

"Do you anticipate requiring the entirety of your fortune on this adventure?"

"Indeed not. But I'd like to know that I have access to it all the same."

"You won't find me unreasonable."

"No. I don't believe I will." She folded her documents into her reticule, then met his eyes. "You've been absolutely lovely about all of this. Very kind and generous. Indeed, I believe I owe you an apology."

"You don't."

"I think I do." She didn't wish to make him uncomfortable, but she couldn't leave the words unsaid. "I hope you can forgive me for misjudging your motives. It's one of my chief failings, you know, always assuming that people are trying to get the better of me. To lord it over me in some way. I daresay it comes from spending so long as a companion. But I won't make excuses. The fact is, you've been terribly helpful, when I know that you'd much rather be back at your office."

"Don't be absurd. I'm exactly where I wish to be."

She gave a doubtful laugh. "On a train to Dover in the middle of the business day?"

"Why not? I enjoy your company."

Her cheeks warmed. "And I yours."

"Well, then, the two of us appear to be in harmony. No apologies necessary."

Jenny didn't argue with him. How could she when he was being so gallant? Instead she turned the subject to the Channel crossing. To Calais and Marseilles and beyond.

The hours flew by, the two of them engaged in companionable conversation until the train pulled into the station at Dover.

The porters saw to her trunk and Tom hired a carriage to convey her to Admiralty Pier. Jenny waited, her stomach roiling with an unsettling combination of nervous excitement and something very near dread. Was this where he would leave her? Would he help her into the coach and then bid her farewell?

The answer was no, thank goodness. After Tom assisted her into the carriage, he didn't bid her goodbye or wish her safe journey. He climbed into the cab after her.

Jenny couldn't hide her relief. "I thought we were parting ways at the station."

"Whatever gave you that idea?"

"Common sense. You could have caught the next train back and been home by nightfall."

"I'm in no hurry to return to London."

"What about the case you're working on?"

"The land dispute? It's been going on for nearly eleven years. There's no urgency at the moment. Besides, if my client finds himself in desperate need of counsel, he can always call on Fothergill. The old fellow would enjoy the diversion. Possibly even more than he'll enjoy raking me over the coals when I return."

"Surely he can't begrudge you a little time off?"

"He begrudges me anything that takes me away from my practice."

"But…he's not your superior anymore, is he?"

"Not in the strict sense of the word. He retired two years ago. Unfortunately, he still likes to keep his hand in. When he discovers I've gone, he'll be apoplectic."

"I don't see why. It's only the space of a day. You'll be back by morning."

Tom didn't say anything.

Jenny didn't press him. It was plain enough that the law was his life. The sum total of his entire existence. For a man with such a work ethic, taking off a day to escort a friend to Kent must be the equivalent of a long holiday.

"Have you ever been to Dover?" she asked.

"Once or twice."

"I daresay you're much more well traveled than I am. You must be. I've never been anywhere at all."

"You're more well traveled than you realize. Most people born in a country village never see the city. But you've not only lived in London, you've traveled all the way to the Devon coast."

"And now to Dover." She smiled as she turned her gaze back to the window.

It was only a short distance to the pier. When they arrived, they were greeted by the prospect of a churning sea. A handful of travelers were gathered on the dock, all of them bundled up against the frigid weather.

Tom disembarked first. "Careful. Mind the step."

Jenny clung to his hand as she stepped down from the carriage. The wind whipped at her skirts and at the ribbons of her bonnet. It was cold as ice, biting at her face and stinging her eyes.

After months of living on the North Devon coast with Helena and Mr. Thornhill, she was accustomed to the smell of sea air and the peculiar force of the wind as it blew in from over the water. But like everything else, this was different.

The beach at Greyfriar's Abbey was isolated. Lonely. Dover, by contrast, was teeming with industry.

A steamer ship was docked in the harbor, near to where the crowd of people were gathered. Men in rough coats and wool trousers moved up and down a narrow wooden gangplank, loading the ship with crates, leather cases, and great waterproof trunks like Jenny's.

"The *Onyx*," she said. "That's my ship, isn't it?"

Tom stood close at her side. "It is." He cast her a look. "Scared?"

"No."

The carriage was stopped behind them, the driver hunched over on the box. He likely couldn't hear them over the wind. And he certainly didn't seem interested in what it was they were saying or doing.

Gathering her courage, Jenny turned to face Tom. "Please don't walk me to the ship," she said in a rush. "I'd rather say goodbye to you here."

Tom's expression was guarded. Almost unreadable. He cleared his throat. "As to that—"

"Please. I don't think I could bear it if you were to stand on the dock waving me off. It's difficult enough as it is."

"Why should it be difficult?"

"I don't know." The wind blew the silk ribbon ties of her bonnet across her mouth. She brushed them away. "You and I are a puzzle, aren't we? To me, anyway. I've resolved to chalk it up to one of those unfortunate pangs that we discussed last evening."

Tom gave her an arrested look. "Longing, do you mean?"

"Yes. I suppose that's it."

"For me?"

She flushed. "Why not?" And then, before she could talk herself out of it, she stood up on the toes of her boots and pressed a kiss to his cheek. "Goodbye, Tom. Perhaps, someday— if you ever have the inclination—you might write to me in India."

Tom stared down at her, his Adam's apple bobbing on a swallow. When at last he replied, his voice was deeper than usual. "I won't be writing to you, Jenny."

Her stomach dropped. "Oh." She took a step back from him. A surge of embarrassment clogged her throat, making it difficult to speak. "Yes, of course. I perfectly understand."

"No, you don't. There won't be any need to write because... I'm coming with you."

Tom grimaced. He hadn't planned to blurt it out like that. He'd planned to walk her to the ship, at which point he would introduce her to Ahmad and Mira. The pair of them had taken an earlier train. They should already be here, pre-sumably among the crowd on the docks. It was difficult to tell when everyone was wrapped up in overcoats, mufflers, and hats; virtually indistinguishable from one another.

Once Jenny met Ahmad and Mira, she'd be trapped. There would be no polite way to refuse their escort. She'd be obliged to accept them as manservant and maid. And then she'd be safe. Ready to embark on her travels properly escorted.

That was his plan, anyway.

A plan that had all gone out the window when Jenny Hol-loway had kissed him.

No. That wasn't precisely true. The plan, in its original form, had first met its demise when he opened his eyes this morning, the memory of Jenny's touch emblazoned on his brain.

He'd been on the plump sofa in the parlor at Half Moon Street, his collar loosened and a blanket draped over his legs. And he'd known—he'd simply known—that the sweet memory he had of the previous evening hadn't been a dream. Far from it. Jenny had removed his spectacles with uncommon care and then smoothed her fingers over his brow. It had been a caress. Something tender. Almost loving. And something done when she'd believed he was asleep.

It had changed everything.

At least, he'd thought it had. But now, his cheek still burning from where her soft pink lips had pressed against his skin, he felt as if his world had been knocked off its axis once more.

Jenny Holloway felt a pang of longing...for *him*?

He stared down at her, a little dazed. She looked beautiful. Almost wild, with flashing blue-green eyes and stray locks of waving auburn hair escaping from beneath her bonnet to whip in the wind.

"What did you say?" she asked.

"I'm coming with you. The railway sent my luggage ahead. I expect it's already loaded on the ship."

"You're joking." She gave a nervous laugh. "You can't come with me. You...you don't even have the right papers. You wouldn't have had time—"

"I know a gentleman in Fleet Street. He arranged for my travel documents to be expedited from the Foreign Office." Tom shrugged. "He owed me a favor."

The look of amused disbelief froze on Jenny's face. "Even if that were true, you know very well that it wouldn't be proper for us to travel together. If anyone ever found out, I'd be ruined."

"It's not improper for a lady to travel with a member of her own family."

"Oh? And who am I to claim you as? My husband? You presume a great deal, sir."

"I would never presume such intimacy. As far as Keane knows, you're my sister. It's an easy enough fiction to maintain."

Jenny's lips parted in astonishment. "Good lord. You're serious, aren't you?"

"I'm sorry to disappoint you, but yes."

Some of the sparkle left her eyes. The air of anticipation that had clung about her since they departed London dimmed, and then, much to his alarm, disappeared altogether.

Tom's chest tightened. He was painfully reminded of an injured dove he and Neville had found outside the orphanage when they were boys. They'd put it in a cage. It had been an act of mercy, done to save its life. Even so, Tom had never forgotten the way the dove had behaved as they'd closed the door of its prison. The wildness had gone from its eye. It had become small and still, giving up all hope.

"I suppose," Jenny said, "that you expect me to change my mind. To say I won't go at all."

"I'm not bluffing."

"Good, because I intend to board that ship and go to Marseilles and Alexandria and Delhi just as I planned. And if you think you're going to stop me—"

"Pray keep your voice down. I'm not going to stop you. I'm only coming along to make sure you're safe. To look after you."

"Why? Surely Helena and Mr. Thornhill never expected you to—"

"I'm not doing it for them. I'm doing it for you." *And for myself,* he added silently.

Because she was beautiful and full of fire. Because he enjoyed talking with her. Confiding in her. Feeling the touch of her hands and the press of her lips. Because, quite simply, he couldn't let her go. Couldn't let her board that ship and disappear from his life forever.

"This is madness!" she cried.

"It's no madder than your desire to find the missing Earl of Castleton. Which, by the way, you're not likely to accomplish without a little help."

"From you?" she scoffed. "What can you achieve that I can't on my own?"

"I'm a man. What can't I achieve?" His tone was bored. Casual. And particularly designed to get a rise out of her.

It worked better than he'd anticipated.

Jenny's gloved hands clenched into fists at her sides. The sparkle returned to her eyes. Indeed, she fairly glittered with fury. "Oh, the nerve of you. The unmitigated nerve."

Tom suppressed a surge of relief. He'd disappointed her—hurt her, even—but the damage wasn't permanent. She was as fierce and determined as ever. Once she recognized that he didn't mean to stand in her way, she'd regain some of her excitement over the impending journey. It would just take a little time.

"To think I trusted you," she said. "That I actually believed you when you—"

"Ah, look," Tom interrupted. "There's Ahmad and his cousin."

"Who?"

"The servants I hired on your behalf."

She turned to look down the pier. "What servants? I specifically told you that I didn't wish to travel with servants."

"No. What you said was that you didn't wish to travel with British servants." He raised a hand to Ahmad and Mira.

They were standing a short distance away, looking at Jenny with vague suspicion.

A native of Delhi, Ahmad Malik was a tall, muscular fellow with jet-black hair and obsidian eyes. Up until last evening, he'd been employed as a bully boy at Mrs. Pritchard's establishment in Whitechapel. On any given day, he could be found tossing unruly clients out into the alley. It was how Tom had made his acquaintance. Ahmad had tossed a wealthy baronet a tad too roughly, breaking the gentleman's shoulder in the process. The baronet had tried to have Ahmad sent away for it. And he might have succeeded if Tom hadn't intervened on Ahmad's behalf.

Tom's acquaintance with Ahmad's cousin, Mira Malik, was of shorter duration. She was a quiet girl. Slightly fairer than Ahmad, with eyes of a singular olive green. She too had been born in Delhi, and she too worked at Mrs. Pritchard's, first as a maid, and then as a laundress. Word was that the proprietress was anxious to promote her to another position—one to which Mira was most vehemently opposed.

Both had been more than ready to abandon Mrs. Pritchard's for the employ of Jenny Holloway. Though judging by the looks on their faces, they were still reserving judgment on their new mistress.

"Jenny?" Tom said as they approached. "This is Ahmad and Mira Malik. I've taken the liberty of employing them to act as manservant and maid during your journey. Ahmad. Mira. This is Miss Holloway."

Jenny sent Tom a look that could have withered an oak tree. "Indian servants, I see."

"And very well suited to their new positions."

She didn't respond to him, turning instead to address Ahmad and Mira. "And how is it that the both of you know Mr. Finchley? I don't suppose he saved one of you from being hanged?"

"No, madam," Ahmad said solemnly. "It was from transportation."

Jenny gave a tight smile. "Of course it was."

Chapter Five

Calais, France
February, 1860

Crossing the English Channel was every bit as miserable as Tom had warned. Even worse, in fact. The rain
started not long after departing Dover. The roiling sea seemed
to rise up to meet it, tossing the ship about in a most alarming fashion.

Huddled in her cabin with Mira, Jenny strove to endure
the tempest with creditable fortitude, trying her best to set an
example for her newly acquired maid. It wasn't easy. Indeed,
several times she feared she might disgrace herself. Fortunately
for her stomach, the entirety of the journey was completed
in less than two hours.

Their party disembarked at Calais looking somewhat the
worse for wear. Jenny's silk dress was wet with rain and sea
spray. Mira was faring little better. Her skirts were drenched
and her hat appeared to have wilted on her head.

Tom took one look at the pair of them and decided that they would all stay the night in Calais. After clearing their baggage at the Custom House, he found them lodgings at a little hotel situated near the marketplace.

"Rest awhile," he said when they parted ways at the door of her room. "We can have supper later, if you like."

Jenny was still angry but didn't have the strength to argue. She was tired and hungry and chilled to the bone. If Tom wanted to take charge for the evening, he could do so with her good wishes.

Once in her room, she quickly stripped out of her wet clothes. "There seems little point in engaging a cabin," she muttered, "when one gets this wet regardless."

Mira hovered around her. "Shall I help you, madam?"

Jenny stepped out of her skirts "You may help me by taking care of yourself. You're wet through, Mira. You'll be no use to anyone if you catch your death." She unfastened her crinoline. "And do cease calling me *madam*. I was practically a servant myself until last year."

Mira looked doubtful.

"It's true," Jenny said. "I was companion to Lady Helena Reynolds, daughter of the 5th Earl of Castleton. She married in September and no longer has any need of me."

Mira unhooked her jacket bodice and struggled out of her wet sleeves. "You were dismissed?"

"No. I left with her blessing. She even settled a sum of money on me. It's how I'm able to afford this trip." Jenny draped her wet things on a wooden chair near the fireplace. "I hadn't planned on hiring any servants until I arrived in India."

Mira made no reply as she finished undressing. She was an uncommonly reserved girl. Indeed, she'd scarcely said a word since their introduction on the pier. Whenever she did speak, it was quiet and respectful, her voice lilting ever so lightly.

"How long have you lived in England?" Jenny asked. "You've scarcely any accent."

"I came to London when I was a girl," Mira said. "With my cousin, Ahmad."

Jenny removed her corset hook by hook, her lungs expanding fully for the first time in hours. Clad only in her chemise and drawers, she sat down on the edge of the bed to remove her stockings. "Is he your only family?"

"Yes, madam."

Jenny didn't bother correcting her this time. It was difficult enough extracting information from the girl. It wasn't going to help to pepper her with reprimands.

She heaved a sigh. "I know I said I didn't want any servants, but now you're here, I don't wish you to be frightened of me or to feel unwelcome. I'm not an unreasonable person, truly. You'll learn that soon enough. In the meanwhile, you're not to make yourself uncomfortable on my account. And if there's anything you require, anything at all, you must speak out directly. Do you understand?"

"I understand."

"Good. Now, tell me, have you ever worked as a lady's maid before?"

Mira's hands froze on the tapes of her petticoats.

"It's all right if you haven't," Jenny added hastily. "In truth, I don't really need a lady's maid. I can dress and undress myself perfectly well and I'm capable enough at arranging my own hair."

Not that anyone would know it from the current state of her coiffure. The voyage across the Channel had left her tresses in disarray. She plucked out the remaining hairpins, letting the plaited coils unravel to fall halfway down her back.

"You don't require me to act as your lady's maid?" Mira sounded confused. "What is it you wish me to do?"

"Nothing at the moment."

"But what about my duties?"

"What were your duties at Mrs. Pritchard's?"

Mira's face tensed.

"It was a lodging house, wasn't it? Somewhere in the East End, Mr. Finchley said."

"Off of the High Street, yes, madam. I laundered the linens and the women's underthings."

"Hmm." Jenny considered. "You can launder our things, I suppose. And if you'll occasionally assist with sponging and pressing my gowns, that would be tremendously helpful. I only brought the four of them. *Bradshaw's* advised packing light."

"Bradshaw?"

"The overland travel guide to India and Egypt. I've a copy in my reticule if you'd like to read it." Jenny rose to drape her stockings over the back of the chair along with the rest of her things before returning to the bed and drawing back the thin woolen blanket.

"Are you retiring, madam?"

"Just a short lie-down before dinner." Jenny slipped under the coarse sheets.

As much as one romanticized travel, the realities of the business were exhausting. How many miles had she traveled in the past two days? First from Devon to London and then from London to Dover and on to Calais. And now here she was, out of England at last, and all she wanted was to curl up in a warm bed and sleep.

"I'm so dreadfully tired," she said. "It was the Channel crossing, I expect. It wasn't very long, but it seems to have taken it out of me. Something about the sea, don't you think?"

Whether Mira answered or not, Jenny never knew. She was asleep as soon as her head hit the pillow.

A long time later, she was awakened by the chime of church bells in the marketplace. Sunlight filtered in through the half-raised window shade.

Her stomach grumbled.

As if by magic, Mira appeared. "Good morning, madam." She leaned over the bed, a tray in her hands. "Mr. Finchley has sent you breakfast. He's waiting on you downstairs."

Jenny struggled to a sitting position. "What time is it?"

"Eight o'clock."

Good lord. She must have slept straight through. "Didn't he come to fetch me for dinner last night?"

"Yes, madam. He said I mustn't disturb you." Mira set the tray on Jenny's lap. It held a steaming pot of tea along with boiled eggs, toast, and some manner of jam. "Should I have wakened you?"

"No, no. You did the right thing. I daresay I needed the sleep."

Jenny made short work of her breakfast and then rose to wash and dress. A half hour later she emerged from her room, garbed in an unflounced green skirt and a black caraco. The loose, thigh-length jacket nipped in at her waist and flared down over her hips. It was one of her favorite ensembles. Sensible yet absurdly flattering to her figure.

She felt the need to look her best today. It was stupid, really, but after her actions at the Dover pier, she couldn't bear to be thought of as an unattractive old maid.

If only her departure had gone according to plan. Under different circumstances, the final words she'd said to Tom and the kiss she'd pressed to his cheek might have been romantic. A grand farewell gesture, the memory of which she could return to down the years.

Instead, such actions had to be viewed in the starkest terms.

She'd been impulsive. Immodest. And she'd made herself needlessly vulnerable in front of a gentleman who had more than once run roughshod over her feelings.

The whole of it left her feeling more than a little ridiculous.

If Tom was experiencing anything remotely similar, he gave no sign of it. She found him waiting in the hotel's reception area with their luggage, looking as cool and composed as ever. His gaze flicked over her. "Good. I was just about to send Ahmad up to hurry you along."

"Are we in a hurry?"

"The train to Marseilles leaves in half an hour."

She blinked. "So soon?"

"Surely you didn't expect us to linger in Calais? There's nothing to see here."

"No. I suppose not."

Outside, Ahmad and one of the hotel porters were loading their luggage into a hired carriage. The sky was gray, the sunshine drifting through just enough to brighten, but not enough to warm.

"Thank God the rain has stopped," Tom muttered.

It was the last thing he said to her for a long while.

When next he spoke, they were settled opposite each other in their first-class compartment on the train to Marseilles. They were absent Ahmad and Mira. Servants of first-class passengers were obliged to travel in the second-class carriage.

"We could have insisted that Mira remain with you," Tom said. "It's not unheard of for a lady's maid to travel with her mistress."

Jenny removed her wide-brimmed straw hat and lay it on the seat beside her. "To what purpose? I have no need of her at the moment. And she'd far rather travel with her cousin. That was plain enough to see."

Doubtless the pair of them had a good deal to talk about, not the least of which would be on the subject of their new employer. Jenny prayed she hadn't disappointed them entirely with her ramshackle ways. Servants wanted to be proud of their masters and mistresses. Helena always said it was one's duty never to let them down.

"I trust you're getting on," Tom said.

"With Mira?" Jenny smoothed her gloves. Thus far, she'd had great success in avoiding Tom's gaze. It didn't alleviate all of the embarrassment occasioned by yesterday's behavior, but it certainly helped make it more bearable. "As well as can be expected. She's rather shy, isn't she?"

"She'll warm to you."

Jenny hoped so. As for Ahmad, she didn't have any inkling whether they'd suit. She'd hardly interacted with the man since boarding the steamship in Dover. That hadn't stopped her from forming an impression, of course. If Mira was shy, her cousin was downright surly. "Were they long at Mrs. Pritchard's establishment?"

"Since they first arrived from India, I believe. Ahmad claims that there haven't been any prospects for more respectable employment. Not if they wish to stay together."

"Mrs. Pritchard's isn't respectable? I thought it was a lodging house or a hotel of some kind."

"It is a hotel, in a manner of speaking. One that, ah, caters to gentlemen."

Her eyes jerked to his. "Do you mean to say you recruited my servants from a—"

"Regrettably, yes. But Ahmad and Mira have no connection with the more sordid aspects of Mrs. Pritchard's establishment. They're honest workers. Capable, as well. I can speak for Ahmad in that regard. You could wish for no better protection on your travels."

"You can't speak for Mira?"

"I only know her through her cousin. Ahmad came to me last year. Some business over a baronet's injured shoulder."

"And you saved him from being transported." Jenny frowned. "But how? You're not a barrister. You don't argue cases in a court of law. Not that I'm aware of anyway."

"No. That's correct. I don't argue cases."

"Then how—"

"I write. Briefs. Letters. Contracts. That sort of thing."

She felt as if she were missing something. "That's all very well, but I don't see how writing a brief or a letter can save a man from being transported. Or from hanging, come to that."

Tom smiled slightly. "My writing is very persuasive."

Jenny regarded him with a furrowed brow. Not for the first time it occurred to her that there was something sinister about Thomas Finchley. He'd told her himself that he found strength in knowledge. That he'd learned from a young age how to accumulate it. And how to leverage it too, apparently.

Good heavens, he didn't threaten people or...or blackmail them, did he?

She very nearly asked him, but it wasn't the kind of thing one just blurted out. It would be a scandalous accusation to make. And in very poor taste, too. Gentlemen didn't take kindly to questions about their honor. To even imply that Tom had broken the law—and in such a despicable manner—could very well damage her friendship with him forever.

Such that they had a friendship.

Her spirits sank. "Is that what you do? Entangle your adversaries with words?"

"That's one way of looking at it."

She could think of no other. "I'd rather you not do that to me."

"You're hardly my adversary, Jenny."

"No, but I've fallen victim to your machinations as surely as they have. Worse, I think. For I didn't even know that we *were* adversaries."

Tom fell silent. She had the sense that her words had taken him off his guard—and that he was determining how best to counter them.

She gave him no chance to formulate a reply. "I'm not a child, you know. You could have told me straight out that you wouldn't release my funds unless I agreed to be properly escorted on my travels. I'd have railed at you, of course, and probably lost my temper, but we would have compromised in the end. We're both sensible people, more than capable of finding common ground. You didn't need to draw a net around me and trap me."

He might have flinched at that, but he didn't dispute the charge. Neither did he try to defend against it. He merely looked at her, an expression in his eyes that was hard to read.

"It didn't feel very good, what you did to me. And after I'd kissed you goodbye, as well. I'll wager you found *that* vastly entertaining."

His face went taut. "Is that what you think of me?"

"What else am I to think?"

"That I was doing what was best for you. That I had your best interest at heart."

"So you've said. But you didn't listen to me. You didn't mark my feelings at all. You simply did what you wanted. And you waited to tell me about it until I was wholly ensnared by your scheme. Until I had no choice."

"There was no solution that would have been ideal. And there was no time for talking things to death. You needed me to solve your problem and I did so, as quickly and efficiently as I could."

"I'm not one of your legal problems, Tom. I'm a person. Your friend, or so you claim."

He leaned forward. "You *are* my friend. Which is precisely why I couldn't permit you to traipse halfway round the world unaccompanied. Anything might have happened to you, Jenny. *Anything.*"

She exhaled. "I know that. I even accept that you were right to some degree. But that's all beside the point."

"Forgive me, I seem to have lost the point. If you agree that having servants accompany you was the right thing to do, then what the devil are we arguing about?"

"About the fact that you went behind my back. That you maneuvered me like a token on a board. And then…" Her cheeks flushed with heat. "You let me say those things."

He looked stricken. "Good God, Jenny, do you think I knew you were going to say anything like that?"

"I only said it because I thought I was never going to see you again."

He gave a sudden huff. "Well, if that isn't the most illogical thing I've ever heard."

She bristled. "What's illogical about it?"

"If you have a longing for a fellow, you don't confess it five seconds before bidding him goodbye forever. You don't leave him standing on Dover pier like a—"

"I never said I longed for you. I only admitted to a pang—"

"Of longing."

"Oh, what difference does it make? It was a ridiculous thing to have said. Had I known you were coming with me, I'd never have mentioned it at all. I'd have taken these dratted pangs or whatever they are—and that kiss I gave you—straight to my grave."

Tom's mouth hitched in a reluctant smile. "If that's truly the case, then I'm glad you didn't know."

Jenny's heart skipped a beat—or several. That lopsided smile of his did unsettling things to her constitution. It made her feel breathless and quivery and quite unlike herself. She wasn't at all sure she cared for the sensation.

She turned her gaze to the window until she regained her composure. It was raining out, the French countryside passing by in a blur of gray skies and brown winter landscape. "Why did you come with me? You needn't have. Not now I've got Ahmad and Mira." She shot him a narrow look. "And don't say it was to keep me safe or to help me find Giles. We both know that's nothing but convenient flummery."

"It also happens to be the truth. Though, I'll admit those concerns weren't at the forefront of my mind when I first made the decision to accompany you."

"What, then?"

"It was an impulse, initially."

"Rubbish. You're not impulsive."

"Not generally, no. But when I woke in the parlor at Half Moon Street, I realized that I had to go with you. It was a feeling more than a thought. Nothing particularly logical about it."

She stared at him. "Do you mean…you only made the decision to accompany me yesterday morning?"

"I told you it was an impulse. A powerful one, too. I got straight up from the sofa and took myself off to book my passage and arrange for my travel documents."

"My goodness, that *was* impulsive. And quite unlike you. I can't think what could have prompted such rash behavior." Her brows drew together in concern. "I trust it wasn't Mrs. Culpepper's visit."

"It wasn't Mrs. Culpepper."

"Then why?"

He shrugged. "I don't know." A faint flush appeared high on his cheekbones. "Perhaps I've been having a similar pang to the one you described in Dover."

Chapter Six

The train rattled noisily along the track through acres of rain-soaked pastures, forests, and vineyards. But in the first-class compartment where Jenny sat across from Tom Finchley, the passing French landscape, the jolt of the brakes, and the sounds of the whistle and the hissing steam all faded from her awareness. She heard nothing, saw nothing, but him.

His words sent a shockwave through her body, stunning her as surely as a shock from one of those newfangled electrical machines she'd lately had experience with. She went perfectly still; her gloved hands clasped tight in her lap. Even her breath seemed to have stopped. "Do you mean to say that you have *feelings* for me?"

"Is that so hard to believe?"

"It is, rather." Her gaze dropped to her hands, her heart and her mind battling for supremacy. The very notion that he bore some small affection for her was as bitter as it was sweet. "I wish you hadn't told me."

"Why?"

She raised her eyes back to his. "Because nothing can come of it."

"Who says so?"

"I do. You know I don't wish to marry. Not you or anyone. I haven't earned my freedom only to exchange it for another form of servitude."

"I'm not proposing to you, Jenny."

A blush bloomed in her cheeks. "I *know* that. I didn't mean—"

"Indeed," he said. "Marriage needn't even enter the equation."

And just like that, all of the oxygen seemed to leave the railway carriage.

Jenny stared at him, lips still half parted on words that had evaporated the instant he uttered what had to be the most incendiary sentence she'd ever heard in her life.

Marriage needn't enter the equation?

Great God almighty, had Tom Finchley lost his mind?

He didn't appear to be suffering from any visible head injury. Nor did he seem to be under the influence of strong spirits. He was regarding her calmly, steadily, as if he hadn't just uttered those seven fateful words. Except…

No. He wasn't calm at all. Any semblance of such was only the thinnest veneer, beneath which he was unnaturally still, his muscles taut as he waited for her to say something. Anything.

She moistened her lips. "What is it that you're suggesting?"

Tom's breath gusted out of him. He pushed his fingers through his hair. "I don't know. But we're together now and will be for a long while to come. There will be ample time for us to explore this…attraction…or whatever it is between us."

Jenny's heart threatened to hammer straight out of her chest. Her voice dropped to a scandalized whisper. "Do you mean…?"

A rush of scalding color swept up his neck. "My God, no. Nothing like that. I wouldn't presume… That is… What I'm talking about… What I propose—what I very much wish— is that we might dispense with this pretense of being indifferent to one another. That we might…"

"What?"

"Find some degree of solace in each other's company."

"Solace," she repeated.

"By which I mean companionship."

"Oh." The single word was no more than a breath. A *disappointed* breath. She'd expected something more daring. Holding hands or sharing a kiss, perhaps. Both actions would be highly inappropriate, of course. They weren't an engaged couple. Neither was he courting her. Nevertheless…she privately admitted to a distinct curiosity.

What would it be like to be kissed by Tom Finchley?

Her mouth went dry at the thought. She liked to think herself an adventurous person. A bold female who didn't let society's rules dictate her every behavior. But to kiss a gentleman who wasn't her intended? It passed beyond the scandalous and into the realm of the outrageously wanton.

She didn't wish to be thought of as shameless. And yet…

Her gaze lingered on Tom's lips. It took an effort to raise her eyes back to his.

"Or," he said, "if you like, we can agree to forget this entire conversation."

"Are you jesting? You must be, for I don't believe I'm capable of forgetting a single word you've said."

His expression turned rueful. "That shocking, was it?"

"That's certainly one way of putting it."

"Forgive me. I spoke too boldly. I beg your pardon if I've offended you."

The rain beat a steady rhythm against the velvet-curtained windows. Jenny contemplated accepting Tom's apology, if for no other reason than to put this incident behind them. They needed to be comfortable in each other's company. Awkwardness and embarrassment during a journey of this length would be unbearable. Far better to brush off his bewildering proposal and set her mind to the prospect of her forthcoming adventures.

But a liaison with Tom would be an adventure, too.

"You haven't offended me," she said. "Quite the opposite. I find myself intrigued."

Tom's gaze found hers. "Do you?"

"Yes, but...I'm not entirely certain what you mean by companionship. Something more than friendship, I gather. But how much more? And in what form?"

He cleared his throat. "In general terms? Closeness, I suppose. Familiarity. Even tenderness, if we're so inclined."

"You're speaking of romance."

"If you like."

Doubt infiltrated her thoughts—and her voice. She shook her head. "We scarcely know each other."

"At this moment, you know more about me than almost anyone on earth."

She gave him a startled look. "Do you mean because I know about Mrs. Culpepper? Oh, but surely—"

"You *know* me," he said. "And we know each other. Better than most courting couples, I'd wager."

Her pulse accelerated, even as her stomach clenched. Was there ever such an unsettling feeling? It was equal parts fear and breathless anticipation. "Now you're speaking of courtship."

"Must we put a label on it? Isn't it enough to say that we're fond of each other?"

"I *am* fond of you. Enormously fond, as I believe you're well aware."

A slow smile spread over Tom's face. "And I'm fond of you. Enormously fond. As for the rest of it…we have plenty of time. An abundance of it. Hours until we reach Marseilles and then six days at least on steamer ships to Malta and Alexandria. After that…"

"However long it takes to journey to Calcutta. Another three or four weeks, I think, depending on the trains and the weather at sea."

"Come. We can do better than that sad estimate." He rose and crossed the short distance to sink down at her side. She had only a fraction of a second to snatch away her hat before he crushed it beneath him. "Where's your *Bradshaw's*?"

She stared at him, her cheeks flushed with color.

"Jenny?"

"It's in my reticule."

"Fetch it, will you? We can go over our route."

She retrieved the little cloth bag from its place at her feet, opened the drawstring mouth, and withdrew her battered travel guide. Each of her movements caused another part of her to brush against him, from the curve of her arm to the swell of her skirts. It was maddeningly intimate—and surely as disconcerting for Tom as it was for her. Indeed, he seemed to have stopped breathing altogether.

"Let me see," she murmured, flipping through the dog-eared pages. "Ah. Here it is." She angled the book for him, her finger pointing to a miniscule line of print. "Calcutta."

Tom leaned closer, drawing his head near to hers as they pored over the train schedule. "And here we are." He set his own gloved finger to a point on the accompanying map.

"We have thousands of miles to go yet," she said. "Weeks and weeks of travel."

"Every one of them taking us farther away from our lives in England."

Jenny detected an odd note in his voice. "Are you having second thoughts?"

"A few," he admitted. "Third and fourth ones as well."

"It's not too late to turn back."

"And leave you to continue on alone?"

"I wouldn't be alone. I have Ahmad and Mira now. You said yourself that they're more than capable of looking after me. And if you have doubts—"

"It's not that. It's just…I still can't quite believe I've done it. That I've left so much of my life behind. Being here with you—on a train rolling through the French countryside…it doesn't seem quite real."

"No," she agreed. And then she smiled. "But what an adventure."

Tom had it on good authority that there wasn't a sleeper train in the whole of France. Instead, railway passengers embark-

ing on overnight journeys were obliged to sleep sitting up—
if they slept at all.

As for himself, he didn't feel much inclined to slumber.
It was a quiet, moonlit night, intermittently interrupted by a
shower of rain, the blackness of a long tunnel, or the sounds
of raised voices and feet pounding down the corridor as the
train stopped and started. New passengers boarded and old
ones were ushered off, all to the accompaniment of the train's
whistle and the upraised voice of the porters.

At Paris, he'd suggested they disembark. They could break
their journey. Stay a night or two and enjoy the benefit of fine
food and comfortable lodgings. Wouldn't that be a nice diversion? But Jenny had been unmoved. She was set on reaching
India without delay.

"We've already wasted a day by overnighting in Calais,"
she'd said.

Tom had an argument prepared for just such an objection,
but he'd refrained from using it. There was no point wasting
all his rhetorical ammunition this early in their journey. No
doubt he'd need every argument he could muster to keep
Jenny's worst impulses in check once they reached India.

She was such a determined creature. So full of courage
and certainty. Justin had called her a managing female, but
Tom recognized what his friend could not. In the absence
of family and friends, Jenny Holloway had become accustomed to relying on herself. To trusting her own judgment
and valuing her own opinions.

What need had she of a man?

He looked at her in the darkness, feeling the same peculiar tightening in his chest he'd felt the first day they'd met.

A small oil lamp swung from the corner of their compartment, casting a flickering glimmer over her dozing form. She was facing the window, one arm draped loosely over the swell of her green silk skirts. He couldn't see her eyes—had no idea whether she was awake or asleep. From his seat beside her, he could only see a shadowed glimmer of her profile. The soft curve of her cheek, the firm line of her jaw, and the delicate shell of her ear.

She'd removed her hat shortly after they boarded the train. Her head was uncovered, her hair bound up in a large, haphazard roll at the nape of her neck. It looked as if her pins could scarcely contain it. Several curling auburn tendrils had already sprung lose to frame her face.

He wanted to reach out to her. To brush the stray strands back from her cheek. It would be no more than what they'd already discussed. An act of familiarity. Of tenderness. She wouldn't object, surely.

But great as the temptation was, Tom resisted. He was in no hurry. He'd learned to wait for what he wanted.

He settled back in his seat, folding his arms. A short moment later, Jenny turned her head to look at him. Their eyes met in the shadows. "I thought you were asleep."

"No. Just woolgathering." She yawned behind her hand. "What time is it?"

Tom withdrew his pocket watch. "Quarter past eleven."

"It feels later."

"It does." He returned his watch to the front pocket of his waistcoat. "What about?"

"Hmm?"

"Your woolgathering. Was it on any subject in particular?"

"Oh that." She paused. "I was thinking about Giles."

A pitcher of ice water upended over his head couldn't have been more effective.

Giles Reynolds, 6th Earl of Castleton. Damn him to Hades and back. He was the proverbial ghost at the feast. A gentleman against whom Tom could never hope to compete.

A gentleman who was very probably no longer alive.

"What about him?"

"Mr. Thornhill hasn't spent very long trying to find him. Just since the business with Helena's uncle was settled last October. The inquiry agent he hired hasn't even traveled to India yet. And Mr. Thornhill himself has only written letters."

"I wouldn't say *only*. Those letters Thornhill wrote to his acquaintances in India produced the only creditable lead we have on the last days of the late earl."

"You're speaking of Colonel Anstruther? The officer who witnessed Giles's death?"

"I assumed he's the reason you're so set on reaching Delhi."

"He is. I mean to question him. To look him in the eye and ask him straight out what happened to Giles at the siege of Jhansi. After that, I intend to question anyone else I can find with a connection to the siege, all the way down to the officers' batmen and servants. The only trouble will be in locating them all."

"Anstruther might be of help in that regard."

"And if he tells us nothing?"

"Someone else will. We've only to ask the right questions."

"I don't hold out a great deal of hope," Jenny said. "But that won't stop me from exhausting all of my efforts. Helena is so certain that her brother is alive. She says she'd know it if he were dead. That she'd feel it somehow."

"What about you? Would you feel anything if Giles were dead?"

"I don't see how I should."

"You've kissed him."

"*He* kissed *me*. And the experience was hardly enough to inspire an affinity for one another. Indeed, when the letter came with news of Giles's death, I had no reason to doubt it. After all, why would Colonel Anstruther lie about such a thing? Unless he was confused or suffering some sort of injury himself. In which case—"

"Giles was rumored to be having an affair with Anstruther's wife."

"*What?*" She drew back from him. "Who told you that?"

"Thornhill. One of his friends in India wrote him with the local gossip. Apparently, there was no love lost between Giles and Anstruther. Whether that has any bearing on Anstruther reporting Giles dead, I have no idea. But it's an interesting fact, nonetheless."

"Helena never said anything."

"Perhaps she was embarrassed? The tale doesn't cast her brother in the best light."

"You knew about it."

"Only because Thornhill wished me to do what I could to find out if Giles might still be alive."

"Did you discover anything that might be of use?"

"Regrettably no. I have little influence in India. My power—such that it is—reaches only so far as the English shore. And possibly into Le Havre."

"Why Le Havre?"

"I had a case there once. A lengthy matter. I developed a dozen or so contacts in the area." Tom frowned. "No. When it comes to India, it's Thornhill who has the reach. And even that's limited by the events of the uprising. He left Cawnpore with a black cloud over his head. I don't expect he'll ever go back."

"He would if Helena asked him to."

"Is she likely to do so?"

"No," Jenny admitted with a sigh. "Not even for Giles. Which is why it's up to me to discover what happened to him. There's no one else to do it. No one who has the mettle—and who knew Giles as I did."

"You needn't look so oppressed. You're well on your way."

"Yes, but to what end?

"The truth, I trust. Whatever that may be."

Her brow creased. "I suppose."

"You don't sound entirely convinced."

"I am. That is, I *was*. Things were much clearer to me in the daylight. They always are. When night falls, I...I have a terrible habit of second-guessing myself. It's one of the reasons I find it so hard to sleep."

He smiled at her confession. She'd made it so quietly. So haltingly. As if self-doubt were something to be ashamed of it.

"And now you're laughing at me."

"No," he said. "*No*. But you're not the only one who suffers from a lack of certainty. I have moments of self-doubt myself on occasion."

"Yes, but at my age—"

"At your age? You're eight and twenty, not eight and eighty. I'm years older than you and I still—"

"How many years?"

Tom stopped, midsentence, feeling his face heat. Was there no end to the blushes Jenny Holloway could wring out of him? "Three and thirty. I look older, I know. A consequence of my profession. You should see Fothergill."

"Nonsense. You don't look old at all." She raised a hand to his face, her fingers brushing the edge of his hairline. "You've no trace of gray hair."

He looked at her intently, holding his breath as the pads of her fingertips touched his temple, lingering just above the metal arm of his spectacles. It was the briefest contact. Seconds, merely. But it fired his blood and set his heart to racing.

She withdrew her hand, her face coloring in the light of the oil lamp. "Forgive me, I—"

"Don't apologize."

"I feel foolish being so forward."

"Don't," he said again, his voice gone gruff. "Everything you do is pleasing to me."

Her expression softened. "Oh, Tom. You say that now…"

The rest of her words were lost in the shrill whistle of the train. It slowed as it approached the next station, the shriek of the engine and the screeching brakes piercing the darkness.

A guard shouted: "*Dijon! Dix minutes d'arrêt!*"

Jenny sat forward in her seat, the thread of their conversation seemingly forgotten. "Ten minutes? That's not very much time."

"No." But it was more than had been allotted at the last stop. There, they'd only been given six minutes to disembark and avail themselves of the buffet. Several of the passengers hadn't completed their business fast enough. Tom had seen them running alongside the train, shouting and cursing as it departed the station without them.

"Can we get out?" Jenny looked hopeful.

"That depends. Are you very hungry?"

"Famished."

"Then yes. But you have to stay close to me. We don't want the train to leave with only one of us on board."

"No, indeed." She retrieved her hat, securing it on her head with a dangerous-looking hatpin.

Tom glanced out the window at the smoke-engulfed platform. It was too late for dinner and not early enough for breakfast. Nevertheless, when they disembarked, it was to find the railway refreshment room fully stocked. Two very tired-looking ladies worked behind the counter, doling out comestibles to the equally tired passengers. For six francs, Jenny purchased two baskets, each containing a cold meal of breads, meats, and cheeses. Another two francs bought a bottle of burgundy wine.

Tom's efforts to pay for their food and drink were politely—and rather firmly—rebuffed. Under other circumstances, he might have been offended. But Jenny was determined to embrace her newfound independence. He wouldn't begrudge her the privilege.

"I won't be beholden to you," she said. "It will only confuse things between us."

"At least allow me to carry this for you." He lifted the second basket of food from her arms.

A German gentleman complained loudly at the counter. "You have a nerve charging these prices for food of this quality. Is it any wonder *Baedeker* advises us to see to our own sustenance?"

"*Bradshaw's* made no mention of bringing our own food," Jenny whispered as they exited the refreshment room.

"An unfortunate oversight. We'll have to remember it for the journey back."

"Much good that will do me. I may not be coming back."

Only six short words, but they were enough to knock the breath out of him. He couldn't recover it, not even when Jenny's hand came to rest on his arm.

"Oh look, there's Ahmad and Mira." Jenny waved at the two servants. "I do hope they haven't been too uncomfortable in second class."

Ahmad and Mira crossed the gaslit platform to meet them. They looked rumpled and tired, their faces drawn from lack of sleep.

"I've bought a basket of food for you both," Jenny said.

Ahmad took one of the baskets from Tom's arms and peered inside.

"Thank you, madam," Mira said.

"Don't thank me. I'd no idea we were meant to bring our own food along. Have you been very miserable? One of the porters said there was no water available on the train. And we all must sleep sitting bolt upright. Perhaps we should have—"

"They're fine," Tom interrupted. "They've done this all before, remember?"

Ahmad's mouth pulled up at one corner, but he said nothing. He and his cousin had endured far worse conditions than those in a second-class railway car. Tom didn't know every particular, but he knew enough to realize that their employment as servants to Jenny Holloway was something of a godsend for them. They'd never complain, least of all over some minor discomfort.

"Come," he said. "We all of us must get back on board. These tyrannical railway fellows have no qualms about leaving passengers behind."

The scream of the whistle gave truth to his statement, urging them all off in their separate directions up and down the platform, through the billows of steam. Tom and Jenny had no sooner entered their compartment and sunk into their seats than the train began to depart the station.

"That was cutting it rather close," he said.

Jenny didn't seem to hear him. She was immediately occupied with opening the basket she'd purchased. After a brief rummage about, she withdrew a hunk of bread and cheese, the quality of which could best be described as indifferent. Her nose wrinkled. "I thought French food was supposed to be superior to all others."

"Not the sort purchased at a railway buffet."

She took out a wrapped package of cold meat. "How very disappointing."

"Best accustom yourself to being disappointed. It's the better part of travel, or so I understand."

"I don't accept that. Nor should you. Just because you've had bad experiences with travel in the past doesn't mean—"

"I have no experiences with travel. I've been no farther from England than Le Havre. Didn't I say so?"

Jenny's brows shot up. "You're not serious."

"Is it so hard to believe?"

"Well….yes," she said with her characteristic frankness. "I was sure you were well traveled. At least as well traveled as Mr. Thornhill."

"Thornhill was a captain in Her Majesty's Army. There's no comparison."

"Yes, but…you said you wanted to look after me. To keep me safe. How can you when you don't know anything more about India than I do?"

"I know what Thornhill's told me. And what I hear from my clients and read in the papers."

"That's hardly enough."

"No," he acknowledged. "What's enough is the mere fact that I'm a man."

"Oh—!"

"I know you don't like to hear it, but it's true. You'll have an easier time of it now that I'm with you." He uncorked the bottle of wine. "And I'll have an easier time as well."

Her blue-green eyes kindled. "Men generally do."

"Undoubtedly. However, in this case, I'll have an easier time of it because I can keep an eye on you. I won't be stuck back in London, sitting in my office, imagining all of the dreadful things that might have happened to you had you ventured out on this adventure alone."

"And for this small peace of mind, you're willing to upend your entire life and accompany me around the globe?"

"Who said it was small? Besides, it's not forever. I'll have to return to London eventually."

"When?" she asked. "After we find out what happened to Giles?"

"I don't know." It was the truth. He hadn't thought that far ahead. For the first time in his life, he'd been impulsive. He hadn't planned things out to the last degree. There'd been no time to strategize. No opportunity. All he'd known was that she was leaving and that he must do something. Anything.

There were no pressing legal matters to constrain him. For years, the tortuous case between the Viscount Atwater and the Earl of Warren had formed the bulk of his practice. Now that it was settled at last, Tom's immediate future was his own to do with as he wanted. And what he wanted was to be with Jenny.

"So this journey with me is nothing but an interlude. A time out of time. In other words, not part of your real life at all."

Tom's hand stilled on the wine bottle.

"But it's part of *my* real life. Indeed, it's just the beginning of it. I meant what I said about not coming back. If the mood strikes me, I may very well remain in India or Egypt or even here in France. Can't you understand? I feel as though I've walked through a door. Until two days ago, I'd only ever caught glimpses of what lies beyond it. And now that I'm here—now that I've passed through to the other side—I can't imagine ever going back to all that bleakness and misery."

"It doesn't have to be that way," he said.

"Perhaps not, but it's how I feel about it."

"Why should you? You're not a companion anymore. You're a woman of means. There'd be nothing bleak about your settling in London or somewhere in the English countryside. Nothing miserable about remaining close to your friends."

"Haven't you ever wanted a fresh start?"

"One needn't move thousands of miles away to start anew. Trust me, the world's not that much brighter on this side of the door."

"Not to you. You've existed here your entire life."

"Not quite my entire life, but I take your meaning. You're restless and dissatisfied. I won't minimize such feelings. But I warn you, these far-off vistas you crave are likely nothing more than a mirage in the desert. They only dazzle when you view them at a distance. An unknown place in some distant land can't undo the tragedies of the past. If it could, we'd all be travelers, spending our natural lives on steamer ships and trains."

"And yet," she said, "my future is my own. My travel plans mine and nobody's else's. You won't force me to return to England simply because it's your idea of what's right and proper."

"I've no intention of forcing you to do anything."

"And you won't employ any of your legal tricks to try and persuade me?"

"Legal tricks, Jenny?"

"You know precisely what I mean. Don't pretend that you don't."

He didn't answer. Couldn't answer. Because he knew exactly what she meant. He had, in fact, planned to ply her with arguments. To weaken her resolve. To convince her to come home once her adventure was over. Back to England where a future between them might actually be possible.

It was the same manner of manipulation he employed against his adversaries. Zealous advocacy administered so subtly, so smoothly, that they were often left believing the idea he'd argued for was their own.

I'd rather you not do that to me, Jenny had said this morning.

A twinge of guilt pricked at Tom's conscience.

She didn't want to be managed and manipulated. Not by him. Not by anyone.

If he wanted her in his life, he couldn't win her with plotting and trickery. He would have to win her on his own merits. Not as a solicitor, but as a man.

The idea terrified him.

"Tom?"

"Of course I won't employ any tricks against you," he said gruffly. "Legal or otherwise."

"Do you promise?"

His palms were damp on the cool glass of the wine bottle. He had the vague sense that he was signing away his soul. But there was nothing for it. Not when they'd already come so far. "Yes," he said. "I promise."

Chapter Seven

Marseilles, France
February, 1860

Jenny hadn't realized how much of travel depended on the quantity of one's linens. And yet, it was linens—or the lack of them—that occupied the majority of their last day in France. Upon arrival in Marseilles, they'd taken rooms at the Hotel des Ambassadeurs. It was there they'd met Mrs. Plank. The redoubtable lady was bound for India along with her two daughters and had wasted no time in extolling the importance of sufficient linens for the journey.

And not only linens. She'd also emphasized the necessity of additional chemises, stockings, and soap. The sum of items mentioned was far greater than anything Jenny had brought with her—a fact which had provoked a minor panic.

"One trunkful," Mrs. Plank declared from her place near the fire. "No less, mind. You and your brother will need every bit of it."

Jenny lowered her diminutive cup of coffee back to its gilt-edged saucer. She was seated beside Tom on a tufted settee in the hotel's lavish salon. They'd gathered there, along with several of the other guests, after dinner. "I have more than a trunkful now," she assured Mrs. Plank. "Indeed, I bought so much linen today that I was obliged to purchase more luggage."

Tom had accompanied her from shop to shop, up one cobbled street and down another, never uttering a word of complaint, though Jenny knew he must be exhausted after their rail journey. She certainly was. When they'd arrived in Marseilles, she'd wanted nothing more than a warm bath, a hot meal, and a nap. But the dire pronouncements of Mrs. Plank and the other matrons residing at the hotel—all waiting to board the steamer ship to Malta the next morning—had made an impression. And Tom had agreed. Additional linens and luggage must be bought while they still had the opportunity.

At least the rain had stopped. It wasn't even particularly cold in Marseilles. Certainly not in comparison to London.

"More luggage?" Mrs. Plank's eyes narrowed. "Not another of those enormous sea trunks, I trust."

"No, ma'am," Jenny said. "I took your advice and bought three of the smaller leather portmanteaus. The ones with waterproof covers."

"Excellent." Mrs. Plank nodded her approval. "And you mustn't forget to pack what you'll require for immediate use in a carpetbag. The steamers don't allow trunks and portmanteaus in one's cabin. They're secured away on the ship until it reaches port."

Mrs. Hardcastle, another of the overbearing matrons in residence, nodded along from her seat across from them. She and her husband were traveling to India as chaperones to their eighteen-year-old niece. "Before the railway was extended in Egypt, one had to transport all one's luggage in a van across the desert. Portmanteaus and carpetbags were a necessity."

"Now there's rail, one can bring whatever one likes," Mr. Hardcastle said. He was half-reclined in a chair at his wife's side, his eyes heavy-lidded from drink. "We've brought a full complement of pots and pans for Dulcie. And a bathtub as well. No worries about the natives having to haul it from Alexandria to Port Suez."

"You'd have done better to buy her households goods in India," said Mrs. Plank. "It's the linens that must be bought here. One can't have too many for the sea voyage."

"Exactly how many times have you made this journey, Mrs. Plank?" Tom asked.

"Let me see." Mrs. Plank clucked her tongue. She was a large woman. The formidable, bullying sort Jenny had often encountered during her time as Lady Helena's companion. "I accompanied my eldest daughter in '54. She married Sir Anthony Tiverton, a diplomat of some importance. I made another trip out in '57 not long before the mutiny. On that occasion, my second eldest was wed to the youngest son of the…"

Jenny's finished her coffee as Mrs. Plank droned on. She would have preferred a cup of tea. Something to settle her stomach. Their luxurious hotel dinner, comprised mainly of bouillabaisse and entrees swimming in rich cream sauces, had made her feel a trifle ill. She was beginning to worry that, despite her normally strong constitution, the rigors of travel didn't agree with her.

It didn't appear to have any effect on the other guests staying at the hotel. Like Jenny and Tom, most of them had arrived in Marseilles by rail. And yet they looked none the worse for wear. To be sure, the younger girls seemed inordinately bright-eyed and eager. Mrs. Plank's daughters especially. They sat beside their mother, listening to her with rapt attention. They were pretty girls, though no one would call them beauties.

"She's taking them to India to find them husbands," Tom said a half hour later as he escorted Jenny to her room on the third floor. "And she won't be the only gimlet-eyed mama we encounter during our journey. The ship is likely to be full of them." His lips quirked in a tired smile. "They call them the Fishing Fleet."

"Who does?"

"Everyone, apparently. According to Mr. Hardcastle, the bachelors come to the harbor to meet the boats. There's a scarcity of Englishwomen in India."

"Yes, but the Fishing Fleet? It's not very flattering."

"Rather apt, though." Tom unlocked her door and held it open for her. "Mrs. Plank and her daughters have been eyeing you all evening. Trying to determine if you're competition."

She gave him a sharp look. "They most certainly have not."

"Oh, but they have. Mr. Hardcastle came right out and asked me if I was taking you to India to find you a husband."

"Impertinent. I hope you left him with a flea in his ear." Jenny stepped into her room.

Tom remained at the door. "I told him the truth."

She turned to face him. "Which is?" Considering the fact that he'd told everyone they met that she was his sister—a product of his mother's second marriage, no less—she wasn't entirely certain what the truth was anymore.

"That we're going to look for a friend who disappeared during the uprising."

"Oh."

"Did you think I'd make something up?"

"I don't know. I feared you might." She paused before admitting, "I hate the lies we've told."

"One lie," he said. "A necessary one. And one on which we'd already agreed."

"Yes, but...I didn't expect you'd embellish it quite so much."

"How else to account for our having different last names?"

He was right. Of course he was. But Jenny still felt uneasy about it. She'd been known to withhold the truth now and then, when the occasion required it, but outright lying was another matter. It troubled her that Tom had such an innate facility for it. This morning, when first they'd met Mrs. Plank, he'd uttered that rot about her being the child of his mother's second marriage so smoothly, so easily. It hadn't appeared to bother him at all.

"Yes, but—"

"It's your reputation, Jenny. Would you rather I told them the truth?"

She compressed her lips. "I haven't any choice, have I? You've put me in a devilish position."

"I know. And for that I can only beg your pardon." He glanced past her into the empty hotel room. An oil lamp was lit, illuminating a bed that was presently heaped with half-packed luggage. "Where's Mira?"

"Still at dinner with Ahmad, I expect. He said he was taking her to a café."

Tom's eyes met hers. "Shall I wait with you until they return?"

Jenny's stomach fluttered. Wait with her? Here? It shouldn't sound so shocking. They'd just spent a whole day and night together in a railway carriage after all. And yet…the very idea of Tom keeping company with her in a hotel room was too scandalous to contemplate.

Scandalous and quite deliciously tempting. Like a piece of forbidden fruit offered to her on the flat of his hand. All she need do was reach out and take it.

But she was not wholly lost to propriety. Not yet, anyway.

"No, thank you," she said. "I'm going to order a bath."

The words were out before she'd fully considered them. *A bath?* Good lord.

Tom cleared his throat. "Well. I'll, ah, leave you to it, then."

Jenny bid him a swift goodnight, shutting the door a touch more firmly than she'd intended. She had no strength of will, that was the problem. When it came to Tom Finchley, she was ready to fling her hat over the windmill. To abandon her principles, her very reputation, and throw herself into his arms.

Marriage needn't even enter the equation, he'd said.

But he hadn't been speaking of *that*. He'd been speaking of companionship. Of tenderness.

No one had ever accused her of being an overly tender person. Strong and forthright, perhaps. Temperamental and stubborn and loyal to a fault. But tender? Affectionate? She wouldn't know where to begin.

Everything you do is pleasing to me, he'd said.

The memory of if sent a nervous tremor through her veins.

What exactly was it that he wanted from her? He knew she didn't wish to marry, that she didn't wish anything to interfere with her newfound independence.

But he was already interfering. She should be thinking of Giles—of her adventure—not worrying over her feelings for Tom.

She called for a bath and, after a long soak, wrapped herself in a woolen dressing gown and proceeded to finish packing away her new purchases. There were more than ten sets of linens, a dozen chemises and thin cotton stockings, and a full fifteen bars of fine-milled white Marseilles soap.

Next to so much, the dresses Jenny had brought seemed inadequate to the journey. But there was no time to visit the dressmaker. Her meager wardrobe would have to suffice until they reached India.

She'd nearly finished packing when Mira returned, full of apologies for the lateness of the hour.

"Don't apologize," Jenny said, struggling with the latch on one of the new portmanteaus. "But do help me shut this. I believe one of us may have to sit on it."

When the final portmanteau was closed, the two of them retired to bed only to be awakened a mere six hours later by the sound of a maid rapping sharply at the door.

Jenny sat bolt upright amidst her tangled blankets. Her eyes were bleary, her hair in disarray. But no amount of fatigue could keep her abed. It was time to go. To get up, get dressed, and finally start her adventure.

The Peninsular and Oriental Steam Navigation Company kept a veritable fleet of ships. Their fastest steamship, the *Valetta*, regularly made the mail journey from Marseilles to Malta.

Jenny's stomach was awash with butterflies as she boarded the magnificent vessel.

Ahmad and Mira had gone ahead with the luggage. As on the train, most of the servants were obliged to travel second class. The rest of the passengers—more than one hundred by Jenny's count—were comprised of well-to-do ladies and gentlemen and their daughters, granddaughters, and nieces. The Fishing Fleet in all its glory.

Tom's hand came to rest at the small of her back as Jenny stepped onto the deck of the ship. Mrs. Plank was already there, shouting orders to the crew while her daughters looked on with wide, unblinking eyes.

"She's not the largest ship," a crewman was saying to Mrs. Plank, "but she has paddles and engines big enough for a vessel three times her size."

"What use are paddles and engines when there aren't enough private cabins to accommodate the guests?" Mrs. Plank retorted. "See here, young man…"

Tom guided Jenny past them. "You have a private cabin," he said when they were well out of earshot. "It's small. They all are. But it will give you some privacy until we reach Malta. The captain says it should take no more than three days to arrive in port."

Jenny nodded mutely. She was certain she must look as goggle-eyed as the Plank girls. She'd never been on a ship of this size before. It was terribly exciting. A bit overwhelming, too.

The wind off of the sea whipped at her skirts and teased at the ribbons of her velvet bonnet. It was salty and sharp, and smelled, rather appallingly, of fish. Her stomach recoiled at the pungent reminder of last night's bouillabaisse. She silently commanded it to settle, having no wish to disgrace herself before the ship had even left the harbor.

In short order, a young crewman approached to take them to their quarters. He was a robust young chap who claimed to have made the journey to Malta more times than he could remember. "The *Valetta's* one of the fastest steamers running. Why, last month we made port in fifty-four hours. And that was despite a heavy gale."

Jenny found her tongue at last. "Is she safe?"

"Safe, ma'am? Why, she's one of the safest vessels ever built. That's what the captain always says."

His assurances did nothing to assuage Jenny's sudden onset of nerves. But her fears made little matter in the end. By half past ten, the *Valetta* was steaming out of the harbor at speed, leaving the Port of Marseilles far behind them.

After a brief visit to her cabin, Jenny returned to the deck with the other passengers to watch the city disappear from view. Mira and Ahmad stood beside her at the railing.

"Do you remember this part of the journey?" Jenny asked. "Seeing Marseilles in the distance as you arrived?"

Ahmad was staring out at the water, his expression somber. "We came by a different route. Around the cape. It took four months to reach Southampton from Bombay."

"Four months?" Jenny had known it was a longer journey around the cape, but she'd no idea it was a full third of a year. Her stomach gave another rebellious quiver. "And all that time on a boat?"

"Most of it. The soldier who took us from India—"

"What soldier?"

"An Englishman," Mira said. "A colonel retiring from service in Delhi."

Jenny eyes went first to Mira's face and then to Ahmad's. "Do you mean to say, this soldier—this Englishman—brought you here against your will?"

Ahmad shrugged. "We were children."

"And he just...*took* you?"

"On sufferance. He only wanted Mira. He was acquainted with her mother before she died."

Mira's cheeks darkened. "She made him promise to bring me to England. To give me a better life."

A flicker of anger sharpened Jenny's voice. "Where is he now?"

"Dead," Mira said.

"Dead," Ahmad agreed. "Many years since."

Jenny's anger died as quickly as it had flared to life. Frustration took its place. "Did he make no provision for either of you?"

Ahmad smiled dryly. "He died of drink, Miss Holloway. And it was on drink that he spent his last coin."

"You needn't worry so, madam," Mira said. "Ahmad took care of me."

Jenny looked at her two new servants. It was difficult to think of them as such. Mira was dressed as smartly as Jenny was herself in a dark skirt and jacket bodice, a bonnet covering her sleek tresses. Ahmad was turned out just as well in a sharp tweed jacket and trousers, his thick black hair swept back from his brow with pomade. They were a handsome pair, and Jenny suspected, as British in their thoughts and habits as anyone else in England. How could they not be when they'd come to London as children?

She wondered if she was doing them a disservice by taking them back to India. What if they had no wish to return there?

No desire to be reminded of the life they'd lived before? What if they were merely acquiescing because they desperately needed employment?

"Are you looking forward to our visit to Delhi?" she asked.

They were quiet for a long moment. "It will be interesting to see it after so many years," Ahmad said at last.

"Then...you don't mind it? Traveling there with me, not knowing when we might return?"

"Oh, but Mr. Finchley said—"

Ahmad cut Mira off before she could finish. "We are quite content, Miss Holloway."

Jenny would have questioned them further, but she was stopped short by the arrival of Tom. He emerged from the mass of passengers on the deck in the most peculiar fashion. One moment he was simply *there*. As if he'd materialized out of the ether.

Her heart gave a few hard, hopeful thumps at the sight of him. She didn't know why. There was nothing particularly remarkable about Thomas Finchley. He was, admittedly, taller than her and respectably broad of shoulder—though nowhere near as formidable in size as Mr. Thornhill. He was, instead, the sort of man who could blend easily into a crowd or disappear into the shadows.

It wasn't that he was plain or ordinary. Not in the usual sense. Indeed, there was something almost sinister about the unremarkable quality of Tom's countenance. Perhaps because it wasn't entirely natural. It was something she suspected he'd cultivated. A quality he used to his advantage, the way a predator might employ a convenient camouflage.

Oh, but she was being fanciful, surely. Tom Finchley wasn't dangerous. Certainly not where she was concerned. Unless, of course, one counted the very real threat he posed to her virtue.

He joined them at the rail, one of the few gentlemen on deck to have foregone a hat. His hair flopped over his forehead, giving an almost boyish air to his rather too-serious face.

"How did you find your cabin?" she asked.

Tom pushed his hair back from his brow. "I don't have one."

"What? Why not? Was there some mistake with booking our passage?"

He gave her a grim look. "No mistake. There are only enough single and double berth cabins to accommodate the ladies and married couples. We bachelors must bunk together."

"Oh, Tom. I'd no idea. Is it going to be dreadful for you?"

"I've endured worse. Besides, it's only for three days."

"Unless," Ahmad said, "we hit bad weather in the Strait of Bonifacio."

Tom shot him a look. "You've been listening to the sailors."

"Ahmad wanted to be a sailor," Mira volunteered. "If not for me, he would have joined Her Majesty's Navy."

"Is that true?" Tom asked.

Ahmad didn't look pleased at his cousin's revelation. "When I was a boy. Not any longer."

Jenny's hand tightened on the rail as she turned to address the two men. "Is the strait dangerous?"

Tom and Ahmad exchanged a weighted look.

She didn't have to be a mind reader to realize that they were keeping something from her. "Whatever it is you're not telling me—"

"There was an accident there long ago," Tom said. "It's nothing to trouble yourself over. Ahmad should never have made mention of it."

"How long ago?"

"Five years." He hesitated before adding, "The French lost a frigate there during a storm. It hit a reef and sank. There were no survivors."

A chill of foreboding shivered down Jenny's spine. "What time of year was it? Not February, I hope." Her question was greeted with an awkward silence. Her stomach sank. "February, then." She lifted her gaze to the clear blue sky. "But there's no storm coming now."

"And the ship is powerful." Mira directed their attention to the churning water. "See how it cuts through the waves?"

Jenny gripped the rail with both hands. "That's comforting."

Tom came to stand beside her. "Even if there were a storm, it's not likely to sink us."

"I pray it won't. I'm not a very strong swimmer."

His hand rested next to hers on the rail. Their gloved fingers touched. "I am."

"And that's supposed to reassure me?" She huffed. "I suppose if everything goes to the devil, I must rely on you to rescue me."

Tom's blue eyes were solemn behind the lenses of his spectacles. "And I will. Every time."

Chapter Eight

P & O Paddle Steamer Valetta
Marseilles to Malta
February, 1860

Tom didn't see Jenny again for the rest of the morning. She retired to her cabin, pale and drawn, not long after they left the Port of Marseilles. When he knocked on her door at luncheon it was opened the tiniest crack by Mira.

"Miss Holloway has retired until dinner," she informed him. "She asks not to be disturbed."

Tom put his hand on the door, only just preventing her from shutting it in his face. "Don't be ridiculous. She's clearly ill. If you would step aside—"

"She doesn't wish to be disturbed, sir."

This time, when Mira snapped the door shut, Tom made no move to prevent her.

Good lord, only a few days in Jenny's employ and the blasted girl was already as starchy and intractable as her mistress.

He ran a hand through his hair in frustration before making his way back to the upper deck. Ahmad was there, engaged in conversation with one of the younger sailors. When he saw Tom, he detached himself, his stride surprisingly steady on the rolling deck of the ship.

"Do you have need of me?"

"As a matter of fact, I do. Your cousin has barred me from Miss Holloway's cabin. She's plainly unwell."

"She's seasick," Ahmad said. "They both are. The same thing happened when we crossed the Channel."

The young sailor strolled over to join them. "It comes on like that with some of the ladies. Some of the gents, too."

"Shall I summon the ship's surgeon?" Ahmad asked.

"There's naught he can do, sir. It has to run its course."

Tom looked at the sailor. "And how long is that?"

"Two, maybe three days."

"In other words, the entire length of our journey to Malta." Tom sighed. "Never mind the surgeon. I'm sure the ladies will rally."

Or so he thought. In fact, Jenny made no appearance at dinner. This time, when he called at her cabin, Mira opened the door only enough to pop her head out. Her complexion was decidedly green.

"Miss Holloway says she will send for you if she requires anything. She bids you goodnight, sir."

"Do either of you need a doctor?" His words bounced off the cabin door as it was shut in his face. "Damn and blast," he muttered under his breath. He'd hired a veritable guard dog to act as Jenny's companion. Is this what the rest of the journey was going to be like? Doors shut in his face and messages sent through surly maids?

Hat clutched in his hand, he sought out the ship's surgeon for a word. The man was in the ship's saloon enjoying an after-dinner pipe. "All quite normal, I assure you," he said between puffs. "They'll be better tomorrow after they've voided everything in their stomachs. If not, come and fetch me and I'll have a look at them."

Tom spent a restless first night on the *Valetta*, bunked in with the handful of other single gentlemen. He tossed and turned in his berth, the pitch and yaw of the ship rocking him asleep only to jolt him back awake again.

It had been well over two decades since he'd slept in a room with so many other males. Not since his days in the orphanage in Abbott's Holcombe. There, it had been two boys to a narrow bed. The mattresses had been vile, the straw stuffing damp and frequently teeming with fleas. For warmth, they'd each been allotted a single blanket—a scratchy woolen scrap, which did nothing to keep out the icy air that seeped into their tiny bones.

Justin had shared his bed with Neville, while Tom had spent his nights in the orphanage huddled next to Alex Archer. They'd all been friends. As close as brothers. But in his youth Tom had always been closer with Alex. Perhaps it was because they were the same age, both arriving at the orphanage as infants sometime in the winter of 1827. They'd been playmates. Companions in both mischief and misery. Tom couldn't remember a time when Alex wasn't there, until... suddenly he wasn't.

Or perhaps not so suddenly.

There had been signs, after all. Warnings of what was to come. As a grown man, Tom could see them quite plainly. As a child, he'd been completely in the dark. Too much of his days and nights had been caught up in fear and worry. There had been little opportunity for examining subtleties. Little time for anything save the business of surviving.

When Fothergill had fetched him from the orphanage and taken him London, Tom had, for the first time, been given his own room. Privacy had been a rare luxury in the orphanage. An uncommon privilege. But under Fothergill's tutelage it became a right. An absolute necessity. Within a year, he'd spent so much time alone, reading through law books and copying out papers, that he was far more comfortable with his own company than that of others. At last, the world had quieted down. He had finally been able to focus. Organize his thoughts into some semblance of order.

After the orphanage, solitude had been a godsend. It was only lately that his solitary existence had begun to pall. And it was no great mystery why. Indeed, he could trace his dissatisfaction with his life back to the very day.

At dawn he rose with the crew, and after washing, shaving, and dressing, called at Jenny's cabin again only to find that she and Mira were still terribly seasick. The night, it seemed, had done nothing to calm their stomachs. The very pitch and yaw that had kept him awake had served to exacerbate their symptoms. And today it was worse. The wind was high and the sea a churning stew of white-capped waves.

Tom sent Ahmad for the ship's surgeon. The pair of them waited outside the cabin while he examined Jenny and Mira. When he emerged from the room ten minutes later, his expression was grave.

"Your sister's maid has a fever. She must be taken to the infirmary."

"What's wrong with her?" Ahmad demanded.

The surgeon flashed him an irritated look. "A fever, boy, didn't you hear me?" He turned back to Tom. "Is your servant capable of carrying her to the infirmary? Or shall I summon the steward?"

Ahmad glowered at the man. "I'm capable, sahib."

Tom inwardly grimaced. "This isn't helping."

The surgeon didn't appear to register either remark. He was an elderly British gentleman, oblivious to any offence he might have caused. He continued talking without pause while Ahmad ducked into the cabin to retrieve Mira. "The maid doesn't appear to be contagious, but best to be careful. I'll keep her in the infirmary tonight under observation. As for your sister—"

"Yes?"

"She has no fever as yet. If she comes down with one, send your lad for me."

"How is she otherwise?"

"Seasick. Give her some beef tea when she can keep it down." The surgeon's tone was dismissive. He stayed only long enough for Ahmad to return from the cabin with Mira. She was huddled in his arms, her flushed face turned against his shoulder.

"Anything she needs," Tom said to Ahmad. "Do you understand?"

"Does *he*?"

"She'll have whatever she requires," the surgeon snapped. "Now come along, boy, before she catches her death."

When they'd gone, Tom rapped lightly on the door to Jenny's cabin. He wasn't going to force his presence on her. If she desired privacy, that's exactly what he intended to give her. But she was ill, even if it was only seasickness. On receiving no answer, he had no compunction about letting himself in. In times like these, one didn't wait for a gilt-edged invitation.

He found Jenny in her berth, curled half on her side. She was in her underclothes, her legs covered by a long, ruffled petticoat, and her midriff and bosom scarcely concealed by the thin fabric of a cambric chemise.

Tom stopped where he stood. It was all he could do to remember to shut the door behind him. He leaned back against it, his heart pounding so hard he was sure she must hear it.

Good lord. Her hair was down.

He swiftly removed his spectacles. Jenny Holloway's ample charms were instantly transformed into a blur of color and shape. He wasn't entirely blind without corrective lenses, but at a distance, he could no longer see the swell of her hip or the high curve of her breasts. He could no longer see those thick auburn locks tumbling all about her in a fiery tangle.

It gave him a moment to gather his bearings. To calm his racing pulse and catch his breath.

"Tom?" she croaked.

"I'm here." He steeled himself before shoving his spectacles back onto his nose.

She turned over on her back. Her face was drained of all color. He saw it for only an instant before she covered it with both hands and muttered something wholly unintelligible.

He picked his way across the cabin. There was clothing draped over every surface and two unpacked carpetbags littering the floor. A pitcher, basin, and cloths sat at the ready on the washstand. "What did you say?"

"I said...go away."

"Don't be ridiculous. Mira's gone to the infirmary with a fever. You need someone to take care of you."

"Not you."

He winced. "Would you prefer Ahmad?"

"Anyone," she mumbled.

"Anyone but me, you mean." He stood, frowning down at her. "Have you any particular objection to my helping you?"

"Yes. I look awful. Now would you please go?"

A weight lifted from his shoulders. "You're right. You look dreadful."

Jenny groaned behind her hands. "Oh, just leave me alone."

Tom stripped off his coat and tossed it over the back of a chair. It was warm inside the cabin, the air oppressive for lack of ventilation. He rolled up the sleeves of his linen shirt. "You also look thoroughly indecent. What the devil are you doing in your underclothes? Don't you have a nightgown or a dressing gown or—"

"Please stop talking."

He filled the basin with water and wet a cloth. "I suppose, if Mira doesn't rally before we reach Malta, I'll be obliged to play lady's maid."

"I don't need a lady's maid. I—" She broke off. "Oh God. I think I'm going to be sick again."

Tom sank down on the edge of her berth. He pressed the wet cloth to her brow. "You're not going to be sick." To his knowledge, she hadn't eaten since they left Marseilles. He doubted whether there was anything left in her stomach.

Her hands slid from her face. She looked absolutely wretched. "I'm so disappointed," she said. And then, much to Tom's alarm, her blue-green eyes puddled with tears.

His heart clutched. "About what?"

"Adventuring."

"Ah." He bathed her face, moving the cloth over her skin as gently as he could manage with a hand that was damnably unsteady. "Not quite what you expected, is it?"

"I don't have the constitution for it. I'm not strong enough."

"Nonsense. It's only a bit of seasickness. You'll be better tomorrow."

Her lips trembled. "I was getting dressed. That's why I'm in my underclothes. And I couldn't even do that without disgracing myself. I can't seem to—"

"You're being too hard on yourself."

"I'm not. I should have known—"

"You are. I have it on good authority that even the strongest men have been known to succumb to seasickness on their first voyage."

"You haven't done."

He moved the cloth down the slender column of her throat. She was wearing the same fine gold necklace she'd worn when they dined in Half Moon Street. It pooled between her breasts, half sticking to her skin. She was damp with perspiration, strands of auburn hair clinging to her face and neck like curling tendrils of seaweed. "It doesn't affect everyone in the same way. A fact for which you should be grateful. Imagine if we were all ill."

Her fingers encircled his wrist, stopping the downward progress of his hand. "Tom—"

His eyes found hers. "Would you like me to stop?"

"No, it's just…"

"What?"

"My stupid pride." Her words were thick with unshed tears. "I didn't want you to see me in such a state."

A wave of tenderness assailed him. "You have nothing to worry about."

"I do. I look dreadful, you said. And now you'll always remember—"

"Hush. I only said that because I was trying to rile you. To get your spirits up. The truth is..." He cleared his throat. "The truth is, you're so beautiful I'm finding it rather difficult to look at you."

Under other circumstances, Jenny might have blushed. He'd seen her do so several times during the course of their journey. But this time, she was too pale and weak to lose her pallor. She merely looked at him, a notch working its way between her brows as her eyes searched his. "Perhaps," she said at last, "you need new spectacles."

"I don't need spectacles at all when I'm this close to someone."

"Don't you?"

"No." He took them off. "There, you see. Now we're both undressed."

Her throat rippled in a visible swallow. "Is that what it feels like to be without them?"

"To a certain degree. I've worn them as long as I can remember. Without them...I suppose I feel vulnerable. Foolish of me, but there it is."

She lifted a hand to his face and traced the bridge of his nose with her fingertip. There was a bump on the ridge. Evidence of the break he'd suffered as a boy. "How did it happen?"

"It was a very long time ago."

"Don't you remember?"

"What I remember is that Cheevers tried to set the break himself. Had he summoned the village doctor, I might not be the sad specimen you see before you today."

"I think you're very handsome."

Tom's heartbeat quickened, even as his mouth hitched in a wry smile. "Perhaps I'm not the only one who needs spectacles."

The ship chose that precise instant to rise up in the water and pitch back down. Jenny's hand abandoned his wrist and moved swiftly to cover her mouth. She stifled another groan.

Tom pressed the cloth back to her forehead. He couldn't recall when he'd last felt so utterly useless. She was in anguish and here he was doing nothing more effective than dabbing at her face with a wet cloth. It wouldn't do at all. He was going to have to find a way to help her acclimate.

"Don't you feel anything?" she asked.

"Yes. Keenly. But it doesn't affect my stomach."

"I despise your stomach."

"Undoubtedly. The ship's surgeon suggested a cup of tea to settle yours. Shall we try it?"

"I couldn't."

"Let's. And then, when you're a little more yourself, I'll escort you up onto the deck for some fresh air." He folded the cloth, leaving it draped over her brow as he put his spectacles back on. "But first, for my own peace of mind, I think we'd better get you into a dressing gown."

Much to Jenny's relief, the first dose of tea remained firmly in her stomach. Encouraged by the result, Tom plied her with weak tea and toast throughout the day. He even tidied her cabin, causing no little amount of mutual embarrassment as he folded away her corset and stockings.

Jenny watched him from where she lay propped up in her berth. She'd never seen him in his shirtsleeves before. It seemed an extraordinary intimacy. Then again, considering he'd only this morning encountered her in her petticoats and chemise, they were already on rather intimate terms.

Still, she couldn't tear her eyes away. He'd rolled up his sleeves, revealing leanly muscled forearms that were lightly dusted with hair. He appeared to be leanly muscled everywhere, from the broadness of his linen-clad shoulders down to the cloth waistcoat he wore buttoned over his trim midsection.

A gentleman who spent most of his day at a desk shouldn't be in such fine form. He should be soft about the middle, gone to fat from too much sitting and self-indulgence.

"Do you take exercise?" she asked.

"I beg your pardon?"

"You're extraordinarily fit."

"I don't know that there's anything extraordinary about it." He closed her carpetbag after packing away a final stack of folded linens.

"For a solicitor?"

"Why not? We all of us are always running somewhere or other. I've spent the better part of my career chasing after hansom cabs and omnibuses, trying to get papers to Fothergill or to clients or to file them with the court."

"I would think that's what a clerk was for."

"I don't keep a clerk."

"And you don't box or fence or anything else to keep fit?"

His lips quirked. "Do I look like I box or fence?"

"You do, rather."

"I shall take that as a compliment." He crossed the cabin to stand over her berth. "How are you feeling? Any better?"

"Much better, thank you."

"You don't have to thank me."

"I believe I do. It can't have been pleasant to spend so much of your day in here with me. Not when I was so ill and being such a poor patient."

"I'd far rather be here with you than socializing with Mrs. Plank and the rest of the Fishing Fleet."

"Have you heard anything more about Mira?"

"She's improving. Still a little feverish, but it doesn't appear to be anything serious."

"And Ahmad?"

"He's camped outside the ship surgeon's door, being completely unreasonable. She's in no immediate danger. There's nothing he can do for her now but allow her to get some rest."

"I daresay he's hoping to be of some use. To help Mira get well in the same way you helped me."

"The difference being that you didn't have a fever. If you had, I'd have—"

"What?" She stared up at him.

"I don't know. Probably camped outside the surgeon's door and been completely unreasonable." He smiled wryly. "It's stifling in here. Will you let me take you up on the deck?"

It sounded a lovely idea, but… "I'd rather not see anyone else. I'm still not steady enough to manage polite conversation."

"It's after sunset. We'll be quite alone." He held out his hand. "Come. You can lean on me if you need. I won't even require that you talk."

"Oh, very well." She slipped her hand into his. It fit there perfectly. As if it had been made to settle in the warm curve of his palm, to be held fast by the strong clasp of his fingers. Her heart thumped hard. "I have to dress first."

Tom helped her to her feet. "Do you need assistance getting into your gown?"

There was nothing suggestive in the tenor of his voice. Nevertheless, Jenny felt the thrill of his question all the way to her toes. She pulled her hand free. "What I need is a few moments of privacy."

A hint of a smile touched Tom's mouth. "As you wish." He retrieved his coat from the back of the chair. "I'll wait for you outside."

Jenny watched him go, then made the speediest toilette of her life.

She rinsed her mouth in the basin and cleaned her teeth, raked a comb through her tangled tresses and bound them up in a hasty arrangement of plaits and pins, and—after a brief moment of indecision—slipped on her corset, closing the hooks with trembling fingers. There was no way to forego the dratted thing. Without it, none of her dresses would fit properly. Certainly not the fitted jacket bodice and skirt she chose.

When she was finished dressing, she swept up a shawl and exited her cabin, forgetting her gloves and bonnet in her haste. True to his word, Tom was waiting outside. He offered her his arm and Jenny took it gratefully. She wondered if she would ever become accustomed to the way the deck of the ship rolled beneath her feet. She braced for the motion to echo in her stomach, but—much to her relief—her tea and toast stayed down.

Tom led her up to the deck. The sea air was cold on her face, a delicious feeling after spending so much time in her cabin. It wasn't dark yet. The sun was just sinking beyond the horizon, streaking the sky and the water below it in a dazzling array of oranges and reds. She stood at the rail, her arm still linked through his.

"It's magnificent, isn't it?"

She nodded, her gaze fixed on the endless prospect of the sea. "I've never seen anything like it."

"Nor have I."

They watched the rest of the sunset in silence, saying nothing else to each other until it had slipped completely from view. Jenny heard the swell of far-off voices, the sounds of the crew shouting to each other, and passengers talking and laughing. She and Tom weren't alone on the deck. It was impossible to be so on a ship of this size.

And yet, as they stood side by side at the rail, she had a sense of privacy. Of intimacy. As if they were the only two people on board.

Tom seemed to read her mind. "No one can see us here. Not now it's dark."

"It's not *that* dark." A full moon was coming up. It wouldn't be long before it was shining, luminous in the sky above them, as bright as a line of oil lamps arrayed on the deck.

"No matter. There's nothing untoward about a fellow standing at the rail with his sister."

Jenny suppressed a grimace. She was beginning to hate that particular lie. "I don't think I like being your sister."

"No more than I like being your brother. But it's a necessary fiction if we want to protect your reputation." He nudged her. "What were your real brothers like? Were you fond of them?"

"If you must know, they were absolute pains in the backside."

Tom was surprised into a bark of laughter.

"It's true." She let go of his arm, placing both of her hands on the railing. "They take after my father."

His expression sobered. "They weren't—"

"Drunkards? No. They weren't bad men. They were just men. Selfish and dictatorial, never lifting a finger to look after themselves—or me." She recalled the years she'd lived in her father's house. All the time she'd spent praying that something would change. That someone would come and save her. "My brothers wanted to get away as much as I did. They had plans, you see. To marry and start families of their own. They expected I would stay at home forever, taking care of my father. It was my duty, they said."

"Why yours and not their own?"

"Because I was an unmarried woman, and therefore, a burden on the family. To them, I was no more than a drudge. An unpaid housekeeper. They didn't love me. Not like Giles loved Helena. I daresay I wasn't very loveable."

"And so you left."

"Not without a plan, but yes. I wrote to Helena's father, imposing on our tenuous familial connection to beg employment from him. He replied within the month, offering me a position as Helena's companion. As soon as I had his letter in hand, I packed my case and boarded the next mail coach to London." Pride rose within her at the memory of it. "One grows tired of waiting for knights in shining armor. Sometimes nothing will do but to rescue oneself."

Tom looked at her, his face half-shadowed in the darkness. "How little I know of you."

"Don't you? And here I thought you knew everything about everyone."

"As a general rule."

"How do you usually find things out? By planting spies in people's houses as you did with Helena's uncle?"

"Sometimes."

"I daresay, if you were interested enough, you could have found out plenty about me."

"Who says I wasn't interested?"

She gave him a weighted glance. "And yet you claim to know nothing."

"It didn't seem fair to delve into your past."

"You considered it?"

"More than once." He laughed at her expression. "I'm a curious man."

"Not curious enough, it seems."

His smile faded. "No." He looked out at the roiling sea, his arms folded over the railing. "I was content to keep you a mystery."

"There's nothing mysterious about me."

"Isn't there? You've managed to surprise me a time or two since we left London."

Jenny felt the beginning of a blush creeping up her neck. She was glad of the darkness. "Were you terribly shocked by what I said at the pier?"

They'd been to several piers since that first one in Dover, but Tom asked for no clarification. She didn't suppose he needed one. The memory of her impulsive declaration was no doubt burnt into his brain. "A little."

"Only a little?"

"Very well, it was more than a little." He set his hand beside hers on the rail. "But you see...I already had an inkling that you cared for me."

"As a friend."

"As more than a friend." His fingers brushed hers. "When I was falling asleep on the sofa at Half Moon Street, I felt you touch me."

Jenny went still. Her bosom rose and fell on an unsteady breath. "Did you? How mortifying."

"Please, don't be embarrassed. The truth is...it meant a great deal to me. I haven't had much tenderness in my life. There's been no softness. No sweetness. Not even when I was a lad. Lately, I've begun to feel the lack of it."

"You make it sound as though any female would fill the void."

"Hardly. If that were the case, I wouldn't have spent the past years living alone. I would have married or..."

"Or."

"Quite. But I haven't. It's never been the right time. There was too much work to do. Too many commitments. It's only these past months that something in me has changed."

"Hence, the pangs of longing." She sighed. "Oh, Tom, we're both lonely, that's all. And we've only come to realize it since Helena and Mr. Thornhill were married."

"Is that what you think?"

"It must be, mustn't it? Theirs is one of those great love affairs. It casts the rest of us in the shade. Makes us feel as though we're missing something important in our lives. Or someone."

"That's not the reason."

"It is," she assured him. "An unmarried person always feels inadequate in such circumstances. It's perfectly natural."

"It's not that."

"What else could it—"

"It's you, Jenny. All these feelings. They all started with you."

She turned her head to look at him, brows knit in confusion. "What?"

"I felt something for you long before Thornhill and Lady Helena were married. Long before they even met."

"I don't understand how—"

"From the moment you walked into my office last year, inquiring after that blasted matrimonial advertisement in the *Times*, I felt something…" He took her hand in his and pressed it to his chest. "Here. This is where I felt the first pang for you."

Jenny's hand rested flat on the breast of his waistcoat. His heart thumped strong and fast beneath her palm. He was nervous. Surely as nervous and uncertain as she was herself.

"I'm not a romantic, Jenny. And I'm certainly no knight in shining armor. What I am is desperately fond of you. I believe I'd do anything in the world to make you happy."

She swallowed hard. Her voice, when it came, was a mere thread of sound. "Oh, Tom, what am I to do with you?"

"For now? Just let me be with you. I don't require anything else."

"That's easy enough. You're stuck with me for the foreseeable future." She brought her hand up to cup his cheek. "Whatever possessed you to board that steamship in Dover? You might be in your office now, writing up one of your legal papers."

"Do you know, at the moment, the prospect holds no appeal at all." He gazed down at her. "May I kiss you?"

Jenny's throat went dry. All she could do was nod.

He took a step forward and set one arm about her waist, drawing her against the leanly-muscled length of his body.

She was at once enveloped by the heat and strength of him. Caught up in the scent of bay rum, linen, and clean male skin. Her pulse fluttered as he touched her face.

"How extraordinary you are," he murmured.

She trembled in his arms, too overwhelmed by the moment to speak. What in the world could she possibly say when every nerve ending in her body was firing with anticipation?

But Tom was in no hurry. He was slow and deliberate, his fingers tracing down the edge of her jaw to gently cup her chin. He tilted her face up to his.

She felt his breath whisper over her lips as he bent his head to kiss her. And then—

And then Mrs. Plank's voice echoed down the deck, as unsubtle as a trumpet blast. "Mr. Finchley, is that you lurking about? And who's that with you there? Is that your sister?"

Tom froze, his mouth hovering a fraction of an inch over her own.

For the barest instance, Jenny thought he might ignore the interruption. That he might actually press his lips to hers and kiss her.

But there was no chance of that.

He withdrew from her all at once, releasing her from his arms and moving a full two feet away from her.

Jenny suppressed a cry of frustration. Curse Mrs. Plank! The dratted busybody. "How long do you suppose she's been there?"

"I don't know." Tom's voice was grim. "Not long, I hope."

She turned away from him, setting her hands on the rail of the ship to steady herself as he answered Mrs. Plank. The woman didn't come and join them. That was something, at least. But not enough. Not when he'd come so close to kissing her only to draw back at the final moment.

It left Jenny feeling oddly off-kilter, awash in emotions she couldn't begin to understand.

She didn't hear Tom approach. Suddenly he was just… there, standing at her side, a great wall of masculine warmth. It took all of her will not to lean into him. Not to burrow back into his arms like some desperate, affection-starved spinster.

"Forgive me," he said.

"For what, precisely?"

"My lack of foresight. When it comes to matters of importance, I usually plan things out a bit better."

"Is kissing me important to you?"

"Everything about you is important to me. I'd have thought that would be obvious by now."

"Not to me it isn't. That is——" She broke off. "I know you care for me, but…I don't like to assume anything more."

He brushed a curling lock of hair back from her face, tucking it behind her ear with gentle fingers. "You're so full of fire. So capable and confident. Sometimes I forget just how innocent you are."

She huffed, even as she quivered at his touch. "I'm not a child, Tom."

"I didn't say you were a child. I said you were an innocent."

"I'm not—"

"You are. The worst sort. The kind that doesn't even realize how innocent she is."

Jenny did look at him then. How could she not? "I know I'm inexperienced. Dreadfully so. That's what all this is about. This journey so far from home. I mean to broaden my understanding. To have experiences out of the common way. But I don't intend to make myself ridiculous in the process."

Tom's gaze held hers. "I see."

"I don't know that you can." Her hands gripped the rail as she tried to explain. "There's a kind of woman in my world. An unmarried female of a certain age. The sort who imagines that every gentleman who does her the smallest service is in love with her. People laugh at her behind their hands. Such a sad, dried-up old dear with her foolish romantic fancies."

Tom didn't say anything. Didn't give any sign he objected to her characterization—or agreed with it, either. His silence prompted her to continue.

"There's an opposite to that pathetic spinster. A young lady whose fate is far more common. She gives in to the expectations of her family—of society—and signs her life away in marriage." A gust of wind off of the sea rustled Jenny's hair and skirts, filling her lungs with the scent, the very taste, of an adventure that lay just beyond her grasp. "I feel I've spent all of my life caught between those two poles. Struggling to maintain some semblance of independence. But society's expectations are a powerful force. Almost as powerful as the romantic fancies of a spinster."

"You fear you'll succumb."

"More than anything."

"There's only one problem."

She cast him a glance. "Which is?"

"Your whole concept is wrongheaded. You're no more likely to make yourself ridiculous over a gentleman than you are to bow to the dictates of society."

"Oh, but I am. Indeed, I already have. Do you remember the first letter you wrote to me? It wasn't even truly a letter, only a note to fix the time and day we'd meet to discuss Mr. Thornhill's matrimonial advertisement. There was nothing at all familiar about it. And yet I kept it as surely as any love token."

He gave her a look that was hard to read. "Did you?"

"After we first met face-to-face, I couldn't bring myself to discard it. How kind he is, I thought. Surely the attention he paid me must be out of the ordinary. Surely he was as moved by me as I was by him." She smiled bitterly. "A spinster's yearnings."

"But I *was* moved by you. I fancied you from the first moment I set eyes on you."

"Perhaps that's only because bachelors of a certain age are subject to a similar tension."

"Societal pressure versus private desperation? Rubbish. You're putting too much thought into this. And that's coming from me, a fellow who puts too much thought into everything."

Jenny opened her mouth to respond, but there was no opportunity. Another shout from Mrs. Plank put an end to their conversation, this time for good.

"Do come and join us, Mr. Finchley," she called out. "We're woefully short of gentleman."

The sounds of the ship swelled in the background. The call of the sailors and the laughter of the Fishing Fleet. With the dinner hour over, many of the passengers had come up on deck for a breath of air or a stroll in the moonlight. Any semblance of privacy was gone.

"I suppose we'd better do as she asks," Tom said. "It would be odd of us not to, all things considered."

"Yes." Jenny took his arm as they reluctantly moved to join the others. "We must keep up appearances."

Chapter Nine

P & O Paddle Steamer Indus
Malta to Alexandria
February, 1860

There was no storm in the Strait of Bonifacio and no rough water to pitch them onto the reef. They made port in Malta a mere fifty-five hours after leaving Marseilles. The prospect of the capital city, with its magnificent domed church, steepled cathedral, and ancient fortifications, beckoned to them from the harbor. But there was no opportunity for exploring. Their stop in Malta was brief, only long enough to change ships. Within an hour, they were settled on the *Indus*—a larger and far more comfortable vessel on which they would make the journey to Alexandria.

Unlike the *Valetta*, the *Indus* boasted English stewards and stewardesses, comfortable cabins with sweet-smelling sheets, and a well-appointed saloon with plenty of good food served at table, including a generous selection of oranges, grapes, and other fresh fruits taken on board at Malta. It was the closest thing Tom could imagine to a pleasure liner, and the British subjects on board treated it as such. There was music and laughter and games of cards and charades. One might think they were in attendance at a country house party rather than on board a ship steaming toward Egypt.

Tom and Jenny were obliged to take part in some of the activities, if for no other reason than to show themselves sociable and prove that their relationship as brother and sister was aboveboard. After their inauspicious meeting with Mrs. Plank on the deck of the *Valetta*, Tom sensed some doubt about the latter. It didn't help that he and Jenny were as opposite in appearance as two people could be. With her flaming auburn hair and sea-colored eyes, she looked nothing at all like his half sister, nor even his cousin or second cousin once removed.

"Where did you say the pair of you are from again?" Mrs. Plank asked on their second evening on board the *Indus*. The wine served at dinner had loosened her tongue to an unfortunate degree. "I don't recall having met any Finchleys in London, nor any Holloways."

Tom was seated next to Mrs. Plank and her daughters at the table, half-finished plates of mutton and potatoes still poised in front of them. Jenny sat across from him, her face a studied blank.

He took a swallow of his wine, well aware how much she disliked it when he lied. "We're from Devon, originally."

"Whereabouts in Devon?"

"Abbot's Holcombe." In Tom's experience, the best lies were the ones that adhered closest to the truth.

"A resort town, isn't it? And the pair of you live there together?"

"I reside in London, ma'am. My sister's only recently come up from Devon."

"Your sister still looks a bit peaked," Mrs. Plank said. "Not in poor health, is she?" She raised her voice to address Jenny. "India isn't the place for people in poor health, my dear. They sicken and die there at an alarming rate. Why, I know of a lady who's been twice widowed since she arrived in Calcutta five years ago."

"I'm perfectly well, ma'am," Jenny said.

Mrs. Plank took no notice. "This gentleman you're looking for in Delhi. Went missing, did he? During the mutiny?"

"At the siege of Jhansi," Tom said. "He was reported dead."

"And does this gentleman have a name?"

Jenny looked at Tom, a question in her eyes.

Tom was silent. In truth, he didn't know how useful it would be to share the subject of their search with someone like Mrs. Plank. There was, of course, a small chance it might generate more information about Giles. However, there was a better chance it would result in gossip about Jenny. Once her connection to Giles and Lady Helena was revealed, it wouldn't take much effort to deduce who she was—and who she wasn't.

"Come now," Mrs. Plank prompted. "It's a small world in India, Mr. Finchley, as you'll soon find out. We're a tight-knit group when we're in residence—far more so than when we're at home. A proper English village, Mr. Plank liked to call it. We none of us have any secrets there."

Jenny's chin lifted a fraction. "His name was Giles Reynolds. He was the 6th Earl of Castleton."

Was.

Tom hadn't any wish to damn the man before they'd even begun their search, but in the deepest recesses of his heart, he hoped that Jenny's tense was correct. It was selfish of him, he knew. Lady Helena would be delighted to find her brother alive, as would Justin, by association.

But Tom could see nothing positive about the late earl's resurrection from the dead. Not for himself, at any rate.

Giles had kissed Jenny. He'd written to her. He'd referenced marriage, for God's sake. Granted, the reference had been in the negative. There was no real indication he'd ever wanted to wed his sister's companion. But he'd *kissed* her.

Tom couldn't get the thought out of his head.

He recognized it for what it was. It was possessiveness. A masculine instinct of the most primitive kind. He was reacting as if Jenny belonged to him. As if he had some claim over her heart—and her body. The impulse unsettled him deeply.

"*The Earl of Castleton!*" Mrs. Plank's voice carried throughout the saloon. The other guests turned to stare, craning their necks in curiosity. "Why, I never. Do you mean to say that you *knew* his lordship? That you have reason to believe him *alive*?"

"His body was never recovered after the siege," Tom said.

"Oh." Mrs. Plank visibly deflated. "Is that all."

Jenny's own face fell. "You think it makes no difference?"

"It was madness during the mutiny," Mrs. Plank replied, as if that explained all.

"Are you acquainted with the earl's family, sir?" one of the Plank girls asked in timid tones. She was seated at Tom's left. A sparrow-faced girl who couldn't have been any older than seventeen.

"After a fashion," Tom said.

"No need to be coy, sir." Mrs. Plank pointed her fork at him. "We shall get the story out of you one way or another."

"There's no story to tell, I'm afraid. We had a passing acquaintance before he left for India. My sister and I hope to question those who knew him there. With any luck we may discover something to put the matter to rest for his family."

"A great expense of time and money with little chance of success. But it needn't be a wasted journey. You must visit us in Delhi after we've settled. Any acquaintance of the Earl of Castleton will be most welcome."

Tom exchanged a glance with Jenny. He hadn't realized Mrs. Plank and her daughters were traveling all the way to Delhi. He'd hoped to part ways with them earlier. "You're very kind, ma'am."

Mrs. Plank gave a dismissive wave of her fork. "Nonsense. We must stick together. It isn't safe to be striking out on your own. Even if you have brought a pair of natives with you."

Jenny's fingers tightened on her glass. "My servants are from London. They're as English as you or I."

"Oh, my dear." Mrs. Plank laughed heartily. "You fool no one by dressing them in frock coats and gowns. Mark my words, the instant we step foot into Calcutta, they'll shed their clothes like any savage. The natives loll about in Egypt and India in a frightful state of undress. One must accustom oneself."

Tom went still. He was grateful that Ahmad and Mira weren't present. Not that he could hope to shield them from such opinions for long. Indeed, the closer they got to India, the more pronounced the English passengers' prejudice. It was as if they'd crossed some invisible line. A through point after which anyone who wasn't a British colonial was—as Mrs. Plank had claimed—a savage.

"I don't believe," he said, "that one can accurately be called a savage if one is inhabiting one's own country."

Mrs. Plank's smile turned thin. "It is not their country, sir. It is ours. But I will not argue the point. This is your first visit to India. You will see for yourself soon enough."

"I met the Earl of Castleton once," the younger Plank girl said.

Everyone at the table turned to look at her.

"Don't boast, Ursula," Mrs. Plank warned.

"I wasn't boasting, Mama. I only said I'd met him. Which is true. It was last summer. He was walking down Bond Street—"

"That would be the current earl, not the young one who died in India." Mrs. Plank resumed cutting her meat. "The sixth Earl of Castleton left England before you were out of the schoolroom."

"The gentleman I met *was* quite elderly. But very civil. He bid me good morning—"

"Mr. Finchley," the older Plank girl interrupted. She was as sparrow-faced as the first, albeit sporting a bit more town bronze. "Why are you not married?"

Tom's glass froze in the air, midway to his mouth. Being together on a ship conveyed a false impression of intimacy between the passengers, it was true, but it was unheard of for an eligible young lady to be so bold with a single gentleman.

"Lydia," Mrs. Plank said sharply. "Mind your tongue."

Miss Plank continued, unperturbed. "I would think it a fine thing to be a London solicitor's wife. Especially if that gentleman had an acquaintance with the Earl of Castleton."

"Lydia has no wish to settle in India," the younger Plank girl said.

"I'd rather settle in London. I cannot abide the heat." Miss Plank looked at him from beneath her lashes. "Do you intend to remain in India, sir? Or will you be returning to London?"

Jenny stood abruptly, her chair scraping back on the floor. "I beg your pardon. I'm not feeling at all well."

Tom rose to assist her, but he wasn't quick enough. No sooner had he gained his feet than Jenny was striding out of the room.

"Oh dear," Mrs. Plank said with a laugh. "She doesn't have the stomach for travel, does she? What a shame. When I was last in India…"

Tom didn't remain to hear the rest of Mrs. Plank's tale. He lingered only long enough to make his excuses before setting off after Jenny. However, upon exiting the saloon, there was no sign of her anywhere.

In the end, he found her in the most logical place. She was inside her cabin.

Mira cracked open the door. The young maid's fever had broken before they changed ships in Malta. Only the faint blue shadows under her eyes attested to the fact that she'd ever been ill in the first place. "Good evening, sir."

"Good evening, Mira. May I speak with Miss Holloway?"

Jenny's voice rang out from within. "Oh, do come in, Tom. You needn't stand on ceremony."

Tom remained at the door.

After a moment, Jenny joined him there. She was still dressed in the pale green gown she'd worn at dinner.

His gaze drifted over her. "Are you unwell?"

"Not unwell, merely tired of spending day after endless day listening to Mrs. Plank spout her odious opinions and watching those insufferable Plank girls flirt with you." She paused. "Will you not come in?"

"It's not a good idea. I—" He broke off, realization dawning slowly. Good lord. Was she *jealous*?

"Because we might be observed? Very well. But I must say, if I were an interfering busybody, it would seem less suspicious to me if a brother entered his sister's cabin on occasion than if he made a point of never entering it at all." She moved to close the door.

Tom stopped it with his hand. "They weren't flirting with me."

Jenny snorted.

"And even if they were…" He sank his voice. "Do you think it would matter to me one jot?"

Her own voice dropped to a whisper. "It matters to *me*. And if they intend to continue casting out lures for you, I'd just as soon spend the rest of this voyage in my cabin."

"Under the auspices of seasickness."

"Why not?"

"Because I'd like to see you now and then. You're the only reason I'm here."

"And yet you won't step one foot into my cabin."

Tom lowered his voice yet again. "And have a repeat of what happened on the deck of the *Valetta*? No thank you."

Jenny drew back as if he'd struck her. "Well! If that's how you feel—"

Tom held the door firm against her further attempts to shut it in his face. "Don't be absurd. I'm not referencing our embrace. I'm referencing the possibility of being caught. Of stirring up a shipboard scandal. I should think that was abundantly clear."

She didn't reply, merely looked at him, a mulish expression on her face.

He was at a loss for how to proceed. No woman had ever found him worthy of a jealous temper. At least, none that he'd been aware of.

In truth, it had never even occurred to him that Jenny *could* be jealous, of the Plank girls or anyone. There wasn't a female on board the *Indus* who could hold a candle to her. Indeed, next to Jenny Holloway every other lady he encountered seemed colorless and insipid. He was beginning to suspect that that was going to be the case for the remainder of his life. Who could possibly come after her? The short answer was no one.

"Do you want to argue?" he asked. "To rip up at me?"

"No."

"What do you want?"

"To get off this ship. I didn't come all the way to wherever it is we are to endure a battalion of British mamas and their hopeful daughters. This isn't at all what I—"

"Somewhere off the coast of Egypt," he said.

She blinked up at him. "What?"

"That's where we are. Somewhere in the Mediterranean, closer to Alexandria than to Malta by this point."

"Not close enough." She folded her arms at her waist. Some of the tension left her face, leaving in its wake a vague expression of desolation. "Is this all a fool's errand, Tom? Do you think Giles died at the siege just like Colonel Anstruther said?"

"I don't know." It was the only answer he had and one he knew was wholly inadequate. "Fetch your shawl, Jenny."

"Why?"

"Just because I won't come into your cabin, doesn't mean we can't talk. Come with me for a walk on the upper deck. We can have a little privacy there."

"What about the risk of stirring up a scandal?"

"I think I can manage to resist you for the space of a walk." He added dryly, "Providing it's a short one."

As they strolled along the deck of the *Indus*, Jenny had to wonder if Tom had accounted for the moonlight. Or the stars. Or the way the cool evening breeze whispered over them from atop the rippling, deep blue waves of the Mediterranean. It was dreadfully romantic. Like something out of a lady's novel. The sort of scene inhabited by beautiful, raven-haired young heroines with melting voices and alabaster brows.

It was definitely not the setting for a hardened spinster of eight and twenty. Not one with auburn hair that, in some lights, could pass for red—a thoroughly unfortunate shade. And certainly not one with a short temper and a streak of stubbornness as wide as the Thames.

She tilted her head back to gaze at the stars. There were fashionable fortune-tellers in London who claimed that a lady's future was written there. Either there or in tea leaves or among the lines in the palm of her hand. At the moment, Jenny would have paid a great deal to know what her future held.

Despite the more than two thousand miles they'd already traveled, she still had the sense that she was on the cusp of an adventure. That it hadn't quite started yet. Indeed, with each stage of their journey, it receded farther beyond the horizon, shimmering there just out of her grasp. On the train to Marseilles, Tom had called it a mirage. What if it was? A terrible thought. Because then she would be forced to admit that the dissatisfaction she had with her life had little to do with the setting of it and everything to do with herself.

She refused to believe it. If she was dissatisfied with her adventure it was only because of her bout of seasickness. And because of the dratted Fishing Fleet. All those mamas and daughters, so very British and proper—and so very interested in the marital status of one Tom Finchley.

"Do you think Mrs. Plank is telling the truth?" she asked. "Is India the same as an English village, with everyone knowing one another's business?"

"In some places, I expect. Thornhill says the colonials have created British life in miniature. They keep themselves set apart, fraternizing with each other at their clubs, having dinners and dances and tea parties. It's quite the social whirl-wind, apparently."

"What of the Indians?"

"He says there's more prejudice against them in India than at home. Even more so after the uprising."

"It *was* a great tragedy."

"For all concerned—the oppressed and the oppressors."

Jenny gave him a curious look. "You share Mr. Thorn-hill's opinions?"

"On British rule in India? I tend to agree with him, yes. Does that surprise you?"

"Why should it? I've never been to India. I have no views on the subject one way or the other."

"None at all?"

She ignored the smile in his voice. She wouldn't apologize for being opinionated. "What do you wish me to say? That I abhor cruelty and unfairness, wherever it manifests itself? That I'd no more judge an Indian for rebelling than I would an Englishwoman? That we all of us have our God-given rights, even if the law doesn't see fit to grant them to us?"

"The Mrs. Planks of the world would disagree."

"I'll wager you already know how I feel about the Mrs. Planks of the world."

Tom laughed softly. "Here," he said, stopping near the rail. "I brought something for you."

She let go of his arm, watching as he reached into the pocket of his gray woolen topcoat. "What is it?"

He withdrew something and placed it in her palm, closing her fingers around it. It was round and firm, with pebbled skin.

Her lips tilted upward. "An orange!"

"One of the last we took on board at Malta."

"Thank you, Tom. How very thoughtful."

"Would you like me to section it for you?"

"I can manage." She set to work at once. Within seconds, the fragrance of freshly peeled orange swirled deliciously about them. They shared the sections, eating them in contented silence as the sea breeze ruffled their hair. When they'd finished, Tom gave Jenny his linen handkerchief to clean her hands. "They're very sticky," she said.

"And very sweet."

"Wonderfully sweet." She handed him back his handkerchief as they resumed their walk. "I apologize for being greedy. I didn't finish my dinner."

"I noticed."

"You notice everything."

"An irritating habit of mine." Tom thrust his hands into his pockets. "Jenny..."

"Yes?"

"You need to prepare yourself for the very real possibility that Giles is dead."

Jenny's spirits sank. The orange, it seemed, was only a bribe. A bit of sweetness to leaven the grim conversation to come. "I'm prepared enough."

"Are you? It doesn't appear so. The closer we get to India, the more often I see you distracted. Troubled."

"If I am, it's not over myself. It's Helena that worries me."

"What about her?"

"Isn't it obvious? She wants to find him so badly. She's never lost hope that he's still out there somewhere. If we discover undeniable proof that he's dead, she'll be devastated. And when I think of all that she's already endured—"

"None of which was your fault."

"Of course not, but I saw what the loss of her brother did to her. It wasn't right or fair. She's one of the finest people I know. The first person I could truly call my friend. If I can repay her in some small way—"

"Lady Helena doesn't expect repayment from you. She'd be offended at the very thought. She gave you an independence to set you free, not to put you in her debt."

Jenny knew he was right. Even so... "I don't know what I would have done if I hadn't been hired as her companion. My life would have been so very different. She never intended to exact any payment from me, it's true. She would, as you say, be appalled at the very idea of it. But I do owe her, Tom. I owe her everything. It's both a blessing and a burden. You can't imagine what it's like."

"Oh, can't I?" He gave a short laugh. "Would you like to know how many times Alex Archer took a thrashing for me during my years in the orphanage? Or how many times Thornhill intervened when I was being bullied by the other boys? Without the pair of them to protect me, I daresay I might have died."

Jenny stopped where she stood, turning to look at him. "What?"

He came to a reluctant halt, facing her. "I was the smallest and thinnest among us. Not strong enough to withstand the beatings and the deprivations."

"They beat you?" She couldn't conceal her dismay. "And what do you mean by deprivations? What were you deprived of?"

Tom said nothing for a long while. When he finally spoke, his voice was brusque. Businesslike. "It was food, mostly. Cheevers withheld it for the smallest infraction. He didn't like children. He ran the orphanage only because Sir Oswald appointed him to the post. The entire enterprise was badly mismanaged. The bread moldy, the mattresses ridden with insects. The worst part—" He broke off, his jaw clenching. "The worst part was that Cheevers wouldn't allow fires in the dormitories. During a particularly harsh winter, a boy froze to death in his bed. Many a night after that, I feared I would suffer the same fate."

Emotion welled in Jenny's chest. She felt her lips tremble. "Oh, Tom. I can't imagine. It all sounds so horrible." She touched his sleeve. "But you survived it. You made it through somehow."

He shrugged. "Thornhill and Archer protected me. They protected Neville Cross as well, until he outgrew them both."

"Helena says that Mr. Thornhill protects everyone in his care."

"To the point of folly."

"It sounds as though your friend Mr. Archer was the same."

"He was," Tom said. "And he wasn't. He could be heroic when he chose. Even more heroic than Thornhill. The four of us used to climb down the cliffs at Abbot's Holcombe.

Thornhill, Archer, Cross, and me. One day, Cross slipped and fell into the sea."

Jenny was familiar with the cliffs. They were some of the most treacherous in North Devon, only a smattering of rocky outcroppings breaking up what was otherwise a sheer, vertical drop into the sea. Mr. Cross's fall from them as a boy had left him permanently damaged; slow of speech and prone to drifting off in his head in the midst of conversations.

"The weather was abysmal, the water churning like a maelstrom. Thornhill dove in, but he couldn't find Cross in the water. In the end, it was Archer who saved him. To this day I still don't know how he managed it. Raw courage and sheer strength of will, I imagine. Admirable qualities, to be sure. But there was a darkness in Archer, too. A selfishness that Thornhill never had." Tom gave an eloquent grimace. "I don't know how we arrived at this morbid subject."

"We were talking about Giles. You told me I must prepare myself. But you've lost someone close to you just as surely as I have. I don't see why we can't share the burden."

"The loss of Alex Archer is no burden to me."

"You're not troubled at all by the past?"

"Not any longer. Sir Oswald is dead. Cheevers is dead. The orphanage has been razed to the ground." He gave her a long look. "It was I who bought the place. I who had it destroyed."

"You must have hated the place."

"*Hate* is a strong word. Suffice to say, I have a long memory. It's much like your imagined debt to Lady Helena. Both a blessing and a burden. For many years I never forgave an injustice. I was somewhat ruthless when it came to balancing the scales. And as for those men behind it all…"

The fine hairs rose on the back of Jenny's neck. There was something in Tom's eyes. An expression she couldn't interpret. It chilled her to the bone. "I know that Sir Oswald fell from the cliffs one night outside the Abbey. The whole of the village still talks about it. There was an inquest, wasn't there?"

"He'd been drinking to excess. His death was ruled an accident."

She searched his face. "Was Mr. Cheevers's death an accident, too?"

Tom's mouth curled into a smile. A smile that didn't reach his eyes. "Quite the reverse. Unlike Sir Oswald, Leonard Cheevers met his end very much on purpose."

There was nothing to laugh about when it came to the memory of Leonard Cheevers. And yet, at the horrified look on Jenny's face, Tom felt his lips twitch. Good lord, did she think he'd murdered the man? "He was hanged, Jenny. Arrested, sentenced, and hanged in the public square."

She did a creditable job of hiding her relief. "On what charge?"

"Something to do with stolen property."

"And for that he was *executed*?"

Ah. And there was the crux of it. "It was a discretionary sentence. The judge might have pardoned him if he wished, but given Cheevers's long history of villainy…" Tom shrugged.

Her brows knit. "Did you have anything to do with it?"

"Very little. I merely submitted a few facts about Cheevers's character to the judge before sentence was pronounced."

Understanding dawned slowly in her eyes. "One of your very persuasive legal documents."

Tom stared down at her. "You sound disappointed in me."

"Not disappointed, no. Just…" She looked at him as though she were trying to solve a puzzle. "Did you feel better afterward? After he was dead?"

"I didn't feel any worse."

"Don't be flippant."

"It was a long time ago, Jenny. Over a decade."

"But you have a long memory. You said so yourself. You can't have forgotten."

Tom ran a hand over the back of his neck. "No," he said at last. "I didn't feel any better. The man's death changed nothing. How could it? His crimes were in the past. There's no way to undo them. No way to go back. All I can do is go forward."

She continued to gaze up at him. As if she were waiting for something.

He didn't plan to kiss her. When he'd attempted to do so on the *Valetta,* it had very nearly exposed her to gossip. He'd promised himself then that he'd keep a respectful distance. It wasn't worth the risk, neither to his sanity nor her reputation. And yet…

As he stood on the *Indus,* the deck rolling beneath his booted feet and the crisp sea air ruffling his hair, his good intentions all melted away. He didn't want to talk about the past. Not when there were stars and moonlight and the sound of lapping waves.

Not when there was her.

He bent his head and kissed her very softly on the mouth. She tasted of oranges. Sweet and warm and citrus tart. She swayed against him, her hand still clutching his sleeve. Their breath mingled, their half-parted lips clinging for a long moment.

And Tom felt it everywhere, surging in his blood and pounding in his heart. This was no ordinary kiss. No dutiful bus on the cheek or chaste peck under the mistletoe. This was a *kiss*. The kiss to end all kisses. Rich with meaning and trembling with tenderness. It robbed him of breath. Set his entire body alight.

Jenny must have felt it, too. Her hand found its way to his neck, her fingers curling into the hair at his nape.

He circled his arms around her waist to steady her, holding her so close that her heavy skirts swirled all about his legs. Every fiber of his being told him to keep kissing her. Lord knew he wanted to. Indeed, for several throbbing moments, it seemed the single most important occupation of his entire life.

But good sense ultimately prevailed. It had to.

He pulled back, just as he had on the *Valetta*. "We shouldn't—"

"No." Her hand fell from his hair. "You're right."

"Forgive me, I didn't look about first. We might have been observed." He cast a belated glance around the deck. "I don't see anyone. Not now, anyway."

Jenny's face was flushed, her lips swollen from his kisses. She looked a bit dazed. A bit breathless. As if she didn't quite know where she was.

Tom had no doubt he appeared equally affected. His pulse was still struggling to regain its normal rhythm. "Jenny—"

"Please don't apologize again, Tom. It isn't very nice to have someone beg your pardon every time they embrace you."

"I wasn't going to beg your pardon. I was going to try and explain—"

"You needn't. It's all perfectly plain."

"I don't believe it is." He took her hand and tucked it through his arm. "Let's walk, shall we?"

Jenny permitted him to guide her back out along the deck. There were sailors and stewards in the distance, passengers laughing, and even a fiddle player perched somewhere below. The jaunty notes of a Scotch reel drifted up into the night, as out of place on an Egyptian-bound steamer as they were to the seriousness of what Tom had to say.

"On the *Valetta*, you told me about the sort of woman you didn't wish to be, do you remember? Neither powerless wife, nor ridiculous spinster."

"Of course I remember."

"I have a similar quandary. A sort of a man I never wish to become." He voice was quiet and—considering the erratic thumping of his heart—surprisingly steady. "In the orphanage I grew up surrounded by unwanted children, all products of liaisons between irresponsible men and desperate women. Men like Sir Oswald who used women, often against their will. And women like my mother, poor and ignorant, who gave in to the blandishments of men, hoping they might provide them with affection or some manner of security."

He felt Jenny's eyes upon him, but he didn't return her gaze.

"You often lament the fact that men hold all the power. And you're right. They do. Power in law and power in strength. I may not have been born a gentleman, but I resolved long ago that I would never use that power to take advantage of a woman. I promised myself I'd be better than that. That I'd never do to anyone what was done to my mother or the mothers of Thornhill, Archer, and Cross."

Jenny's hand tightened on his arm, pulling him to a halt.

He at last turned to look at her. Their eyes met in the flickering light of an oil lamp that hung overhead. "The closest I've come to breaking that promise has been with you. I'm here now, a part of your adventure, only because I gave you no choice. I forced my company on you, as careless of your feelings as any brute. When it came to the point, my principles couldn't withstand my desire to be near you. They crumbled at the first test." He gave a humorless laugh. "So much for principles."

"Oh, Tom. It wasn't like that at all."

"It was. And each time I take you in my arms, I'm reminded—"

"It hasn't all been one-sided. Surely you know that."

"I do, and I thank God for it, but it doesn't change how I've wronged you." He regarded her steadily. "I want you to know that I'm sorry—truly sorry—that I didn't respect your wishes at Dover. But I can't be sorry I'm here. Being with you on this journey…I wish I could say I was sorry for that, but I can't. If I did, it would be a lie. And I won't lie to you, Jenny."

Her mouth curved in a rueful smile. "We've become a pair of liars during this journey, haven't we? I daresay we shall have to make some sort of penance for it when we return to England."

Tom's heart stopped in his breast. *When* they returned to England. Not if, *when*.

But Jenny didn't appear to register the import of what she'd said. She continued on as if she hadn't just upended his world once more. "You're right. I didn't want you to come. I only ever envisioned this adventure as happening to me alone. It never occurred to me that I might have a companion. Someone to share it all with."

"It wasn't part of your dream."

"No."

"Which is why I find it so difficult…Knowing that we're only here together because I drew a net around you and trapped you." It was the very way she'd described his actions on the train to Marseilles. And she'd been right. It was exactly what he'd done to her. "How can you ever get past such a breach of trust?"

"Quite easily," she said. "I can accept your apology. And I can forgive you."

A spasm of emotion contracted his throat. "Jenny…"

"You see? It's not difficult at all."

Tom bowed his head, his forehead coming to rest lightly against hers. Her forgiveness was a gift he hadn't expected—and probably didn't deserve. He couldn't understand how she gave it so freely. Life, as he knew it, was built on long-held grudges. The notion that the slate could ever be wiped clean was foreign to him.

He wanted to ask her how she could do it. How she could absolve him for ruining her plans. For forcing himself into her adventure.

But Jenny, being Jenny, anticipated that, too.

"It's true," she confessed, her voice sinking to a whisper. "In the beginning, you weren't part of my dream. But now…" She touched his cheek. "I couldn't imagine any of this without you."

Chapter Ten

Alexandria, Egypt
March, 1860

Jenny stood on the deck of the *Indus*, watching the ancient city of Alexandria come into view. The weather had turned warmer. It was still nothing like the baking heat she imagined in India, but it was warm enough that most of the other passengers had come up on deck to join her. Some were still bundled up against the cold. Others were already garbed in their muslins and linens.

As for herself, she'd dressed in her black caraco jacket and skirt, a wide-brimmed straw hat pinned to her rolled and plaited coiffure.

Tom emerged from the crowd across the deck. When he saw her, his mouth hitched into a lopsided smile.

She smiled back at him, a little foolishly, she feared. No doubt she looked like a love-smitten schoolgirl. It was impossible not to after the kiss they'd shared. She watched as he made his way toward her. He'd gone no more than a few steps when Lydia Plank caught at his arm.

Tom looked down at Miss Plank. His face was solemn, his attention fixed on whatever she was telling him. And then, much to Jenny's chagrin, he turned and walked off with the girl.

Jenny stared after them, chewing at her lip. It was stupid to be jealous. The Plank daughters were young and pretty, it was true, but Tom had shown no particular fondness for them. And even if he had, what of it? Who was Jenny to get in the way of a shipboard flirtation? Or any flirtation, for that matter. She and Tom had no formal understanding. Rather the opposite. She'd made it plain to him that she didn't wish to marry. That she had no desire to become entangled with a man.

Having firmly established her independence, was she now going to play the part of dog in the manger every time Tom looked at a young lady?

And Miss Plank *was* young. No more than nineteen, at Jenny's guess. She tried to recall what she'd been doing at a similar age. Still living at the vicarage in Chipping St. Mary, cooking and cleaning for her father and brothers and trying to scrape up enough money to pay the tradesman's bills. She hadn't had the time for flirtations. Her entire focus had been on finding a way to get out. To get free.

Her hand moved reflexively to the gold chain at her neck. It was half-hidden by the collar of her jacket, the bottom looping down to rest at the top of her corset busk. No one could see it, not when she was in ordinary day dress. But it wasn't meant to be seen. It was enough that she knew it was there. An ever-present reminder of why she must guard her independence.

As if she needed reminding.

She folded her arms at her waist, focusing her gaze on the view of the bustling city. Whatever happened with Tom, she was free now. Freer than most spinsters of modest fortunes could ever dream of being. Heaven's sake, she was in Egypt! She, Jenny Holloway, former lady's companion, was on the greatest adventure of her life. No man could spoil it, and no woman, either. Certainly not one of the feather-headed Planks.

The *Indus* docked not far from a multitude of other ships, all of them busy with activity. *Bradshaw's* described the Port of Alexandria as being the foremost port in Egypt, a fact to which the crowded harbor appeared to attest. Situated at the meeting of the Nile River and the Mediterranean Sea, it was fringed in a reef of rocks and smelled—in its way—no more pleasant than had the harbor at Marseilles.

Ahmad and Mira appeared at Jenny's side, both of them clutching carpetbags. The luggage was going ahead to the steamer at Port Suez. The contents of the carpetbags were the only articles they would be carrying with them on the rail journey through Egypt.

Tom arrived shortly after, giving Jenny a smile so faint she couldn't even be sure it was a smile and not a trick of the sunlight on his face. "Miss Plank had some difficulty with one of the stewards."

Jenny refrained from commenting on the subject, saying instead, "Our train leaves in five hours, I believe."

"Four and half," Tom said. "Ample time to take rooms at a hotel and order something to eat."

"Enough time to see any of the sights?"

"Which ones did you have in mind?"

"*Bradshaw's* mentions Pompey's Pillar and Cleopatra's Needle." Jenny fumbled for the guide book in her reticule.

She flipped through to the dog-eared page on Alexandria. "It says here that they're both reachable by carriage or donkey."

Ahmad gave Tom a doubtful look.

"Carriage it is, then," Tom said. "Providing we can settle our other affairs in a timely manner."

There wasn't a great deal to settle. As passengers of the Peninsular and Oriental Steam Navigation Company, their luggage and railway passage were already taken care of, as was the passage for their P & O steamship journey from Suez to Calcutta. All that was required was for them to book in at one of the hotels. After disembarking, they fought their way through a multitude of shouting donkey drivers all battling for the passengers' attention, and boarded an omnibus bound for the grand square.

A short time later, they arrived at their destination, only to discover that the first three hotels they called upon were already full.

The fourth hotel—the Hotel d'Angleterre—had two rooms available, which they booked at once. Tom ordered their dinner for three hours hence and Jenny ordered baths for both herself and Mira. They then departed by carriage for Cleopatra's Needle.

Along the way, they passed through crowded, zigzagging streets of well-trod sand, adorned here and there with feathery palm trees. Jenny had never seen such a diverse collection of human beings. British travelers, garbed as anyone might be in the English countryside, mingled with olive-skinned Greeks and Spaniards, black-bearded Arabs in gracefully flowing robes, and veiled women with babies riding on donkeys. There were men puffing long pipes, and merchants bartering with customers in swiftly uttered French and Arabic. She even saw her first camel—a whole string of them—being led through the street by an Egyptian in a tasseled hat.

It was a cacophony of smoke and sound and stimulating scents.

Some of the residents of the city were, indeed, as semi-clothed as Mrs. Plank had foretold, but there was nothing of savagery in it. The streets were dusty and the sun was shining bright. The city was vivid. Wholly alive. The diversity of language and skin color—of dress and undress—was as well-suited to the setting as anything Jenny could imagine.

And yet she couldn't be entirely at ease. No sooner had they climbed into their hired carriage than a flock of children began to run after them with desperate pleas for "*baksheesh*."

Jenny gave Tom an anxious glance. "Can't we give them something?"

Tom hesitated a moment before calling out to the driver. "Stop the carriage!" And then again in French, "*Arrêter le chariot!*"

The carriage came to a jolting halt on the street. It was at once surrounded by beggars. Not only the children, but grown men and women, too; all of whom seemed to materialize out of nowhere.

"Don't get out," Ahmad warned. "Unless you wish to have your pockets picked clean."

Mira peered warily out the carriage window. "We shouldn't have stopped, madam."

Jenny had to admit they were right. The money she'd withdrawn from her reticule seemed dreadfully inadequate now, even when combined with Tom's contribution. As he tossed the coins from the window, a crippling sense of helplessness assailed her.

The experience made it near impossible to enjoy seeing Cleopatra's Needle. There were beggar children there, too. A small group of them, following along as she and Tom circled the red granite obelisk.

It was a beautiful relic. One of the most fascinating sights Jenny had ever seen—and also one of the saddest. Instead of standing upright, it was half buried in a ditch. A European gentleman in a cloth-covered helmet was perched atop the exposed end of it, breaking off a portion of the inscribed stone with a small mallet and chisel.

She suppressed a cry of protest. "Is that permitted?"

Tom frowned. "Judging by the state of the thing, I'd say it's encouraged."

The obelisk was indeed missing several chunks. As if countless tourists had taken pieces away with them as souvenirs.

"It belongs to Britain," she said under her breath. "He has no right to deface it."

"I don't recommend we tell him so."

Jenny had no intention of saying anything to the man. But she wasn't averse to scowling at him as they passed, giving him a look so sharp with disapproval that it briefly stopped the trajectory of his mallet.

As they walked, the beggars kept pace with them, calling out, and—every so often—tugging at Jenny's skirts or touching the velvet of her caraco with curious fingers. It became more and more difficult to ignore them. They weren't hardened criminals. They were just children, some of them scarcely more than babies, toddling along in the wake of their elders. One of them looked up at her, giving her a gap-toothed smile. Jenny smiled back at him, alarmed to feel the sting of tears in her eyes.

Tom didn't fail to notice. When they paused to examine the hieroglyphics, he discreetly pressed her hand. "There are desperate people in every capital of the world, Jenny. It helps no one if you make yourself wretched over it."

"I can't just ignore them. It's too cruel. If there were children like this at home—"

"What do you mean *if*? Have you never been to the East End? To St. Giles or any of the other neighborhoods in London where people live in poverty and despair? You must have heard of such places."

"I have. Of course I have. But I never thought... I never considered..."

"It's nothing to rake yourself over the coals for. When you—" He broke off. "*If* you decide to return to England, there are things you can do to aid the poor. But while we're here, we shouldn't interfere."

Jenny didn't understand how Tom could call it interference. He'd been an orphan. He knew what it was to go hungry. "You believe I should refrain from giving them coins?"

"Give them coins, by all means, but don't fall into the trap of thinking only we can help them. We're visitors to their country, not their saviors."

They returned to the hotel in grim silence. Jenny and Mira retired to their room. After they'd both had their bath, Mira patiently combed the tangles from Jenny's freshly washed hair.

Jenny felt suddenly much younger than her eight and twenty years. Young and woefully ignorant. "I mustn't involve myself," she said. "But how can I not? Am I to just walk past it all, as if it were of no more consequence than an exhibit at the Zoological Gardens?"

"Madam?"

"There will be more children begging in India, won't there? I shan't be able to give coins to all of them."

Mira met her eyes briefly in the looking glass before swiftly dropping her gaze.

"What is it?" Jenny asked. "I'd value your opinion on the matter."

The maid hesitated. "My mother…"

"Yes?"

"She said we must not give them money. That it is better to give them food and clothing."

"Did your mother do so?"

"Often."

"That was very kind of her."

"She was a very kind lady."

There was a note of sadness in Mira's voice that touched Jenny's heart. "Were you quite young when she died?"

Mira's olive-green eyes brightened with unshed tears. "I was not yet nine years of age."

Jenny reached up to clasp her hand. "My own mother succumbed to fever when I was just ten years old. It broke my heart. I was still grieving when my father came to me and said that I must be the little mother of the family now, for my brothers' sake."

"Babies," Mira said with a nod of understanding.

"Hardly. My two brothers are much older than I am. Older, and I must confess, terribly useless as far as household matters are concerned."

"What did you do, madam?"

"What could I do? I grew up. Far too quickly, I expect." Jenny gave Mira's hand a final squeeze before releasing it. "Females are incredibly resilient."

"Strong," Mira agreed.

"Yes. But not infallible. I shall have to find my own way out here. I can only hope I don't make too much more of a mull of it."

After a leisurely dinner at the hotel, they all boarded the omnibus to the Alexandria railway terminus. There, they encountered many of their fellow travelers from the *Indus*—including the Planks and the Hardcastles.

"I knew we'd see you again," Miss Plank said. "Didn't I say so, Mama?"

Tom did his level best to ignore the young lady's batting eyes. Why she'd singled him out for attention, he had no idea. Unless she truly was that desperate to avoid marrying some chap in India. In which case, he'd better remain on his guard. Trapping unsuspecting fellows into marriage to their daughters was the stock-in-trade of women like Mrs. Plank. All it would take was one compromising moment—one ill-thought familiarity—and the hammer of wedlock would be brought down upon him.

"So you did, my dear." Mrs. Plank eyed him with interest. "And where have you got to today, sir? We didn't see you at the Hotel d' Orient. I trust you and your sister have dined?"

"We have, thank you." Tom looked to Jenny. She was standing with Mira a short distance away, the pair of them flipping through the worn pages of Jenny's dratted travel guide.

Mrs. Plank followed his gaze. "Your sister will want to avail herself of the refreshment hall. One can't have too many provisions for the rail journey. I shall advise her. Ursula, come with me. Lydia, you may wait with Mr. Finchley. Mind you don't wander off."

"Forgive me, ma'am," Tom said, "but I must away for a few moments. I have business to conduct before we depart."

"I can accompany you," Miss Plank offered. "Mama wouldn't mind."

"I'm obliged to you, but my business is of a personal nature. If I can trouble you to look after my sister?"

Mrs. Plank could do nothing but acquiesce. "Never fear, sir. We shall keep her with us. Come, girls."

Miss Plank reluctantly followed after her mother and sister, her lower lip stuck out in a pout.

Tom waited until they'd collected Jenny and Mira before taking himself off to the telegraph office to send a wire to Devon. It was short and to the point:

ACCOMPANYING MISS HOLLOWAY
TO INDIA VIA OVERLAND ROUTE.
ALL PRECAUTIONS TAKEN. LETTER
TO FOLLOW. FINCHLEY.

He then posted the referenced letter, thankful that at the moment he and Justin Thornhill had a continent between them. Justin wouldn't take kindly to Tom's accompanying Jenny to India. Not with her reputation to consider. And not with her being his wife's distant relation and dearest friend.

After settling his business, Tom joined Mr. Hardcastle in waiting for the ladies. Hardcastle was a heavyset man on the shady side of forty with receding hair and lavish side-whiskers. He stood outside the refreshment hall, smoking a cheap Egyptian cigar he'd procured at the bazaar.

"Are you certain you won't try one, Finchley?"

Tom politely declined.

"Don't say as I blame you." Hardcastle puffed smoke with a grimace. "Damned Oriental tobacco. Never have grown accustomed to it. Don't know why I buy the stuff. Can't bring it along without paying a hefty duty."

"Have you made the journey to Port Suez by rail before?"

"Not as yet. It's bound to be a blessing for the ladies. Nothing worse for them than traveling across country in a van. Your *sister* wouldn't enjoy it."

Tom cast him a sharp glance. "Do you have something you wish to say, Hardcastle?"

"About your sister? I wouldn't dream of it."

The muscles in Tom's arms and shoulders tensed. He wanted nothing more than to smack the knowing smile off of Hardcastle's face. But violence rarely solved anything. Instead, he extracted his pocket watch to check the time. "You wouldn't happen to be a relation of Frederick Hardcastle, formerly of Christchurch Street?"

Hardcastle withdrew his cigar from his mouth with a scowl. "Are you trying to make a point, Finchley? To threaten me in some way?"

"With my knowledge of Frederick Hardcastle? What in the world would give you that idea? At this moment, I don't even know if you're related to the man."

Hardcastle put out his cigar under his foot. "Blackmail is a dastardly business, sir."

"As I'm well aware. Indeed, I believe it may be one of the first things I learned when I was articled to Josiah Fothergill." Tom watched the color drain from Hardcastle's face. "Mrs. Plank was right," he said mildly. "It is a small world in these parts. One never knows who one might meet."

Chapter Eleven

Egyptian Railways
Alexandria to Suez
March, 1860

The train rattled along the tracks, the window sashes rolled up on each side to let in the late afternoon sun. Jenny loosened the top button of her caraco. It was a seven-hour rail journey to Cairo. They'd only departed Alexandria an hour ago and the weather was already getting warmer. "Is there any lemonade left?"

"Let me see." Tom rifled through the hamper of food she'd purchased in the refreshment hall. His own collar was unbuttoned, his coat and cravat long discarded.

They were alone together in their compartment in one of the train's first-class carriages. Lined with well-worn buff leather, it was made to seat six; however, unlike some of the other passengers, they hadn't been obliged to share. A lucky occurrence, Tom had called it.

Jenny suspected luck had nothing to do with it. At the station, she could have sworn she'd seen him passing money to one of the porters. A bribe, no less. Mrs. Plank claimed that the bureaucratic wheels of Egypt were greased with them.

"We have lemonade, cakes, nuts, and…whatever this is…" Tom withdrew a scrap of white fabric from the basket.

She swept it from his hand. "It's a covering for my hat. They were selling them at the station. *Bradshaw's* says a lady must protect against the sun during this part of the journey."

"Why aren't you wearing it?"

"In truth? It seems a nuisance." She folded it into a square. "Besides, I'd as soon get a little color than go about shrouded in draperies. Did you see the way those Egyptian gentlemen at the port were dressed? They looked far more comfortable, to my mind."

"Undoubtedly. They were half-naked."

"Nonsense. You sound as prudish as Mrs. Plank." Jenny thrust her veil back into the basket, her hand briefly touching Tom's as he simultaneously reached for the flask of lemonade. "By the by, in future, I'd prefer you not convey messages to me through your young lady."

His gaze lifted to hers. "You're referencing Miss Plank, I presume."

"Who else? She had the nerve to say that you'd sent her to look after me. As if I weren't a grown woman of eight and twenty and she the veriest chit."

"She's not my young lady, as well you know."

"I'm glad to hear it. As your sister, I'd have to object to her."

"And as your brother, I'd be curious to know why."

"For obvious reasons. She's not at all the right type of female to be your wife."

Tom's lips quirked. "Jealous, Jenny?"

"Why should I be? We've already established that I have no wish to marry."

"And yet you consider yourself an expert on what kind of lady I should take to wife."

"Not an expert, no, but I daresay I have a better grasp of your needs than most."

He gave her an ironic look, even as a faint flush of color crept up his neck.

Jenny felt her own cheeks heat. She was vividly reminded of the kiss they'd shared on the *Indus*. "I didn't mean anything untoward. I only meant that I understand what sort of man you are."

"Do you?" He offered her the flask of lemonade. "Pray enlighten me."

She took it from him and poured them each a small glass. "I certainly won't. Not if you're going to laugh at me."

"I'm not laughing." And he wasn't. Not anymore.

Outside the windows of their compartment, the flat Egyptian landscape rolled by. On the right was a brown strip of desert, Lake Mareotis glimmering in the distance. On the left was a prospect of the Mahmoudia Canal, a waterway of the Nile which flowed through Alexandria and out to the Mediterranean Sea. There was nothing more to see, save the occasional short palm tree or Egyptian villager traversing the sands on his donkey.

"Very well. If you really wish to hear it." She handed him his lemonade before settling back into her seat with her own. "You're a serious man, devoted to your work. You're at the office from dawn until well past dusk. Some evenings you don't go home at all. Do you deny it?"

"There's no reason to. It's the truth, more or less."

"Which is precisely why you shouldn't marry a woman who will make unnecessary demands on your time. What kind of life would that be? Trying to get on with your work, when all the while, your new bride was troubling you with her megrims? You'd never bear it."

"You paint a grim picture."

"So it is. But you wouldn't be the first gentleman to ruin his life by marrying a girl just out of the schoolroom."

"Miss Plank is twenty, I believe. Hardly a child. And I've no wish to marry her or anyone."

His words stung. Jenny couldn't understand why. Hadn't she expressed the selfsame sentiment to him? It shouldn't hurt to hear it directed back at her. Shouldn't make her feel as if she was being rejected.

She forced herself to finish her lemonade. "Your wishes are of little matter when a determined lady has set her sights on you."

"I'm not troubled by the prospect."

"Why not? Do you think you can't be caught? When I was Helena's companion, I saw dozens of girls like Lydia Plank, and dozens more of their calculating mamas. They'll have you standing in front of the vicar so quickly your head will spin."

"If Miss Plank is capable of that, she has more depth to her than I'd realized. Perhaps I should marry her after all."

"I'm glad the idea brings you so much amusement."

"It amuses me because it's so damnably unlikely. I mean it, Jenny. When it comes to dealing with calculating females, you may trust that I know what I'm about. I've no intention of being trapped." Tom's mouth hitched in a lopsided smile. "But it warms my heart to know you care."

"Of course I care." She took his empty glass and returned it, along with hers, to the hamper. "You should be in no doubt of that by this point."

"Sometimes I wonder," he admitted. "You were cross with me when we left Cleopatra's Needle."

"I wasn't."

"You were. You scarcely said five words to me during the drive back to the hotel. And you were equally quiet at dinner."

"It had nothing to do with you. I was just…lost in thought."

"Anything you'd care to share?"

"Only that I thought myself prepared for this adventure, for seeing all the sights and encountering all the people. I read so many books and travel guides. But now I'm here in one of the most fascinating countries in the world and I realize…" She gave him a rueful look. "It's nothing like a plate in a history book, is it?"

"Would you rather it was?"

Jenny considered the question. "Do you know, I don't believe I would. Because then…then it wouldn't be real. And it's the reality of it that makes it so magnificent. The city and the people and Cleopatra's Needle. There's a sense of history here. Of something almost magical." She flushed with embarrassment. "I'm putting it badly."

"Not at all. I expect anyone of sensibility would be similarly affected by their first trip to Egypt."

"Has it affected you?"

"To some degree. It's made me want to know more. About the history and the culture. There's a great deal to learn here if one has the time."

"A very great deal. It's all rather overwhelmed me," she confessed. "The journey and the people and all the changes in my life. There are times I feel completely at sea."

"You've struck me as being rather determined."

"In some respects. I know what I want and what I don't want. I suppose I've always known that. As for the rest…"

"What else is there?"

"Only the entire world. I have to discover my place in it. To figure out how to move about here without becoming like every other British female who barges in and tramples all over everyone."

"There's no chance of your doing that. For one, you're not like other British females. None that I've ever known."

"In other words, I'm an eccentric oddity."

"In other words, you're perfect just as you are."

Jenny's heart swelled, the beat of it becoming almost painful in her chest. "That's very sweet of you to say, but—"

"There's nothing sweet about it. It's the truth. I realized it not long after meeting you. You're the most imperfectly perfect woman I've ever encountered."

"Imperfectly perfect." She tried to laugh but couldn't. "I haven't the slightest idea what that means."

"It was you who found Thornhill's advertisement in the *Times*. You who arranged for Lady Helena to escape from London. I daresay some might call it managing. I call it down-right heroic. You take care of people. You help to solve their problems."

"And you don't?"

"The difference being that I'm paid for it. Very *well* paid by people who often don't deserve to be helped."

"Did Mr. Thornhill pay for your help?"

"No, but—"

"Yet it was you who placed the matrimonial advertisement in the first place. You who determined the method for saving Helena and her fortune from her uncle."

Tom frowned. "That was different."

"I don't see how."

"What I did for Thornhill I did for a friend. A man who's like a brother to me. A decent, honorable fellow who deserves a chance at happiness. The rest of my clients are neither decent nor honorable."

"Not all of your clients fit that description, surely. What about Ahmad? What about Mr. and Mrs. Jarrow's son?"

"Those cases were different, too."

"Different how?"

"Out of the common way. Not representative of the bulk of the cases I take." Tom briefly removed his spectacles to massage the bridge of his nose. He looked suddenly tired, his blue eyes even wearier than they normally were. "Several years ago I began to become somewhat disenchanted with the work I was doing for Fothergill. In the main, I didn't like my primary client."

"The gentleman engaged in the land dispute?"

Tom nodded. "His case and its various offshoots had come to form the bulk of my practice and...I was tired of it. I decided then that I'd start taking on additional cases of my own. That I would use the skills I'd learned from Fothergill, employ the knowledge he'd given me, to help those who actually deserved to be helped."

"A laudable goal."

"Fothergill thought it foolish. Especially as the cases I took on usually involved the poor. Those stuck in untenable situations. I could often solve things for them with a letter or a word dropped in the right ear. It was no great sacrifice of my time."

"Still, it's very generous of you."

"Hardly. Helping people like Ahmad and the Jarrows' son is selfish. I do it because of how it makes *me* feel. Since Fothergill's retirement, I've taken on more cases like theirs. Some days, it's the only thing that keeps me going."

"Do you dislike your client so much?"

"What I dislike is being used as a weapon."

Jenny's brows shot up. "Is that how you view the work you do for him? I thought you loved the law."

"I do, but there are aspects of my practice that have little to do with it."

"What aspects?"

Tom settled his spectacles back onto his nose. At first it seemed as though he wouldn't answer her; however, after a weighted pause, he finally spoke. "I told you once that in the orphanage I learned that there was strength in knowledge."

She remembered. It had been the night he came to Half Moon Street. "You said that you'd developed a propensity for keeping secrets."

"Sometimes I think that's why Fothergill chose me. He recognized the habit in me. Because he was the same, you see. He listened to everyone. He accumulated scraps of information. People's darkest secrets. Their deepest desires. He used the knowledge to make himself powerful—and to help those who could afford his fee."

Jenny moistened her lips. On the train from Marseilles, she'd hesitated to voice her suspicions. She'd been too afraid of offending him. Of harming their friendship. But now, after all they'd been through together, it seemed foolish to remain silent. "You're speaking of blackmail."

Tom's brow creased. "No." He shook his head. "Never that. He didn't need to resort to such foul tactics. It was enough that people knew that he knew. By the time he took me on, he'd developed a reputation. He was a man to be feared. People called him the spider behind his back. Though nothing was ever truly behind Fothergill's back. He knew very well what was said about him. I daresay he liked being thought a spider, one with a vast web stretching out over London and beyond."

Jenny suppressed a shudder. "He sounds a dreadful man."

"He is. And he's as responsible for saving my life as Thornhill or Archer. He taught me all he knew. Molded me in his image."

"I don't believe that. You're nothing like the man you describe. You're your own person."

"What I am is his successor." A dry smile edged Tom's mouth. "Though no one's assigned me a moniker yet."

She managed a faint smile in return. There was nothing of humor in it. "Thank heaven. If anyone started calling you the spider, I'd have to cut your acquaintance."

"Jenny…"

"Do you know, I always suspected you were dangerous in some way. It's the way you carry yourself. So purposefully unremarkable."

"I'm hardly dangerous. Certainly not to you."

"I know that."

"Then why are you looking at me that way? As if I've suddenly become a stranger?" Tom didn't give her an opportunity to answer. "He's dying, Jenny. Wasting away from the inside out. He won't last another year."

His face was taut, almost cold, but Jenny detected a flicker of genuine sorrow in the depths of his gaze. She softened immediately. Whatever his secrets, this was no stranger. This was Tom. *Her* Tom. "I'm sorry. Truly."

"He's an infuriating old devil. I can't help but think I've let him down."

"How could you have?"

"By having doubts. By occasionally doing what was right instead of what was necessary."

She stretched out her hand to him over the hamper. He took it without hesitation. Neither of them was wearing gloves. Their fingers threaded together in an intimate clasp. "What will you do?"

"When he's gone? I shall continue as I am. And one day, if I hold fast to my resolve, the worthy cases will have replaced the unworthy ones entirely." Tom raised their joined hands to his lips and pressed a kiss to her knuckles. "I must confess, I'm heartily looking forward to it."

Jenny's pulse skittered. She watched, a little breathless, as he kissed her hand once more before drawing it to his cheek. He'd been clean shaven when they arrived in port this morning, but it was nearly six in the evening now. His jaw was shadowed with stubble. It tickled her skin in the most thrilling way. "Tom?"

"Hmm?"

"Did you bribe the railway porter?"

He regarded her steadily. "I did."

"Why?"

"I wanted to be alone with you." His thumb moved over the curve of her finger. "Do you disapprove? Would you rather we'd forced Mira and Ahmad to remain with us? Or been obliged to share the compartment with the Hardcastles or the Planks?"

"No indeed, but..."

"But?"

"The more time we spend together like this, the harder it's going to be to say goodbye."

Tom went still, his Adam's apple bobbing on a swallow. The weight of his gaze conveyed both so much and so very little. "What would you have me do?"

"I don't know."

"Shall I refrain from touching you? From holding your hand or—"

"No." She squeezed tight to his hand, refusing to let him go. "I don't want any of this to stop. Unless you—"

"I don't want it to stop either, damn me."

"Shall we agree not to think of it? The end of things, I mean."

"You're proposing we suspend reality. That we pretend—" He broke off abruptly. "For how long?"

"Until we find out what happened to Giles. And then… we must agree to part as friends."

"As if none of this ever happened."

"No," she said. "I don't plan to forget a single moment. I'll always remember—"

"And that's what you want from me? To help you to create a memory? Some colorless shadow you can look back on fondly long after I've gone?" Tom's voice was rough with something very like anger. "I could never be content with such a bloodless version of what we've shared. Never."

She stared at him, uncertain what to make of his tone. "You'd prefer not to remember at all?"

"I won't remember. Indeed, when we part, I intend to make a concerted effort to forget you, Jenny. If we ever meet again someday in London or Devon, it shall be as common and indifferent acquaintances. Make no mistake. I won't waste my time pining for something I cannot have."

His words skewered the most vulnerable part of her with ruthless precision. It was all she could do not to jerk her hand from his. "Why would you pine? You don't want me. You said yourself you'd no desire to marry. It isn't as if I'd be rejecting you, nor you me. We neither of us have any wish to become entangled."

"I know that. But this attraction between us. I've never—"

"You've no cause to be angry with me over it. I made it clear from the beginning—"

"I'm not angry. I promise you." He pressed another kiss to her hand. "I just…"

"What?"

"I don't like being out of control of things. Feeling so bloody powerless."

"Well, I don't like it any better than you do. But I don't see what can be done about it. Either we part ways now and try to forget each other or…" She laughed bitterly. "I suppose we could marry and settle down to a brood of children. Wouldn't that be shocking?"

Tom looked at her, an expression his eyes that was hard to read. "Yes. Terribly shocking."

"We'd both be miserable. And God help our poor offspring. What sort of mother would I be? Always feeling trapped. Always dreaming of running away to some far-off land."

Tom didn't reply. He merely held her hand against his cheek as the train rattled on toward Cairo.

They reached the railway station in Cairo at a quarter past eleven. There, they were obliged to break their journey for the night. Ahmad and Mira seemed in far better spirits than Tom was himself. Especially when given the opportunity to purchase skewers of spiced meat from one of the crowds of Egyptian peddlers shouting out to them in Arabic and broken English.

Jenny, by contrast, gravitated to a peddler selling sweet cakes. Her purchases were wrapped swiftly into a handkerchief. "How does one say thank you in Arabic?"

The peddler answered, "*Shukraan*."

"*Shukraan*," Jenny repeated in tentative accents.

The peddler grinned broadly, rewarding her pronunciation with another rapid string of Arabic.

Jenny smiled at him in return. She was still smiling when they climbed into the carriage Tom had hired to take them to their hotel. "One day, I shall come back here and stay a good long while."

"What about India?" he asked. "I thought you intended to settle there?"

"I intend to find Giles. As to the rest…who knows where my heart will lead me?"

Who indeed, Tom thought grimly.

He'd been in a foul mood since they left Alexandria. The business with Hardcastle hadn't helped. It was bad enough that the man had stooped to making vulgar insinuations about Jenny. But the fact that he'd forced Tom to mention Fothergill by name had left a bad taste in his mouth.

This journey was meant to be a time out of time. Something above the sordid business of his life in London. Yes, it had been impulsive of him. He'd never had any desire to travel the world. But now that he was here, every stage of the route—every steamship, train, and foreign hotel—seemed almost sacred. It was *theirs*. His and Jenny's. The only places they would ever be together. Unless…

I suppose we could marry and settle down to a brood of children, she'd said.

The phrase had been ricocheting around in his head since first she'd uttered it.

He'd told her on the train that he had no wish to marry. It hadn't been entirely true. Not when it came to her. With every mile they traveled, he wanted more of Jenny Holloway—more of her confidences and more of her kisses. When she'd uttered those fateful words, his heart had given a leap of furious joy.

Yes, he'd wanted to say. *Please*.

But he hadn't done. He'd simply held her hand as if he'd never let her go, knowing all the while that the train was taking them closer and closer to the end of their…whatever it was they were doing together.

It seemed inadequate to call it a romance. And he certainly couldn't think of it as a love affair. Thus far, they'd been chaste.

Thus far.

Tom tugged at his collar. The darkened streets of Cairo were narrow and unpaved, the carriage bouncing sharply along, jostling Jenny against his side at every turn. She briefly rested a hand on his thigh to brace herself. He sucked in a breath, feeling the fleeting contact everywhere.

Jenny didn't appear to notice. "It's a pity we won't be here long enough to go to the bazaar and the Turkish baths. And I'd dearly love to visit the pyramids."

"At this stage," he grumbled, "we shall be fortunate to make it to our hotel in one piece."

Ahmad cast him a perceptive glance. It only served to irritate Tom further.

"I thought I caught a glimpse of them as the train approached Cairo," Jenny went on. "They were visible just outside of the right window. Did either of you see them?"

"It was dark," Ahmad said.

"Too dark," Mira agreed.

Jenny sighed. "Yes. But I was sure I saw *something*."

"Perhaps," Tom said, "it was a mirage brought on by hunger. We've had nothing but cake and nuts since Alexandria."

"You're probably right. We must have a proper dinner when we arrive at the hotel. Traveling brings on a furious appetite."

Shepheard's Hotel was a grand Cairo establishment, known far and wide for its opulence. They arrived to find musicians playing in the illuminated court at its front. A smattering of people were seated at outdoor tables, the smell of smoke and the echo of conversations in English, French, and Arabic swirling up into the night.

After checking in at the desk, they dined in Tom's hotel room, along with Mira and Ahmad, too exhausted to stand on ceremony. Waiters garbed in clean-pressed linen served them soup, fish, and *boeuf à la bourgoise*, followed by salads, fruits, and Turkish coffee.

Jenny ate with unabashed enthusiasm, but when she was done, she didn't linger. She bid Tom goodnight and disappeared with Mira to her bedroom across the hall.

Tom was left alone with Ahmad, who once again gave him a look that was all too perceptive.

"Not a word," Tom warned.

Ahmad was a taciturn fellow at the best of times, but he had, after all, spent years working at Mrs. Pritchard's establishment. Lord knew what pearls of wisdom he might dispense on the subject of gentlemen who grew too infatuated with a particular lady. He'd likely seen all manner of fellows making fools of themselves.

"There are murmurings among the servants," he said.

Tom rested his head in his hands. By God, he was weary. "What kind of murmurings?"

"Suspicions."

Tom wasn't entirely surprised. He could only wonder that it had taken them so long to voice them. "Anything specific?"

"That you don't look like your sister."

"Half sister."

"Shall I remind them of that fact?" Ahmad asked.

"Do," Tom said.

Not that it would make any difference at this point. Between Mrs. Plank—who might well have seen him embracing Jenny on the *Valetta*—and Mr. Hardcastle, it was only a matter of time before such murmurings developed into full-blown gossip. He'd have to find a way to counter it. A strategy that didn't involve separating himself from Jenny. He wasn't ready to part from her yet. Couldn't bear to contemplate keeping his distance, even if that distance was nothing more than the space of a railway carriage.

The train to Suez left at eight in the morning. They departed the hotel much earlier, all of them tired and worn, blinking up into the sun like newborn kittens.

"I hardly slept," Jenny confided. "I was far too excited."

"You can sleep on the train," Tom said as he bundled her back into the carriage.

And sleep she did, curled up against him in their private railway compartment, her head on his chest and her skirts spilling all over his legs.

Tom's arm was around her, holding her close, his face turned into her uncovered hair. Gossip be damned. He was glad he'd closed the blinds when they boarded. Glad he had her to himself, if even for a short while.

I suppose we could marry and settle down to a brood of children.

If they were married, he could hold her like this whenever he wanted. He could wake with her in his arms. Could press his face into her unbound hair. Could kiss her as he had on the *Indus*.

But he wasn't blind. And he wasn't stupid.

Though their journey had started with seasickness and self-doubt, Jenny had rapidly grown into her adventure. He saw evidence of it every time she gazed about her in wonder. Every time she smiled at shopkeepers, porters, and peddlers. The farther they traveled from England, the more she brightened. By the time they reached Delhi, she would surely be incandescent.

One day, I shall come back here and stay a good long while.

A good long while in Cairo. How long was that, he wondered. A month? A year? More, perhaps?

He pressed his nose into her hair, seeking the clean herbal scent she'd had in London. The practical, no-nonsense fragrance that was so unmistakably Jenny Holloway. But it was gone. Replaced somewhere during their journey with the redolence of the sun, and the sea, and the delicate perfume of Marseilles soap.

She stirred against him with a sigh, bringing one hand to rest on his midsection.

And I am in hell, Tom thought. *This is hell.*

Jenny woke in Tom's arms, the motion of the train nearly lulling her straight back to sleep again. She knew she should sit up. Should make some effort to straighten her gown and repair her hair. But Tom was holding her so closely. If she withdrew from him now, she didn't know when he might do so again.

His cheek brushed over her plaited hair. "Are you awake?"

"Mmm."

"We'll be in Suez in an hour."

She tilted her head to look at him. His face was bare, his blue eyes fixed on hers without any barrier between them. "Where are your spectacles?"

"In the pocket of my waistcoat."

Her hand was resting low on his midriff, her fingers half-curled over one of his buttons. She slid it up to his chest, feeling the outline of his spectacles just where he'd said they'd be.

If she were sensible, she'd have stopped there. She'd have dropped her hand and sat up, withdrawing back to her side of the compartment. But Jenny wasn't feeling very sensible at the moment. Her hand drifted up to his cheek as if it had a will of its own.

Tom's gaze held hers. He didn't say a word. She suspected he was holding his breath. Waiting to see what she was going to do next.

Jenny was quite curious to find out herself.

On the single occasion they'd kissed, it was Tom who had initiated the intimacy between them. *He* had kissed *her.* Which had been lovely and thrilling; a thoroughly knee-weakening experience. But this time…

This time, she didn't wish to wait for him to kiss her. Who knew if he ever would? He'd been acting so oddly since they disembarked from the *Indus*. At war with his principles, no doubt. Trying to resist doing anything that might seem as if he were taking advantage of her.

It was ridiculously noble of him. It was also wholly unnecessary.

She cradled his face in her hand, her thumb moving over his cheekbone in a slow caress.

Tom's brows knit into a troubled frown. "Jenny…" He sounded as though he was going to object. And yet his arms tightened around her, holding her against his chest, so close she could feel the rapid drumbeat of his heart.

She curved her hand around his neck and tugged him down to her. He didn't resist. Indeed, he readily obliged her, dipping his chin until his brow came to rest gently against hers. Jenny stretched up to meet his mouth.

Her lips brushed his. And then again, searching, seeking, until he angled his head and their mouths fused together in a kiss so perfect it nearly brought tears to her eyes.

She twined both arms around his neck. And she kissed him and kissed him. Warm, soft kisses with the slightest taste of desperation in them. Kisses that promised him she would never forget him, even if he was resolved to forget her.

When at last their lips parted, Jenny didn't pull away from him. She buried her face in his neck, holding him as fiercely as he held her in return.

Only a few weeks ago, she'd have quailed at such intimacy. An unmarried lady didn't embrace an unmarried gentleman. She certainly didn't kiss him or caress his face.

But an unmarried lady didn't travel alone with an unmarried gentleman, either. She didn't share a private railway compartment with him or dine in his hotel room. She didn't allow him to enter her cabin on board a steamship and tend her while she was ill. And she certainly didn't permit him to see her in her underclothes.

The rules were there for a reason. They were meant to keep young ladies safe from harm. To protect their reputations and preserve their virtue. But the rules, such that they were, didn't seem to apply anymore. She and Tom had, effectively, been alone together since they stepped on the train to Dover. At each stage of their journey their familiarity had increased. They'd broken the rules one by one. All of them, in quick succession.

Well. Not quite all of them.

There were some rules Jenny wouldn't break, no matter the temptation. Because if she did, there would be no going back. She'd be trapped as surely as Tom would be. Sentenced to a life together that neither of them wanted.

He pressed a kiss to her hair. "What's all this about?"

"I don't know." She tried to laugh, but couldn't. "Pangs of longing, I suppose."

His hand moved on her back, his voice a rough murmur against her ear. "For what, precisely?"

He didn't need to ask. He already knew. What he wanted was reassurance. Jenny understood because it was the same thing she wanted. A kiss. An embrace. A soft word telling her that it was all going to be all right.

"For you, Tom. For you."

Chapter Twelve

S.S. Bentinck
Suez to Calcutta
March, 1860

They'd spent too much time alone together, that was the problem. All those evenings walking together on the decks of the *Valetta* and the *Indus*. All those hours spent in a private compartment on the train from Alexandria to Suez. It hadn't gone unremarked. Jenny had endured too many years as a lady's companion not to recognize the knowing looks.

It wasn't full-blown ostracism. Not yet. But as she and Tom settled into life on the P & O steamship *Bentinck*, it became clear that the veneer of their simply crafted fiction had worn thin.

Mrs. Plank and her daughters had boarded the *Bentinck* in Port Suez along with Mr. and Mrs. Hardcastle and their niece. Jenny recognized other passengers as well, most of them unmarried ladies in the company of their parents or other relations. They were going to India to find eligible husbands. The last thing any of them wanted was to be tainted by scandal.

"I'm fast becoming a pariah," Jenny said as Mira helped her to dress for dinner. It was their third night on the *Bentinck*, and though Jenny had had no recurrence of the illness she'd suffered on the *Valetta*, she was heartily sick of the sea. It had little to do with the motion of the ship and everything to do with its passengers. "If we were in London, they'd have already cut my acquaintance."

Mira tightened the laces of Jenny's corset. "Because of Mr. Finchley?"

Jenny pressed a hand to her abdomen, beginning to feel a little lightheaded. "It's not underserved. I've been incredibly foolish over him."

"He's a good man." Mira gave one last tug to Jenny's corset laces before knotting them tight. "He saved Ahmad."

"I know." Jenny exhaled an uneven breath. "Good heavens, does it need to be so snug?"

"For your gown, madam."

Mira had mended Jenny's dinner dress after it had been torn during the journey across Egypt. In the process, she'd taken it in, creating a more fashionable—and far more unforgiving—silhouette.

Jenny hadn't had the heart to criticize her. Not when Mira had such an uncommon talent with the needle. Still… "I've never laced it this tightly before myself."

"It's the fashion."

"In Paris, perhaps." Jenny waited beside her berth while Mira fetched the altered dress. It had fit Jenny well enough to begin with, but now, as Mira helped her into it, Jenny privately conceded that her maid had worked wonders.

With the aid of a brutally cinched corset, Jenny's figure had become distinctly hourglass. The pale green fabric skimmed close to her curves, giving the illusion of a generous bosom and a waist so narrow that a suitably impetuous gentleman might be able to span it with both hands.

She smoothed her full skirts. "Where did you learn to sew so beautifully, Mira? Was it from your mother?"

Mira's cheeks darkened. "From Ahmad."

"Ahmad! Does he sew?"

"He sometimes helped to stitch gowns for the ladies at Mrs. Pritchard's."

In other words, Jenny had received the same style of alterations enjoyed by the female residents of an East End gentlemen's establishment. "That must have made them feel very special."

"Oh yes." Mira brightened. "Everyone wanted Ahmad to alter their gowns. He taught me the skill so I could make myself useful to them."

"Is it something you enjoy?"

"I'm learning to enjoy it," Mira said. "And one day, when I am married—"

"Married? To whom?"

"I have not had the fortune to meet the gentleman yet."

"But you know you wish to marry?"

Mira gave Jenny a bewildered look. "Yes, madam. What else am I to do?"

Jenny could think of one hundred things that were preferable to marriage. But she didn't enumerate them. What would be the purpose? Mira didn't deserve to have her head turned by thoughts of travel and independence. She had no fortune to speak of. No means to make such dreams come true.

A rap on the door of her cabin heralded Tom's arrival. Jenny answered it herself, one hand still pressed to her midriff.

Tom stood on the threshold, clad in the same sack coat and trousers he'd worn the day they left London. His hair was combed into meticulous order. He even appeared to have used a little pomade.

His gaze roved over her, leaving a trail of heat in its wake. "Are you ready for dinner?"

"Yes." It was the only word she could manage with her corset laced to mere inches. A godsend, really. She was terrible at subterfuge and even worse at feigning politeness toward those who thought ill of her. It would be better for all concerned if she didn't speak at dinner.

But a loss of words wasn't the only consequence of a too-tight corset. It affected her appetite as well. Once seated at one of the tables in the *Bentinck*'s elegant saloon beneath the quarter-deck, she could do nothing but pick at her food.

"Is that a new frock, Miss Holloway?" Miss Plank examined Jenny's dress with envious eyes. "Did you purchase it in Egypt?"

"I wouldn't have thought there was time to visit a dressmaker," Mrs. Plank said.

There was no avoiding the conversation. The *Bentinck* was a larger and far more luxurious ship than the *Indus*. At present it carried one hundred and fifty passengers along with the crew. And yet privacy was well-nigh impossible. Especially among those who had traveled other stages of the route together. "There wasn't," Jenny said. "My maid saw to the alterations herself."

"Your native maid? She sews, does she?" Mrs. Plank grunted. "That's something."

Beside her, Mr. Hardcastle poured himself another glass of wine. He'd been eyeing Tom warily through most of the meal, but now, for the first time, he turned his attention to Jenny. "I brought a native servant back with me when I left Bombay in '49. The laziest devil I've ever encountered. Disappeared in London two years later."

Jenny gritted her teeth.

Later that evening, when she was alone with Tom, she asked, "Was it common for colonial men to bring back Indians in that way? As if they were curiosities to collect?"

They were strolling along the spar deck, a magnificent walk which ran the full length of the ship. They weren't the only ones. The sun was setting on the Gulf of Aden, the water luminous in its brilliancy and the wind warm and fair. Passengers had no reason to stay below.

The Plank girls stood at the rail with Miss Hardcastle, whispering and giggling together. Two young gentlemen conversed nearby and, a distance away, Mrs. Plank and Mrs. Hardcastle walked side by side, keeping a close eye on their charges—and everyone else.

It was for the best, really. She and Tom daren't risk being caught in an embrace. Since boarding the ship in Port Suez, they had taken care to avoid any appearances of undue intimacy. Jenny suspected their efforts came too late to make a difference. Nevertheless, the unhappy pantomime continued.

"Some of them did," Tom said. "They weren't all as irresponsible as Hardcastle and the fellow who brought Ahmad and Mira to London."

"Do you know anything of him? The mysterious colonel they sometimes mention?"

"Only that he had some connection to Mira's mother."

Jenny nodded. "Mira said that her mother extracted a death-bed promise from him. That she made him swear to bring Mira back to England with him and see that she had a better life."

"Thornhill spoke of soldiers who took Indian wives and sired children by them. The practice is frowned upon, but not at all uncommon."

"Are you suggesting that the colonel was Mira's father?"

"I think he might have been. Whether or not Mira's mother was his wife, I've no idea."

Jenny chewed her lip. "And Ahmad?"

Tom shrugged. "He is what he is. A concerned cousin. Too noble to let Mira be taken away from India on her own."

"Did you know he's something of a seamstress? Or a tailor, I suppose you might call him. He alters dresses and has taught Mira to do the same."

Tom's mouth curved upward. "Nothing would surprise me about the man." He cast Jenny a sidelong glance. "Is he responsible for what you're wearing?"

"This was Mira's doing." She pressed a hand to her waist, still struggling to adapt to the tight lacing. "She was only meant to repair a ripped seam."

"You don't like it?"

"It's very fashionable. It's also exceedingly uncomfortable." She sunk her voice. "My corset is cinched nearly two inches tighter."

Tom's eyes dropped briefly to her midsection. "What in God's name for?"

"The dress wouldn't fit otherwise."

"No wonder you ate so little at dinner. I thought you might be getting seasick again."

"I'm surprised you noticed. You scarcely looked in my direction."

"I'm trying not to." He paused, staring briefly out at the water. "Ahmad says that I don't look at you the way a gentleman looks at his sister."

Jenny let his words sink in.

"The trouble is," Tom said, "I don't know how to stop looking at you however it is I look at you. It's become as natural to me as breathing."

"So you've decided not to look at me at all?"

"If it means preserving your good name, then yes. I intend to refrain as much as I'm able." Tom thrust his hands into his pockets. "You look beautiful, by the way."

"Thank you."

"I hate that we can't be together."

Her gaze flew to his face. Did he mean here, on the *Bentinck*? Or was he talking about their lives in England?

"It feels as though a year has passed since we were alone."

"Not quite a year." She brushed her shoulder against his arm in what she hoped presented as a sisterly nudge to the other passengers on deck. "It will be easier when we reach Calcutta."

"You don't know that."

"No, but—"

"There's every chance it will be worse."

The next twenty days at sea passed at an unbearably slow pace. Their journey to Calcutta was an endless stretch of wind and waves, broken only by the *Bentinck's* stops to take on coal and the occasional bout of stormy weather. The passengers were restless. It hadn't taken long for card games and promenades above deck to pall.

Fortunately their meals and other creature comforts were still well above average. There was plenty of livestock on board, including chickens for the pot and dairy cows to provide milk. The *Bentinck* even boasted hot and cold shower baths. As for the surfeit of time, the passengers had taken to filling it as best they could. Some decorated their cabins. Others engaged in modified games of sport on the deck. Still others embarked on furtive shipboard romances. Indeed, there had been a minor crisis near the Bay of Bengal when Miss Hardcastle had been caught in the arms of a young ship's steward.

It was this incident more than any other that prompted Tom to visit Jenny in her cabin. He could think of no better time to do so. The attention of Mrs. Plank and the other gossips was fully on the catastrophe at hand. They would have no interest, at present, in the rather dubious relationship between a boring London solicitor and his alleged half sister.

Or so Tom hoped.

He and Jenny had been making a particular effort to be careful. Since leaving Port Suez, they'd restricted themselves to public promenades on the spar deck in the morning and evening and equally public meetings in the grand saloon.

The closest they'd come to being alone was the long afternoon they'd spent in the ship's library going over Jenny's finances. It had been an arduous and personally painful task. She'd not only wanted to know her expenses thus far down to the penny, she'd also inquired about budgeting the remainder of her funds so that she might maintain a household somewhere when her adventures were over.

Where? he'd asked.

India, probably, she'd said. *Or Egypt. I haven't decided yet.*

Tom had known her answer wouldn't be to his liking. Nevertheless, on hearing it, his already fractured heart had splintered a little more.

He was falling in love with her. Had been since somewhere between Calais and Alexandria.

It had started with a fondness. A mere attraction. He'd thought it powerful then. Powerful enough, at least, to provoke those damnable pangs of longing. But during their train journey across Egypt it had taken on a life of its own. Mere longing had transformed into an ache so acute that some nights he thought he would die from it.

It was not in his nature to want something he couldn't have. Futile yearnings were the grim stuff of his boyhood. All those years in the orphanage at Abbot's Holcombe, wanting so many things but having none of them. No sense of safety or belonging. No warmth. No tenderness. He'd promised himself long ago that he'd never again be so vulnerable. And yet...

Here he was, pining as surely as any schoolboy.

He sat on the edge of Jenny berth, legs stretched out in front of him, watching while she ran a comb through her long tresses. It wasn't the first time he'd seen her with her hair down. That had been on the *Valetta*—a memory that still made his heart clench. The flaming auburn locks were wavy and thick, falling almost to her waist. A wild tangle more suitable to a mermaid or an Arthurian princess than a former lady's companion. Tom didn't think he'd ever grow accustomed to the sight of it.

"Have you ever cut it?" he asked.

She stood in front of the marble-covered basin stand, struggling to unknot a tangled section. "I'm tempted to cut it right now."

He made a low sound of disapproval. "Come here."

Jenny glanced at him. She was dressed for dinner, wearing the same gown Mira had taken in for her nearly three weeks before.

They would have to join the others in the saloon shortly. But not yet.

He patted the berth.

Her mouth turned up at one corner. "Very well." She crossed the short distance, placing her tortoiseshell comb in his hand before sinking down at his side.

Tom angled himself behind her and set to work. "The trouble is you have no patience."

"And you do?"

"An infinite amount."

Jenny bent her head forward. "You wouldn't have if you had to comb this dratted tangle every day. It's a terrible nuisance. I'd have it sheared off at the shoulders if I wasn't so vain."

"You're the least vain woman I know."

"I am about my hair."

He smiled to himself. "With good reason." After working the knot loose, he ran his fingers through her tresses. They were heavy in his hand, soft as raw silk and smelling of the now-familiar scent of Marseilles soap. "Has anyone else ever seen you with it down?"

The question was out before he could catch himself. It sounded just what it was: the uncertain query of a jealous lover.

Jenny looked at him over her shoulder. "A man, do you mean?"

He could have cut his own tongue out. "You don't have to answer."

"Why wouldn't I? It's no great secret." Her expression softened, as if she could see straight to the heart of his insecurity. "The answer is no, Tom. You're the first."

The knowledge of it settled warm in his chest. A rare treasure which, under other circumstances, he would have guarded zealously. But what was he to do with it now? He could scarcely extract a promise from her never to show her unbound hair to another man.

After they parted, who knew who she might meet? Granted, she didn't wish to marry and settle down to a family at present, but what of three years from now? What of ten? At some point she would meet a man for whom she would gladly give up her freedom.

A man who wasn't him.

A lump formed in his throat. He handed her back her comb. "I'd offer to plait it for you, but I'd only make a mess of it."

"I can do it quick enough." She moved to rise, and would have done if he hadn't encircled her wrist with his hand. She turned to him, brows knit as she searched his face. "What is it?"

He shook his head. "Melancholy. Pangs of longing. I don't know."

She sank back down, facing him. "Oh, Tom. We've been too long at sea, that's all."

"You sound very certain."

"Only because I'm restless, too. But it's not much longer until we reach Calcutta. Just two days, the captain says."

Tom slid his hand from her wrist to clasp her fingers. She wore no enameled bracelets or rings set with gemstones, as was the fashion. She was all smooth skin and delicate bones.

More delicate than one might expect for a lady of Jenny's strong temperament.

"I've been thinking of how we might proceed," she said as he held her hand. "It's nearly one thousand miles from Calcutta to Delhi. Four times greater the distance than the one we traveled across Egypt—and in far less comfortable weather. Mr. Hardcastle suggests we stop awhile in Calcutta. Perhaps take a house there for a week or two."

Tom lifted his gaze. "You've spoken to Hardcastle?"

"Shouldn't I have?"

"I'd rather you stayed clear of the man."

Not that Hardcastle had said anything untoward since Tom issued his warning in Alexandria. But the fellow was a heavy drinker. Who knew what impertinences he might utter—or liberties he might attempt—if given the chance?

"Why?" she asked. "Has he done something?"

Tom hesitated before admitting, "He's made insinuations."

Her brows lifted. "Has he? When?"

"In Egypt. It doesn't matter. I've taken care of it." Tom moved the pad of his thumb over Jenny's knuckles. "He's not likely to say anything more. Even so, I'd as soon you refrained from being in company with the blackguard."

"It's difficult to avoid it when we're all stuck together at sea." She gave him a nudge with her knee. He scarcely felt it beneath the layers of her petticoats and crinoline. "Did you have words with him?"

"I did."

"Well?" she prompted. "What did you say?"

He saw no reason to dissemble. "I asked him about his father."

Her brow creased. "I don't understand."

Tom exhaled. "The man was a forger. It was kept out of the papers, but I remember the incident well enough from my early days in Fleet Street. Why do you think Hardcastle spends so much time abroad? He has no wish to be associated with his father's crimes. I'd wager that no one in India knows his family name has a stain on it. With his niece's future hanging in the balance, he must be particularly keen to keep it a secret."

"You threatened him with exposure?"

"Not explicitly. I merely mentioned his father. And then I mentioned Fothergill. It was enough."

Jenny looked both intrigued and appalled. "You never let on that you knew anything about the man, let alone his father. I thought he was a stranger to you."

"I recognized him in Marseilles." Tom gave her a fleeting, dry smile. "I told you I had a long memory."

She didn't appear to be amused. "But you were so civil to him. You even played cards with him of an evening."

"Why not? I had no dispute with him then."

Her eyes narrowed. "Is there anyone else in our party you recognize? The distant cousin of a murderer or the grand-nephew of a horse thief?"

"A few of the surnames are familiar to me. Then again, they're common enough. Those that bear them likely have no connection to anything untoward."

"Which names? Not Mrs. Plank, surely? Or any of the others we met in Marseilles?"

"You can't truly expect me to answer that."

Her lips compressed. "You keep far too many secrets."

"A consequence of my profession." He brought her hand to his lips and pressed a brief kiss to her palm. "And of my character, I'm afraid."

"I would have you share some of them with me."

"You know I—"

She forestalled his objection. "Not the ones about your clients. Only the secrets about yourself."

"*Only?* Good lord, Jenny, we haven't the time. We'd miss dinner. And believe me when I say that my secrets are not worth going hungry over."

"I'll be the judge of that."

Tom set her hand to his cheek, just as he'd done on the train to Cairo. Her fingers curved against him, cradling his face with a tenderness that made his pulse stutter.

In that perfect moment, he'd have given her the moon if she asked for it.

"Very well," he said. "What would you like to know?"

"To start?" Jenny shifted her hand to brush the tip of her finger over the bridge of his nose. "I want you to tell me how this happened."

"Ah." He wasn't entirely surprised by her request. Nevertheless, it sent a stab of ice through his vitals. "Is that all?"

"You wouldn't confess it when we were on the *Valetta*."

"There's nothing to confess. It wasn't a crime. It's merely an old tale, hardly worth the telling."

"Don't you trust me, Tom?"

"As much as I trust anyone."

She frowned. "That's not very comforting."

"Is it so important to you how a boy of twelve had his nose broken?"

"Yes," she said.

"I can't fathom why."

"Because I'm too curious for my own good. A dreadful failing, I admit." Her fingers were soft on his cheek, a slow caress. "And because I care for you, Tom Finchley, most awfully."

His throat bobbed on a swallow.

"It makes me want to know everything about you. All of your secrets."

"Greedy of you," he managed to say, his voice hoarse.

"Undoubtedly." Jenny's expression sobered, her hand stilling on his face. "Was it Mr. Cheevers who did it?"

Tom could think of no name more designed to dispel the mood between them. One mention of it and the warm glow resulting from Jenny's declaration receded into the shadows, leaving nothing but desolation in its wake. "No, it wasn't Cheevers."

Though the man had hardly been above such behavior. He'd enjoyed nothing more than punishing perceived wrongdoers by caning them or taking away their rations—no matter how small and vulnerable those perceived wrongdoers might be.

But there was no cause to tell Jenny any of that. Nothing could come of burdening her with the full breadth of Cheevers's cruelties. It was his own cross to bear. His and Justin's and Neville's and—

"Then who?" Jenny asked. "Sir Oswald? Or another of the men involved with the orphanage?"

"No, it wasn't any of them. It wasn't a man at all." Tom pressed her hand. The truth of his injury didn't come easily. He'd kept it too long and held it too close. But Jenny coaxed it out of him with her soft words and even softer caresses. She wanted his darkest secret. His very soul.

And so he gave it to her.

"It was another boy," he said. "It was Alex Archer."

Chapter Thirteen

Jenny stared at Tom, trying her best to understand what it was he was telling her. "Do you mean to say that the pair of you engaged in a bout of fisticuffs?"

It wasn't uncommon among boys of a certain age. Her own two older brothers had regularly pummeled each other senseless. She'd seen so many black eyes, bloody noses, and injured limbs as a girl, that for a time, she'd considered taking up nursing.

"It wasn't fisticuffs," Tom said. "It was a beating, more or less. A fairly brutal one."

"A beating?" Jenny couldn't hide her confusion. She'd thought they'd been friends. As close as brothers, wasn't that how Helena had described them? Four orphans united against the world? "Why?"

"There was an incident. A confluence of events leading up to Archer's disappearance." Tom removed her hand from his cheek, but he didn't relinquish it. He held it fast in his as if it were his lifeline. "Whenever we climbed down the cliffs at Abbot's Holcombe, we'd row up the coast to the Abbey. We did it at least once a week, even after Cross had his accident. You'd think that would have stopped us, but it didn't."

Jenny couldn't imagine what would be so powerful as to draw the remaining boys back to the cliffs after their friend had been so grievously injured. "Was it because of Sir Oswald? Because you'd discovered he was Mr. Thornhill's father?"

"In the beginning, yes. But that wasn't our only motivation for braving the cliffs." The corner of Tom's mouth quirked wryly. "There are ghost stories about the Abbey. Just the sort of nonsense to appeal to young boys. You must have heard them."

She grimaced. "In all their infinite variations." It was difficult not to when one was residing in the very house that featured in the local legends. "Helena mentioned vengeful pirate ghosts and smugglers' treasure. And one of the serving girls in the village said something about mad monks and papists' gold."

"There are dozens more, each version a little different. Ancient structures like the Abbey often inspire such tales. But in this case, all the old stories have one thing in common."

Realization dawned slowly in Jenny's brain. When it came, it left her almost speechless. "The treasure?"

"The treasure," Tom concurred.

"Do you mean to say there really was such a thing?"

"I never believed it myself, not even as a boy. It was merely a dream. A childish fancy. And then, one day, not long after Cross's accident, Archer and I rowed to the Abbey. Thornhill wasn't with us. He was keeping vigil at Cross's bed."

"What did you do?"

"The usual mischief. We went down to the storerooms. We'd been digging there for some time already. But this time, we didn't dig. Archer saw a loose stone in the wall. It gave us the idea to start checking all of the loose stones."

"You don't mean to say you found something?"

"We did, much to our astonishment."

"Well?" she prompted him. "What was it?"

"A rotted leather pouch with one hundred pounds in gold coins inside of it."

"One hundred pounds!"

"A king's ransom, or so it seemed to us. And that wasn't all. There was some jewelry in the pouch as well. An old ruby ring and a diamond pendant. Very old, if the cut of the stones are as I remember." His thumb moved over the back of her hand, idly stroking her skin. "I was ecstatic, of course. Right away, I began planning our futures. We'd leave the orphanage. Buy ourselves new clothes, procure passage on the mail coach, and go to London. And we'd eat whatever we wanted, whenever we wanted. None of us would ever go hungry again."

Her mouth curved in a smile. "It sounds a reasonable plan."

"I thought so. Archer saw it differently. He didn't want me to tell anyone. Not yet. He asked me to wait a week until he'd decided what to do."

"He thought it his decision alone?"

"I don't believe he thought anything. The moment we opened that pouch, he lost all sense of proportion. I think it scared him to suddenly have so much money in his grasp. I told him we must bring it back with us, but he refused. When I tried to take it, he hit me. And he kept hitting me until I let it go. Until I promised I wouldn't say a word to the others." Tom's expression hardened at the memory. "My God, but I hated him in that moment. He'd never before used his strength against me. Two days later, when Fothergill came to the orphanage, I was still seething with rage. He asked me who was responsible for my injuries and I wouldn't tell him. Within the week, he'd taken me away to London."

"Why on earth didn't you say anything?"

"I'd given Archer my word to keep silent on the subject. I'd promised him a week. After that...I suppose I could have told Thornhill and Cross, but by then it was too late." Tom met her gaze, his own eyes weary. "Archer didn't just disappear, Jenny. He disappeared with the money. He took it for himself, Thornhill's and Cross's one chance at freedom and security. How could I ever tell them what he'd done? What I'd *let him* do?"

"Has Mr. Thornhill no idea?"

"No." Tom shook his head. "Thornhill believes in loyalty above all things. The betrayal would break his heart."

"And what of your heart?"

He gave her a smile that was as weary as his eyes. "Bruised, but not broken. I had Fothergill and the promise of a profession. It was Thornhill and Cross who were left behind."

"You can't blame yourself."

"Can't I?"

"You were a boy. An honest boy trying to honor your promise to a friend."

"Alex Archer *was* my friend. My best friend, I daresay. He was also selfish and desperate—a dangerous combination, as my nose can attest."

Jenny leaned closer to him, her words a soft suggestion. "You should tell Mr. Thornhill."

"To what purpose?"

"Because it's the right thing to do. And because there are some secrets that shouldn't be kept. It's a burden on your conscience. Such things weigh heavily after a time."

"You speak from experience?"

"Hardly. I haven't any secrets worth telling."

"I'll be the judge of that," he said, echoing her earlier words to him.

She laughed. "Truly I haven't. Ask me anything you like. You'll see."

Tom regarded her for a moment, his expression solemn. And then his gaze dropped down her throat to the bare expanse of skin above the scooped bodice of her dinner dress. "Do you always wear that necklace?"

Her smile faded, her free hand moving reflexively to touch the gold chain at her neck. "Yes."

"Any particular reason?"

"It belonged to my mother."

"Ah. I see." His eyes met hers. "It means something to you."

Jenny privately cursed herself for an idiot. What had she been thinking to open herself up to Tom's questions? He was the most observant man she'd ever met. A man trained to identify the chinks in his adversaries' armor. Had she truly believed, even for a moment, that he'd fail to notice her own vulnerabilities?

"Yes, it does. But that's not why I wear it." Her fingers threaded through the end of the chain. "There used to be a pendant. Just here. An emerald medallion. It was passed down in my family from mother to daughter for generations. On my mother's death, it came to me. It was the only piece of jewelry she owned. The only thing she had to leave me save her childhood Bible."

Tom didn't press her to say any more. He only listened, his gaze holding hers as gently as he held her hand.

"My father was dreadful with the accounts. We were always behind on something, always coming up short. The winter before I left to become Helena's companion it was the worst. He'd spent the last of the housekeeping money on drink again. The tradesmen were threatening to summon the bailiffs. And the church was making noises about taking away the vicarage. I daresay it was the latter that frightened him. Being a vicar is his only measure of respectability. Without that..." Her shoulder lifted in a faint shrug. "Of course, he decided that something must be done to wipe the slate clean. And being the head of the family—and a man who, by law, had rights over me and my property..."

"He sold the medallion."

Her stomach tightened with nausea, just as it always did at the memory. "He knew how much it meant to me. How it was all I had left of her. But none of it mattered. My feelings didn't matter. My mother didn't matter. He simply took it from me and...I couldn't do anything. Not to stop him, and not to get it back after it was gone."

"I'm sorry," Tom said.

"Don't be. It's an all-too-common tale. There are countless women who have been similarly treated by their husbands and fathers. In any case, I still managed to keep the necklace. It's not very valuable. Not in terms of money. But it did belong to my mother."

"Is that why you wear it? To remember her by?"

"I wear it to remind myself what it feels like to be powerless. I don't ever wish to feel that way again. And I won't," she vowed. "Not so long as I live." She gave his hand one last squeeze. "Are you satisfied now?"

"That depends. Have you any other secrets I should know about?"

"The rest will have to wait. We've dinner to get to. And I still haven't arranged my hair."

He at last relinquished her hand. She rose from the berth and crossed back to the basin stand, where she swiftly plaited her hair in sections and twisted it into a roll at her nape. The coiffure took mere minutes to achieve, her hands manipulating her tresses with practiced skill. When she'd finished, she looked at him over her shoulder as she secured the last pin. He was watching her, his countenance solemn.

"What is it?" she asked.

His lips twisted into a humorless smile. "I'm memorizing you."

Jenny's heart contracted. But she refused to give in to the brooding melancholy that had lately overtaken Tom's spirits. Yes, they must part eventually. That had always been the plan. Until then, she wouldn't succumb to sorrow.

And she wouldn't let him succumb, either.

"There's no need." And then, with a smile, "Our adventure together isn't quite over yet."

Chapter Fourteen

Calcutta, India
March, 1860

The *Bentinck* reached the Port of Calcutta two days later, exactly as the captain had promised. Jenny stood on the spar deck, the heat of the morning sun blazing down upon her as the ship navigated the murky, vegetation-filled waters of the Hooghly River.

She'd read that Calcutta was known as the City of Palaces and she could certainly see why. The river was lined with elegant mansions and grand, dome-topped buildings. The largest sported a figure of Britannia atop it. She was holding a spear in her fist, as if to announce her supremacy over the city to all who ventured near.

There was no sign of any humbler sort of native dwellings made of mud or bamboo. Not from this side of the Hooghly, at least. The view from the ship was all European wealth and luxury. Only the harbor gave a true glimpse of the city's character. It was a hive of industry, crowded with people of all descriptions.

As the *Bentinck* drew closer, Jenny saw scantily clad Indian gentlemen in small boats, rowing out to meet the docking ships. Some came to assist with transporting luggage and passengers. Others were washermen, come to collect the dirty linen, or peddlers seeking to sell their wares.

Exotic sights and sounds abounded. It was impossible to become used to such things. Nevertheless, since their departure from Suez, the element of wonder with which Jenny had first beheld the sights of Egypt had largely been replaced by a quieter appreciation. She'd seen so many things during their voyage. Pearl divers off the coast of Ceylon when they'd stopped to take on coal. Dolphins leaping out of the water in the Bay of Bengal. And an islet near the mouth of the Hooghly inhabited entirely by alligators.

Indian men of all ages bathed in the river, and Indian women draped in colorfully printed cloth carried baskets in their arms as they traversed the water's edge with their children.

All of this—from bejeweled merchants to shouting donkey drivers—set against the ever-increasing heat that had come to replace the cool sea breezes they'd enjoyed when they'd first departed Egypt.

Perspiration dotted Jenny's brow and trickled down the back of her neck. She was envious of the Indians and their sparse clothing. The lightest garment she'd brought with her was a linen day dress; however, once paired with her corset, petticoats, and crinoline, it wasn't light at all. She resolved to purchase new gowns while they were in Calcutta. Without lighter clothing, she'd never bear the heat during the train journey to Delhi.

"That's Fort William," Mrs. Plank said, coming to stand at her side. The angle of her lace parasol cast a lattice-work shadow over her face. "When the sepoys rebelled, the British residents were forced to hide inside to escape the slaughter."

Jenny stiffened. She'd thought herself quite alone. "Were they?" Her gaze drifted over the city, taking in the elegant fortress-like structure and the equally grand, Grecian-style buildings along the riverside. The latter were ornamented with colonnades and verandahs, more like princely homes of Europe than Indian villas. "It's difficult to imagine."

"Were you expecting something more exotic?" Mrs. Plank asked.

"I had no expectation. Every aspect of this journey has been a surprise to me."

"Your first trip away from England, isn't it?" Mrs. Plank gave Jenny a smile that was almost feline. "Your *brother* said you'd only recently come up from Devon."

Jenny's skin prickled. She had the vague sense that Mrs. Plank was baiting her. "I did, ma'am. In preparation for traveling with him to India."

"Then this is all new to you."

"It is."

"Allow me to offer some advice."

Jenny inwardly sighed. She'd known something of this nature was coming. She'd met enough old-cattish matrons like Mrs. Plank during her time as Helena's companion. They loved nothing better than issuing dire warnings to ladies they deemed less fortunate than themselves. She steeled herself for the worst.

"Calcutta is not as vast as it appears," Mrs. Plank said in confidential tones. "We all of us socialize with each other.

It will not be long before your liaison with Mr. Finchley is common knowledge."

Jenny's body went still as stone. She continued to stare out at the docks, her stomach trembling as if Mrs. Plank had dealt her a physical blow. It was worse than she'd expected. Far worse. But she refused to give Mrs. Plank the satisfaction of knowing how thoroughly she'd rattled her. "You are mistaken, ma'am."

"I don't believe I am, Miss Holloway. Last month, when I came upon the pair of you on the deck of the ship we took to Malta, I'm certain you'd been embracing."

"There's nothing untoward about a sister embracing her brother."

"Come, my girl. I've seen the way he looks at you. Only a fool would believe you were his sister. If you care for him at all, you will take my advice and leave Calcutta before the scandal of your conduct touches on his reputation. He may yet still make a success of it out here. But with you at his side, he is sure to be shunned from polite society."

"I haven't any idea what you're talking about."

"Don't play the innocent with me, dear. Do you think I'm the only one who's noticed? Mrs. Hardcastle saw him leaving your cabin only two days past and my own daughter observed him kissing your hand on the promenade."

Jenny inhaled a steadying breath before turning on Mrs. Plank. As a lady's companion, she'd been obliged to tolerate the barbs of such women. She'd bitten her tongue time and again, never once allowing her anger to get the better of her.

But she wasn't a lady's companion anymore.

"These are grievous sins, to be sure," she said.

Mrs. Plank's bosom swelled. "Can a woman in your position afford to be glib on the subject of her own honor?"

"My honor is unblemished. I haven't engaged in any indiscretions, nor have I been spending my time spying on the private moments of others."

"Spying! Why, I—"

"You should be ashamed, madam. I realize your daughter has set her cap for my brother, but threatening me with your evil gossip is no way to advance her suit. You may believe me when I say that he would as soon die a bachelor than join his future to that of a family of gossipmongers and sneaks."

Mrs. Plank's face went white as milk. For an instant, Jenny feared the woman would either faint dead away or commence some sort of apoplectic fit. She did neither. Instead, she drew herself up to her full height. "How *dare* you? You impudent, brazen—"

"I beg your pardon, ladies."

Jenny turned with a start to find Tom standing at her right shoulder. She'd been too caught up in her disagreement with Mrs. Plank to hear his approach. How long had he been there? How much had he overheard?

It was impossible to tell from his expression. He merely stood there, looking perfectly at ease in a suit of lightweight cloth. The chain of his pocket watch glimmered in the sunlight.

"Mr. Finchley," Mrs. Plank spat. "Your *sister* has insulted my daughter and myself most grievously. You will understand if I withdraw my invitation for you to stay with us in Delhi. This woman's presence would not be welcome under any circumstances." She gave a stiff inclination of her head. "Good day to you, sir."

Tom's gaze followed Mrs. Plank as she sailed off in the direction of the stairs that led belowdecks.

"I should have held my tongue," Jenny said. "She'll tell everyone now."

"Tell them what?"

"That I insulted her. That I—" She suppressed a groan. "That I said you'd sooner die a bachelor than marry her daughter."

Tom's mouth hitched. "Yes, I heard that part."

"I trust you didn't have any intentions toward Miss Plank? If so, I regret to inform you that I've just damaged your prospects with the girl beyond repair."

All traces of amusement faded from Tom's face. "What did that woman say to you?"

"That everyone knows I'm not your sister. That, if I cared for you, I would leave you here in Calcutta before I damage your reputation beyond repair."

"Like hell you will."

Jenny looked out at the city, scarcely registering the impropriety of Tom's language—or the vehemence of his tone. The captain had commenced the arduous process of docking the ship. Soon the little boats would arrive to take them to shore. And then...

"Gossip about us can't spread any further, Tom. Not here in India. If it does, we'll have no hope of being received anywhere. And then how are we to go about finding Giles?"

"We'll just have to see that it doesn't spread."

"How?"

"By being careful."

"Avoiding each other, do you mean? Restricting our contact to public view? We've tried that already and it hasn't worked at all."

"Rubbish. If anything, we've been too careful. Had I showed myself to be fonder of you in public, perhaps no one would have taken notice of the—"

"It wouldn't have made one jot of difference and you know it. These society matrons love nothing better than discovering a scandal. And it's worse because...because you're eligible and comfortably off. There will be any number of mothers and daughters anxious to reel you in. If they see me as an obstacle—"

"You speak as if I have no say in any of this at all. I'm not a fish to be reeled in, Jenny, no matter how cunning the angler."

"Perhaps not, but it's a ruthless business. I'd as soon be well out of it."

He took her arm, forcing her to look at him. "What are you saying? Because if you're asking me to grant you permission to go to Delhi alone, you may as well know right now that I've no intention—"

"*Grant me permission?* You have no say over anything I do. If I wish to continue my journey alone—"

"We're back to this, are we?"

"And will be," she said. "Every time you attempt to assert your will over me."

"I'm not asserting my will. All I'm saying is that I won't allow the opinions of Mrs. Plank or anyone to separate us before our time. We're going to go to Delhi together, and wherever else we need to travel to put an end to this mystery about Lady Helena's brother. After that—"

"Must we speak of what happens after? I don't even want to think about it."

"What *do* you want?"

"To get off this ship and away from these wretched people. I can't bear it anymore."

He looked at her for a long moment before giving a curt nod. "Done."

Tom took care of everything; paperwork, passports, luggage, and accommodations. Bureaucracy he could handle. Even bribes. It was emotion he was beginning to find difficult.

The last three weeks on the *Bentinck* had pushed him to the limits of his control. To have Jenny so near and yet be forced to maintain a distance from her was torture. Even worse was the knowledge that the end of their journey together was rapidly looming ahead. Whatever the fate of Giles Reynolds, 6th Earl of Castleton, Tom would soon be returning to England.

He had no choice. His life and his work were in London. It had been bad enough to abandon his responsibilities temporarily. The very idea of abandoning them permanently was unthinkable. How could he? Traveling the world was Jenny's dream, not his. He preferred the familiarity of London. The fog and the drizzle. The way the gas lamps illuminated the street as he walked home of an evening.

It wasn't that their adventures thus far had held no appeal. Indeed, the exotic sights, sounds, and smells were things he was not likely to ever forget. But there was nothing about them that tempted him to continue on this journey.

Nothing, save Jenny Holloway.

When he at last emerged from the Custom House, he found her on the docks in the same place he'd left her, seated on her trunk beneath an azure sky, holding a dainty satin parasol half-tilted over her head to block out the unrelenting rays of the sun.

A small group of native children had gathered round her. Some crouched at her feet. Others stood. They all appeared to be eating something.

"Candied fruit," Jenny said when he approached. "I've bought some for the children. And some for you."

He took the paper of sweets she extended to him. Inside were sugary, yellow-orange chunks. Mango, he suspected.

"My first taste of India," Jenny said, popping one into her mouth.

The children giggled.

Ahmad and Mira stood nearby, nibbling on candy of their own. They looked as overheated and travel worn as Tom felt himself.

"Come," he said. "Let's get out of the sun."

"And go where?"

"I've hired a gharry to take us to a hotel outside the European quarter of the city." The horse-drawn carriage had looked a little worse for wear, but it was serviceable enough. The native driver—or gharry-wallah, as he was called—was waiting for them on the street.

Jenny stood, giving her skirts a brisk shake over her crinoline. She looked vaguely intrigued. "Are there no other British travelers there?"

"We'll find out."

The hotel in question turned out to be a modest establishment, nothing like the grander Calcutta hotels in which the rest of the passengers of the *Bentinck* were likely to be staying. Nevertheless, it was comfortable, and the gentleman at the Custom House had assured him that it was perfectly safe.

The proprietor was a cheerful Indian fellow named Mr. Vidyasagar. He spoke creditable English and was a veritable fount of information about the city. As he escorted them to their rooms, he talked of the botanical gardens and other popular sights they might see during their stay.

"It all sounds lovely," Jenny said. "But my brother and I won't be here long enough."

"You can see much in a short time, Miss Holloway." Mr. Vidyasagar opened the door to Jenny's room. Easily triple the size of a hotel room in England, it boasted white-painted walls and a matted floor. At its heart stood a large bedstead curtained with mosquito netting.

Jenny and Mira entered along with two of the hotel servants carrying their luggage.

If not for Mr. Vidyasagar's presence, Tom would have followed. It would be easier—and far more private—to speak with Jenny in her room than to discuss their plans in one of the common areas. But this time he was resolved there would be no hint of impropriety. No moonlit walks. No discreet holding of hands. And absolutely no visits with Jenny in her bedchamber.

His own room was situated next door. It was almost identical to Jenny's, down to the large bathing room with a spacious tub. There were even accommodations for his valet.

Ahmad gave him a wry look. "Is this mine? Or am I to sleep outside Miss Holloway's door like a native servant?"

"One of us may have to." Tom's words were spoken only half in jest. Jenny didn't want to spend any more time than necessary in Calcutta. Though she wasn't likely to bolt, Mrs. Plank's accusations had plainly shaken her. They had shaken him, too. Gossip was a poison that could spread with surprising rapidity. Unchecked, it could easily find its way back to England.

He wasn't so much concerned about himself as he was about Jenny. She was only in this predicament because of him.

After washing and changing, he joined her at one of the small tables in the courtyard. It was cooler there, inset with tiles and adorned with potted palms, exotic plants, and other greenery. The sound of rippling water emanated from a three-tiered marble fountain at the center of the room.

Mr. Vidyasagar himself served them tea. No sooner had he gone than Jenny asked, "You don't intend us to remain in Calcutta for any length of time, do you?"

"No more than four or five days," he said.

"*Four or five days?* Heaven's sake, Tom. Didn't you hear what I said on the ship? I don't want to remain here any longer than necessary."

"I heard you perfectly well."

"Then why in the——"

"Because we're not prepared. We haven't sent letters to Anstruther, or to anyone else associated with Giles's regiment. We haven't purchased clothing appropriate to the climate. And, most importantly, we haven't rested. We've been traveling nonstop for well over a month. The voyage on the *Bentinck* alone was in excess of three weeks. It seems only reasonable that we take the time to become accustomed to dry land again." He paused before adding, "I'm thinking of your health in this, and the health of Ahmad and Mira."

Jenny frowned at him. It was a variety of frown Tom had begun to recognize. One that said she resented his arguments but couldn't disagree with the logic of them. "You're right, as always," she said. "Not but that I wouldn't gladly forgo new dresses if it meant avoiding Mrs. Plank and the rest of them."

"With any luck, we won't see the other passengers for the remainder of our stay. They don't strike me as the sort who'll stray from the European quarter."

She took a grudging sip of her tea. "I suppose I must thank you for arranging lodgings so far away from them. I don't know how you managed it."

"The usual way. Talking to people. Asking questions. The gentlemen I encountered at the Custom House were happy to be of service."

"Mr. Vidyasagar is certainly very pleasant."

"And very helpful as well." Tom withdrew a folded piece of paper from an inside pocket of his coat. He opened it on the table, revealing the faded lines of a map of greater India. "I asked him if he had a map we might use during our stay."

Jenny set aside her teacup. "Gracious, how vast it is!"

"It's a large country. We'd be wise to plot our journey beforehand. The last thing we need is to be forever doubling back and covering the same terrain."

She leaned forward in her seat to get a closer look. "What do you suggest?"

"To start, we should consider whether there are any other officers worth talking to in addition to Colonel Anstruther."

"I have considered it," she said.

"And?"

"It seems to me that we must pay a visit to Fort William."

Tom couldn't disagree. "I'll send a note round."

"You may address it to the Deputy Adjutant General. A fellow by the name of Sir Eustace Tavernier." She smiled slightly. "You're right. Mr. Vidyasagar *is* very helpful."

His mouth hitched. "Let's pray Sir Eustace is equally so."

"We needn't only question soldiers," she said. "There are bound to be others who encountered Giles at one point or another. Friends and passing acquaintances—and the servants in their households. Though it has been two years. Perhaps they won't remember him?"

"Why shouldn't they? He was a nobleman. Wealthy—and handsome, I presume."

"Very handsome."

Tom suppressed a sharp pang of jealousy. "Yes, well…a gentleman so well-favored isn't likely to have been forgotten."

Unlike himself, a man who made it a practice to be— as Jenny had described him—purposefully unremarkable. It was a useful enough trait in gathering information to help his clients. However, when it came to romance, the last thing a fellow wanted to be was easy to forget.

Would Jenny remember him when they parted? Would she look back on their romance with an ache of longing? A twinge of regret that she hadn't returned to England with him? Or would the memory of their time together slowly fade away, replaced by newer and better adventures?

Tom hated to think of it.

"The only difficulty is in knowing where to begin," Jenny said. "Giles never mentioned any of his friends or acquaintances in his letters. Not with any regularity. He only ever described the weather and the food. That sort of thing."

"What did you say to him in your letters?"

Her brows lifted. "In *my* letters? Goodness. I hardly know. Though I doubt it was anything more profound than what he wrote to me." She gave him a curious look. "Why do you ask?"

Because he begrudged Giles Reynolds every word that Jenny had ever written to him. It was ridiculous—and so was Tom for fixating on such trifles. "Just trying to get a better picture of the man. Speaking of which…you don't happen to have a likeness of him, do you?"

A faint blush seeped into Jenny's cheeks. "I do, actually."

Tom stared at her, a pit of lead forming in his stomach.

"It's a daguerreotype," she said. "Giles had it made for Helena before he left London."

"Do you have it with you?"

She nodded. "It's upstairs in my carpetbag. Shall I fetch it?"

"There's no urgency." He forced a reassuring smile, certain it must look more like a grimace of pain. "You were wise to bring it along."

"I hoped someone would recognize him, even if they didn't remember his name."

"And so they may. If not here, then in Delhi or somewhere else along the way."

"It's going to be a dreadfully long journey. And not very comfortable, I fear."

"No," Tom agreed. "Which is why we must take our time. The heat is only going to get worse as we move farther inland. We won't be able to keep the same hectic pace we kept when we traveled through France and Egypt."

Neither would they be able to keep such agreeable company with each other. The romance of their shared compartment on the train to Suez was a thing of the past. There would no repeat of their embraces on the rail journey to Delhi. Tom was resolved upon it.

This time, no matter what it cost him, he would resist this cursed longing for her.

Chapter Fifteen

Fort William was a formidable structure, designed along the lines of a somewhat irregular octagon, with five sides facing the land and three facing the river. The whole of it was surrounded by a moat which could be crossed by six separate drawbridges that led to six separate gates.

Jenny and Tom entered by the Chowringhee Gate. Their appointment with Sir Eustace wasn't for another half an hour, which left a little time to explore—but only a very little.

"I don't suppose we can wander about asking questions." Jenny tipped her silk parasol back to better shade her face from the midmorning sun. "Not without making ourselves conspicuous."

Tom strolled along at her side. "No. Though I expect Sir Eustace may permit us a little leeway after we've spoken to him."

She looked all about them as they walked deeper into the compound. There were warehouses, officers' barracks, and a little Roman Catholic chapel. Farther down the avenue, the Garrison Church resided, a Gothic structure bearing a brass dedication to St. Peter.

"Perhaps we might question the Garrison Chaplain?" Tom suggested.

"Oh, let's. But Tom—" She tugged at his arm, her voice dropping on a whisper. "If we must speak with a man of the cloth, I'd prefer we not lie to him about who are."

Tom's mouth quirked. "That goes without saying."

She exhaled a breath of relief. It was one thing to tell Mrs. Plank and the other travelers on the overland route that she and Tom were half siblings, but spouting that lie to a chaplain was something else entirely.

Tom opened the door of the church, waiting as she preceded him inside.

The wide skirts of her gown brushed his legs as she passed. Warmth crept into her cheeks. Lately, even the slightest contact between them seemed to have taken on new meaning. It was rare that the air about them wasn't thick with unspoken words and unexpressed emotion.

Her hand slowly found its way to her necklace, tucked safely beneath the modest neckline of her bodice. A jolt of memory brought her back to her senses. She'd do well to keep her head. Otherwise...

Well.

This was how ladies fell into making bad decisions.

An older gentleman looked up at them from behind the high altar. A stone depiction of the Last Supper decorated the wall at his back. "Good morning."

"Good morning," Tom said. "Are you the chaplain?"

"I am, sir. Reverend George Proudfoot at your service." He made his way down the aisle. The sides of the church were flanked with marble figures of angels. They appeared to be gazing down at him benevolently as he passed. "How can I be of service?"

Tom performed the necessary introductions, giving the reverend a brief explanation of what had brought them to Calcutta.

"The Earl of Castleton," the reverend murmured. "The title is not unfamiliar to me, but I can't seem to recall the man himself."

Jenny reached into her reticule and withdrew the small, folding daguerreotype case she'd taken from Helena's dressing table before leaving Greyfriar's Abbey. It was covered in gold leaf, worn at the edges. She offered it to him. "Would seeing a likeness help?"

"It may at that." The reverend took the case and opened it. Inside, a portrait of Giles was displayed under glass. He looked very much as Jenny remembered him. Fair and slim and devil-may-care in his regimentals.

Tom stared at the portrait in silence as Reverend Proudfoot examined it.

Jenny stared at it, too. It had always been impossible *not* to stare at Giles. He was fairer than Helena, his hair nearly blond, and so perfectly handsome that young ladies were forever swooning at his feet or going into palpitations.

When first Jenny had seen him, her own heart had fluttered so badly, she could scarcely put two words together. And when he'd begun to pay her attention—goodness! She'd felt as if she must be the most beautiful, fascinating young lady in the world. How else to have caught the eye of a gentleman so handsome?

More fool her.

Giles had had no more thought for her beauty and character than he did for the next young lady. She was merely an entertaining diversion while he was home on leave and restless from the tediousness of his obligations.

You deserve better than a fellow like me, he'd written in his final letter.

And she *had* deserved better. She still did. But that didn't mean she couldn't acknowledge his attributes, such that they were.

"Ah, yes," the reverend said. "Captain Lord Castleton."

Jenny brightened with expectation. "You knew him?"

"I met him briefly some years ago. A charming fellow. I was grieved to hear of his death." He folded the daguerreotype case and handed it back to Jenny. "As for anything more… I'm sorry to disappoint you, ma'am. You would do better to speak with Sir Eustace."

Her countenance sobered as she returned the case to her reticule. "I didn't truly expect he'd know anything," she admitted as she and Tom left the church. "Still, it is rather disheartening."

Tom was oddly quiet.

She looked up at him. "What is it?"

"I've seen him before," he said.

"Reverend Proudfoot?"

"Giles."

"What?" Jenny's eyes flew to his. "When? You never said so."

"Eight or nine years ago. I hadn't a name to put to the face."

Her steps slowed. If not for the soldiers all about them, she'd have stopped right in the middle of the curving avenue that led toward the Deputy Adjutant General's office. As it was, she could only sink her voice. "Under what circumstances did you meet?"

"We didn't meet. Not formally. He came to the office in Fleet Street along with another young society gentleman. They were in the way of being moral support to a third young man who was demanding to see Fothergill. He was the son of one of the parties to a case of ours."

"Your client?"

"No." Tom's jaw hardened. "Our adversary."

"Heavens."

"The case only just settled the day you came to see me in Fleet Street."

Jenny blinked in surprise. "The land dispute? My goodness. It is a small world." She hesitated. "What did you make of him?"

"The encounter didn't last long enough for me to form a set opinion. We never spoke. It was Fothergill they were focused on. I was likely discounted as being no more important than a clerk. It's doubtful he'd even remember seeing me."

"At this rate, we'll never know what Giles remembers."

"You're not giving up already?"

"Hardly." She stiffened her spine. "I still have hopes that Sir Eustace might tell us something new."

But much to Jenny's disappointment, the meeting with Sir Eustace proved no more illuminating than their meeting with the chaplain. A jovial gentleman with thinning hair and an impressive black mustache, he was all things civil to them, offering them tea in his office and regaling them with anecdotes. However, when it came to the fate of the missing earl, he was of no help at all.

"As I informed Mr. Treadway, Colonel Anstruther is the fellow you should be speaking with."

Jenny blinked. "Mr. Treadway?"

"Thornhill's inquiry agent," Tom supplied.

"Quite right." Sir Eustace nodded. "I received a letter from the man some months ago. As I explained to him in my reply, it was Anstruther who witnessed Lord Castleton's death. If it's a firsthand account you're after—"

"But surely he isn't the only witness," Jenny said. "There were other soldiers at the siege. One of them must have seen something."

"Not necessarily, Miss Holloway. Jhansi was the site of the second bloodiest battle of the rebellion. Not optimal conditions for making an identification. It's a stroke of luck that Anstruther saw his lordship struck down."

Her lips compressed. She didn't believe in strokes of luck. And even if she did, there was certainly nothing lucky about Giles falling in battle. "Are there any men presently at Fort William who were in Jhansi during the uprising?"

"One or two, I should think."

"May we speak with them?"

"Of course." Sir Eustace rose from his chair and went to his desk. "Let me see what I can arrange."

Two hours later, Jenny and Tom left Fort William with no more information about Giles than when they'd arrived. The soldiers to whom they'd spoken had admitted to knowing the late earl, but they had no secret knowledge to impart about how he'd died or what had happened to his body.

"Last I remember, he was right up with the engineers when they breached the walls," one young man had informed them. "First to the fight, that was Captain Castleton."

"There was smoke everywhere," another had said. "I don't recall much else, aside from the cannon fire."

Jenny passed back through the Chowringhee Gate at Tom's side, her hand tucked in his arm. "None of them were very forthcoming, were they?"

"They mightn't have had anything more to tell."

"You believed them?"

"I see no reason we shouldn't. Unless you suspect a conspiracy. Though what the military could achieve by faking the death of the Earl of Castleton, I haven't the slightest idea."

She shot him a quelling glance. "I don't suspect anything of the sort."

"In any case, we're not done yet. There are more soldiers to speak with. Friends and acquaintances of Giles's—if we can find them."

"Do you suppose Mr. Treadway will have written to them as well?"

"Unlikely. He doesn't seem to have been very productive. Though if he wrote to Sir Eustace, he's probably written to Anstruther. Other than that…" Tom shrugged. "I've a mind to ask Thornhill to discharge the man. There seems little use for him now that we're here."

"I agree. Not that we've found out very much. No one seems to remember anything more than the smoke and cannon fire."

"It was a battle. They were fighting for their lives."

"I know that. I do. It's only…I suppose I was hoping it would be a little easier. That we'd actually learn something we didn't already know." She frowned. "The only new fact I've learned thus far is that Jhansi was the site of the second bloodiest battle of the mutiny. Where was the first, I wonder?"

Tom answered without hesitation. "Cawnpore."

"Where Mr. Thornhill was stationed?"

"He was right in the thick of it. When news reports of the massacre first reached London, there was a time I believed he was dead."

"Goodness. It wasn't for very long, I hope?"

"Ten days. On the eleventh, a letter arrived from him, telling me he was coming home on the next steamer. It seemed a miracle."

She curved her hand more tightly about his arm. "Perhaps it was."

As a consequence of the heat, the majority of businesses in Calcutta were only open during the morning and evening hours. The middle of the day was a time for rest—and staying well out of the sun. Jenny passed the time in her room, having a long bath and washing her hair.

Tom had disappeared shortly after they'd returned from Fort William, retiring to his own rooms to write letters to Colonel Anstruther, Mr. Keane, Mr. Fothergill, and Mr. Thornhill. He'd been in a strange mood since they disembarked from the *Bentinck*. A consequence of Mrs. Plank's threats, no doubt. And of Jenny's reaction to them.

She wished she'd been more circumspect. That she hadn't shown him how much that vile woman's words had bothered her. As it was, he was more concerned about preserving her reputation than ever. He wouldn't enter her rooms. Wouldn't touch her hand. Wouldn't look at her any more than was polite and necessary.

Even luncheon—or tiffin, as the locals called it—was a public affair. Rather than dine at a table alone, they joined the other guests for a meal comprised of cold beef, rice, curry, and iced ale.

Mr. Vidyasagar's establishment presently played host to a variety of military gentlemen. Two of them had wives— redoubtable memsahibs, as familiar with the weather and customs of India as any native lady. They were a jovial bunch, talking and laughing with each other as if they were guests at a country dinner party rather than strangers meeting for the first time at an obscure Calcutta hotel.

"The hotter the climate," one of the soldiers declared to Jenny, "the hotter the food."

Jenny's eyes watered at the spiciness of the curry. "That seems an odd philosophy," she said as she hastily downed another swallow of ale.

"It's a matter of body temperature. One only confuses it by eating cold food in a hot climate. The food must be equally as hot as the weather. You'll soon see the sense of it."

At the moment Jenny wasn't certain she could ever grow accustomed to food so filled with scorching spices. And yet… the flavor was like nothing she'd ever experienced. Upon arrival in Calcutta, she'd thought that candied mangoes were her first taste of India, but here—in the curry served at Mr. Vidyasagar's hotel—was the true essence of the country. Hot, spicy, and bursting with flavor. How could any food that came after ever hope to compare?

"I've taught my cook to make a decent enough curry at home," one of the wives told her. "There aren't many who can replicate it."

"You must order the spices through the mail," the woman's husband said. "Direct from India."

After tiffin, Jenny retired to her room for a short nap until sunset. Mira was already there, fast asleep on her net-draped bed in the corner. Jenny didn't wake her. She wasn't entirely used to having a maid of her own yet. And Mira, with her quiet ways and elegant bearing, felt more like an equal than a servant. When given the option, Jenny still found it easier to shift for herself.

She stripped down to her chemise and drawers and lay down on her bed atop the soft woven coverlet. The sheer white mosquito netting hung all about her, dull and oppressive in the heavy heat of her room.

A fine dew of perspiration dotted her brow and bare limbs. She was tired but couldn't sleep. Her mind was too busy with thoughts of travel—and her heart too full of her romance with Tom.

And it *was* a romance.

She hadn't any qualms about admitting it to herself. Had she been plain old Jenny Holloway, resigned to a dull life in Chipping St. Mary, she'd have been dreaming of marrying him. Of settling down to a house and a family.

It was an ordinary sort of dream. So commonplace as to be no dream at all. Even so, the idea of it settled warmly in her stomach and heavily in her heart. It wasn't what she wanted of life, but the temptation of it was powerful. She felt, at times, it might be worth it to give up her dreams of adventure. That *he* might be worth it.

Not that Tom had shown any desire to propose to her. Indeed, on the train to Suez, he'd come right out and said he didn't wish to marry anyone. She supposed that he was, in his way, wedded to the law.

Whatever it was he did for Mr. Fothergill consumed his life. There was only a small corner of it left for himself—and for those he cared for. She could number the lucky recipients of his regard on one hand. There was Mr. Thornhill, of course. And Mr. Cross. Helena might even merit a mention. But what of Jenny herself? Was she among those he cared for? One of the fortunate few to command his loyalty and affection?

Tom's words would have her believe so. He'd said he was fond of her. That he'd do anything to make her happy. However, in her experience, a gentleman's words were untrustworthy at the best of times—especially when uttered in relation to women. In the presence of a pleasing face or a neatly turned ankle, he might spout the most tender phrases. It never meant anything. It was simply how men behaved.

But Tom wasn't like other men. Not any that she'd ever known.

At sunset, she rose and dressed, still feeling a little sluggish from the heat. She and Mira made their way down to the mosaic-tiled lobby where Tom was waiting along with Ahmad.

"Mr. Vidyasagar has given us the name of a seamstress and tailor," Tom said as they climbed into a waiting gharry. "They're not far from where most of the British do their shopping."

"I'd as soon we went to a native tailor," Jenny replied. "There'd be less chance of encountering the Planks."

"We'll be safe enough from them."

Jenny had her doubts, but as the gharry bounced through the busy streets, her worries about running into Mrs. Plank and the other gossips from the overland route were replaced by a growing sense of wonder.

Calcutta was a different kind of city than Alexandria, more modern in its way but no less fascinating in its diversity. Among the wide streets and avenues of trees there was no evidence of the rebellion that had savaged the land three years before. Instead, there were a surfeit of Europeans, many of them parading in elegant gigs as if it were the fashionable hour in Hyde Park. There were also Turks, Arabs, and Indians of every class, dressed in all manner of clothing—from flowing robes and turbans to loincloths and sandals.

The gharry-wallah deposited them at the gates of the marketplace near the Chowringhee Road. There, European-run establishments vied for custom with Chinese shoemakers, Indian peddlers, and the colorful stalls in the bazaar.

Jenny took Tom's arm as they proceeded down the crowded street. It was lined with gas lamps as modern as those in London or Paris. The jets illuminated the storefronts of chemists' shops, jewelers, and cloth emporiums. She saw liveried Indian servants waiting outside of the doors right along with scantily-clad ones carrying baskets atop their heads.

Ahmad intermittently spoke in a halting language to the peddlers who approached. When she cast him a questioning look, he admitted, "My Bengali is out of practice."

"Do you know any other of the regional languages?"

"Enough to get by."

"What about you, Mira?" Jenny asked.

Mira's cheeks colored. "I speak only Hindustani, madam. But it has been a very long time. I fear I've forgotten more than I remember."

"Mrs. Pritchard wouldn't permit any language but English spoken in her establishment," Ahmad explained. "And Mira was quite young when we arrived in London."

"I wouldn't worry," Tom said. "Nothing learned is ever gone completely. It's always there somewhere, lurking in the back of your head. You need only find a way to draw it out again."

"Spoken like a man who remembers everything." Jenny squeezed his arm. "We're not all of us blessed with a mind as vault-like as yours."

Tom gave her a grim smile. "A fact for which you should be thankful. There are some things best left forgotten."

The seamstress and tailor's shops were located next to each other midway down the road. They shared an entrance between them which led to a showroom containing bolts of fabric, varied trimmings, and a polished counter stacked high with pattern books.

The proprietors, Mr. and Mrs. McTavish, were a hearty Scottish couple with accents as thick as porridge. Mrs. McTavish took charge of Jenny at the outset, bustling her into the back room to strip her down to her underclothes and take her measurements.

"You'll be wanting muslins," she said as she plied her tape measure. "And, if you'll take my advice, a summer-weight corset to wear beneath them. Anything thicker isn't suited for the heat."

Jenny didn't argue with the woman. "What kind of muslins do you recommend?"

"I've a good selection of worked muslin. There's also mull muslins and printed muslins. Any of them would make fine dresses for a lady of your age and coloring."

In other words, Jenny thought, a rather antiquated spinster with an unfortunate shade of red-auburn hair. "How long will it take to run them up?"

"That depends on the quantity you order and how soon you have need of them."

"My brother and I plan to leave Calcutta no later than Friday," Jenny said. "Will that give you enough time to finish five gowns?"

"I can have seven finished for you by Thursday evening."

"Seven!" Jenny couldn't hide her surprise.

"Oh, aye. I've got three girls stitching in the back. I'll set them all to work on your order. They'll have it finished in a trice."

Two hours later, Jenny and Tom emerged from the McTavish's shop. Mira's arms were full of Jenny's purchases—including new corsets for the both of them. Jenny had also purchased three muslin dresses for Mira, a trifling expense, but one that was very well worth it.

"If you don't like how she finishes them," Jenny said as they waited for Ahmad to fetch a gharry, "you're welcome to re-stitch them as you please."

Mira inclined her head. "I am most grateful, madam."

"You'll both be more comfortable in lighter clothing," Tom said. "Mr. McTavish claims that within a week the heat will be unbearable. He says it takes most newcomers several months to acclimate."

"Nonsense," Jenny scoffed. "We four are made of sterner stuff than that."

Mira chose that precise moment to sway where she stood.

"Heavens!" Jenny caught her swiftly round the waist to steady her. "You're not going to faint, are you?"

"I don't think so," Mira said in a small voice. But when Ahmad appeared with the gharry, she visibly sagged into his arms, permitting him to hoist her into the cab without a word of protest.

"The heat," Ahmad said. "She's no longer accustomed to it."

"She needs tea and a lie-down." Jenny followed after them, casting a brief, longing glance back at the Chowringhee Road. There were so many things yet to see. She wanted to remain and explore them all. But she wasn't alone in her adventure. It would be selfish to put her own desires over the needs of the rest of their party.

Resigned, she moved to climb into the gharry only to be stopped by the pressure of Tom's hand at her elbow. She turned to look at him, her brows lifted in inquiry.

"Mira will be fine with Ahmad," he said. "Let them go on ahead. It will be easy enough for us to find another gharry or a palanquin to take us back to the hotel."

"You wouldn't mind staying here with me awhile longer?"

"No." Tom's eyes were soft on hers. "I wouldn't mind it at all."

Chapter Sixteen

The gas lamps lining the Chowringhee Road cast a dim glow over the crowds of people hustling and bustling along the pavement. It was a rush of a single-minded energy, everyone focused on their own endeavors. Ladies stopped to duck into brightly lit shops. Gentlemen haggled with peddlers. And servants, with their arms full of packages, darted toward waiting vehicles.

Jenny's hand settled firmly on Tom's arm as they strolled among the fray. "Could you ever have imagined, when you were a little boy, that one day you'd be strolling down a gaslit road in Calcutta of all places?"

"With an auburn-haired beauty on my arm?"

Jenny burst into laughter. An unladylike reaction that was, fortunately, muted in comparison to the general noise of the street. "Rubbish. No one else would describe me thus."

"No one else knows you as I do." Tom looked down at her, his eyes smiling. "Could you have imagined it? Being here like this?"

"In Calcutta? No. When I was a little girl, I never dreamed of a specific city. All I knew was that I wanted adventure. Somewhere far away from home. I'd have taken any chance to get it."

"I felt the same way about stability. The boring day-to-day toil of a clerk's life in London. That was my dream."

"You can't be serious."

He shrugged a shoulder. "When a boy spends his childhood never knowing from one day to the next whether he'll have food to eat or a roof over his head, the prospect of steady work and dependable wages *is* something to dream about. Even if taking that work means your life is less adventurous than it otherwise might have been."

"I've never had the impression that your life was lacking excitement. Not with all of your mysterious secrets and dark dealings."

"You make me sound far more interesting than I am."

"You *are* interesting. I could talk with you all day and never get bored."

His mouth quirked up at the corner. "A rare compliment."

"I mean it. I wish…"

"What?"

"That we had more time together."

His smile faded. "We have to be careful. For your sake, Jenny."

"Yes, I realize, but…" She gave him a speaking glance. "Had I known that evening in my cabin would be our last moment alone, I wouldn't have been so preoccupied with arranging my hair for dinner."

Tom regarded her with a solemn frown, his blue eyes lit with a peculiar intensity. "What would you have done instead?"

The street was noisy—everyone too consumed with their own business to trouble with eavesdropping. Jenny nevertheless sunk her voice. "Kissed you, probably."

"As you did on the train to Suez?" He covered her gloved hand with his. "If you had, we'd never have made it to the saloon for dinner."

A shivery thrill ran through Jenny's midsection. "What a scandal that would have caused."

"The worst kind of scandal." His words took on a husky edge. "You'd have had no choice but to marry me."

"Because I'd be ruined? I daresay that's one way to trap a husband."

"Or a wife."

Jenny wished the thought of it didn't stir so many emotions within her. "But we'd never do that to each other, would we? No matter what anyone said."

"You may feel differently if the gossip about us worsens."

"If it does, I shall simply keep traveling until I reach the farthest edge of the world."

Tom guided Jenny around a pair of bickering Indian shopkeepers. They were shouting at each other, gesticulating wildly. "A place where gossip doesn't exist? Best of luck with that plan."

"Must you be so grim?" She tugged at his arm. Ahead of them was what had to be the most dazzling storefront on the entire road. It was all twinkling glass and sparkling wares of gold and silver. A jewelers' shop with a distinguished Bengali gentleman waiting at its door to receive them. He caught

Jenny's eye and made her an elaborate bow. "Oh, do let's go in, Tom," she said. "Please."

"If you like."

For the next half hour or more, Jenny stood at one of the tall counters as the proprietor, Mr. Chowdhury, showed her glass bangles, gold and silver bangles, and bangles set with precious gemstones. Tom stayed at her side awhile before wandering off to speak with the shop assistant. When he was out of earshot, Jenny bent her head closer to Mr. Chowdhury. "Do you have anything a gentleman might wear?"

Another half hour and she and Tom were back on the street, her purchases tucked securely into her reticule. She'd never spent so much money in one place in her entire life. It wasn't going to bankrupt her. Not by any means. Still…

"You've gone pale," Tom said, searching her face. "Is it the heat?"

"It's not the heat." She gave him a weak smile. "I bought a jeweled bangle. It was terribly expensive."

"Ah."

"Would you like to see it?"

His hand came to rest on the small of her back, guiding her along the pavement. "Not on the street. You can show me in the gharry."

"Did you find anything you liked?"

"In the jeweler's shop? I'm afraid not. However, the shop assistant did give me the name of a cobbler at the end of the street. Claims he makes better boots than Hoby."

"Do you need new boots?"

"I don't need anything."

"I see. Just gathering information, were you?"

He smiled. "About boots, Jenny?"

"Who knows when such knowledge might be valuable?"

Tom endured her teasing with good grace even as he hailed a gharry to take them back to Mr. Vidyasagar's hotel. It was a sagging contraption with windows curtained against the heat. Tom helped her into it before climbing in himself and shutting the door.

Jenny settled back on the shabbily cushioned seat as the gharry sprung into motion. An oil lamp swung from the corner of the cab, casting an intermittent light over Tom's face.

She opened her reticule and withdrew a small wooden box, extending it to him in her suddenly trembling hand.

He took it, still half smiling from all of her teasing. "The jeweled bangle, I presume."

She watched with growing anxiety as he opened it.

Tom went still.

"It's a pin," she said. "For your cravat."

He continued to look at it, his face wiped of all expression.

"I know it's not proper to be giving gifts to a gentleman, but I thought…that is…I wanted you to have something special to remember all of this by." She was rambling and couldn't seem to stop herself. "It's quite understated. Nothing too gaudy. And look…" She rummaged in her reticule, pulling out the second box and removing the wooden lid. "Mr. Chowdhury said it was made from a chip of the same sapphire used to make my bangle."

Tom looked at her bangle and then back at his pin before, finally, lifting his gaze to her face. "Jenny…"

"Do you hate it? Is it too awfully sentimental? You don't have to wear it if you don't want to. I promise it won't hurt my feelings."

"I don't hate it," he said, his voice gone gruff.

"Don't you?"

"No, I…" He swallowed hard. "I shall treasure it."

Jenny's heart swelled with warmth—and no little relief. "You were so quiet. I was afraid I'd presumed too much."

"You surprised me, that's all."

"And you're not easy to surprise, are you?" She smiled at him. "I shall consider it an accomplishment."

What she would consider it was an unmitigated success. She'd never given a gentleman a gift before. It simply wasn't done. Not by unmarried ladies. Who knew how such things were meant to proceed? Her pulse had been pounding since she climbed into the gharry, the little voice in her head warning her that she was risking too much. Revealing too much.

But it was dark and they were alone together, side by side in the little cab, their legs touching through the vast thickness of her petticoats, crinoline, and linen skirts. She took the small box from his hands and removed the elegant little cravat pin. It was nothing more than a single sapphire chip atop a needle of gold.

He cleared his throat. "The same stone, did you say?"

"That's what Mr. Chowdhury told me. I trust it wasn't just a ruse to get me to buy both pieces." She leaned closer to him, the sapphire glittering between her gloved fingers. "May I?" When he nodded, she reached up to his throat and carefully stuck the pin through the folds of his neckcloth. "There." Her hands brushed over his shirt and waistcoat. "Not too garish at all."

Tom stared down at her. When she would have pulled away from him to move back to her seat, he stopped her by the simple expedient of framing her face with his hands. "Do you have any notion how difficult you make this?"

A blush rose warmly in her cheeks. "What?"

"Being with you."

Her own hands rested flat on his chest. She could feel his heart thumping heavily beneath them. Almost as heavily as her own. "Because I gave you a gift?"

"Because you're you. Because I can't be near you without losing all of my good sense."

"You've behaved perfectly well since we left Egypt."

He bent his head to hers. "When I brushed your hair in your cabin? When I kissed your hand?"

Jenny stretched up to nuzzle her nose against his. "Both of which were lovely."

"You're lovely," he said. And then he leaned down and kissed her, his lips capturing hers so softly and so sweetly that she could do nothing more than melt against him and kiss him back.

The gharry-wallah kept the horse to a walk. Anything faster would have been unconscionable in the heat. It gave Tom ample time to enfold Jenny into his strong embrace, to press tender kisses to her cheeks and temple, and to murmur to her the most delicious things she'd ever heard in her life.

"My dear girl," he said. "You'll drive me mad with wanting you."

She slid her arms around his neck, returning his kisses with anything but passivity. "I don't care," she murmured back. "I don't care."

Which wasn't true in the slightest, but in that moment—safe in his arms—nothing of the world seemed to matter. She had no thought for respectability or for keeping up appearances. There was only Tom and an ache for him so acute that nothing would do but to kiss him and hold him and burrow deeper into his embrace.

He pressed his face into her hair. "You will if I harm your reputation any further. We both will."

She smoothed a hand over the back of his head. "I hate gossip, I do. And I've no desire to be ostracized, but really…I can't see that any of it matters much anymore."

Tom slowly drew back from her to look her in the eye. His hair was rumpled, his face flushed high at his cheekbones. "What are you saying?"

"Only that we've already suffered our fair share of talk. Knowing that, what difference can it possibly make if we—"

"What?" He searched her face, his fingers tightening at her waist, pressing into the hard bones of her corset. "Surely you're not suggesting—"

"Not *that*." A rush of heat swept up Jenny's neck, setting her face aflame. "I'm not lost to all propriety." Her hands slid down to the front of his waistcoat. "All I'm suggesting is that…" She plucked at one of his buttons. "Perhaps we might consider traveling to Delhi in the same way we traveled across Egypt?"

"Alone. In a private compartment."

It was the very thing she'd resolved against that morning on the deck of the *Bentinck*, the shock of Mrs. Plank's accusations still fresh in her mind. Gossip was dangerous to a single woman, even more so to one traveling alone in a strange land. Jenny had promised herself then she'd do nothing to exacerbate the situation.

But now, in the darkened cab of the gharry, her lips still swollen from Tom's kisses, such concerns carried no weight at all.

"Yes," she said. And then again, more softly, "*Yes*. I want to be with you like this. I'm not ready for it all to end."

"Nor am I, but…we're playing with fire, Jenny. This attraction between us is strong. Stronger than anything I've ever experienced."

"Which is why it's no use fighting it all the time."

"We haven't fought it enough. I know I haven't."

"It isn't only you." She gave him a look, half embarrassed and half foolishly tender. "I've tried, but I can't stop thinking about you."

His own expression softened. "You never show it."

"Don't I? I feel as if it must be plain for the whole world to see."

"Perhaps it is. Perhaps it's just me who's too stupid to recognize it." The color in his cheeks heightened, his voice deepening on a husky admission. "I haven't much experience with any of this."

"And you think I have?"

"What I think is that neither of us have exercised any restraint since we left England."

"Not for lack of trying."

"But we haven't tried very hard, have we? And it's my fault. I'm the one who proposed that we explore this attraction between us." He exhaled a frustrated breath. "I suppose I thought I could exert some control over it. That I could manage these feelings for you the way I manage everything else."

"Do you regret coming with me?"

"I should."

"But do you?" she pressed.

"No. And that's the devil of it. I don't enjoy feeling powerless any more than you do. I've spent the past two decades of my life crafting a world in which I'm always in control. Not only of myself, but of my work and my environment. And now, here I am, halfway round the globe, with no control of anything."

"You're out of your element, that's all."

"To put it mildly."

"But so am I."

He smiled. "The difference being, you relish it."

"Not without reason." She smoothed his waistcoat. "Up until now, my entire life has been a study in self-control. Of biting my tongue and blending into the background. The same rigid rules and expectations that give you strength were a prison to me. They didn't make me feel as if I had power. They robbed me of my power. Perhaps it's so for all women. Our lives are a series of cages: daughter, wife, mother. It isn't a structure designed for being oneself. For discovering what truly makes one happy."

His hand moved gently over the curve of her spine. "Could you never be happy in any of those roles? As a wife or a mother?"

"I don't know. I haven't lived enough yet as a whole person. I haven't experienced enough."

"How much is enough?"

"I don't know," she said again. "But it must be something longer than a few months abroad looking for Giles, mustn't it? I've yet to lose this restless feeling in my chest. And it's all mixed up with my feelings for you, making everything a wretched tangle."

"What do you anticipate will calm your restlessness?"

"More travel, I expect."

Tom's voice lowered, making her pulse throb and the butterflies in her stomach soar. "And what about your restlessness for me?"

She slid her arms around his waist, bringing her cheek to rest on his lapel. Tom's arms encircled her firmly in return. "More of this."

His lips brushed over her temple in the barest whisper of a kiss. "It's not wise to continue in this manner. You said so yourself."

"I never did."

"On the train to Cairo, you said that the more time we spend together, the harder it's going to be to say goodbye."

"Which is true, but still no reason we can't—"

"Your reputation seems a good enough reason to me."

"Rubbish. We'll simply have to be more careful."

"By sharing a private compartment all the way to Delhi? It will never do."

He was right. She knew he was. And yet his pronouncement felt like a rejection not only of her travel suggestions, but of herself and the tenderness she bore for him. "Don't you want—?"

"My God, yes. But we daren't risk it. You know that as well as I do. If we continue on as we are, it will only be a matter of time before there's more talk. Before your reputation is damaged beyond all hope of repair."

"Mrs. Plank would claim that it already is. She'd say I was ruined from the moment we boarded the ship together in Dover. If it wasn't for—"

Tom abruptly set her away from him. His blue eyes were no longer weary. They were sharp and clear, regarding her with an unsettling solemnity. "Do you believe I've ruined you?"

Her mouth tilted upward. "I don't feel ruined."

"It's no joke, Jenny."

She could see that it wasn't. Not to him. "I know that, but I don't understand how—"

"If you feel—if you suspect for even a moment—that our journey together has irrevocably harmed your reputation, then I'll—"

"You'll what?"

"I'll redeem it," he said.

Jenny's breath stopped in her chest. She moistened lips that were suddenly dry. "How do you propose to do that?"

He gave her a wry look. "How do you think?"

As marriage proposals went, it was an unmitigated disaster. Especially when made after she had so passionately explained her need for more travel and more independence—and so eloquently expressed her lack of interest in the roles of wife and mother. Had it been a legal strategy, Fothergill would have decried it as being impetuous, poorly thought out, and destined for failure from the first word.

Tom couldn't disagree.

This was what came of sharing kisses in the darkened cab of a Calcutta gharry thousands of miles away from the rigid certainty of his life in London. A man forgot how to plan things properly. How to strategize for a successful outcome.

As if a man could think at all while holding Jenny Holloway in his arms.

But this was no time for unfettered emotion, no matter how much his pulse was pounding and his stomach tying itself in knots. This was the time for serious business. For taking responsibility for his actions.

"I was the one who made the decision to join you on this journey," he said. "I've no intention of leaving you alone to face the consequences of my rash actions. Even if that means I must marry you."

Even if that means I must marry you?

Good lord, could he make any more of a mull of this?

"What I mean to say is that you may rely on me. If you feel the situation warrants it, I would gladly make you my wife." It sounded a little better, but not much, Tom feared. He gave a rueful grimace. "More than gladly, obviously."

Jenny gazed up at him. Her face was pale in the lamplight, her expression wholly unreadable. "But you don't wish to marry anyone. No more than I do."

"You're not just anyone, Jenny. As for the rest of it, I know you're reluctant but..." He was at a loss. She already knew how much he cared for her. To say anything more on the subject would be a gross miscalculation. Even a fool could see rejection was looming. There was no point in him making an impassioned declaration. No use in dropping to one knee. He soldiered on in a businesslike tone. "But in some cases, personal wishes are secondary to the demands of the moment. Especially where a lady's reputation is concerned."

"A lady's reputation is a serious matter indeed," she acknowledged. "And yet you must have known that mine would suffer when you decided to accompany me to India. I certainly knew it. I told you as much on the pier at Dover."

"You did."

"Then nothing has changed. Unless..." Her brows knit into an elegant line as she looked at him. Really looked at him. "Were you already resigned to marrying me when we boarded the ship to Calais?"

Tom's heart hammered in his ribcage. "If it came to that."

Astonishment flickered for an instant on Jenny's face before being replaced once more by that same unreadable mask. She slowly drew back from him, out of his arms. "I see."

"You don't. If you did, you wouldn't look like that. As if I've tricked you or trapped you in some way. I swore to you on the train to Marseilles that I wouldn't do that to you again. I'd never have made such a promise if I couldn't keep it."

She sat back against the seat of the gharry as the rackety vehicle rolled on through the crowded city traffic. Her hands, which had only moments ago stroked his hair and clutched at his shoulders, folded primly into her lap. "I believe you. And I'm grateful for your offer, Tom, truly."

"I don't want your gratitude." He tugged at his cravat, only to feel the prick of the cravat pin against his fingers. A spasm of soul-clenching emotion contracted his chest. He was going to lose her. If not now, then a month from now. And there wasn't a blasted thing he could do about it. The promise she'd extracted from him had effectively tied his hands, binding him up so thoroughly he was powerless to act.

"You have it anyway," she said. "My gratitude. My affection. My heart, too, I daresay."

"*Jenny*—"

"But I'd never do that to you, or to myself. It could only end badly. The two of us want different things from life. There's no reconciling them. Not even to save my reputation." She forced a faint smile. "Besides, I'd rather weather the storm of scandal. In time, people will find something else worth gossiping about. And if, in the meanwhile, I continue to insist that you're my brother——"

He muttered an oath he'd never before used in the presence of a lady.

Jenny's brows shot up. "Gracious, Tom. It was *your* idea."

"I should be drawn and quartered for ever suggesting such a thing." A fate which would be a damn sight more comfortable than the torments of hell he was suffering at present. "And it was Keane's idea, if we're being precise. He's the one who put the blasted notion into my head, always referring to you as Miss Finchley."

"Yes, it's so much ridiculousness, but better we act the part of siblings and pray the scandal will die down than that we do something hasty. You must agree."

The logical part of his brain—whatever small fragment of it was still functioning after kissing her—knew that she was right. It would never work between them. A woman like Jenny could no more be content trapped in London than he would be spending the rest of his life traipsing about the globe. They wanted different things—needed different things in order to thrive.

Affection wouldn't be enough. *Love* wouldn't be enough. One couldn't derive happiness entirely from another person, no matter how fond of that other person one might be. In the absence of all else, how long before such fondness turned to bitterness and regret?

Tom knew this. Recognized it as plainly as the nose on his face. But such knowledge amounted to less than nothing when compared to the ache he felt when he looked at Jenny Holloway.

He'd given up too much in his life. Suffered and gone without from the time he was a lad. Surely fate couldn't be so cruel as to make him go without her as well.

"If that's what you wish," he said.

"I'm only being sensible." She paused before adding, "And trying to prevent you from being unnecessarily gallant."

Tom managed a humorless huff of laughter. *Unnecessarily gallant.* That was one way of describing it.

She regarded him steadily. "Are you cross with me?"

"Do I look cross?"

"You do, rather." She extended her hand to him, slim and elegant in a fine kidskin glove.

He took it, holding it in both of his as if it were something fragile and infinitely precious. "Do I have your heart, Jenny?" he asked quietly.

Her thumb moved over his palm. "Yes."

The gharry rolled to a rattling halt. Even if Tom had been able to think of something to say, he had no time to say it. He scarcely had a moment to press her hand before the door was thrust open and the gharry-wallah unceremoniously ushered them out into the street in front of Mr. Vidyasagar's hotel.

The night was balmy and rich with the scent of coffee, smoke, and curried meat. Voices filled the air, the sounds of guests laughing and servants talking together in brisk tones as the table was laid for the evening meal.

Tom walked with Jenny through the gates, only just remembering to drop her hand a fraction of a second before the appearance of one of the soldier's wives they'd met at tiffin.

Later, he wondered how it was that he and Jenny ended up dining with the other guests rather than dining alone.

Neither of them had voiced any preference. It had just happened, as if by some unspoken agreement.

The same way it happened five days later when they boarded the train for Delhi.

There was no more mention of marriage. No more talk of private compartments so they might embrace or kiss at will. When they left Calcutta, it was in a first-class compartment which they shared with Ahmad, Mira, and two strangers.

Tom sat beside Jenny in pensive silence as the train departed Howrah Station in a cloud of smoke and steam. A weight of inevitability settled over his shoulders. Their romance wasn't over yet, but for the first time, he could see the ending of it. And it didn't end happily. Not for him.

Chapter Seventeen

East Indian Railway
Calcutta to Delhi
April, 1860

The well-to-do strangers with whom they had been obliged to share their compartment disembarked at the first stop, leaving Jenny alone with Tom, Ahmad, and Mira. She leaned forward in her seat, raising the Venetian blinds a fraction to peer out the window at the lush Bengal landscape. Hedges of aloe, tall *sirkee* grass, banyan trees, and bamboo nearly overshadowed the small native cottages and their inhabitants—some of whom had come to watch as the train went by.

It was baking hot. Far too hot to be making any sort of journey. Jenny was damp all over beneath her new day dress. That it was made of a sensible light muslin made little difference. Not when one was roasting in an Indian railway car.

The first-class compartments of the East Indian Railway were as comfortable as could be made in the heat. Designed to seat six, they were large and roomy with white-painted double roofs and projecting shades to protect from the sun. The stations they'd stopped at thus far were equally accommodating to the climate. Native water carriers of the region, known as *bhishtis*, supplied them with cool drinking water. For an additional sum, passengers could purchase earthen jars of it to keep with them on their journey.

There were presently two such jars in their compartment, along with a tiffin basket Jenny had purchased at one of the railway station refreshment rooms. Nobody had eaten yet. The oppressive heat didn't inspire much of an appetite.

She settled back in her seat, plying her paper fan with renewed vigor.

Tom sat beside her, reading the same page of the same English newspaper he'd been reading for the past hour. She doubted whether he'd absorbed a single word of it.

Their relationship had been strained since that night in the gharry. Indeed, it seemed that they'd each privately come to the same unhappy conclusion. No matter how ironclad their resolve or rational their good sense, they couldn't be alone together. Not anymore. Every time they'd risked it, they'd failed the test.

During their final days in Calcutta, whenever they'd set out from Mr. Vidyasagar's hotel, Ahmad had accompanied them. He'd been with them as they met with more of the soldiers who had known Giles. With them as they questioned the soldiers' batmen and servants. He was, ostensibly, their interpreter. That's what they said, anyway.

In truth, he was their chaperone.

The attraction between them was simply too powerful. Tom had admitted as much himself. That it was stronger than anything he'd ever felt. It was making them both foolish—and careless.

Was it any wonder unmarried ladies and gentlemen were obliged to be chaperoned? Clearly a single man and a single woman couldn't be left alone together without succumbing to their basest instincts. Not this single man and woman, at any rate.

But that wasn't entirely true, was it? Last year, she and Tom had spent many a civil and perfectly proper evening drinking tea together in the parlor at Half Moon Street. They hadn't been in danger of falling into each other's arms then. It was only when their mutual feelings had been acknowledged that the danger had manifested itself. That acknowledgement had given them a form of permission. An excuse to behave in a way they would never have done before. Certainly not when Tom was still Mr. Finchley and she was still Miss Holloway.

She cast him a thoughtful glance. His hair was rumpled, some of it falling over his forehead in that soft way it did. A surge of emotion tightened her throat. How dear he'd become to her over the past months, every aspect of his face and figure evoking a now-treasured memory.

Sometimes, when she lay awake in her bed, she could still feel his breath against her cheek. The way he brushed kisses over her temple and the strength of his fingers pressing into her waist. The memories were that strong. That potently real.

Even more real was the way he was always there to take care of her. To see that she had precisely what she needed, all without bullying her or stifling her. She had only to tell him what she wished and he made it his mission to fulfill it. Granted, most of her wishes had been fairly mundane of late. Tickets for the train, transportation from the hotel, and tedious arrangements to be made for their luggage. But Tom never complained about filling out forms, mapping routes, or dashing off letters. On the contrary, he seemed glad to be of use to her.

It shouldn't have been the least romantic, but somehow it was.

As a girl, she'd never dreamed of being rescued by a hero skilled at managing legal and bureaucratic inconveniences. However, as a mature woman of eight and twenty, Jenny found Tom's talents far more useful than those offered by the white knights and swashbuckling pirates that populated penny novels. Dragon slaying and derring-do were all well and good, but in the modern world, a lady required a different kind of heroism.

Which wasn't to say that Tom was incapable of slaying the occasional dragon.

She still had the sense that he was dangerous. Whatever manner of legal business he conducted with Mr. Fothergill was of a ruthless sort. Part of her didn't want to know the full extent of it. After all, it didn't matter outside of London, did it? Tom had said himself that he was powerless here. Whatever he might have been in England, in India he was hers.

"Are you quite done with your paper?" she asked.

He looked at her, his blue eyes keen, leaving no doubt in her mind that he'd been fully aware of her perusal. "Would you like to read it?"

"Not at present." She wafted her fan. "Aren't you hot?"

"Extremely."

Her gaze drifted over his cravat, coat, and waistcoat. Ahmad and Mira were no less constrained. Jenny sighed. "Come, everyone. It's hours yet to the next stop. Surely we needn't stand on ceremony."

With that, she dropped her fan to her lap and stripped off her gloves. Her bonnet swiftly followed. She was unbuttoning the topmost button of her bodice before the others finally joined her in removing their outer garments.

Mira disposed of her bonnet and gloves, while both Tom and Ahmad discarded their coats and loosened their neckcloths.

"That's better," Jenny said. "Now, would anyone care for some water?"

A short while later they were all much more at their ease. It was still hot—beastly hot—but Jenny felt a little less like she was being cooked alive inside her own clothing.

As the train steamed ahead, they talked of their plans for what they would do in Delhi, where they would visit, and whom they would question. There was a logic to it, as far as Jenny was concerned. "I daresay it will feel as if we're often retreading the same ground, but we must leave no stone unturned. Even if that means questioning the same people Mr. Thornhill's inquiry agent has already written to."

Tom agreed. "Even the smallest detail may later prove important."

"I only hope there's someone out there who remembers what happened to him," Jenny said. "Or...or to his body."

It was difficult to think of Giles in that way—as a body instead of a person. But she'd be foolish not to prepare herself. From the beginning, she'd understood that this journey might well end in disappointment. There was every likelihood that

Giles was indeed dead. That he had been cut down at the siege of Jhansi just as had been reported.

"Ahmad can show the daguerreotype to Colonel Anstruther's servants," Tom said. "They may prove to be more forthcoming than their master."

Ahmad looked doubtful but made no objection.

"Do you have reason to think that Colonel Anstruther won't help us?" Jenny asked Tom.

"Only that he and Giles were rumored to have bad blood between them."

"But surely that won't matter now. Not in the present circumstances."

Tom's expression wasn't encouraging. "Some men hold a grudge for a very long time."

Jenny didn't know what to say. It had never occurred to her that Colonel Anstruther might prove difficult. The very notion was enough to make her stomach twist with anxiety.

As if she hadn't anxiety enough.

Her nerves showed no sign of relenting during the course of their journey. It was several days to Delhi by rail, with a few brief stops each day for passengers to dine and stretch their legs. At night, those in first-class compartments were able to convert their seats for sleeping. The seat itself made one berth and the padded back, when strapped up to the ceiling, made another. It was really rather efficient, though somewhat intimate in nature.

This posed no difficulty for the many compartments filled with gentlemen. Likewise for the few ladies Jenny had seen traveling in the company of their fathers, husbands, or brothers.

Had Tom truly been Jenny's brother, the sleeping arrangements wouldn't have been the least awkward. As it was, when night fell and the compartment went dark, she could scarcely relax on her upper berth for the thought of him sleeping beneath her.

Tom appeared to be facing a similar struggle. He didn't lie down at all, choosing instead to remain seated on his lower berth, his arms folded over his midsection, his legs stretched out in front of him, and his head tipped back against the wall.

Ahmad and Mira, by contrast, didn't seem uncomfortable at all. They were fast asleep in their berths on the opposite side of the compartment.

Jenny tossed and turned awhile longer before, finally, sitting up.

Tom's hushed voice sounded in the darkness. "Can't sleep?"

"No," she whispered back. "Can't you?"

"Not sitting bolt upright."

"Why don't you lie down?"

"Why do you think?"

Jenny sighed. "This is ridiculous. We've two more days to Allahabad. We'll have to sleep at some point." She moved to climb down from her berth. Tom rose to assist her, his hands closing firmly on her waist. When her stocking feet touched the floor, he didn't release her.

His voice sounded softly against her ear. "Are you still wearing your corset?"

She blushed. "What a thing to ask."

"No wonder you can't sleep," he chided.

He was right, of course. She should have changed into her nightgown and robe before retiring. The other ladies in the first-class carriage had done so. She'd seen them, emerging from the washroom, garbed in sensible nightcaps and dressing gowns with shawls draped round their shoulders.

"I'd feel indecent if I removed it," she said.

"Why?"

"I don't know. This entire arrangement feels indecent. Sleeping in the same compartment."

"We slept in the same compartment on the train to Marseilles. And again on the train to Suez."

"Yes, but…we weren't in beds." She paused before adding, "I know that must sound silly, but—"

"It doesn't."

"No?"

"It makes perfect sense to me, unfortunately." The train rattled and shook as it hurtled through the darkness. Tom put a hand on the wall to brace them. "We'd better sit."

Jenny sank down on the lower berth. Without its padded back, it was much deeper and far less comfortable than in its normal state.

Tom sat down beside her, leaving enough room between them to have easily accommodated another person. Was he trying to maintain some measure of distance? Or were his actions merely inspired by the cloying heat?

She turned to face him, wishing she could see his expression more clearly in the darkness. "Will you be too warm if I move a little closer?"

"Probably." He extended his arm to her. "Come here."

Jenny didn't require an engraved invitation. In an instant, she was snuggled against his chest, his arm holding her close. He *was* warm. Deliciously so. She felt as if she were surrounded by him. His strength and his scent. Her nerves ceased their jangling. *At last*, her body seemed to say. *At last*.

"Is this better?" he rumbled.

"Mmm." She slid her arm around his waist, feeling her eyes drift close as sleep finally beckoned.

The last thing she was aware of was the feeling of Tom's cheek on her hair as she drifted off, his breath a soft whisper against her temple.

"Five days," he murmured. "That's how long it took before you were back in my arms."

There was nothing like a long journey in the sweltering heat to promote intimacy between the inhabitants of a railway carriage. Tom had seen gentlemen in various stages of undress rushing onto station platforms to get their breakfast and ladies swathed in shawls and colorfully patterned dressing gowns hurrying into the first-class carriage washroom only to emerge minutes later looking as neatly garbed and coiffed as they might in any British drawing room.

His own lady—such that Jenny was—took a bit of convincing before she would admit to any level of comfort for herself. It was only on their second night on the train that she properly dressed for bed. She returned from the washroom in a prim flannel robe, her hair disposed in a long auburn plait over her shoulder. Her face was freshly scrubbed, her cheeks rosy.

"After all," she said, "you are my brother."

Tom didn't know whether to grin or to grumble. He settled for helping her up into her berth, trying not to notice how soft she was without her usual underlayers of whalebone and crinoline.

After their first night on the train, they'd managed to resist the temptation to sleep in each other's arms. It had been disconcerting enough to do it once, awakening as they had to Ahmad and Mira bustling about.

Tom had felt like the veriest cad. It was one thing to indulge his affection for Jenny when the two of them were alone, but to do so in front of others was worse than ungentlemanly. It was the sort of thing a fellow did if he held a woman cheaply. If he didn't respect her. That they'd both been fully clothed hadn't mattered one jot.

What must Ahmad think of him? What must Mira? The pair of them hadn't said anything, but he didn't expect that they viewed his conduct in a very good light. Especially not after having worked so long at Mrs. Pritchard's establishment.

Fortunately, the sheer length of the journey made many such concerns secondary to one's comfort. Both he and Ahmad spent a great deal of their time in the compartment coatless, with loosened neckcloths, opened shirt collars, and uncovered heads. Jenny and Mira were no less willing to forego their bonnets and gloves in the ever-increasing heat.

When the train at last stopped for twelve hours in Allahabad, they stepped out onto the busy platform in various stages of exhaustion. The famous city, with its Moorish arches and grand structures of white marble, was situated at the junction of the Ganges, Jumna, and Sarasvati rivers and, therefore, of particular religious meaning to those of the Hindu faith. Many pilgrims had come to bathe in the sacred waters. Among the crowds Tom saw very few Europeans, save for a British soldier or two on horseback.

He shepherded Jenny through the station, their progress intermittently delayed as she stopped to purchase sweetmeats from peddlers or to clasp the hands of the curious children who dogged their every step.

They put up at a native hotel for the day, too tired from their journey to summon any desire to explore the famous fort or the botanical gardens. Instead, he and Jenny dined on curried meat, rice, and ale with some of the other passengers in the hotel's small dining room.

Among the British travelers making their way to Delhi, the talk was solely of the mutiny.

"The railway station was burned," said Mrs. Goodwin, a widow traveling with her son and daughter-in-law. "And the tracks torn right out of the ground. The natives would have burned the trains as well had they not been frightened of them."

"Were you here at the time, ma'am?" Jenny asked.

"I was not, Miss Holloway. But I've read all about it in the papers. The city was devastated. One wouldn't know to look at it."

"No indeed, madam," Mr. Walters said. He was a quiet gentleman. A missionary, Tom suspected. He'd seen him reading the Bible on occasion. "The burned houses have been rebuilt and new roads have been laid. The resiliency of the native residents is really quite something to behold."

"Everyone has been very friendly toward us," Jenny said. "Ever since we arrived in Calcutta."

Mr. Walters smiled. "That is because you're very friendly toward them, Miss Holloway. Anyone who treats the Indians with kindness and respect will find them a welcoming people. That has been my own experience."

Mrs. Goodwin's son narrowed his eyes. "How then does one account for the atrocities committed by them during the mutiny?"

"In the same manner one accounts for the atrocities committed by us." Mr. Walters resumed eating his rice. "We have not come out of the mutiny with clean hands, sir. In many cases, it would be as fitting for us to ask forgiveness as to extend it."

"Do you mean to compare the slaughter and cruelty that they—"

"I say, sir," an older gentleman at the end of the table interjected in a booming voice. "My lady wife is present. I'll thank you to turn the subject to one fit for females."

Tom exchanged a glance with Jenny. She smiled at him. One of her private smiles, a faint upward tilt of her lips and a glint in her sea-colored eyes. A smile reserved only for him. It never failed to make his heart beat faster, even now, surrounded by strangers in the sweltering heat.

"A subject fit for females," she murmured to him as they left the dining room. "How dreadfully dull."

His mouth quirked. "Don't you enjoy discussing the weather?"

"Hardly. How many ways can one express an opinion on the heat?"

Tom walked Jenny to the door of her room. "You have time for a nap before dinner."

"I don't think I'll sleep." She brushed her skirts. "What I need is a bath. I've never encountered so much dirt and grime in my life."

"Order one, by all means. We've plenty of time."

After settling into his room next door to Jenny's, Tom took his own advice. Four servants clad in loincloths carried up the large copper tub and filled it with cans of hot water. When they'd gone, Tom stripped out of his dusty clothes and gratefully climbed in.

As a boy, baths had been few and far between, and hot baths even fewer and farther. He'd never forgotten the deprivations of his youth. All these years later, a hot bath was still a luxury to him.

His head came to rest on the rolled back of the tub, his eyes falling shut as the warmth and heat worked on his tired muscles. He imagined Jenny enjoying the same pleasure, her slim, shapely limbs relaxed and pliant beneath the steaming water, suds of Marseilles soap clinging to her skin.

Would she wash her hair? Or would she leave it pinned up in its carefully plaited sections?

He tried not to think of it. It wasn't right or proper—certainly not while he was in the bath.

But it was impossible not to think of it. Not to think of *her*.

Sometime later, as the sun was lowering over the horizon, Tom emerged from his room freshly washed, shaven, and in a slightly better frame of mind. He made his way downstairs to the lobby. He'd seen Ahmad from his window, standing on the street, smoking a cheroot as he talked with an Indian gentleman in a turban.

Outside the hotel there was no sign of Ahmad. Instead, Tom saw Jenny.

And an elephant.

It was an enormous creature, gray and whiskery, with a thin tasseled tail and fringed ears that twitched as Jenny stroked its shoulder. Beside the elephant stood its keeper, a rather grand-looking Sikh fellow garbed in dramatic white and scarlet.

"She belongs to the rajah." Mr. Walters was seated beneath the veranda at the front of the hotel, a small sketchbook open on his lap. The pencil in his hand moved in short strokes over the page. "He often lends her to honored guests for transport from the railway station."

Tom stopped beside him, trying to keep his mouth from falling open.

"Have you never seen an elephant, Mr. Finchley?"

"Once or twice in a menagerie, but never like this."

Jenny laughed as the elephant touched her with its trunk. Her face glowed with pleasure, her plaited auburn hair radiant in the sun.

Tom's chest tightened at the sight of her—even more so when Mr. Walters gave voice to his thoughts.

"Your sister appears well suited to India, if you don't mind my saying so."

"Yes, she—"Tom broke off. "She has an adventurous nature."

Mr. Walter's tilted his sketchpad in Tom's direction. "I'm not a professional portraitist by any means, but I do believe I've managed to capture something of her spirit."

Tom stared down at the pencil sketch. His mouth went dry. Indeed, it wasn't a proper portrait. And yet…somehow, Mr. Walters had caught the very thing that made Jenny so captivating. It was there in the arch of her brows and the stubborn uptilt of her chin. There in the curve of her soft lips and in the way tendrils of hair determinedly escaped from her carefully pinned coiffure.

"The elephant was more difficult, surprisingly." Mr. Walters examined his drawing with a frown. "Something about the legs. I shall have to study the proportions and try again." He tore the sketch out of his book and offered it to Tom. "With my compliments."

"Thank you." Tom looked at the piece of paper a moment longer before folding it carefully away into a pocket of his waistcoat.

"Happy to be of service." Mr. Walters gathered his things and stood. "If you'll excuse me, I must ready myself for dinner."

Tom bid him good evening.

In the street, the elephant's keeper drove it onward. Jenny stood awhile, watching it go. And then she looked at Tom, still smiling. "Did you see her, Tom?"

He crossed the short distance to join her. "She was hard to miss."

Jenny met him halfway, dusting her hands on her skirts as she walked. "Wasn't she marvelous? And so intelligent, too! She understood everything her handler said to her."

"Are you sure it wasn't a trick? Like the whist-playing dog at Cremorne Gardens?"

Her eyes twinkled. "I'm surprised you remember."

"How could I forget?" They had encountered the famous Learned Dog Lily last year while visiting the pleasure gardens with Justin and Lady Helena. The memory of dancing with Jenny that evening, of laughing with her and squiring her about on his arm, was one of Tom's most treasured.

"An elephant is smarter than a dog, surely," she said. "One only has to look into its eyes to know that it's thinking profound thoughts."

"That may be taking things a bit far."

"Nonsense. You'd have seen it yourself if you weren't hanging back with Mr. Walters."

Tom smiled down at her. "I was admiring you. I've rarely seen you look so happy."

A flush rose in her cheeks. "You make it sound as though I'm gloomy all the rest of the time."

"Not at all." His gaze drifted over her face. "Did you realize that you've begun to freckle from all of this sun?"

She looked vaguely horrified. "Have I?"

"It's rather charming."

"It's careless, is what it is." She touched her nose. "If I were smart, I'd have been carrying a parasol every day and employing a lemon juice wash every night."

"Alas, we can't all be as intelligent as an elephant."

She burst out laughing. The sound of it warmed him from the inside out. "On that chivalrous note," she said, taking his arm, "you'd best escort me back to the hotel for dinner."

What Tom wanted to do was to take her in his arms and kiss her laughing mouth. They hadn't kissed since their memorable ride in that Calcutta gharry—and he had a sinking feeling that they never would again. It was for the best, really. But that didn't stop him longing for her.

They dined with the other guests, seated far away from each other at the table, and then—at nine o'clock—boarded the train that would take them through Cawnpore and on to Delhi.

There were delays, of course. It seemed, when it came to Indian rail travel, that there were always delays. However, within an hour they were rattling along the tracks at a good rate of speed, all of them tucked snug into their berths for the overnight journey.

"We'll be in Delhi by tomorrow afternoon," Jenny said into the darkness of their compartment. "The end of our quest, for good or ill."

Tom lay on his narrow berth beneath her, one arm bent behind his head. How familiar it had all become. The intimacy of having her with him. Of hearing her voice after the carriage lamps had been doused. "Who's to say it's the end?" he asked. "It may well be just the beginning."

Chapter Eighteen

Delhi, India
April, 1860

Jenny clasped her hands in her lap to keep them from trembling as she and Tom waited in the study of Colonel Marcus Anstruther's villa. It was a marble-faced monstrosity on the outskirts of Delhi, decorated with furnishings of wood, leather, and varnished bamboo. Hunting trophies and weaponry adorned the walls. Elephant and tiger heads, and even the mounted head of a rhinoceros. The whole of it made Jenny distinctly uncomfortable.

"Do you suppose he killed all of these animals himself?" she asked Tom in a whisper.

Tom's face was expressionless. Clothed in a dark three-piece suit, he appeared every inch the formidable London solicitor. He had done since their arrival in Delhi yesterday afternoon. While she'd been restless with anticipation, he'd been calm and focused, addressing the preliminaries of their visit to Colonel Anstruther with solemn efficiency.

At first it had all seemed to be going according to plan. In response to Tom's note informing him of their arrival in Delhi, the colonel had sent a terse response, inviting them to call on him the following morning.

Jenny had been up most of the night pacing her hotel room, riddled with anxiety and excitement, only to be disappointed when they had at last arrived at the colonel's villa and found the man not at home.

Fortunately, the Anstruther's majordomo—or Khansama, as he was called in India—had not turned them away. He'd bid them wait in the colonel's study. And wait they had, for the past twenty minutes, surrounded by the carcasses of dead animals.

"He did kill them," a trilling feminine voice sounded from the doorway. "My husband is adept at killing things. There's no sport he enjoys better."

Tom and Jenny both stood as the owner of the voice floated into the room in a sea of flounced, floral-printed muslin. Her fair hair was arranged in ringlets that framed a face of waxen beauty.

"Mrs. Anstruther," Tom said, bowing.

"And you're Mr. Finchley, the solicitor come to ask after Lord Castleton. The late Lord Castleton, as we must call him. Why, it seems only yesterday I saw him in Poona. So young. So vigorous." She motioned for Tom and Jenny to resume their seats, arranging herself in the chair across from them. "Your letter to my husband said you were acting on behalf of Lord Castleton's family."

"Indeed, ma'am. May I present Miss Holloway, Lord Castleton's cousin?"

Mrs. Anstruther turned her doll-like eyes on Jenny. "Are you? I can see no resemblance."

Jenny returned the woman's gaze with a measuring look of her own. She'd often heard that the climate in India didn't agree with Englishwomen and here, in the face of Mrs. Anstruther, was visible proof. She was beautiful, to be sure, but she was also oddly colorless. As if the very lifeblood were drained from her body. "We're distant cousins, ma'am."

"Lord Castleton never mentioned any cousins. It was only his sister he spoke of." Mrs. Anstruther looked about the room. "How stifling it is today. Did Khansama offer you refreshment? Ah, but here he is with the tray. Khansama? Is my husband back?"

The Anstruther's majordomo entered the room carrying a pitcher and three tall glasses on a brass tray. "No, memsahib."

Mrs. Anstruther's face tensed. "He'll return soon, I daresay. He knew you were calling."

"He must be a very busy man," Tom said.

"Oh yes, he has many responsibilities, though he is quite retired now." She poured out three glasses of lemonade. Her hand, clad in an ecru openwork mitt, shook as it gripped the handle of the pitcher. "Have you been in Delhi long?"

Jenny watched the unsteady progress of the pitcher with growing concern. A spill seemed imminent. "We arrived yesterday afternoon on the train from Calcutta."

Mrs. Anstruther looked to Tom, as if she hadn't heard Jenny's response. "Are you staying nearby? With friends or—?"

"We've taken rooms at the Westbrook Hotel," Tom said.

"The Westbrook! Why, that must be very fine. I've frequently wished I might stay there for a night or two. It has been a long while since I've enjoyed a holiday. Not since my wedding trip." She lowered the pitcher back to the tray with a trembling clatter. "Travel is so difficult nowadays."

Jenny handed Tom a glass of lemonade before taking one herself. "With the expansion of the railway, you can surely visit wherever you like."

"But this is no season for rail travel, Miss Holloway. That's what my husband is forever telling me. I've tried to convince him to leave India now he is retired, but it is never the right time to make the journey, what with the heat and the monsoons." Mrs. Anstruther gave a hollow laugh. "We're trapped here, I fear."

"Are you unhappy in India?" It was an impertinent question, but Jenny couldn't help asking it.

Mrs. Anstruther laughed again, a short, brittle sound. "Oh, to hear me complaining! I'm very happy here, as you see. I have every luxury." She lifted her glass of lemonade to her lips only to return it back to the tray without drinking. "You…you must ask me whatever you like about Lord Castleton while we wait."

Tom looked steadily at Mrs. Anstruther. "Did you know him well?"

"Quite well. He was a dear, dear friend to me when Colonel Anstruther and I were newly married."

A dear, dear friend.

Jenny briefly wondered if the rumors were true. Had Mrs. Anstruther and Giles really been lovers? The lady didn't seem at all Giles's type. She was too frail and flighty. The fragile sort of woman who required a great deal of looking after. Surely Giles wouldn't have had the patience to indulge her. "When did you see him last?"

"In Poona, sometime before the mutiny began. He often came to dine with me." Mrs. Anstruther smiled for the first time. "He was a young gallant, Lord Castleton. He knew just how to lift my spirits."

"Yes," Jenny said. "His lordship always knew precisely what to say."

"Indeed, Miss Holloway." Mrs. Anstruther reached into her sleeve for her handkerchief. "I was ever so grieved to hear of his death. For such a gentleman to be cut down in the prime of his life. It's one of the great tragedies of the mutiny." Her eyes filled with tears. "When I think of how he was—"

"My dear," Colonel Anstruther said from the doorway. "You have entertained our visitors long enough."

Jenny and Tom rose, but neither of them so fast as Mrs. Anstruther. She was on her feet in seconds, nearly knocking over her chair.

"Have a care, madam," the colonel said sharply. He was a big fellow, tall and wide, with a heavy, drooping mustache. His skin was baked brown from the sun, his black hair peppered with gray. He looked, Jenny thought, exactly like the sort of man who would take pleasure in hunting a tiger or an elephant. The sort of man with not an ounce of finer feeling within him.

She regarded him with a frown as he unceremoniously ushered his much younger wife from the room. He shut the doors to his study behind her before coming to join them.

Introductions were dispensed with and they returned to their seats, Anstruther taking the chair lately vacated by his wife. "You must excuse my wife. She's been unwell for some time."

Tom's brow furrowed with concern. Whether or not it was genuine, Jenny couldn't tell. "Nothing serious, I trust?"

"The heat. She's never adjusted to it. Many wives don't." Anstruther crossed one leg over the other. "But you haven't come to Delhi to discuss my wife. You have questions about Captain Lord Castleton, I understand."

"We do, sir," Jenny said.

"Seems dashed strange. I've already had a letter on the subject from a fellow called Treadway. It was delivered some-time in late January."

Jenny stifled an inward groan. In Calcutta, Tom had written to Mr. Thornhill and asked him to discharge Mr. Treadway. Unfortunately, Mr. Treadway's own letters—written to the upper echelons of the Bengal Army—had been dispatched months ago. As a result, Jenny and Tom were forever tripping over his name.

"We'd hoped to learn something more than Mr. Tread-way," she said. "You must know that yours is the only account of Lord Castleton's death."

"I'm aware."

"Would you—that is—if you could please tell me what it is that you observed that day, I—"

"It will be no different from what I wrote in my report and subsequent letters. One to his sister, if memory serves. Which is precisely what I told this Treadway fellow."

"Yes, but I'd very much like to hear it from your own lips."

Anstruther's brow lowered. "Have you reason to doubt my report?"

"No one doubts your account," Tom said. "Miss Holloway and Lady Helena are only hoping to discover some minor detail that might have been missed."

"To what purpose?"

Jenny leaned forward in her seat. "To discover if there is any small chance Lord Castleton might have survived the fall of Jhansi."

Anstruther's lip curled. "You may dispense with that notion, ma'am. Castleton is dead. I saw the death blow delivered with my own eyes."

"You said as much in your condolence letter to Lady Helena," Jenny said. "But you gave no further details other than that he had been cut down by a rebel sepoy. How can you be certain that the blow he received—"

"My good man," Anstruther interrupted her to address Tom. "Can you countenance such a discussion in front of a lady? I wouldn't permit it in the presence of my wife. Too upsetting, you know. Not quite the thing."

A burst of helpless frustration flared in Jenny's bosom. It was the same sensation she'd felt in Allahabad when the gentleman at luncheon had demanded they limit the conversation to subjects fit for females. Only this was worse. Far worse. She hadn't come all this way merely to be excluded at the final hour on account of her sex.

Her mouth opened on a sharp retort.

Before she could utter a single syllable, Tom replied in her stead. "Miss Holloway is a lady of impeccable sense. She's fully prepared to hear every detail. You may take my word on it."

At his words, some of the tension went out of Jenny's body. In its place came a swell of affection for Tom so great that it nearly stole her breath. He was on her side. He would *always* be on her side. The knowledge was enough to strengthen her faltering resolve.

"These details you speak of are graphic in nature," Anstruther warned.

"I'm not likely to faint," she assured him. "Yours won't be the first account of the uprising I've heard."

He made no effort to disguise his disapproval. "Let it be on your head, then."

Tom withdrew a small notebook and pencil from the interior pocket of his coat. In his experience, even the best memory was no match for the written word. And, unless he was much mistaken in his impression of the man, Colonel Anstruther was about to embark on a rambling military reminiscence, the substance of which would later have to be plumbed for meaning. Tom had encountered such fellows before. Retired officers who spent the remainder of their lives reliving former glory.

Anstruther had initially objected to recounting the siege, but it was clear that he relished the opportunity to do so.

The only question was whether Jenny was prepared to hear it.

Tom believed she was. Jenny Holloway was made of sterner stuff than females like Mrs. Anstruther. She wasn't going to wilt at the first mention of blood and slaughter.

And yet she'd been fraught with anxiety since they arrived in Delhi. He wanted to question her about it. To get to the heart of what it was that troubled her. But there was no opportunity for privacy. Even traveling to Anstruther's villa, they hadn't been alone. Ahmad had been with them. With any luck, he was even now questioning Anstruther's servants.

As for Jenny, she looked as though she were on the brink of a momentous discovery. Her body was listed forward in her chair, her gaze riveted on Anstruther's sun-beaten face.

She was beautiful in a sprigged-muslin gown, her thick tresses secured in an arrangement of plaits with what must have been more than a dozen hairpins. One had sprung out in the carriage on the journey up the hill to the villa. Tom had swept it up from the matted floor with his fingers and discreetly deposited it in his pocket. He fancied that he could feel it there now—just as he could feel the weight of the sapphire cravat pin in his neckcloth.

"Will you tell me what happened that day?" she asked. "How you came to determine that Lord Castleton was dead?"

Anstruther's face settled into severe lines. "You're speaking of the day our forces stormed the walls of the city. A damnably hot day. You can understand nothing until you understand that."

"I do understand," she said.

"My dear lady, you couldn't possibly. It was 110 degrees in the shade of our tents and 130 degrees everywhere else. We were losing as many men to the heat as we were to the sepoys. And they knew it, cunning devils. They saved their attacks for the middle of the day when the sun was at full strength."

Tom's pencil moved over the pages of his notebook, jotting down the particulars of the tale.

"We'd encamped on a plain," Anstruther went on, "with no shelter from the sun of any kind. The Rani of Jhansi was a clever woman. A brilliant military strategist, I must admit. She'd had all of the trees destroyed in advance of us marching on the city. The sun beat down on our heads, and scorching winds swept over us. Along with the roar of the cannons, it felt as if the full furies of hell had been unleashed. Within two days some of the men began to suffer from abdominal complaints. Others were afflicted with heat madness. A man can't function in temperatures of that degree. It addles the brain."

Tom could well imagine. Temperatures hadn't reached such a hellish degree during their own journey, but it was hot enough to give him a taste of what the soldiers might have suffered. "Was Lord Castleton one of those affected?"

Anstruther frowned deeply. "Can't say that I noticed him suffering any more than the others. He'd taken to India better than most."

Jenny nodded. "That's the impression I had from his letters."

"That's not to say he was comfortable. None of us were comfortable. Even the best of my men were failing. It was in that state our column stormed the city walls. We planned our attack for midnight, by the light of the moon. The enemy fired upon us without mercy. Three of our engineers braved the musketry and cannons to set ladders at strategic positions against the walls. Castleton was one of the first to go over the top. He always did fancy himself a hero."

"Did you see him, sir?" Jenny asked.

"Clearly." Anstruther's lips thinned beneath the bristles of his mustache. "He leapt over the wall and into the midst of the enemy. When I next encountered him, he was battling on all sides, surrounded by rebel sepoys slashing out with bayonets and swords. One of them laid him open from here to here." Anstruther drew his finger from his shoulder down to his midsection. "Lopped off his arm. Damn near cut him in half."

Jenny's hand flew to her mouth. She made a soft sound behind her fingers; a gasp of horror, perhaps, or a whimper of distress.

Tom's pencil stopped on the page of his notebook. "Miss Holloway—"

"No," she said. "I—I want to hear the rest."

Anstruther required little prompting. "Castleton fell down where he stood in a pool of blood. There was no one to administer aid. The town was in flames, the entire place a conflagration of smoke and cannon fire. We were fighting for our lives. When at last we triumphed, I saw him lying there in the dirt, but it was too late—for him and all the rest of the men we lost."

"He was dead?" Jenny's voice trembled.

"Long dead," Anstruther replied in clipped tones

"But...what happened to his body? Could someone have taken it? Stolen it or—"

"Stolen it? For what purpose? No, ma'am. His body would have been burned. No one wanted disease spreading. Our chaplain read the burial service over the pit in which the bodies were thrown. A barbaric business." His lips briefly contorted in a moue of distaste. "It was for the best. Even if they'd pickled him in brine, he'd never have lasted the journey back to England."

Jenny squeezed her eyes shut a moment. "Oh," she whispered. "Oh, Giles."

Tom's heart came to a standstill. There was something in the quaver of her voice. Something in the way she said the man's name.

Oh, Giles.

But no. He must be imagining it, surely. Jenny was only concerned about Giles's fate because of Lady Helena. It had nothing to do with how Jenny felt about the fellow herself.

Or did it?

Anstruther stood. "I can tell you no more of what happened after. I was taken ill myself. Developed a fever from the heat and had to be removed to Simla to recover."

Tom rose from his seat, waiting for Jenny to do the same. She remained in her chair for a second or two longer, hands clenched in her lap. And then she stood, her face pale and expressionless.

"I beg your pardon," she said, "but might I use your washroom?"

Anstruther didn't look pleased at the request. He nevertheless summoned a servant to escort her from the study. "I warned you," he said to Tom when she was gone. "Females aren't equipped to handle such weighty subjects—even when watered down to make them more palatable."

Tom gave him an alert look. "Did you water down the tale of Castleton's death for Miss Holloway's sake? Is there some detail you've left out in order to spare her?"

"Only this." Anstruther came to stand in front of Tom, scowling down at him as if he were an errant recruit. "Castleton was brave—I'll give him that—but the world is no worse for the loss of him. He was a bounder. A poacher on other men's preserves. Had he not met his end at a sepoy's blade, he'd have met it at the end of a dueling pistol."

A poacher on other men's preserves.

The words painted an unflattering picture of the late Giles Reynolds, 6th Earl of Castleton. One that wasn't very much at odds with the image Tom had come to have of the man. "Do you have evidence that he dallied with other men's wives?"

Anstruther stiffened. "I'll say no more on the subject, sir."

Of course he wouldn't. If he did, he'd risk revealing himself as a cuckold. And, unless Tom was mistaken, Anstruther was the last man on earth to admit he'd been played a fool by his wife and another man—especially if that man was as young and vigorous as Castleton had purportedly been.

"We'll be a few days longer in Delhi," Tom said. "If you remember anything else, we're staying at the Westbrook."

Unwilling curiosity lit in Anstruther's eyes. "You and Miss Holloway? Together?"

"And Miss Holloway's servants."

"Huh. Damned odd, if you ask me."

"I don't recall asking," Tom said.

Anstruther's expression hardened. No doubt he would have barked at Tom if Jenny hadn't chosen that precise moment to return from the washroom. The Anstruther's majordomo was at her heels.

"I'm sorry to have kept you waiting," she said.

Tom's gaze drifted over her. He didn't ask if she was feeling better. He wouldn't. Not in front of Anstruther. But he knew Jenny well enough by now to see that she was upset. Her face was ashen and there were damp, curling tendrils of hair at her temples, as if she'd splashed water on her face. Had she been weeping?

The thought unsettled him deeply.

If Anstruther noticed anything odd in Jenny's appearance, he gave no indication. "You'll forgive me for not inviting you to stay longer. Your presence has upset my wife enough." He inclined his head to them in curt dismissal before turning to his majordomo. "Khansama? Show our guests to the door."

"Yes, sahib." The Khansama ushered them from the study and out into the empty hall. "This way, if you please."

Tom walked alongside Jenny in silence, saying nothing until the doors of the villa shut behind them. "Are you all right?" he asked quietly.

"What?" She gave him a distracted look. "Oh. Yes. Quite well."

The carriage they'd hired was waiting outside. It was an odd vehicle. Nothing more than a shabby box on wheels, pulled by a team of two horses. Ahmad stood at the front near the driver, conversing with the man in rapid Hindustani. When he saw them, he broke off his conversation and came to assist them into the cab.

"Did you have any luck with the servants?" Tom asked as Ahmad climbed in after them. The carriage shook as the horses sprung into motion.

"None whatsoever. They're completely loyal to their sahib."

"I can't think why." Jenny withdrew a paper fan from her reticule and flicked it open. The leaves were patterned with a watercolor print of the Himalayas. "He seemed an awful sort of man to me."

"They're frightened of him," Ahmad said. "He's the great white hunter. A larger-than-life figure in their eyes."

Tom considered the matter. "And what of his wife?"

"Equally oppressed, I suspect," Jenny said. "A prisoner in her own home."

"Or a lady of delicate sensibilities unable to adapt to the rigors of life as a colonial."

Jenny frowned at him. "Must you play devil's advocate?"

"If it keeps us from jumping to conclusions, yes."

"There's only one conclusion to make. Giles is dead. He died at the siege of Jhansi, just as the colonel wrote to Helena two years ago. There's no longer any doubt." She turned her face to the window. "Nothing else matters now."

Tom felt a burgeoning sense of unease. He didn't know what to say. Not when they were in company with Ahmad. And even if they weren't, how the devil was he supposed to comfort her? To cushion the loss of a man who—

But that was the crux of the matter. Tom didn't know who Giles had been to Jenny. Not anymore.

He dropped his voice. "Is there anything I can—"

"Could we not discuss it at the moment?" She wafted her fan. "I can't think straight in this heat."

Ahmad fixed his gaze out the opposite window, effectively withdrawing himself from the conversation.

Tom appreciated the man's efforts at invisibility, but it made it no easier to speak with Jenny. She didn't say another word until they arrived at their hotel, and only then to take her leave of him.

"I need some time to myself," she said upon entering her room. "A few hours rest until tiffin."

He stood at the door, one hand resting on the doorframe, the other clutching his hat. "You're worrying me."

She gave him a weak smile. "Don't worry. Nothing that's happened today is any worse than what we expected all along. We both of us knew there was little chance we'd find Giles alive."

Then why do you look so ravaged? he wanted to ask. *Why do you look as if your heart has been broken into a million pieces?*

"You'll summon me if you need me?"

She promised she would, and then slowly, and quite firmly, shut the door in his face.

Tom entered his own room on a muttered curse, hurling his hat at the bed in a flare of frustration. It bounced against a panel of mosquito netting and ricocheted onto the marble floor. "Blast it."

Ahmad emerged from the dressing room, a pile of shirts draped over his arm. "Is Miss Holloway unwell?"

"I don't know." It was the honest truth. Tom had no idea how she was feeling, physically or otherwise.

Good God, but he hadn't expected this. He hadn't anticipated that Jenny would be genuinely grieved at the loss of the man. She wasn't Lady Helena. She hadn't spent the past years hoping and praying that Giles was alive. She'd said herself that she had no reason to doubt the initial reports of his death. That the kiss she and Giles had shared wasn't enough to spark an affinity between them.

But that wasn't all she'd said.

Tom stopped where he stood. His stomach turned over on a wave of apprehension. Hell and damnation. How could he have overlooked it? How could he have failed to recognize—

He turned sharply to Ahmad, his heart thumping hard in his chest. "I must speak with Miss Holloway."

Ahmad's brows lifted. "Now?"

"Yes, now. In her room. If you'll take Mira away awhile, for a cup of tea or a—"

"Mira isn't there," Ahmad said. "She's gone on an errand."

"What?" Tom shot him a look. "By herself?"

Ahmad shrugged. "She knows the city better than a gharry-wallah."

"Nonsense. She was a child when she left Delhi."

"One doesn't forget the streets where one was born. Mira hasn't." Ahmad paused. "I haven't."

"Then you must go and find her."

"And leave you here, alone with Miss Holloway?"

"Miss Holloway will be safe enough with me."

Ahmad didn't look convinced. Though he'd been acting as Tom's valet for the better part of their journey, he clearly hadn't forgotten to whom he owed his allegiance. "What about gossip? You might be observed going into her room."

"I won't be," Tom promised.

For once, the fates seemed to be on his side. The hall that led between his room and Jenny's was empty. There were no nosy guests peeking out of their rooms and no busy servants trotting up the marble corridor with trays of food and drinks.

He rapped softly on Jenny's door.

She didn't answer. Not immediately. It was only some moments later, after Tom knocked again, that he heard the sound of starched petticoats swishing as she made her way to the door.

The bolt was unlatched and the door slowly cracked open to reveal Jenny's tear-streaked face.

Tom's breath stopped in his chest. Every instinct urged him to reach out to her, to take her in his arms and offer his shoulder to cry on. But he didn't. He couldn't. At the sight of her tears for the late Earl of Castleton, something within him froze.

She didn't invite him in, merely turned and walked back into the confines of her hotel room.

He slowly followed after her, shutting the door behind him and drawing the latch back into place. At the scrape of the bolt, she stopped to face him, a question trembling at her lips.

The draperies were closed against the midday heat. It was dim and cool, the net curtains over her bed drawn open to reveal a rumpled coverlet and linens. As if she'd lain there, only seconds before, sobbing into her pillow.

"'Such events loom large in the life of a young woman,'" he said.

She blinked up at him, her eyes swollen from weeping. "What?"

"That's what you told me about Giles's final letter. The one in which he wrote that his kissing you meant nothing. In which he told you he didn't wish to marry you. That's how you explained crumpling it up and throwing it into the coal scuttle. 'Such events loom large in the life of a young woman.'" Tom stared down at her, his voice steady even as his heart fractured. "You loved him, didn't you?"

Chapter Nineteen

Jenny thought she must be hearing things. It wouldn't surprise her. From the instant Colonel Anstruther had concluded his gruesome tale, she'd felt an odd detachment. It had all been far too much to take in—not only the indisputable fact that Giles was dead, but what that fact meant to her and her own future. Her own happiness. "What are you talking about?"

"It's why we're here. Why you wanted so badly to find him. It's because you loved him." Tom was still and solemn as he looked at her. He was also more controlled than Jenny had ever seen him. As if he were holding himself together by sheer force of will. "Do you deny it?"

"You make it sound as though I'm on trial."

"Do you?"

She wiped at her face with her hands. "Of course I deny it. I didn't love Giles. Not in the way I think you mean."

"You're weeping over the loss of him."

"You idiot." Or, at least, it's what she'd meant to say. It came out in a choked sob on another flood of tears. "I'm not weeping for Giles. Not entirely. I'm weeping because it's over. You'll go home now. Back to England. And I'll n-never see you again."

Tom stared down at her, dumbstruck. His Adam's apple bobbed as he swallowed hard, and then again. "Jenny…"

It was only her name, but it was enough to make her face crumple. She hadn't mastered the art of attractive feminine weeping. She was too noisy—too red and blotchy and prone to puffiness about the eyes and nose. "I told you I needed time to compose myself. Why didn't you listen to me?" She fumbled about herself to no avail. "Oh, where is my handkerchief?"

Tom pressed his own into her hands. It was large and clean and smelled of him—of bay rum, fresh linen, and the ink and parchment of his dratted legal papers. Another sob broke as she buried her face into it.

She didn't fight it. Rather the opposite. She sank down in a chair beside the bed and gave herself up to it, crying until her throat burned and her chest ached.

When at last she opened her eyes, Tom was crouched in front of her on his haunches, one hand on his knee, the other hand resting on the arm of her chair. The coldness in his face was gone. He was still solemn and self-controlled. But there was something else there now, too. A tenderness in his weary blue eyes that she'd never seen before.

"Come with me," he said.

She snuffled into his handkerchief, wishing there was a more ladylike way to blow one's nose. "What? Where?"

"Home," he said. "To England. This doesn't have to be the end."

"Lord, I must look a fright."

"Jenny, are you listening to me?"

"Yes, but—" Her face contorted in a spasm of grief. "I can't go with you."

"Why not?"

"Because that's not who I am. It isn't what I want. Not England. Not the life I had before."

"And not me."

"That isn't true. I do want you. I've been crying my heart out, wanting—" She broke off, blinking back another swell of tears. "I *do* want you," she said again, feeling young and foolish and in extraordinarily poor control of her emotions. "I'd kiss you if I wasn't in such a dreadful state."

"You're beautiful," Tom said gruffly. He took his handkerchief from her hands and used it to dry her face. "You're always beautiful."

"Don't dare be kind to me. I'll never stop weeping."

"I can be nothing but kind to you. You're my dearest girl. Don't you know that?"

Jenny looked into his eyes as he dried her tears. Her heart ached to the point of pain. "You're no less dear to me."

His lips quirked. "Which is why you called me an idiot."

He was trying to make her laugh, but Jenny didn't feel much like laughing. She exhaled a trembling breath. "When will you leave Delhi?"

Tom drew back. His expression was grim. "I don't know."

Tears rose in her eyes once more. "Oh, drat," she muttered. "Is there no end to this humiliation?"

He didn't reply. Instead he reached for her, pulling her into his arms. She buried her face in his neck as he stood, lifting her as if she weighed no more than a feather, and carried her to the bed.

Jenny made no objection, not even when he sat down amidst her pillows, his back propped against the wall, and cradled her as she wept.

But she should have. She *should* have.

It was scandalous. Wanton and reckless. The very opposite of how she'd promised herself she'd behave once they arrived in Delhi. Gracious, they were in bed together! He did nothing to initiate greater intimacy, but he might have done. And she might have done. All it wanted was a bit of encouragement. A grain in the balance to tip the scales.

"We can't," she said.

"We won't. Just let me hold you awhile."

His breath was soft on her hair, the pressure of his hand a soothing weight as it stroked up and down over the curve of her spine.

She was an independent lady now. A spinster of eight and twenty, responsible for her own life. Her own happiness. But, oh—! It was so wonderful to be taken care of by him. So restful and easy after so many tears.

Her eyes grew heavy. "I've never wept so much over anything before."

"It's been a difficult day. For both of us."

"You're not weeping. I don't suppose you ever have. Not over a woman."

"You'd suppose wrong." His voice dropped to a low rumble. "When I was a very young boy in the orphanage, I often wept for my mother."

"But you didn't know you had a mother then, did you?"

"Everyone has a mother."

She drew her fingers through the hair at the nape of his neck, gently, ever so gently. "Why did you weep for her? Did you hope she might come for you one day?"

"I knew she wouldn't."

"Then why?"

"Because…even though I'd never known her, I felt the loss of her. The emptiness inside that comes from being abandoned by the person who's meant to love you first and best." Tom's hand moved over her back. "Tears are a rather fatiguing business, but necessary on occasion, I can attest. I never slept so deeply as I did after a good cry. And when I woke, I was famished. As if I'd swum a mile."

"I'm not going to sleep."

"You can if you like."

"I can't. I've so much to do. Letters to write and plans to make."

"There'll be time enough after tiffin."

"There isn't enough time in the world. Not for us. It's all run out. We knew—"

He hugged her closer. "Let me worry about all of that."

She gulped noisily as fresh tears clogged her throat. "I *am* grieved about Giles," she admitted. "I didn't believe he was alive, not truly. But I was beginning to hope. And now…the thought of him suffering as he did. Of his body being thrown into a pit. How will I ever tell Helena?"

"Leave it with me," he said. "You rest now. You'll feel better when you wake, I promise."

Jenny didn't want to sleep. She couldn't. But Tom's body was so warm and he held her so tenderly in his arms. Weeping was exhausting, especially when one hadn't wept in a very long time. Despite her resolve to remain awake—to tackle their problems as expeditiously as possible—her limbs grew heavy and her eyes drifted shut.

And she must have slept. She *must* have, for when she opened her eyes, Tom was gone. She was alone in her bed, hot and miserable, her head resting on a pillow instead of his shoulder.

"Madam?" Mira's voice sounded from across the hotel room.

Jenny pushed her hair from her face. It was no longer tightly plaited and coiled. Someone had removed all of the pins. She blinked bleary eyes, unable to see anything through the white mosquito netting that shrouded her bed. "Where is everyone?"

"Mr. Finchley has gone off with Ahmad to the railway depot."

"*What?*" Jenny struggled to a sitting position. Her sleeves and skirts were tangled around her, binding her limbs. "He's left Delhi? Already? But he didn't say goodbye or—"

"Oh no, madam." Mira hurried to the bed. "He hasn't gone away for good. He said I was to tell you that he would return in time for dinner."

The jolt of panic that had torn through Jenny's breast slowly subsided. "What time is it? Have I slept the whole day away?"

"It's six o'clock. You missed tiffin. I have a tray for you."

"Thank you, but I'm not hungry." Which was a miracle in itself. Emotional dilemmas always made Jenny ravenous. She never ate so much as when she was sad, worried, or angry. But not now. Not after learning about Giles's death. And not when faced with the imminent loss of Tom.

He might not have left her yet, but he was certainly wasting no time in making preparations for his journey home. Nor why should he? He had his work to consider, his clients and his cases and his obligations to Mr. Fothergill and Mrs. Culpepper. Was it any wonder he'd gone straight to the railway station to book his passage?

She allowed Mira to help her up and assist her in straightening her tangled gown. "How long ago did they leave?"

"Shortly after tiffin." Mira tugged Jenny's skirts into order. "I'm sorry I wasn't here when you returned from your outing."

"What?" Jenny cast Mira a distracted glance. "Oh, yes. I hadn't thought. Where had you gone? Shopping, or—"

"Not shopping." Mira's mouth turned down at the corners. "I went to see the place where I lived with my mother before I was brought to England. I expected to be back before you returned, but…I got lost in the city. Ahmad found me."

A flicker of alarm sounded at the back of Jenny's brain. "Goodness, Mira. You should have taken him with you to begin with. Anything might happen to a young woman wandering about a strange city."

"I was safe."

"You just said you got lost. If Ahmad hadn't found you—"

"But he did. He always knows where I am. He'd let no harm come to me."

Jenny felt somewhat mollified. A little jealous as well. Her own brothers had never done much to protect her. "You're very close with him, aren't you?"

"He's the only family I have now. There is no one left. No one who remembers me." Mira smoothed a self-conscious hand over her own fashionable bodice and skirts. Fashionable because Mira altered them herself. "The neighbors didn't recognize me."

"Did you remember them?"

"Not very well."

Jenny nodded in understanding. "England is your home now."

Mira's face tightened almost imperceptibly. "England isn't my home. I thought Delhi was. That I would feel something for the place and for the people. I don't feel anything. It isn't at all like what I dreamed of."

Jenny contemplated her maid with a furrowed brow. "I shouldn't have brought you here, should I? It's only made you unhappy. It's made all of us unhappy. Better we had stayed in Calcutta. Or better still, that we remained in Egypt. We didn't spend near enough time in Cairo. We didn't even get to see the pyramids. Not properly anyway." The prospect of a new adventure perked her spirits a little. "Would you like to go back to Cairo? We could take a house there for a while. There must be something suitable to let at this time of year."

"If it pleases you, madam."

"You don't have any preference at all?"

"So long as Ahmad and I remain together, I shall be content."

"Of course you'll remain together. I wouldn't employ one of you without the other. You must put that worry straight out of your head."

Mira smiled. "You are very kind."

"Rubbish," Jenny scoffed. She gave another tug to her dress before abandoning her efforts. "It's no use, Mira. It's wrinkled beyond repair. I'd better change into something else." Her fingers worked at the hooks of her bodice. "Do you suppose it's too late to have a bath before dinner?"

Mira helped her to strip off her sleeves and then to unfasten her skirts. "There's time. Shall I call for hot water?"

"Yes, if you—"

A brisk knock sounded at the door.

Jenny's hands froze on the tapes of her crinoline. It was Tom. It must be.

Mira hurried to the door and cracked it open. She exchanged words with whoever was on the other side in murmured Hindustani.

Not Tom, then.

"Who is it?" Jenny asked when Mira shut the door. "Someone from the hotel?"

"Yes, madam. He says I'm to tell you that a lady has come calling. She requests an audience with you here in your room."

"Here?" Jenny's brows lifted. "Did this lady give a name?"

"He says she will not."

"That's odd." There were only a handful of ladies it could be. The Planks or the Hardcastles or, perhaps, one of the ladies Jenny had met in Calcutta. But if it were truly one of those redoubtable memsahibs, they'd have surely sent along their card. And they'd have wished to meet in the hotel's salon, not in her private room of all places.

Jenny chewed her lip. "You'd better tell him to send her up," she said at last. "But not now. I'll need time to dress and repair my hair."

Mira conveyed as much to the hotel footman through a crack in the door. She then returned to help Jenny into a dinner dress of fine mull muslin.

When Jenny had purchased the gown from Mrs. McTavish's shop in Calcutta, it had been plain cream in color, but Mira had lately added shimmering black embroidery to the hem and front of the skirts, giving the whole of it a much more striking appearance.

"How it glistens." Jenny smoothed the skirts over her crinoline.

"For dancing," Mira said.

Jenny managed a slight smile. She wouldn't be doing much dancing in Delhi. Not now that Tom was leaving her. "Your talents are wasted on me, Mira. You do know that, don't you? There are hundreds of ladies in London who could show off your creations better than I do."

Mira ducked her head, blushing. "Shall I arrange your hair, madam?"

"No, thank you. I can do it easily enough." Jenny wandered to the pier glass across the room, swiftly plaiting her tresses and rolling them into a chignon at the nape of her neck. The timing couldn't have been more propitious. No sooner had she inserted the final hairpin than there was a soft rapping at the door.

She waited as Mira went to open it, expecting she knew not what. She prayed it wasn't Mrs. Plank or one of the other ladies she'd met on the *Indus* or the *Bentinck*.

However, when the door was drawn open, it didn't reveal Mrs. Plank. A much smaller lady stood on the threshold. She was clad in a frothy, floral-printed muslin gown, her face completely covered by a heavy veil draped down from the brim of her stylish straw bonnet.

Jenny's eyes widened. "Mrs. Anstruther?"

Mrs. Anstruther waited until the door was shut behind her to sweep her veil back from her face. Her complexion was pale, her brow damp with perspiration. "Do forgive the excess of caution, Miss Holloway. I'm counting on no one noticing me. My husband isn't aware I've gone. I must return to the villa before he realizes."

Mira withdrew to the opposite side of the room to give the two of them privacy. It made little matter. Mrs. Anstruther didn't appear to take any notice of the maid's presence.

Jenny motioned to an empty chair. "Won't you sit down?"

Mrs. Anstruther shook her head. "I haven't the time. I shouldn't even be here."

"Why have you come, ma'am? And why all the secrecy?"

"My husband won't permit me to speak of Lord Castleton. I daren't mention his name." Mrs. Anstruther proceeded to pace back and forth in front of Jenny, her skirts stirring a faint breeze in the stagnant heat of the hotel room. "Whatever my husband told you about his lordship——"

"About his death?"

"What?" Mrs. Anstruther cast Jenny a look of blank confusion.

Jenny saw no need to spare the woman. "Your husband said that Lord Castleton was killed while storming the walls of Jhansi. That he was nearly cut in half by a rebel sepoy's blade."

Mrs. Anstruther's countenance went from waxen to white. "Yes, he's told me that. He's said that Lord Castleton's body was thrown into a pit with the bodies of unknown soldiers. Do you... Do you suppose it's true?"

"Have you reason to doubt him?"

"He might have made it up to torment me." Mrs. Anstruther wrung her hands. "My husband has accused me of the vilest things, Miss Holloway. He believes Lord Castleton and I——" She broke off, turning to look at Jenny. "I've come to tell you that it isn't true. Lord Castleton was not my lover. He was my friend. He sought only to lift my spirits when I was at my lowest ebb."

"And that was all?" Jenny shouldn't have asked. This part of Mrs. Anstruther's history with Giles had no bearing on anything. It was their own private business and nothing at all to do with her.

But Mrs. Anstruther seemed eager to speak of Giles. As if she wanted—needed—to exorcise his ghost. "I confess I did attempt to press a greater intimacy on him at one time, but he rebuffed my advances. He was very kind. Very understanding. But he didn't come to visit me so much after that and he didn't respond to all the little notes I sent him. When I tried to call on him at the cantonment in Poona, he wouldn't even see me."

Jenny felt an unwilling surge of sympathy for the woman.

So that's how it had been. A one-sided infatuation that had embarrassed Giles—and Colonel Anstruther, too, if she had any guess. It was somehow worse than a love affair. To have one's wife openly pining after a fellow who didn't want her.

"I get so very lonely, Miss Holloway. The colonel and I have so little in common, you see. He isn't much of a companion for me. How can he be at his age?"

It was none of Jenny's business. She kept reminding herself of that fact. Nevertheless... "He doesn't mistreat you, does he?"

Mrs. Anstruther gave a dismissive flap of her hand. "No, indeed. But I can do nothing without his permission. He controls everything in my life. Even the bit of money left to me by my father." She gave a colorless laugh. "You are wise to remain a spinster, Miss Holloway. Would that I were in your position, to go where I liked and see whom I liked. I would go far away from this place and never come back."

At that grim pronouncement, Mrs. Anstruther lowered her veil back over her face. "You will tell the Castleton's solicitor, won't you? Whatever my husband said to malign him, Lord Castleton was a gentleman until the very end."

Jenny nodded. "I'll tell him."

"And…if you will extend my condolences to Lord Castleton's sister. He spoke of her often in the fondest terms."

"I will. I promise."

Mrs. Anstruther inclined her head. "Goodbye, Miss Holloway."

"Goodbye." Jenny stood in the doorway, one hand at her necklace, watching Mrs. Anstruther as she disappeared down the hall.

The Westbrook Hotel was not only one of the most luxurious European hotels in Delhi, it was also one of the most conveniently located. From the hotel's entrance it was only a short distance to St. James's Church, the legendary Cashmere Gate, the telegraph and post offices, and the railway station.

In the heavy heat of the early afternoon, Tom had walked to the station with Ahmad, but as it had in Calcutta, the dinner hour brought cooler weather. After conducting his business at the station, he hailed a gharry-wallah to take them back to the hotel.

The rickety little vehicle jolted through the busy streets, navigating through carriages, palanquins, and crowds of pedestrians.

Tom gazed out the window at the passing traffic, lost in his own thoughts.

He'd heard Delhi described as the Rome of India. It was said to be the grandest of cities, filled with the remnants of ancient Mughal splendor. He had seen as much during his brief travels about the city. Amidst the ruins of ages gone by stood brilliantly colored architecture, embellished with enameled tiles, gilded domes, and minarets. There were lush gardens, mosques, and the famous Red Fort, a walled bastion of red granite flanked with turrets and sculptured gateways.

It was there, in the Fort, that the last Mughal Emperor had been tried for aiding and abetting the mutiny. The British now used it as a garrison. Soldiers could be seen coming and going amongst the native residents of the city.

There was no sign of latent hostilities. Not that Tom had seen. He nevertheless detected a subtle tension between the Indians and the British. There were hard feelings on both sides, undoubtedly. There must have been. But whatever those feelings were, they seemed to bubble somewhere beneath the surface, sensed but never expressed.

Tom recognized the emotions well enough. Indeed, the vibrations of bitterness and resentment might as well have been a second language to him. He'd come of age butting his head against injustice.

How long before another uprising took place? Before the Indians successfully ejected the British?

No, he thought grimly, India wasn't a place he could ever live comfortably. Not even with Jenny.

"If we're not needed during dinner, I'll take Mira out to see the city," Ahmad said.

"You won't be needed." Tom had things to discuss with Jenny. The more privacy they had, the better.

Back at the hotel, Ahmad lingered to speak to the gharry-wallah while Tom made his way inside.

He passed through the Westbrook's tiled courtyard. Like the courtyard at Mr. Vidyasagar's hotel in Calcutta, it boasted a fountain, tables, and a surfeit of greenery. That, however, was where the similarities ended. Instead of a quiet sanctuary, the Westbrook's courtyard was awash with the sounds of screeching parrots. They flew from one side to the other, screaming and squawking. They weren't alone. Crows cawed from the nooks and corners of the walls and sparrows hopped about the floor, searching for crumbs.

It was exotic in its way.

Exotic enough to tempt Jenny.

She was there near a low palm tree, her head tilted back as she looked up at a green parrot preening itself on the ledge.

He stopped where he stood. His heart stopped as well. She was lovely, simply lovely, in a dinner dress of cream and black, her auburn hair caught up in its familiar roll of plaits.

No one could tell that hours ago she'd been sobbing her heart out.

Sobbing over *him*.

Tom still couldn't quite believe it.

He smoothed a hand over his hair and gave a futile tug to his wrinkled waistcoat. This wasn't how he'd planned it. He'd wanted time to change for dinner. To put on a freshly pressed suit, to shave and apply some Macassar oil to his perpetually rumpled hair. But there was no time to worry about such things. Not with Jenny standing a mere few feet away.

"Jenny?" he said her name quietly as he approached.

She turned her head. Her mouth trembled on a smile. "Tom."

"What are you doing down here?"

"Feeding nuts to this wretched parrot. You wouldn't know to hear him now, but only five minutes ago he took a cashew directly from my palm." She dusted her hands off. "Have you only just returned from the railway station?"

There was an odd catch in her voice. An echo of the emotion she'd expressed earlier when she'd wept so piteously into his handkerchief. He'd never felt such tortured confusion as he had in those moments, crouched down at her feet, at once so indescribably grateful that it was he she was weeping over, and yet, at the same time, so utterly ravaged that he could do nothing to take away her tears.

Nothing that he could think of *then*.

Now, however...

"Yes," he said. "Only just."

"With Ahmad?"

"He's gone to fetch Mira for an outing. And you're already dressed for dinner, I see. I'm unforgivably behind the times, as usual."

"We're not on a schedule." She moved away from the wall, her skirts swaying around her legs like a bell. "Shall we sit down and talk awhile?"

Tom glanced at the tables scattered about the courtyard. Two soldiers sat at one of them, smoking cheroots. At another, an older lady and gentleman engaged in low conversation. The rest of the tables were empty. "If you like."

"It's private enough here."

Not as private as her room. Or his. But Tom wouldn't argue the point. He gestured to an empty table at the far side of the courtyard, opposite the rippling marble fountain.

Jenny preceded him there, waiting as he pulled out a chair for her and cleaned the seat with his handkerchief. "Parrots aren't the tidiest of creatures."

Tom grimaced. "That's one way of putting it."

"Some ladies in London keep them as pets." She sat down, arranging her skirts all about her. "They're quite fashionable. One can even train them to talk."

"Do these parrots talk?"

"Not that I've heard. I daresay no one has taken the trouble to teach them."

He sat down beside her, angling his chair so he could look her in the eye. "Enough about parrots. There's something I wish to tell you."

"And something I wish to tell you. I had a visitor while you were gone."

"Did you?"

"It was Mrs. Anstruther."

Tom listened in stony silence as Jenny recounted the particulars of the lady's visit.

When she'd finished, she sat back in her chair. "Well? What do you think of that?"

What he thought was that, though in this case Giles may not have been the rank seducer he'd been portrayed as by Colonel Anstruther, it didn't follow that his behavior with other ladies had been exemplary. One need only look to Jenny's experience to know that. Giles had kissed her, leaving her to believe Tom knew not what.

True, she hadn't been weeping over the man today. But he had hurt her. Hurt her enough that she'd crumpled up his final letter and thrown it away.

Such events loom large in the life of a young woman.

It certainly put a different complexion on the matter.

"I have several thoughts," he said. "The first of which was what prompted me to visit the railway office."

Some of the color left her face. "You've booked passage back to Calcutta."

"No. Not back to Calcutta. I—"

"To Bombay, then. You could find an East India Company ship there to take you home, even faster than the P & O ship that brought us to Calcutta."

"Not to Bombay, Jenny. Good lord, do you think I'd book passage home without telling you?" He withdrew a folded square of printed paper from an inner pocket of his coat and smoothed it open in front of her.

She stared down at it in surprise. "Mr. Vidyasagar's map."

"I did book passage at the railways station, but not to Calcutta or Bombay. I purchased tickets for all of us on the morning train"—he tapped a location on the map some distance from Delhi—"here."

"To Jhansi?" Her gaze lifted to his. "Why? We already know how Giles died."

"Are you that confident in Colonel Anstruther's account?"

"I don't want to be. He's an odious man. Had I suspected he was being untruthful, I'd have been ready to leave for Jhansi without delay. That was my plan, anyway. But nothing can alter the fact of Giles's death. I suppose we might learn more about what happened to his body, but it isn't as if it will change anything."

"It will allow me to stay with you awhile longer."

Her blue-green eyes softened. "Oh, Tom. Is that what this is about?"

"In part, yes," he admitted. "I said I'd stay with you until we found out what happened to him."

"Which we have."

"We haven't. Not beyond all doubt."

Her brow creased. "You're trying to humor me. You think I'm going to fall apart when you go. To take to my bed sobbing. Naturally you would think so after witnessing my behavior this morning. But honestly, Tom, I can assure you—"

"Perhaps it isn't only your feelings I'm considering. Perhaps I'm being selfish. I'm not ready to part from you, either, Jenny." He cleared his throat. "Besides which, I don't enjoy leaving a task unfinished. There's still more to be done before I can feel confident of Giles's fate."

She held his gaze, her eyes searching his. For a moment it seemed as though she would say something of an intimate nature. Something about the inevitability of his broken heart—and of her own. But when she spoke, it was only of Giles. "Have you a legitimate hope that he's alive?"

"A slim hope. But a legitimate one, yes."

"On what basis?"

"Consider the facts as we know them. It was hot as Hades. One hundred and thirty degrees, Anstruther said. The men were taking ill from it. Their brains were addled. Anstruther himself admits to being unwell after the fall of the city. He had to be removed to the hill country to recover. That alone would be enough to put his memory of Giles's death into question. But there's more."

"Such as?"

"The battle was fought at midnight. It was dark. There was cannon fire and smoke from burning buildings. Even if Anstruther wasn't heat addled, how could he have made a positive identification? I don't doubt he saw Giles on the wall before he fell, but inside the city it was chaos. How certain could anyone be of a man's identification? Or that he was dead and not merely fallen into a faint from loss of blood?"

"Do you really believe all of that?"

"It's certainly a possibility, and Jhansi is only two days away by rail and van. What do you suppose Lady Helena would advise us to do?"

Tom's conscience gave a rebellious quake. On the train to Marseille, he'd promised Jenny he wouldn't manipulate her. Mentioning Lady Helena's name was the closest he'd come to breaking that promise. And it was no accidental slip. He knew full well what he was doing. He was using her devotion to her friend to force her hand. It was badly done of him.

And unquestionably necessary.

"She would tell us to go to Jhansi," Jenny said quietly.

Tom folded the map back into his coat. "And so we shall."

Chapter Twenty

North Western Dak Company
Aligarh to Jhansi
April, 1860

The train chugged into Aligarh Junction railway station, coming to a halt in a screech of metal and steam. Jenny and Tom were obliged to disembark. There was no direct rail access from Delhi to Jhansi. The remainder of their journey would have to be made under the auspices of the North Western Dak Company, a passenger and mail service that transported travelers by means of sturdy, horse-drawn carriages known as *dak* carts.

Ahmad and Mira emerged from the second-class carriage to join them on the dusty railway platform. Mira's face was wan, her posture oddly wilting as she clung to Ahmad's arm.

"What's wrong?" Jenny went to her in concern. "Have you taken ill?"

"No madam," Mira said. "I'm only a little overheated."

Ahmad shot a scowl at his cousin. "She didn't drink enough water."

"Well, have some, do," Jenny urged. "We've a while to go before we can rest. I'll not have you fainting."

Tom regarded Mira with a frown as she drank from one of the enamel-lined iron cups in Jenny's tiffin basket. When she'd finished, she accompanied Ahmad to the baggage car to see to their luggage.

"What it is?" Jenny asked Tom when the two servants were out of earshot.

"She's not very strong, is she?"

"Mira? Why would you say that?"

Tom cast the two servants another thoughtful glance. "She's been ill in one form or another since we left Marseilles."

"Rubbish. She's unaccustomed to travel, that's all."

Tom didn't argue the point.

Jenny thought that was an end to the matter, but as they walked to join the *dak* line, the idea that Mira was in frail health worked its way further and further into her mind, weighing on her conscience in the most awful way. She found herself examining her new maid with greater than usual attention.

After all, she had as much responsibility to her servants as she had to herself. More even, for they were depending on her to make sensible decisions. It was her duty to keep them safe from harm.

If Mira was truly in poor health, what was Jenny to do about it? Was she to summon a doctor? Leave India and return to Europe? To London?

Well, she could certainly do nothing about it now, not in the middle of the open country with a line of *dak* carts awaiting them.

"This way, sahib," one of the drivers called out to Tom. "This way."

The *dak* carts were solid, squarely-built wooden vehicles with sliding doors and rows of windows shaded by awnings. Native *dak* drivers and grooms bustled about them. Most were friendly, with sufficient fluency in English to communicate with the British passengers. The shaggy little *dak* horses were less civil. Within the first two minutes, Jenny observed one of them attempt to take a bite out of Ahmad's arm as he passed.

"Have a care, Ahmad!" Mira cried.

"Do be careful!" Jenny exclaimed at the same time.

Ahmad only laughed, exchanging words with the driver, the pair of them smiling at the antics of the bad-tempered horses. "You'd be cross too if you had to work in this heat," Ahmad said when he returned to them.

"I *am* working," Mira retorted under her breath.

Jenny exchanged a look with Tom as he helped her into one of the *dak* carts. The interior was comfortable but not very large. It could seat no more than two

"I'll ride with Mira," Jenny said.

Tom didn't object. He assisted Mira in, along with the tiffin basket and an earthen jar of water. A short while later, amidst many shouts from the drivers and the grooms, the *dak* cart surged forward

Jenny sat back in her seat, smoothing her skirts. She contemplated how best to phrase her concern for Mira's well-being, but there was no easy way to put it. "Are you very uncomfortable here, Mira?"

Mira's eyes turned wary. "In India?"

"In India or Egypt, or any of the places we've been. It's all taken its toll on you, I daresay."

"It hasn't."

"Truly? You don't find our travels too much of a strain?"

Mira's gaze dropped to her hands. Her narrow shoulders were rigid with tension. "No, madam."

"You'd tell me if you did? If you felt unwell in any way?"

"But I am well. Well enough to perform my duties."

Jenny frowned. "Never mind your duties. I'm concerned about *you*, not whether or not you can sponge and press my gowns. I wouldn't dismiss you simply because you're in poor health. I'd find a way to help you."

Some of the tension eased from Mira's frame. "You're very kind."

"Kindness has nothing at all to do with it. You and Ahmad are part of my household now. Your welfare is my responsibility. You must tell me what's wrong, however unpleasant. I won't be easy until I know."

Mira clasped her hands tight in her lap. "I *was* ill," she admitted at last. "When I was a child."

It was all Jenny could do not to utter a sigh of relief. At last, a little honesty. "What sort of illness?"

"A sweating sickness. It took most of the people in my village."

"Heavens," Jenny exclaimed under her breath. "And you survived it?"

"Yes, but…my mother did not."

"Oh, Mira. I'm so dreadfully sorry. I had no idea."

Mira's throat spasmed on a swallow. "I never said goodbye to her. She made the colonel promise to take me away. Somewhere safe."

"To England."

Mira nodded.

"But if you were still recovering, how did you manage the journey?"

"Ahmad. He insisted on coming to care for me on the ship. When we arrived in London, he stayed near. And then… when the colonel died…"

"He took care of you again." Jenny felt a stab of sadness at the unfairness of it all. "But Ahmad must have been little more than a child himself."

"He was fifteen. Very handsome. Mrs. Pritchard took a fancy to him."

"She *what*?"

A burning blush swept up Mira's neck. "She gave him work and lodging and…she let me have a cot in his room. I did little tasks for her, helping with the laundry and the sweeping, to earn a penny or two. I wasn't strong enough to take a proper job."

"You were a little girl."

"Many little girls work in the dress shops. I could have found a position doing mending if I had had the strength. But I was too weak to keep to a single task for very long." Mira turned her head to look out the window of the *dak* cart. "Ahmad would have left Mrs. Pritchard's long ago if not for me. He hated it there."

"I don't blame him one bit for hating it," Jenny said with feeling. "I hate it for the both of you. I only wish…"

Mira's gaze jerked to hers. "What, madam?"

"That I could do something to help you. Something more than offering you employment."

"But I am content to be your maid. I don't want anything else. If you will keep me on, I—"

"Of course I will." Jenny withdrew her fan from her reticule and opened it with a snap. "And I promise you we won't always be traveling the world like vagabonds. When our search for Lord Castleton is completed, I'll find a villa to let somewhere. A place we can stay put for a while. Things will be easier for you then."

Mira offered no reply.

Jenny didn't press her. She refused to manage the girl, no matter how much she might wish to organize her life—and Ahmad's. There would be time enough to worry about the future of her two servants. For now, she must keep her attention on the task at hand. On Jhansi and on Giles.

And on what she was going to do about her feelings for Tom.

The *dak* journey to Jhansi was a hot and tedious business with stops every five miles for the horses to be changed. By the time they arrived on the outskirts of the walled city, Tom was dusty, tired, and thoroughly parched from the heat.

The things one does for love.

And it *was* love that had prompted him to persuade Jenny to continue their quest. He needed more time with her. More stolen moments in carriages and hotel rooms. It was the only way he could see to winning her.

As for Giles, Tom had only the faintest hope the man was alive.

He found them rooms at a tumbledown guest house not far from the infamous stone fort. Like many of the buildings in Jhansi, it showed signs of the devastation wrought during the siege. But it was comfortable enough, the beds clean and the food hot and plentiful.

In the morning, after a restless night in which Tom could scarcely sleep for the heat, he and Jenny met at breakfast in the establishment's modest dining room. Ahmad and Mira joined them.

The proprietor of the guest house, a native gentleman by the name of Mr. Bhat, poured their tea. "Lieutenant-Colonel Tremaine is head officer," he said in heavily accented English.

"Do you know if he was here during the siege?" Tom asked.

"No, sahib." Mr. Bhat bowed to them and left. He was friendly enough, but showed no inclination to discuss the tragic events of two years before.

Tom sighed. "I'll send a note round to Tremaine, then. Unless any of you have a better idea?"

Jenny sat across from him, clad in a simple dress of rose-colored muslin. Her skin, so pale and fair at the beginning of their journey, had taken on a healthy bronze glow. Along with her glistening auburn hair, it gave her a look of greater than usual vibrancy. Like a candle in full flame.

Tom inwardly grimaced at the fanciful thought. He was smitten, that's what he was. Foolishly, so. He must be to be having such thoughts at this time of day.

"If he wasn't here during the siege," she said, "perhaps he'll be able to direct us to someone who was?"

"We can but ask him." Tom finished his tea. "While we do," he said, addressing Ahmad, "you may as well question some of the townspeople."

Ahmad lowered his fork. "The daguerreotype would help. If they remember him, it probably won't be by name."

"Of course." Jenny rose from her chair, crumpling her napkin onto her plate. "I'll go and fetch it."

An hour later, less both servants and one daguerreotype, Tom and Jenny were seated in Lieutenant-Colonel Tremaine's office inside what remained of the Fort of Jhansi. It was a decaying structure, the fortifications having never been repaired after the siege.

Tremaine surveyed the two of them from over the top of his wooden desk, his fingers steepled in front of him. He was a rangy gentleman, rapidly approaching middle age. "Naturally I remember Castleton. He was a fine soldier. A good man. His death was a great blow to all who knew him."

"But you weren't here in Jhansi at the time of the siege," Jenny said. "Were you?"

"No indeed, ma'am. I arrived later to assist in restoring order. However, I've read Colonel Anstruther's report and have no reason to find fault with it."

Tom hadn't expected any different. Nevertheless… "Were there no additional accounts given of Lord Castleton's death?" he asked. "No details reported by other soldiers or the townspeople?"

"Why should there be when we had an eyewitness? No, sir. Anstruther's word was sufficient. I've learned not to doubt it."

"Do you know the colonel well, sir?" Jenny asked.

"I count him as a friend, yes. More than that, I have enormous respect for the man. He's done more to protect Her Majesty's interests in India than one hundred soldiers combined." Tremaine moved as if to rise. "I'm sorry to disappoint you, Miss Holloway. Had you written in advance, I might have spared you the journey."

Jenny remained in her seat. "I understand that Colonel Anstruther was taken ill after the siege."

Tremaine lips thinned in irritation. "I may have heard something to that effect."

"Because of the heat, he said." She looked at Tom, as if for confirmation.

Tom nodded. "Anstruther told us himself. He said he was removed to Simla to recover."

"And your point, sir?"

Jenny huffed. "Well, isn't it obvious? If the colonel was addled from the heat, how are we to know that his report of Lord Castleton's death wasn't addled as well? For all we know, the colonel might have imagined the whole thing in a heat fever."

"I hardly think—"

"But it does make one wonder," she went on. "What happened to Lord Castleton's body? It isn't like the army to lose track of a member of the peerage, no matter how bloody the battle."

Tremaine shot a glare at Tom. "This can scarcely be productive, sir."

Tom looked steadily back it him. "I don't find Miss Holloway's questions unreasonable. Certainly not in light of her grief over the loss of her cousin." He paused. "Are any of the soldiers from Lord Castleton's old regiment stationed here now? Any who served with him during the siege?"

"Possibly, but I can't imagine what they could tell you. Had any of them seen anything to call Colonel Anstruther's account into question, they'd have reported it at the time." Tremaine turned back to Jenny. "I appreciate the reality of your grief, ma'am, but there is nothing more I can do for you.

Lord Castleton died during the siege. The fact of his death is indisputable. I regret you've wasted your time."

Jenny's expression turned mulish. "I'd like to speak to those soldiers."

"Really, ma'am—"

"I would ask that you oblige us, sir," Tom said. "We *have* come a very long way."

Tremaine exhaled in a grunt of frustration. "Very well." He stood from his desk. "But I warn you, you're in for a very long wait."

Jenny folded her arms at her waist, half resting them on the swell of her muslin skirts, as they trudged down the dusty street that led back to the guest house. It was nearly dinner-time. Her stomach was growling, her head was aching, and her spirits were at their lowest ebb.

They'd spent the entire day at the fort, first waiting for and then questioning three young soldiers who had known Giles—all of whom had been there that night at the storming of the city. Not a single one of them had offered a scrap of new information.

It had been too dark, they'd said. Too smoky. Too chaotic to know where everyone was.

"When the smoke from the cannon fire cleared, I was taken to hospital," one soldier had confessed. "I didn't learn of Captain Lord Castleton's death until I was released two weeks later. I'm sorry for your loss, ma'am."

Interviewing the medical officer, the chaplain, several of the camp's servants, and even one of the field surgeons who had served in the depot hospital during the siege had proved equally disappointing.

"Everyone is very sorry," Jenny said, "but no one can tell us anything about anything."

Tom walked at her side, his hands clasped behind his back. "We expected as much."

"Yes, but I thought there might be something. Some inconsequential detail that would illuminate everything else."

"Perhaps we're merely asking the wrong people?"

"The soldiers, do you mean? Perhaps you're right. We still have the hospital to visit in the morning. And I don't think it would be amiss to stop at the church."

"We'll set out first thing," Tom promised. "In the meanwhile, Ahmad may have had better luck with the native residents."

Unfortunately, when they arrived back at the guest house, it was to find that Ahmad's luck had been no better than their own.

"The villagers didn't have much to say," he told them. "Whenever I mentioned the siege, they became suspicious of me." He flicked an ironic glance at his impeccably tailored trousers and waistcoat. "Not that they weren't already."

Dinner that evening was a subdued affair. They were all tired and overheated and disappointed in the day's endeavors. Even the food served seemed oddly flavorless and lackluster.

Mr. Bhat addressed Ahmad as he directed a servant to clear away their half-eaten dishes.

"He apologizes for the meal," Ahmad translated after Mr. Bhat withdrew. "And says there will be better fare tomorrow. It's market day. Cook promises a special dinner for us."

"Market day?" Jenny's spirits perked.

Tom gave her a questioning look.

"When I was a girl in Chipping St. Mary," she explained, "market day was one of the best days for gossip. The villagers looked forward to it all week."

He frowned. "Did they?"

"Always. It's human nature. And it must be the same here, surely?" She turned to Ahmad. "You must go, of course. Even if the villagers won't talk, the peddlers might. Especially if you make a purchase or two."

Ahmad nodded. "I'll wear something less conspicuous."

"Shall I go too, madam?" Mira asked.

Jenny looked at her maid. The *dak* journey had plainly exhausted her. It was evident in the slump of her shoulders and the faint circles around her eyes. "Absolutely not. You must rest and stay out of the heat."

"We must all rest." Tom pushed back his chair and got to his feet. "We'll want to make an early start in the morning."

"An excellent idea." Jenny stood.

Tom accompanied her to her room. He stopped at the threshold, his hand holding hers a fraction longer than propriety allowed. "Is there anything you need?" he asked quietly. "Anything I can do to make things easier?"

"You've already made things easier. I don't know how I could have handled all of this without you."

A wry smile briefly lit his eyes. "You'd have managed."

An answering smile touched her lips. Tom knew she was a managing female. That he didn't seem to mind it was rather miraculous. She pressed his hand. "Goodnight, Tom."

"Goodnight, Jenny."

She was still smiling when she closed the door.

The next morning, at eight o'clock precisely, she and Tom set out for the hospital in a gharry.

It was a smallish building, housing no more than fifty beds—less than half of which were presently occupied. The entire enterprise was run by a frazzled surgeon-major by the name of Bartlett. He wasn't particularly keen on having his morning routine disrupted.

"Come, come," he said, ushering them into his small office. "I haven't much time to spare." And then—five minutes later: "There's nothing I can do to help you, Miss Holloway. Had Captain Lord Castleton been injured at the siege rather than killed outright, he'd have been treated in the field. At the depot hospital, not here."

"I'm aware," Jenny replied. "We spoke with one of the field surgeons who served at the depot hospital yesterday. He has no record of having treated Lord Castleton."

"Nor do I, ma'am."

"Yes, but…is there no one working here who might have helped care for the wounded after the siege? A nurse, perhaps. Or a native servant."

The surgeon-major massaged his temples. "You'd be well advised to speak with Lieutenant-Colonel Tremaine at the fort."

"We have done. And he—"

"Well, there you have it. If Tremaine can't help you, I don't see how I can do so."

"You can permit us to speak to the hospital staff," Tom said. "The Earl of Castleton was a gentleman of great importance. His sister, Lady Helena, expects us to pursue every available avenue."

"As that may be, sir, I won't have you making nuisances of yourself in my hospital. And I won't permit any aggravation to my patients. However…seeing as how this is a matter concerning the peerage, you may as well speak with the matron. She can direct you to the appropriate medical staff."

Jenny and Tom spent the next four hours questioning the hospital matron and every other person they could find at the hospital who was remotely connected to the siege. No one remembered Giles. Not the nurses or the man in the dispensary. Not even the few natives who were willing to speak with them.

What they did remember was the siege. Each of those willing to talk to them had some version of the same tale to tell about the diabolical brilliance of the rani, the storming of the fort, and the destruction of the city.

Jenny felt she was beginning to know the story by heart. It had only been two years ago, after all, in this very same month. In the bright light of day, amongst so many polite and industrious people scurrying about at their work or pausing to sip from their cups of tea, it was difficult to imagine the blaze of cannon fire and smoke and the screams of the dying and wounded.

It felt as if the full furies of hell had been unleashed, Colonel Anstruther had said.

A nightmarish thought.

"Let's return to the guest house," Tom said as they left the hospital.

Jenny stopped to open her parasol. "What about the church?"

"We can visit closer to sunset. It's too hot to be traipsing all about the town at midday."

She couldn't disagree. Even the gharry they hired to take them back was flagging. The poor horse looked as if he were about to expire. When the gharry-wallah began to use his whip as encouragement, Jenny touched Tom's arm. "We're close enough to walk, aren't we?"

Tom called for the gharry-wallah to stop. After he helped Jenny out, he went back and spoke to the man.

"What did you say?" Jenny asked as the gharry rolled away. The gharry-wallah was no longer plying his whip.

"Very little. My Hindustani is execrable." Tom paused before adding, "I gave him a ridiculously large tip in addition to his fare. One hopes he'll have the good sense to take his horse back to the stable and call it a day."

Her mouth curved in a sudden smile. One of her love-smitten smiles, no doubt. But, at the moment, she didn't care one jot. "Do you always do the right thing?"

Tom gazed down at her. For an instant, she might have believed him as smitten as herself. "Hardly ever."

"Liar."

"Not at all. I told you I was selfish. It upset you for him to strike the horse, so I made him stop."

"How is that selfish?"

"Because it pleases me to make you happy."

His words brought a flush of warmth to Jenny's cheeks. She bent her head as she proceeded down the street, hoping her parasol shielded her blushes from view. Heaven's sake, she was an aged spinster, not a green girl.

Tom walked along at her side. "I wish I could solve all the rest of this with as much ease."

"Perhaps it's already solved. That may well be our problem. We're asking questions about something to which we already have the answer."

"Anstruther's account."

"I don't like it any more than you do, but thus far he appears to know more about what happened the night Giles died than anyone here."

"We haven't spoken to everyone yet."

"No. There's still the chaplain and whoever might have been involved in assisting with burying the dead. As for the villagers, I don't hold out much hope. Giles only arrived with his regiment during the battle. It isn't as if he was stationed in Jhansi before the uprising."

Tom was silent for a long moment. "Perhaps I was too hasty in urging you to come here."

"Nonsense. Though I think you suspected as well as I that it might come to nothing." She glanced at him. "I'm not a fool, Tom. I could tell you were merely placating me. After how I behaved that morning at the Westbrook—"

"I don't make it a habit of placating people, Jenny."

"Not even ladies who cry themselves to sleep on your shoulder?"

"Ah. As to that…" A glint of humor flickered in his eyes. "It hasn't happened often enough for me to make a formal study."

"I trust not. Though I wouldn't be surprised if it had. You have a very supportive shoulder."

"It's yours whenever you need it."

She took his arm. "I'm obliged to you, but with any luck I won't be needing it anytime soon. I've wept enough for this journey."

The guest house loomed ahead, the chipped brick exterior with its shabby awning beckoning to them in the dry heat. It wasn't going to be much cooler inside, but it was better than nothing.

She sighed heavily. "What an absolutely awful way to end our adventures. Stranded in all this dust and heat, at a disreputable little guest house in the middle of nowhere."

"I don't mind it."

"Rubbish. You're miserable."

"How could I be miserable when I'm with you?"

An unexpected surge of emotion rose in Jenny's breast. "How indeed?"

Tom looked at her, seeming to comprehend exactly what she was feeling. How could he not? Surely he must be feeling it, too. The inevitability of their parting. "You and I need to talk."

She moistened her lips. "Yes."

"Perhaps this evening, after dinner? I can come to your room."

No, she should have said. *It isn't a good idea.*

But none of this had been a good idea. None of it, from the very beginning. And yet, here they were. She and Tom, together.

"Very well," she said.

Tom gave her a thin smile. It was one of encouragement. Either that, or commiseration. "Just to talk. And then—"

"At last," Ahmad said.

Jenny looked up with a start. The sun cast a heavy glare. She hadn't even seen Ahmad standing in front of the guest house. He detached himself from the shadows beneath the awning and came to meet them.

"I've been waiting for you to return for the last two hours."

She dropped Tom's arm, her pulse quickening. "Have you discovered something?"

Ahmad's face lit with a rare smile. "That I have, Miss Holloway."

"Well? What is it? Have you—"

"Let's go inside, shall we?" Tom's hand came to rest on the small of her back. "None of us will be of any use if we expire from the heat."

Jenny followed Ahmad through the doors and into the coolness of the reception area, Tom close at her side. There were no other guests about. Only a native servant was present, an elderly man garbed in a *dhoti*, engaged in sweeping the floor.

"What did you find out?" she asked again.

"Initially, nothing. But you were right about the market. I met a gentleman there. A healer of a kind, peddling medicinal herbs. He told me that after the siege there was a woman who helped with clearing the dead and the wounded."

Jenny's heart pounded. "The British wounded?"

"Natives, mostly, but he seemed to remember rumors of a white man or two being among those she helped. He couldn't recall the particulars."

Tom's expression was grave. "And he simply volunteered all of that?"

"Not without cost," Ahmad said. "I had to purchase a great many of his herbs."

Jenny looked between the two of them. "Well? Who was this woman? And where is she now?"

"For that information, I had to purchase an entire bag of dried *tulsi*." Ahmad's mouth hitched. "Her name is Mrs. Kumar. She works at the mission. If the peddler is to be believed, she's still there now."

Chapter Twenty-One

The structure that housed the mission at Jhansi was in better repair than the rest of the buildings in the city. Built of brick and lime mortar, it stood, small and efficient, on the outskirts of the city. On entering, Ahmad exchanged words with a young native woman in the vestibule.

"She says that Mr. McKidd is in charge. Has been for the last year. He's away in the village at present, condoling with a family who has a sick child." Ahmad continued to speak with the woman, pausing at intervals to translate for them. "She says that Mrs. Kumar is Mr. McKidd's assistant."

Jenny's stomach tightened. "Is Mrs. Kumar here?"

"She's in the schoolroom." Ahmad inclined his head to the native woman. She gave Jenny and Tom a wary look before departing down the hall. "We're to follow her."

Jenny took Tom's arm as they trailed after her. She led them through a painted archway and into an open room with a matted floor. There was a table along the wall with food and drink arrayed upon it. A wizened elderly lady in a sari leaned over it, covering a dish of rice with a piece of cheesecloth.

The young woman approached her, speaking to her in hushed tones, and pointing in their direction.

The elderly lady turned to look at them. Her hair was liberally streaked with gray, her face adorned with a thick pair of spectacles.

"Mrs. Kumar?" Ahmad approached her, offering a greeting in Hindustani.

"I speak English well enough, young man," she replied, her voice rising and falling in a musical lilt. "Bibha says you have come to ask me about a British soldier?"

"We have." Ahmad withdrew the daguerreotype from his pocket and snapped open the case. "Miss Holloway is cousin to this man. His body was lost after the siege."

Mrs. Kumar adjusted her spectacles before peering down at the portrait. "Ah. Him. He was a handsome gentleman. I remember."

Jenny's pulse pounded. But she wouldn't hope. She daren't. "You saw him?"

"I treated him," Mrs. Kumar said. "Not here. This mission is newly built. We had another mission then, closer to the city. It was destroyed during the rebellion. For a time we housed the wounded there. Until the roof was caved in and then…" Her mouth tightened. "So much death and destruction. A terrible tragedy." She looked up at Jenny. "Was he an officer, then? He had no coat when he was brought to me. No insignia. I sent word to the depot hospital, but no one came to claim him."

"Yes, he…he was a captain. He was also the Earl of Castleton, a gentleman of some importance."

"We are all important in God's eyes."

"Yes, of course, but he—" Jenny broke off. "You said no one claimed him. Do you mean…no one claimed his body?"

"He wasn't dead, Miss Holloway. Not when I attended him." Mrs. Kumar crossed the room to a wooden desk. She proceeded to shuffle through a pile of papers, as if she hadn't just knocked Jenny's entire world on end. "He was in a terrible state. But worse was to come. We had an outbreak of cholera that spring. The men who had not yet been stricken were removed."

"He was one of them?"

"He was unconscious. He had lost much blood. We did not expect him to last a week." She shrugged. "I assume he died upon arrival. If not from his wounds, then from the cholera. God rest his soul."

Jenny's mouth went dry as ash. "Arrival where?"

Mrs. Kumar looked at her as if she were a simpleton. "To the hill stations. It is where many go to recover their health. The climate is cool and the air is fresh."

Tom stood at Jenny's side, his hand at her back. "Which of the hill stations?"

"Him? To Darjeeling, probably. At the time of the siege, I had an assistant—Zaina—whose parents worked at a tea plantation there. She escorted the wounded on their journey. A good girl. Smart. She never came back, more's the pity."

"But he was alive when you last saw him?" Jenny pressed. "He was alive and…you're sure—absolutely sure—it was the man in the picture?"

"I am old, madam, as you see," Mrs. Kumar said. "But there is nothing wrong with my memory. Yes, the man I treated after the siege was the man in this portrait of yours. And when I last saw him, he was very much alive."

Tom leaned against the wall, arms folded, watching Jenny pace the confines of her room on the second floor of Mr. Bhat's guest house. Since leaving the mission, she'd been too restless to be still for more than a few seconds at a time.

He should have known then that keeping his promise to come to her room was a bad idea. When he'd first broached the subject, he'd thought the search for Giles was near its end. He'd hoped they could finally have a serious discussion about their future. There was so much he'd wanted to tell her. So many things he'd planned to say in order to persuade her to come home.

Instead, from the time he'd discreetly entered Jenny's room half an hour ago, the conversation between the two of them had revolved entirely around Giles.

"We must go to Darjeeling, obviously," she said. "We've come too far to give up now."

He raked a hand through his hair. Somewhere between meeting Ahmad outside the guest house and leaving the mission, he'd lost control of the situation. He was at a loss as to how he might get it back. "Let's just… Let's wait a moment. We need to properly think this through."

"What's there to think through? Mrs. Kumar recognized Giles from his portrait."

"An unreliable identification at best. The woman must be pushing eighty. And did you see the lenses of her spectacles? They were an inch thick, at least."

"What's that to say to anything? She obviously wasn't blind, else she wouldn't be working at the mission."

"It isn't only her age and eyesight that call her identification into question. The whole account she gave beggars belief."

"It sounded perfectly reasonable to me."

"You truly believe that, if Giles had been alive, even for a day, no one from his regiment would have come for him? She claims to have sent word to the depot hospital, and yet—"

"Perhaps, in all the chaos, her message went astray?"

Tom wasn't convinced. He didn't *want* to be convinced.

"Or perhaps," Jenny continued, "it was Colonel Anstruther who received the message. He didn't strike me as the kind of man who would have given Giles's welfare priority. Not if he believed Giles was a threat to his marriage. Is it so difficult to imagine that he might have ignored Mrs. Kumar's message? If Giles was expected to die regardless, he mightn't have felt any urgency to retrieve him."

"It's possible."

"Exactly. And a possibility is all we've ever had to go on. Not a probability. The entire idea that Giles might have survived the siege has never been more than the flimsiest hope."

"It still is."

"But less flimsy than it was two hours ago, surely. After speaking to Mrs. Kumar, we have more reason to hope than ever, not less."

He exhaled a heavy sigh. "Were time and distance no concern, I'd agree with you. But we've already spent months on this adventure. Were we to travel to the hill stations—"

Jenny stopped pacing to look at him. A hammered-bronze oil lamp stood on the wooden table beside her bed, its low flame illuminating her face in shadows of rose and gold. "I don't expect you to come with me."

"Of course I'll come with you." His voice was harsh, almost angry. "Do you imagine I'd leave you here to make the journey alone?"

"You'll have to leave me eventually. If not in Jhansi, then somewhere else."

"Yes, eventually. But not yet. Not *now*, at any rate."

"Tom—" She broke off, giving him a look. Such a look.

He crossed the room, reaching her in three strides.

"Are you sure?" she asked.

"That I'm going with you? Yes." He framed her face with his hands. The warmth in her eyes went straight to his heart. "About all the rest of it? No."

She circled his wrists with her fingers. "I'd never ask it of you. I'd never expect—"

He bent his head and kissed her.

Jenny's hands tightened on his wrists, even as her lips softened. They parted beneath his, sweet and warm and welcoming.

"I've been wanting to do that since Calcutta," he murmured against her mouth.

"What stopped you?"

He stared down at her, moving his thumbs over the high curve of her cheekbones. "Honor. Decency. The usual sort of things."

"Ah. Them."

"Yes, them. All the noble concerns I've discarded since you came into my life."

Her brows drew together in a disapproving line. "Don't say that."

"Why not, if it's true?"

"Because I don't like to think I'm responsible for you losing sight of who you are. That caring for me—if you do care—"

"*If* I care," he scoffed.

"I never want to presume."

"It's not a presumption. It's a fact. One that may as well be etched in stone."

A soft blush tinted her cheeks. "My darling…" Her voice sunk. "You must know I feel the same way about you."

My darling.

The whispered endearment drifted over Tom like a soothing balm. It warmed him to the heart, seeping into the fractured lines and cracks left from so many years of feeling unwanted, unloved.

"I'm beginning to understand," he said gruffly.

"You mustn't ever doubt it, Tom. When we part, I don't wish you to feel as if—"

"Let's not speak of parting. Not when—"

"We can't pretend—"

"I don't want to pretend. I simply want to focus on the here and now." At that, he stole another kiss. It was deep and fierce. Wholly presumptuous.

Jenny didn't seem shocked at the intimacy. Rather the reverse. She yielded her mouth to him, her lips clinging to his, returning his kiss with innocent abandon.

Desire rose in him like a fire. He wanted to keep kissing her. To take her in his arms and—

But, no. Not here in Jhansi. Not with Giles's ghost hovering over them.

His hands dropped from her face. A breath gusted out of him, half laugh, half groan. "And in the here and now, I'd better take my leave of you before I do something stupid."

Her mouth curved into a smile. "You? Stupid?"

"It's been known to happen on occasion."

"I thought you wanted to talk?"

"Not tonight." He gave her a rueful look. "I'd rather wait until I have your full attention."

She laughed. "Good gracious, Tom. You have it."

No, he didn't. He was sharing it with Giles. Sharing it with her anticipation of the adventure to come. "I'll wait," he said again. "It will be worth it."

Chapter Twenty-Two

Darjeeling, India
April, 1860

Jenny shifted in her seat beside Tom in the back of the wooden cart, her spine stiff from resting it against the metal brackets of one of her trunks. There was no railway line to Darjeeling. A combination of *dak* cart and steam ferry had gotten them as far as the foothills of the Himalayas, but on arriving in the town of Siliguri in West Bengal, they were obliged to proceed the rest of the way by government bullock train.

The bullock carts were heavy and their progress slow. They wound their way up the twisting mountain road on wheels of solid wood at a plodding pace of less than two miles an hour.

Jenny angled her parasol over her head, tilting it just enough that it could provide shade for Tom as well. The sun was setting fast. Soon she'd have no need for a parasol at all.

It was their second evening on the road. The bullock train had only commenced yesterday evening at dusk, traveling all the way through the night before stopping at a rural station. They'd spent the day there resting in a *dak* bungalow, she and Mira together in one apartment and Tom and Ahmad sharing quarters with the servants and drivers in another.

"Did you sleep at all?" Tom asked.

Jenny shook her head. "I was too excited." And too sore. Aching in every limb, in fact. But she wouldn't burden him with her complaints. Not when he was likely aching himself.

"About the possibility of finding Giles?"

"That, and about reaching our destination."

On their final day in Jhansi, Ahmad had gone back to the mission to get the direction of Mrs. Kumar's former assistant, Zaina Chatterjee. According to Mrs. Kumar, the young woman's parents worked at a tea plantation atop the Senchal Ridge.

The native official at the staging area in Siliguri had claimed to know the place.

"Senchal," Ahmad had translated. "He says it means the hill of mist and fog."

The words had sent a thrill of excitement down Jenny's spine. *The hill of mist and fog.* It sounded a magical place. An Indian Avalon, of sorts.

Since learning of its existence, Jenny had been in anticipation of awe-inspiring scenery and cooler mountain weather; however, thus far, it had remained as stifling hot as it had been in Jhansi. As for the sights, she hadn't managed to see very much. The road ran through a tangle of jungle and swamp. The canes and grasses were thrice as high as she was herself, and over the whole of it a heavy mist had settled, obscuring all but the occasional glimpse of the plains below and the majestic mountains above.

"It's not but six miles more," she said. "And yet the gentleman at the bungalow said we wouldn't arrive for another eight hours, at least."

"It's because we're not going in a straight line. The road winds around in a circuitous fashion. It makes the journey four times as long."

"I wonder at what point we'll see a change in the weather?"

"Soon, I expect. We'll be grateful for these." Tom patted the stack of folded blankets that lay in readiness between them. A native gentleman at the last station had been pressing them on the elderly travelers, warning of cooler weather ahead. Ever practical, Tom had insisted they purchase a few for themselves.

It seemed extraordinary that they would need them. At the moment the sun was beating down, unrelenting, on Jenny's parasol. She'd already twice soaked her handkerchief in water so that she might blot her face and throat. The thought of a blanket only made her perspire more.

"I do hope Mira's faring all right." Jenny eyed the cart behind them with concern. Ahmad and Mira rode together in the back of it along with the rest of the luggage. "The heat doesn't agree with her."

Tom looked at Jenny. "What about you?"

"What about me?"

"How are you faring?"

"Oh, I don't mind the heat. It's the dust I can't abide. There's gray grit everywhere. In my hair and all through my clothes. It seems to float straight up from the soil" She gave her skirts a half-hearted shake. "You don't suppose we'll be able to order baths at the plantation, do you?"

"We may not be staying at the plantation."

She gave him a sharp glance. "Do you think they'll turn us away?"

"They might. We don't even know which plantation it is yet. Not to mention the fact that the Chatterjees may have long moved on. It's been two years since their daughter volunteered at the mission."

"Two years isn't so very long."

"It's a lifetime."

Jenny refused to be discouraged. "Well, if they don't welcome us at the plantation, we'll simply have to find lodgings elsewhere. Someplace we can stay while we make inquiries."

Tom's mouth quirked in a faint smile. "Someplace that offers a full bath."

"At this point, even a sponge and basin would suffice." She couldn't bear the grit and dust clinging to her perspiration-damp skin. Some of it had even managed to find a way into her corset, settling there in the most disconcerting way. "If all else fails, I'll find a river to throw myself into."

Within another two hours, the idea of bathing in a river had lost its appeal. The fog dissipated as they ascended the road, and a delicious coolness set in. Another hour more and Tom was draping a blanket over her.

The oil lamps on the bullock cart swung lazily in the darkness, illuminating the path ahead and behind in shifting shadows. No one could see the two of them in any detail. Not enough to object to a slight familiarity.

Jenny slipped her hand into Tom's.

His fingers closed around hers, warm and strong. "Is this enough of an adventure for you?"

"Rattling along a mountain pass in the back of a Himalayan bullock cart? You're teasing me, but the answer is yes. I find it suits me very well."

"You wouldn't rather be back in a railway carriage?"

"Nothing so civilized as that." She paused, almost hating to ask. "Would you?"

"Not at this particular moment." He moved his thumb over the side of hers in a soft caress.

Butterflies stirred in Jenny's stomach at the gentle familiarity of the gesture. "Do you ever stop to consider the sheer distance you and I have traveled since we left Dover?"

"Frequently."

She threaded her fingers through his. "I can scarcely believe we've come so far. Though it hasn't been much of a pleasure trip, has it?"

"I don't know about that. There are certain aspects I've found immensely pleasurable."

Heat bloomed in her cheeks. "As have I. But the journey itself has been so hurried. We've had no time to see the sights or truly get to know anyone."

"We've gotten to know each other."

Jenny met his eyes in the darkness. He looked back at her steadily, his blue gaze solemn—and a little sad—behind the lenses of his spectacles. "We have, haven't we? We're far better friends now than we were in London."

"Is that what you plan to do after I'm gone? Settle someplace where you can get to know people? Make new friends?"

Some of the warmth went out of her at the reminder. But she refused to weep any more over their parting. She was resolved to be grateful for the time they had left together. Grateful for all that they'd shared thus far. "I'd like to. Very much." She rested her head on his shoulder. "Do you know, I've never slept under the stars before."

"You may now, if you like."

"I couldn't possibly. We haven't long to go. We'll be at the ridge by morning. And then we'll finally find out what happened to Giles."

Tom's cheek brushed over her hair. "I don't want you to be disappointed."

"Why should I be?"

"Because there's a good chance we'll learn nothing more about his fate than what we already know."

"I won't be disappointed." She paused. "Well, perhaps I will be a little, but at least I'll be able to write to Helena and tell her I did my best. That I left no stone unturned. Other than that...I couldn't be disappointed in any part of this adventure. It's been everything I ever wanted and more."

"Has it been enough?"

"Enough?" The quiet question sounded a warning bell in her brain. Tom hadn't yet pressured her outright to return to England, but it was always there—that subtle expectation that eventually she would go back to the life she had before. Jenny didn't like it one bit. She nevertheless kept her voice light. "To quench my longing for adventure, do you mean?"

"Nearly three months in as many countries would satisfy most people."

"I don't judge myself by the standards of most people."

"You know what I mean."

"Yes. You're wondering if I'm ready to go home. The answer is no. I won't be, not for a long while I expect. Possibly never. I thought you understood that."

"I do understand. I also understand that people can change their mind in light of new experiences."

"Nothing I've experienced on this journey has made me sour on traveling."

"Not even our present situation?" The bullock cart rattled and shook, jostling them against each other.

"Our present situation is lovely." She closed her eyes for a moment—only a moment, nestling her cheek more comfortably on his shoulder. "You and I, together under the stars. What more could I ask for?"

"What more indeed."

When Jenny next opened her eyes, dawn was breaking and the snow-clad mountains were looming ahead of them. She sat up straight, gazing up at them in wonder.

And then she looked down.

The bullock cart was rattling along the edge of a crumbling precipice with a sheer drop down to the fog-covered plains below.

Her breath caught in her throat.

"Don't look down," Tom advised.

She gulped for air. "Too late."

He drew her close against him. "Are you afraid of heights?"

"No," she said, heart hammering. "What I'm afraid of is plunging down the side of a cliff and being smashed to smithereens."

"You're safe enough."

"Aren't you concerned at all?"

"Of falling? No." His hand moved on her back. "You forget, I grew up climbing the cliffs of Abbot's Holcombe. Whatever fear I might have had of heights died long ago."

"After Mr. Cross fell, I'm amazed you didn't swear off of heights forever."

"If not for Thornhill and Archer, I might have done. But they kept going. They were that determined."

"And whatever they did, you did. Good sense notwithstanding."

"We were young boys with no parents to take us in hand. Good sense was in short supply."

"I can't believe you ever lacked sense, even as a child. You always seem to make the right decisions. It's rather remarkable, really."

"I've simply learned to be cautious. To think things through before I act." He paused, adding, "Until I met you."

"I've been a bad influence on you."

"The worst." A smile crept into his voice. "One moment I was sleeping soundly on the sofa in Half Moon Street and the next…here I am in the back of a bullock cart, clinging to the steep side of a mountain."

The cold air nipped at Jenny's face. She huddled next to Tom, grateful for the security of his arm. "It quite takes your breath away, doesn't it?"

"In more ways than one."

"You don't suppose the drivers have ever misjudged the edge?"

"They seem competent enough."

"But what if—"

"You're safe, I promise. Besides, we're almost there."

"How can you tell?"

"Because I asked the driver half an hour ago. When you feel able, turn and look ahead of us. You'll see."

Jenny waited until the cart had safely navigated the edge of the cliff before kneeling up in all her voluminous skirts and turning to peer over the top of their stacked luggage. Much as the precipice had done, the sight took her breath away. "The hill of mist and fog," she whispered. "That's it, isn't it?"

The driver grinned back at her over his shoulder. "Senchal, memsahib."

From what Tom could see of it, Senchal Ridge was a heavily forested area, wild and beautiful, and so consumed by mists as to be virtually uninhabitable. That much was confirmed when they stopped at the next station.

"He says there's a convalescent depot down the road," Ahmad said, translating his conversation with the station's voluble Khansama. "But the soldiers don't thrive there. Many have…"

"What?" Tom prompted.

Ahmad cast a cautious look at Jenny.

Jenny didn't fail to observe it. She responded with a huff of impatience. "Come. You should know by now that you needn't spare me. Many soldiers have what? Died from their injuries?"

"Many have committed suicide," Ahmad said.

She blinked. "Oh. Oh, dear."

The Khansama continued speaking.

Ahmad translated, "He says that Senchal is too isolated for anyone to recover their health here."

"What about tea?" Tom asked. "Are there any plantations hereabouts run by someone with the name of Chatterjee?"

"He says there's a tea estate on the opposite side of the ridge from the convalescent depot. The old Serracold estate. He doesn't know anyone there, but…he says that Chatterjee is a common enough name and that we're sure to find one or two of them to suit us."

Was Tom not aching in every limb from their days-long bullock cart journey up the mountain, he might have found the energy to laugh. As it was, he wanted nothing more than a hot meal and a warm bed. "Ask him if there's a hotel we might stay at."

Ahmad obliged, and a half hour later, they were on the road again, traveling another mile to what had been described to them as a fully furnished guest house.

Much to Tom's disappointment, on arrival it turned out to be nothing more than another *dak* bungalow run by a sinister-looking Khansama with an avaricious glint in his eye. The cottage-like building was sectioned off into pairs of apartments that could be hired by visitors. Only two such apartments were presently available. Tom was able to secure them by paying what amounted to an exorbitant sum.

"I wouldn't try to negotiate further," Ahmad advised under his breath. "One of the grooms says the Khansama is an ex-convict. He's been jailed on two separate occasions."

"Wonderful," Tom muttered.

"We'll have to make do." Jenny took Mira's arm and walked with her up the steps. "With any luck, before night falls, we'll be invited to stay elsewhere."

Tom wasn't so optimistic. Whoever ran the tea plantation didn't know them from Adam. Even if Zaina Chatterjee's parents still worked there, it was likely only in a menial capacity. What authority could they possibly have to offer lodging to two mysterious British travelers and their servants?

He followed after Jenny into the first apartment. The interior was as grim-looking as the exterior. It boasted a dirty floor and air perfumed with the acrid scent of animal dung. The furnishings were minimal, consisting entirely of a narrow bedframe, stripped of bedding, and a rickety wooden washstand topped by a chipped porcelain basin and pitcher. As if all of that weren't bad enough, the whole of the room was as cold as a butcher's ice house.

Jenny wrinkled her nose. "I suppose we must thank Mrs. Plank for advising us to bring so many linens."

Tom came up beside her, dropping his voice. "This won't do, Jenny."

"It's a little rough, to be sure, but I'm certain—"

"Something's wrong here. It doesn't feel safe."

"It can't be that bad. We aren't the only travelers staying."

"A ramshackle lot of missionaries and the families of injured soldiers? We don't know them any more than they know us. If anything were to happen—"

"Nothing's going to happen."

Tom thrust his hands into the pockets of his trousers. He disliked being out of control of things, and here, in this remote outpost far above Darjeeling, he had less control than ever.

Senchal Ridge was isolated and the visibility was poor. He didn't speak the language with any fluency and he didn't know any of the people outside of the drivers and servants they had traveled with from Siliguri.

How different it all was from London.

There, he knew every jarvey, street sweeper, and petty thief. Information was never out of reach and every problem easily solvable with an eloquently written brief—or the subtle application of a few shillings.

He wondered what Fothergill was doing right now. It had been months since Tom had visited him at his townhouse in Belgrave Square. Then, he'd thought Fothergill on the brink of death. Waxen and wasting away, yet still well enough to order his former clerk about.

Take some time off, he'd commanded.

No doubt he'd expected Tom to retire to his rooms for a few days. To go to the theatre or attend a musicale or two. More than that would have been unthinkable.

India would have been unthinkable.

Tom had posted a letter to him in Delhi, conveying no more than was strictly necessary. There was no need to explain about Jenny or about Lady Helena's missing brother. Fothergill could learn such details easily enough on his own. Even ill and confined to his chair, his spider's web reached everywhere. He'd have known within three hours of Tom boarding the steamship at Dover that his protégé had left the country.

The law is a demanding mistress, my boy. She must come first, last, and always. Take care that you don't forget it.

Tom hadn't forgotten it. Indeed, he was in expectation of returning to his old life very soon.

With Jenny at his side.

"How much time do you require to wash and change?" he asked.

Jenny moved to the door, directing Ahmad where to place her trunk and leather portmanteaus. She glanced at Tom over her shoulder. "A half an hour, at most."

"Is that all?"

"I'd like to visit the plantation as soon as may be."

Ahmad dropped the last case down onto the floor. "Shall I speak to the driver?"

"If you please."

Tom caught Ahmad's eye. "Tell him that after the plantation we'll likely want to visit the convalescent depot. We might have better luck there."

"Am I coming with you?" Ahmad asked.

"We'll need you to translate," Jenny said. "But Mira needs to rest. Do you think she'll be safe here on her own?"

Mira paused in the act of opening one of the portmanteaus. "You mustn't worry about me, madam."

Ahmad ignored his cousin. "I'll speak to the groom."

"But—"

"It will be better this way, Mira," Jenny said, interrupting her maid's protest. "You'll be able to get some rest without worrying about what that Khansama is up to. I don't trust the man. He has a shifty look about him."

Tom exchanged a private glance with Ahmad. "Offer the groom something to keep watch by her door."

Ahmad inclined his head and withdrew. Mira followed after him. Seconds later, his voice sounded outside the door, calling to the driver.

Jenny brushed her hands on her skirts as she walked back toward Tom. Her countenance was grave. "Tom…if we find out what happened to Giles's body—"

"Don't," he said. "You're only setting yourself up for disappointment."

"I realize we probably won't discover anything new, but if—by some chance—we learn where they've buried him—"

"Jenny…" He shook his head.

"I know it sounds morbid, but we must take him back with us. Whatever's left of him. I don't want him resting here alone where no one knows him. His place is with his family. His mother and his father, in the Castleton family vault in Hampshire."

"Even if he *was* the gentleman Mrs. Kumar remembers being removed to Darjeeling—"

"But he *was*. I'm sure she can't have been wrong."

"Very well, let's say he was. And let's say he succumbed to his injuries mid-route."

Jenny looked at him in pale-faced expectation.

Tom's expression softened. "My dear, they might have buried him anywhere from Jhansi to Darjeeling. The odds of finding his remains are—"

"I understand that. But if he's here…" She rested her hands on Tom's waistcoat. "Oh, but I feel he must be. There's something about this place. The beauty of it and the isolation. Giles would have appreciated it. If he drew his last breath here, I think he may have died at peace."

Tom covered her hands with his. "I hope he did. And I hope that—whatever we discover—you and Lady Helena can finally put his ghost to rest."

"That's all I want. It's not too unreasonable, is it?"

"No," he said. "It isn't."

After leaving Jenny, Tom retired to his own room next door. It was in no better shape than hers, but it was serviceable enough for its purpose. He washed and shaved with ice cold water and changed into clothes more suitable to the weather.

Woolen trousers, a waistcoat, and loose-fitting sack coat seemed out of place in the Himalayas; however, it was no dif-

ferent from the garments worn by the other European gentlemen at the guest house.

It had been one of the only constants during their journey.
No matter how far they traveled, by train, ship, or *dak* cart, the
gentlemen were still in coats and cravats and the ladies still in
their corsets and crinolines. After all, Tom thought wryly, a
remote location was no excuse for letting one's standards slip.

He wound his pocket watch as he waited for Jenny outside
her bungalow. Ahmad was already perched atop the cart alongside the driver. The two of them were engaged in murmured
conversation.

Jenny emerged moments later, garbed in a simple woolen
dress with a cashmere shawl wound round her arms. It was
the color of rich cream, the ends adorned with swirls of elaborate red, blue, and gold.

"You look too fine to be traveling in a bullock cart," Tom
said as he handed her up.

She sat down, adjusting her skirts around her. "It's either
this or by palanquin."

Tom climbed in beside her as the cart started forward. "Mr.
Walters called them perambulating coffins."

"How horrible."

"And rather accurate." The palanquins, or *palkee gharries*
as they were called in Darjeeling, were windowless, hearse-
like rectangular boxes in which people traveled lying down.
Pulled by two horses, they were faster than a bullock cart but
a bit unsettling.

"Did you know," Jenny said, "a husband and wife can travel
in one together if they're lying side by side."

"Can they?" Tom gave her a look. "Pity we aren't married."

Her cheeks flushed pink. "Even if we were, I shouldn't like to ride in one. I far prefer sitting upright, even if it is in a bullock cart."

"We could always walk."

"We may have to if the road gets any bumpier."

The Serracold Tea Estate wasn't far from the guest house. It resided farther up the ridge on a vast plateau. As they reached the top, the view expanded to a breathtaking degree. Patches of mist clung to the encroaching forest, and in the distance the snow-capped peaks of Mt. Everest and Kangchenjunga rose up against a clear blue sky.

Tom gazed at them in awe-stricken silence. Jenny was equally transfixed.

"It makes one feel very small and insignificant," she said at last.

"Perhaps we are," he replied. "In the grand scheme of things."

The cart rolled on, coming to a rattling halt at the end of a long, uneven dirt drive. A sprawling bungalow was visible in the distance, the verandah extending out over what appeared to have once been tea fields.

Jenny's brow furrowed. "What happened to it?"

Tom's gaze drifted from the brown fields to the empty huts that had once housed the workers. "It looks as if it's been abandoned."

"It can't be. There's smoke coming from the main bungalow."

She was right. A white vapor swirled up into the sky from one of the bungalow's chimneys.

Ahmad turned in his seat to look at them. "The driver can take us no farther. He doesn't want to risk his cart getting stuck."

"Well," Jenny said. "I was right about us walking."

Tom jumped out of the cart to assist her down. He looked at Ahmad. "Tell him to wait for us."

Ahmad relayed the request to the driver before leaping down himself.

Jenny dusted her skirts off as she peered ahead through the mist. "It's not very far, is it?"

"It's far enough." Tom offered her his arm. She took it, her gloved hand tightening on his sleeve. "Be careful where you step. You could easily twist an ankle."

The three of them proceeded down the road, picking their way carefully around the potholes and mud puddles.

"Do you suppose this is where Zaina Chatterjee's parents worked two years ago?" Jenny asked.

"I think it may be," Tom said.

"Perhaps one of them is still here? As a caretaker or something?"

Tom didn't like to see her get her hopes up. What he'd observed so far of the old Serracold estate seemed to indicate that it had been abandoned a long time ago. There was not a patch of green in the fields to indicate healthy tea growth. Only the smoke from the chimney gave evidence of life. "Anything's possible."

As they drew closer, the mist gradually began to dissipate. The verandah of the bungalow came into better view. There was a native gentleman seated there, his features shaded by a flat-brimmed straw hat. At the sight of them, he rose, very slowly, to his feet.

The midday sun cast a glare on Tom's spectacles. He couldn't see entirely clearly. But it seemed to him that there was something odd about the man. Something vaguely off-kilter.

"Thank goodness," Jenny said. "There *is* a caretaker."

Ahmad called out a greeting in Bengali, but the gentleman didn't answer.

The hair on the back of Tom's neck lifted in warning. And then—

And then realization struck him like a lightning bolt.

The gentleman was no native.

And he was missing an arm.

He gazed down the drive at them, standing stock-still beside one of the pillars of the verandah. "Jenny Holloway," he said at last, in accents straight out of a fashionable London drawing room, "I might have known it would be you."

Chapter Twenty-Three

Jenny's hand fell, nerveless, from Tom's arm at the sound of the man's voice. The next thing she knew, her heavy skirts were clutched in her hands and she was running, full out, the remainder of the distance up the road. All thoughts of propriety—every scrap of caution and good sense—disintegrated the instant she recognized him.

"Giles! Giles!" She reached him in seconds, flinging her arms about his neck and bursting into tears. "It's you. You're alive."

His arm came around her in a tentative embrace. "There now. Let's not make a fuss over it."

"We thought you were dead."

"It wasn't a great loss, I imagine." He drew back from her. "What are you're doing here, Jenny? I distinctly remember commanding you to look after my sister. Don't say you've brought Helena to India?"

Jenny stared up at him. He was still breathtakingly handsome, his dark blond hair streaked with gold and his face as perfectly sculpted as a Greek God. But he was so painfully thin now. Thin and browned by the sun, the linen shirt sleeve of what would have been his right arm pinned, empty, to his chest.

She dashed the tears from her eyes. "I didn't bring Helena. She's home in England with her husband."

His hand spasmed on her arm, almost hurting her. "Helena's married?"

"Oh, Giles, don't you know anything? Haven't you read the papers?"

"I'm lucky to see a newspaper every three months. Time moves more slowly here." Giles looked over her head. "Who are these fellows, then? Your guides?"

Jenny turned as Tom and Ahmad came to join them. She thought Tom would be as astonished to find Giles as she was. She expected some expression of shock or amazement. But Tom's face was completely void of emotion. He looked cold and businesslike. As if he were meeting an adversary rather than finding the object of their months-long quest.

Giles stiffened. "*You.*" He moved Jenny aside with his hand, taking a step forward to face Tom. "I know you."

Tom returned Giles's stare. "I thought you might."

Giles shot a look at Jenny. "What are you doing with this man? Don't you realize who he is?"

It was her turn to stiffen. "I know exactly who he is. He's Thomas Finchley, my solicitor—and that of Helena and her husband."

"My sister has employed this villain? Has the world gone mad in my absence?" Giles's face was the picture of well-bred outrage. "This man nearly ruined the father of one of my closest friends. A cobra couldn't have been more venomous, nor more uncivilized. He's pursued the Earl of Warren for years, destroying his life at every turn, attempting to force the man into compliance." He fixed Tom with an icy glare. "Because of you, sir, the earl's children lost their inheritance. One of them took his own life. All so you might gain ownership of a plot of land."

Tom climbed the steps of the verandah to join her, Ahmad close behind. "Not me," he said. "My client."

"Atwater," Giles uttered the name like a curse. "What sort of solicitor would represent such a scoundrel?"

"Even scoundrels are permitted competent legal counsel, my lord."

"I wouldn't categorize you and your partner as competent legal counsel. The hounds of hell, more like. How much did Atwater pay you to ruin Warren's life?"

"Stop it," Jenny said. "Stop it, the both of you." She turned on Giles. "I can't believe you. We've only just discovered you're alive and all you can do is cast accusations at the gentleman who helped me to find you? I call that very ungrateful."

"You don't know what you're talking about."

"I know that he's an honorable man. And I know that last year he saved your sister from being wrongfully committed to an asylum."

Giles's face fell. "*What?*"

"That's right. You left her alone to fend off your uncle. She knew in her heart you weren't dead. She insisted to everyone that you were still alive somewhere. And he made her suffer for it. If not for Mr. Finchley—"

"It's all right." Tom rested his hand on the small of her back. "You don't have to defend me."

Giles gaze flicked from Tom's hand to Jenny's face. "Did you travel here alone with this man?"

"Oh, for heaven's sake!" Jenny exclaimed. "Haven't we more important things to talk about?"

The door of the bungalow creaked open and a native servant peered out. He was a young, handsome man—no more than five and twenty at Jenny's guess. He addressed Giles in Hindustani, his attitude one of familiarity rather than subservience.

Giles replied in the same language, his cadence sounding almost as natural as Ahmad's did. "This is Hossein," he said when he turned back to Jenny. "My former batman, now my Khansama. He's going to make us some tea. Shall we continue this discussion inside?"

It took a great deal to surprise Tom. He'd been thrown off-balance when Jenny stroked his brow while he dozed on the sofa in Half Moon Street. He'd been dumbfounded when she kissed him on Dover pier, and when she confessed to having feelings for him. And when he'd gone to her room at the Westbrook Hotel in Delhi and found her weeping at the thought of never seeing him again, he'd been stunned. Staggered.

But not now. Not when faced with Giles Reynolds, 6th Earl of Castleton, standing before him in an air of aristocratic disdain—austere, disapproving, and very much alive.

There had always been a chance they'd find him thus. A small chance, admittedly, but a chance nonetheless.

Tom hadn't expected it. He hadn't planned for it. But when confronted with a living, breathing Giles, he felt no sense of shock or dismay, only a grim resignation at the way fate had conspired to thwart his future with Jenny.

The one-armed fellow before him was indeed the same gentleman Tom had encountered in Fleet Street so many years before. It had been at the height of the legal conflict between the Earl of Warren and Viscount Atwater. Warren's youngest son had come to Fleet Street, in the company of two of his aristocratic friends, to rail at Fothergill over a legal maneuver of Tom's that had effectively reduced Warren's shares in a profitable railway venture to nothing.

That was to be my inheritance, he'd said, a vein bulging at his temple. *You had no right.*

Tom had marked the faces of the young man's friends. They were both fashionable gentlemen, clothed in smartly tailored suits and sporting gold-topped ebony walking sticks and jeweled signet rings on their fingers. The blue-blooded sons of other titled lords and ladies. Tom hadn't known who they were by name. It hadn't seemed important.

When he'd recognized the daguerreotype of Giles at Fort William, that hadn't seemed particularly important either. An unsettling coincidence, nothing more. It hadn't mattered. Not truly. Not when Giles was dead.

Not until now.

If Tom lived to be one hundred, he didn't think he'd ever forget the way Jenny had looked when she realized that the gentleman on the verandah was Giles. He'd never forget the way she ran to him, embracing him and bursting into tears.

She clung to Giles's arm as they entered the bungalow, her cheeks still damp. Tom followed behind her, Ahmad at his side.

Ahmad hadn't uttered a single word—neither of surprise, nor indifference—since they'd climbed the steps to the verandah. As always, he seemed content to keep his own counsel. But Tom saw the way his gaze moved about the shadowed interior of the bungalow, taking in the cozy arrangement of chairs and tables and the way Giles's servant, Hossein, navigated amongst them with so much casual familiarity.

"We thought the house abandoned," Jenny said.

"It is, essentially." Giles motioned for her to sit down. "We're cultivating new fields down in the valley. The workers and all of the staff have already relocated there." His gaze cut to Ahmad. "You may join Hossein in the kitchen. He'll be glad of the help."

Ahmad looked to Tom.

Tom gave a brief nod. "Shall I go as well?" he asked Jenny quietly. "If you'd prefer privacy…"

"I don't think that will be necessary." She glanced at Giles, a little uncertain. "Unless…?"

"It makes no difference to me," Giles said.

"Very well." Tom waited until Jenny was seated in a tufted chair by the fireplace before taking a seat himself. Giles hadn't explicitly invited him to sit, but Tom had a feeling that if he waited for an invitation, he'd be waiting until judgment day.

Jenny arranged her heavy skirts. "Giles…you don't mean to say this place is yours, do you?"

"No. I don't own it outright. My own interest amounts to no more than a third. I bought into the venture shortly after regaining my health." Giles flicked an irritated glance at him. "I trust that nothing I say here today will be used for nefarious purposes."

"Really, Giles," Jenny objected.

"Miss Holloway is my client," Tom said. "I'll do as she directs me."

"Your client." Giles gave a short laugh. "Astounding."

"I don't see what's so astounding about it," Jenny retorted.

"Since when does a lady's companion have need of a solicitor?"

"I'm not a lady's companion any longer. I don't work for Lady Helena or for anyone else in your family. I'm wholly independent now."

"Yet, here you are." Giles contemplated her down the aristocratic length of his nose. "Why *are* you here, Jenny?"

"I was already coming to India. It seemed a reasonable enough idea to spend some of my time here trying to find out what became of your body after the siege. We've been all over the country. To Calcutta and Delhi. To Allahabad and Jhansi. And now, here we are. And here *you* are." A notch worked its way between Jenny's brows. "Heaven's sake, Giles, I thought we'd be arranging a method for transporting your bones back to the Castleton vault in England. Why on earth didn't you send word to us? Why didn't you come home? You've no idea the damage you've caused by letting the world think you dead."

Giles's face lost some of its color. "You mentioned something about Helena and an asylum. Is she—"

"She's perfectly safe. She's thriving, in fact. I've never seen her happier."

"You said that she'd married."

"She did. Last September."

"To whom? Was it Lord Caraway or the Marquess of—"

"No, no. None of those gentlemen. She married a former army captain. An ex-soldier who served here in India. His name is Justin Thornhill. He has an estate in North Devon."

Giles's brow creased. "I'm not familiar with the name. Who are his people?"

"He hasn't any people," Jenny said. "None you'd recognize. But he helped to save Helena last year when your uncle was being so ruthless. If not for Mr. Thornhill and Mr. Finchley, I daresay she'd be dead now. Either that or locked away somewhere, beyond all hope."

He ran a hand over his face. "Good God. Was it… Was it because of me? Because of the money I left her?"

Jenny didn't answer. Not directly. "She's fine now, Giles. Truly. It's all been sorted out. And she's kept the money safe. She's always said you would come back one day. That you would need it when you resumed your role as Earl of Castleton."

"The little fool. Perhaps I should have… But I thought it would be easier…less difficult to bear… A clean break, I thought." Giles stood from his chair. "Where's Hossein with that bloody tea?"

Tom exchanged a brief look with Jenny. Her eyes were troubled, her lips compressed into an anxious line. If they'd been alone, he'd have taken her hand. As it was, he could do no more than offer her a faint, reassuring smile.

Hossein entered a moment later with a heavy brass tea tray. Ahmad came in after him, carrying another tray, weighed down with extra cups and a decanter of something that looked to be sherry.

The next quarter of an hour was taken up with Jenny pouring out their tea and dispensing sandwiches and biscuits.

Tom watched her, knowing how hungry she must be after a night spent in the bullock cart and a morning in which they'd yet to partake of breakfast. In the past, she'd never failed to eat with a healthy appetite. But now, in front of the coolly aristocratic Earl of Castleton, she consumed her sandwich in dainty bites, seeming at pains to be as ladylike as possible.

It irritated Tom to no end.

She shouldn't have to change herself for anyone, least of all the blackguard who'd taken advantage of her when she was his sister's companion.

Did Giles even realize how much he'd hurt her? He must have known. He'd referenced the kiss he'd stolen in that letter of his, apologizing for it even as he'd abdicated all responsibility, dismissing any obligation to propose to her or otherwise make amends.

Such events loom large in the life of a young woman.

It did Tom no good to wonder if Jenny would have accepted a marriage proposal from Lord Castleton, but wonder it he did, all through tea.

"The leaf is from the new estate in the valley," Giles said. "It has a delicate flavor and a subtle fragrance, rather like perfume."

Jenny lowered her cup back to its saucer. "I'd no idea you knew anything about tea or tea growing."

"I've spent the better part of the last ten years in India. There's much to learn about the food and drink here if one has a mind to."

"And that's what you've been doing since you've been gone? Making a study of tea cultivation and the culinary arts?"

Giles exhaled. He returned his teacup to the tray. "I'm afraid it's more complicated than that."

"I wish you would explain it to us. We've only been able to discover so much on our own from talking to Colonel Anstruther and—"

Giles brows lifted. "You spoke to Anstruther?"

"And to his wife, and to Sir Eustace Tavernier at Fort William, Lieutenant-Colonel Tremaine in Jhansi, as well as to Mrs. Kumar at the mission there." Jenny ticked the names off on her fingers. "We've questioned everyone we could think of."

"How much do you know?" he asked.

"We know that you were injured after storming the walls of the city. That you…that you lost your arm. After that, the accounts began to differ. Anstruther said you expired from your wounds and that your body had been burned in a pit with the rest of the dead. But Mrs. Kumar said you were saved, taken to the mission and then to one of the hill stations to recover. She said you'd likely died along the way."

"I did lose my arm, as you see." Giles gave his empty sleeve a frowning glance. "But the wound didn't kill me, though I was out of my head for a very long while. Thank God for Hossein."

"Was it he who came to your aid?"

Giles nodded. "He was acquainted with one of the young missionary girls at the school. He took me to her, and thence to Mrs. Kumar. The next thing I knew, the girl was tending to me as we made the journey from Jhansi to Darjeeling. I don't recall much. She fed me ground-up roots and herbs—tinctures to help with the pain and make me sleep. I spent the next five weeks on a pallet, as helpless as a baby."

"Was the girl's name Zaina Chatterjee?" Jenny asked. "Mrs. Kumar said she escorted you to the tea plantation where her parents worked."

"And here I am." Giles made a broad gesture which seemed to encompass the bungalow and all the tea fields beyond it. "Miss Chatterjee, alas, is no more."

Hossein said something to Giles from the doorway. Giles answered back, in the same language, his tone clipped.

"He doesn't like me to speak of her," he explained after Hossein retreated back to the kitchen. "She was like a sister to him."

"Was?" Jenny echoed. "I don't understand. Is Miss Chatterjee dead?"

"It's the price she paid for helping me. As I regained my health, she lost her own. The cholera took her within a week of our arrival here. It took her parents as well." Giles's expression was taut. "No good deed goes unpunished and all that."

"Oh, Giles. I'm so sorry."

He waved off her condolences. "It's going on two years since she passed. A lifetime ago."

"Why in the world did Hossein take you to her and not to the depot hospital? Surely it would have been better to have been treated by one of the field surgeons."

Giles made no reply.

"And why have you stayed on here?" Jenny pressed him. "You seem well enough now, yet you've chosen to live here among strangers rather than go back to your own home. Your own people."

"Have you seen the ridge?" Giles asked abruptly. "Really seen it?"

"Yes, but—"

Giles rose from his chair. "Come for a walk with me."

Jenny looked at Tom.

"Come," Giles said again, making the word a command. "You can be without your solicitor for ten minutes."

Tom stood. "Go ahead, if you like. I'll wait here with the servants."

She gave him a reluctant nod. "Very well."

Tom watched them go. Watched the way Jenny walked at Lord Castleton's side, holding herself with such dignity and rigid self-restraint. Her eyes were still red from crying, her brows still knit with worry. As they exited the bungalow, he saw her take Giles's arm in the same way she'd often taken his.

A jolt of bitter jealousy speared through him.

"Well," Ahmad said, coming to stand beside him, "what are we going to do now?"

Jenny stood atop the ridge next to Giles, her gaze drifting over the snowy mountain range in the distance. The air was crisp and cool, biting at her face and throat. She twisted her cashmere shawl more firmly about her shoulders. "It *is* beautiful here."

"The most beautiful place in the world."

"But it isn't your home. It's not where you belong."

"You don't know the first thing about me, Jenny."

Jenny inwardly winced. It had been a long time since she'd been in company with Giles alone. Long enough to forget how easily he could flay her with a careless word or humiliate her with one of his aristocratic looks.

At one time, such humiliations had been a daily occurrence.

When she'd been fresh up from the country, an unpolished vicar's daughter experiencing her first taste of life in town, how often had he made her feel as if she were something less than the society ladies with whom he regularly associated? How often had he ignored her very presence when she was in the room with Helena, treating her as if she were no more than a piece of furniture?

She'd forgotten how it felt. How it hurt.

"I know enough to recognize that you're being selfish by remaining here. Worse than selfish. Had you cared one jot about your sister, you'd have—"

"You presume to lecture me about my sister?"

"Someone must do so. And as I'm already here—"

"You haven't changed, have you? Always trying to manage other people's affairs." He ran a hand over his hair. "If you must know, I didn't come home precisely because I *do* love my sister. I wouldn't wish my presence on her. Not in the state I was in then."

"She loves you. She wouldn't have minded if you were hurt."

"It wasn't my injuries." He cast an absent glance at his empty sleeve. "Though this has taken some getting used to."

"If not your injuries, then what? What good reason could you possibly have for letting us think what we did?"

"It may not qualify as a good reason, but I—" He broke off. "You know what became of my mother. You know Helena and I have a sadness in us. A melancholy that threatens whenever we let down our guard."

Jenny did know. The sadness had nearly consumed Helena when she first received word that her brother was dead. She'd wept inconsolably, long past the time her uncle believed suitable for mourning.

"Mine has become worse over the years." Giles stared out at the mountains, his mouth set in a hard line. "When first I came here, I was subject to it in the worst way. You can't imagine what it's like for a fellow. This encroaching sorrow. And I had no earthly reason to be sad. Anyone would say I had the world on a platter. It was mine for the taking. And yet…some mornings, I could barely summon the strength to rise from my bed."

"I understand the climate sometimes affects people—"

"It wasn't the climate. It's never been anything but who I am. A sickness I inherited from my own mother." He blinked rapidly. "There's no cure for it, but activity helps to keep it at bay. Within a month of being here, I realized there was no other place I'd rather be. It's something in the air, you see. Something in the food—in the tea—and in living as I do amongst the people. It's taken me outside of myself in a way that nothing else ever could. Hossein understands it. He always has. It's why he took me to Miss Chatterjee instead of the depot hospital. I daresay he thought it was my way out of it all."

"Out of the army?"

"The army. The world." Giles paused, a deep breath expanding his chest. "When I woke up, after the cholera had taken Miss Chatterjee and her parents, Hossein brought me here to this very spot. I sat atop this ridge, my bandages still bloody, and I looked out at this view and I realized…"

"What?" she asked softly.

"That the Earl of Castleton wasn't so very important a man. That there was something bigger out there."

"You're speaking of God."

"God, Allah, Brahman. The name doesn't matter. All I know is that I've found peace here. I've found purpose again. From that moment, my life in England was over."

Jenny thought she understood. He'd had a sort of spiritual awakening. An epiphany of the soul.

Either that or he was simply being self-indulgent.

"What about Helena?" she asked.

"I made arrangement for her to inherit before I left London. In the event of my death, she'd be well taken care of."

"I don't mean the money. I'm speaking of her heart. You broke it, Giles. She's still grieving for you."

"You said she'd married."

"One can experience love and marriage and still be grieving for the loss of a family member. We're not all solid shades of black or white, Helena least of all." She touched Giles's arm, feeling him stiffen beneath her fingers. "She's as subject to these bouts of sadness as you are. How do you think it affected her to lose her brother? The least you could have done was write and tell her you'd decided to remain here."

"It's better this way."

"Better for you, perhaps." She paused, adding, "And don't dare spout any more nonsense about the peace you've found in India. I can't believe any deity would grant you that peace at the expense of your family. God expects us to be responsible. To shoulder our burdens, not to shift them onto people who aren't capable of bearing them."

Giles gave her a scornful look. "A vicar's daughter to the last."

She nearly laughed. "If you think I learned about taking responsibility from my father, you're much mistaken, my lord. My father never met a burden he didn't mind foisting onto me. A gentleman shouldn't behave in such a way. Not if he expects to be worthy of the name."

"You'd have had me return and be miserable. All for the sake of the Castleton family name."

"I don't give a snap of my fingers for your family name."

"Do you know, I don't believe that you do." He turned away from the view. "Where are you staying?"

"At a guest house on the opposite side of the ridge."

"The one with the dubious Khansama?" Giles heaved a sigh. "You'd better put up here."

She searched his face. "Very well. If that's what you wish. I'll send Ahmad to fetch my maid and our luggage."

He shook his head. "You really did it. You came all the way here to find me."

She made a soft sound of disagreement. "I came here for the adventure. Finding you was a secondary concern."

"One for which you brought along the most lethal attack dog you could find."

"I beg your pardon?"

"Mr. Finchley of the notorious Fleet Street firm of Fothergill and Finchley. Damnation, Jenny. Was there no greater villain you could have employed?"

She scowled. "I'll thank you to stop addressing him in those terms. He's been nothing but helpful to me since we left London. I count him a friend."

"A friend?" Giles didn't look convinced.

"A *dear* friend."

"At the very least, I trust he's kept you safe from other nefarious types you might have encountered."

"He has."

"And what about from himself?"

"I've nothing to fear from Tom Finchley."

"*Tom.*"

Indignation rose in her breast. "I don't know what you think you're implying."

"If you were my sister—"

"I'm not your sister, thank heaven. And you have no room to criticize any gentleman when you yourself treated me in the most disrespectful manner when you were last home on leave."

Giles flushed. "As to that—"

"Judging from your letter of apology, I assume you believed I was pining away of love for you. Either that or waiting for you to come home from the wars and marry me." She lifted her chin. "For your information, my lord, your kiss was not at all the sort to make a female weak at the knees. If it was an example of your best efforts, your future wife has my profound sympathies."

Giles gave a sudden laugh. "Good God, *did* I kiss you that day in the library? I'm amazed I survived the experience."

"It's no laughing matter. For a time, I thought that—if you were alive—it might have been that very incident that kept you from coming home."

His expression sobered. "Were it as simple as that."

Jenny took his arm as he slowly turned to walk back to the bungalow. Despite her irritation with the man, she still felt a profound sense of relief to have found him.

Now all that was left was to get him home.

"We'll sort everything out," she promised. "There's no problem so complicated it can't be solved given a bit of feminine ingenuity."

Chapter Twenty-Four

*T*ime moved slowly on Senchal Ridge. That's what Giles had told her. And he'd been right. The next three days passed at a glacial pace. Jenny could sense Tom becoming restless. She didn't wonder. It must take an enormous amount of energy to exhibit the forbearance he'd shown since their arrival. He never rose to Giles's bait. Never spoke sharply to him or put him in his place, even when he most deserved it.

Jenny knew why. Despite the reputation Tom had culti-vated for being in possession of a rather ruthless legal brain, he was, at his heart, a compassionate man. She esteemed him all the more for it.

On their fourth day in residence at the tea estate, she found him alone on the verandah watching the sun rise over the mountains. She came to stand at his side, her shawl wrapped firmly around herself against the morning chill.

They hadn't breakfasted yet. Giles had yet to emerge from his room and Hossein was in the kitchen with Ahmad and Mira preparing she knew not what. It was the first moment she'd had alone with Tom since their arrival. She didn't wish to squander it.

"Would you like to go for a walk?" she asked.

He looked at her, smiling slightly. "Good morning. Did you just wake up?"

She touched a self-conscious hand to her hastily pinned tresses. "Do I look as if I did?"

"There's nothing wrong with the way you look." Tom dropped a glance at his own attire. "Would that I could say the same about myself." He was clad in trousers, a plain waistcoat, and loose-fitting linen shirt. His sleeves were rolled unevenly, exposing leanly muscled forearms. "I thought myself quite alone at this hour, else I would have finished dressing."

"You're dressed well enough for my purposes." She extended her hand to him. "Come, let's be off. If we leave now, we might avoid the others."

His hand engulfed hers. "To where?"

"To anywhere, so long as I get you to myself."

"Ah, well. When you put it that way, how I can I refuse?"

They walked down from the verandah, turning left at the steps instead of proceeding down the road. A narrow, well-trodden path took them past more abandoned tea fields and out along the edge of the encroaching forest where conifers of all sizes stretched up to the endless sky.

And they talked. They talked of the wonder of finding Giles. Of the beauty of the ridge. And of the deep pleasure to be had in resting so comfortably after a journey in which they'd rarely stayed in one place for more than two or three days.

Jenny leapt atop a low boulder, one hand still clutched warmly in Tom's, as she gazed up at the snow-covered peaks. A breath of fresh mountain air filled her lungs. "Is it any wonder they send injured soldiers to the hill stations to recover their health?"

"Do you feel healthier?"

"I wouldn't say healthier. But I do appreciate the cooler weather. Giles says that many of the residents in Calcutta and Delhi remove to the hills in April and May."

"I'm amazed he never encountered anyone who recognized him."

"Oh, he doesn't associate with the Europeans anymore. Indeed, Mrs. Plank would accuse him of having gone native."

"Anyone who met him would know different."

She glanced down at him. "What do you mean?"

"Only that he's retained a fair measure of his aristocratic superiority. There's nothing of the humble native about him, however isolated he may choose to live."

"Which is understandable, really. One can't have been born into such a family and forget it. He's the Earl of Castleton to his core, whether he cares to admit it or not. It isn't something he can shed like an ill-fitting suit of clothes."

Tom's hand tightened on hers as she hopped down from the stone. "Has he shown any willingness to go back?"

"There's willingness. It's the how and when I'm having difficulty pinning him down on." She slid her arm through his. "If only you could persuade him—"

"That's never going to happen, Jenny."

"I don't see why not."

He gave her a look.

"Yes, I know, he's been absolutely beastly toward you." She strolled along at his side as they advanced farther into the woods. "If it's any consolation, he hasn't been much more civil to me."

"He's shown himself quite solicitous of you when we're all in company together."

"Yes, in public, Giles has always been a gentleman. It's in private when he reveals how little he thinks of me and my opinions."

"And that," Tom said, "is something I'd be willing to have words with him about."

She laughed. "Don't dare. I can fight my own battles."

"You shouldn't have to. Not while I'm here."

"Yes, I must take full advantage of you while I have you. Speaking of which…" She tugged at his arm. "I want to show you something. It's just around the corner, if memory serves me. I've gotten to know these paths rather well in the last several days and—"

"Undoubtedly. You've spent hours walking them with Giles."

Jenny's steps flagged. She thought she detected a sharp edge to his words, but wasn't certain. "You might have joined us if you and Giles didn't have so much bad blood between you."

"I've no bad blood with the man. It's his own view of solicitors that makes it impossible for us to be in company together. If he didn't take things so personally—"

"Was any of it true? Any of those things he accused you of on the day we arrived at the ridge?"

Tom's face shuttered. He looked away from her. "You know I can't speak about my cases."

"Not even here, on the other side of the world? Not even with me?"

"It's not a matter of where or to whom. It's simply not done. I'd be breaking one of the foremost rules of my profession."

"Giles said you ruined the Earl of Warren's life. That you drove his son to suicide."

Tom stopped in the center of the path. Her hand fell from his arm as he turned to face her. "The Earl of Warren's son was an opium addict. Whether his death was deliberate or the end result of his addiction is a matter of some dispute. Certainly I had nothing to do with it."

"You didn't do something to affect his inheritance?"

He didn't respond.

Jenny's stomach tightened with apprehension. She had the sense that she should change the subject. That she should cease talking about Giles or giving voice to any of Giles's absurd accusations. But she'd already said too much. There was no point in stopping now. "He said that you boxed Warren in as if he were an animal. That everywhere he turned…there you were. That you destroyed the man's business ventures. Got him ejected from his clubs. That you even exposed his mistress to Lady Warren."

A muscle spasmed in Tom's jaw. "So, this is what you and Giles have been talking about during all of your walks about the grounds. Not about him and how he needs to return to England, but about me and what a ruthless monster I am."

"Don't be absurd."

"Is it absurd? Because it sounds to me as if you're asking me just how much of a villain I am."

"I'm doing nothing of the sort. I haven't any need to. I already know you aren't the calculating figure Giles has made you out to be."

"And yet, I did all of the things he accused me of. I exerted pressure on Warren in every possible way. I didn't care how it affected him or his family. My only concern was gaining his capitulation."

"On behalf of your client."

"It was hardly on my own behalf. I didn't know who the Earl of Warren was before this case began. I had nothing personal against the man. It's *never* been personal. Not with any of them."

Jenny remembered what Tom had told her on the train to Cairo about his clients being dishonorable men. How he'd become disenchanted with representing them. And how he hoped that, one day, worthy clients—like Ahmad and Mr. and Mrs. Jarrow's son—would replace the unworthy ones entirely.

She came a little closer to him. "At Dover, you said this land dispute case of yours had been going on for eleven years."

"A bit longer, in fact. Fothergill would say that I cut my legal teeth on the Earl of Warren. Perhaps I was overzealous initially, but I—" He broke off with a grimace. "I had a great deal to prove."

"I daresay you proved it. The case is settled now, isn't it?"

"For the moment."

"And your client? The Viscount Atwater?"

"Really, Jenny. I can say no more on the subject. Except…"

"What?"

"Except to assure you that I'm no villain. I'm merely a man with a bit of talent for his job."

Jenny choked on a laugh. "A bit of talent? I know nothing about the law, Tom, but even I recognize you must be possessed of more than that." She sought his hand. "In any case, I know you're not a villain."

"You sound very sure of yourself."

"I am," she said. "I could never care for a villain the way I care for you."

His fingers curled around hers. "Well, then."

"Well, then." A smile tugged at her mouth. "If we're quite done arguing—"

"We haven't been arguing."

"So you claim." She took several steps backward on the path, coaxing him along with her. "Talking about what a monster you are, indeed," she chided. "Really, Tom. Do you want to know what Giles and I talk about when we're alone? We talk about *him*. About Helena. About his uncle. And, very occasionally, he stoops to lecture me on my conduct—specifically as it relates to you."

Tom's brow lowered. "He has no reason to do so. From the moment we set foot in his house, we've been avoiding each other like the plague."

"How well I know it." The path curved on ahead of them. She dropped Tom's hand, stepping off of it and crossing the grass, still wet with morning dew. "Through here," she said.

Tom followed after her, ducking through a gap in the trees. On the other side was a clearing of sorts. Small and surrounded on all sides by dense, curving oak trees, maples, and pines. He looked around. "What is this?"

"It's privacy, is what it is. Absolute, unequivocal, privacy."

His eyes found hers. "Ah. I see."

Warmth crept into her cheeks. She backed another few steps into the clearing. "I'm tired of us avoiding each other."

He advanced upon her slowly. "It has been rather wearing, hasn't it?"

"I've found it so." Jenny's heartbeat quickened as he came to a stop in front of her. "So many times, I've wanted…"

He gazed down at her. "What have you wanted?"

"To do this." She curved a hand around his neck. There was no cravat to impede her. His skin was bare and warm beneath her fingers. With a gentle pressure, she urged him down to her at the same time she stood up on the toes of her half boots, reaching to meet his lips.

Tom bent his head, his eyes closing as she kissed him. For several seconds, he let her take the lead, and then, with a low groan, his arms closed around her and he kissed her back, so fiercely it took Jenny's breath away.

Her fingers slid into his hair, clenching there as his mouth moved on hers. He was holding her so tightly, pressing her against him from shoulders to knees. She couldn't tell if the hammering she felt in her chest was his heart or her own. They were that close. That fundamentally connected. It seemed, for those precious moments, that they shared everything; their pulse and heat and breath. The thought of parting was an agony.

But kisses couldn't go on forever.

Eventually, his lips drifted from hers, pressing gentle kisses to her cheek and temple. Conciliatory kisses. Sweet, masculine apologies for putting an end to something that had shaken her so deliciously in heart and limb.

"We don't have to stop," she whispered.

"I do," he said. "I must."

"Why?"

"Because if I don't stop now, I won't be able to stop at all. And then where will we be?"

She knew he was right. Nevertheless…

Her lips grazed the curve of his ear.

"*Jenny*," he growled.

"This mountain air has made me wonderfully reckless. I feel as if I could devour you." It was probably the most non-sensical thing she'd ever said in her life, but when she nipped at his earlobe, the sound he made low in his throat sent a frisson of such excitement through her that she knew it didn't matter. "Kiss me back, Tom. Kiss me *back*."

He did.

And he did.

Until his spectacles were discarded and her shawl was cast off over a nearby boulder. Until his hair was wildly disheveled and her own was half falling from its pins. Until she was nothing more than a mass of melted treacle in his arms, weak at the knees and clinging to his neck and to his lips.

Until he broke away from her at last, setting himself as far apart from her as he had that night on the *Valetta*.

Jenny's legs trembled beneath her. She sank down onto the boulder on which her shawl was draped, staring up at Tom in stunned silence.

He raked both hands through his hair, turning away from her on a muttered word.

"What's that about a chaperone?" she asked, still breathless.

"Having one here might have helped."

She waited for him to turn around, but he made no move to do so. Without seeing his face, she couldn't fathom whether or not he was irritated with her or angry or—even worse—simply embarrassed by her boldness. "Tom, are you—"

"I'm quite all right. I'm just going to stand here for a moment. If you wouldn't mind—"

"Shall I—"

"—staying where you are."

"Oh." The word came out on a disappointed breath. She folded her hands in her lap and waited. After a full thirty seconds of silence, she lost patience and began to re-pin her hair. She had a vague recollection of Tom spearing his fingers through it as he kissed her. Of tugging at her locks in the most demanding way. "I suppose I must apologize for being so brazen."

He gave her a wry glance. "Why? I clearly didn't mind it."

"You look as if you do now."

"I'm trying to regain some semblance of mastery over myself. To remind myself of all the reasons I shouldn't do what I very much want to do."

"Is it working?"

"Not as well as I'd wish." He finally turned and came back to her, crossing the clearing to sink down beside her on the boulder. Her skirts bunched against his legs. "You said you felt as if you could devour me."

A blush threatened. "I don't know what I—"

"I do. It's precisely how I feel about you. About the sweetness you offer every time you kiss me. When there's a lack of something in your life, you want it all the more. It's never enough to have a taste of it. You want to consume it whole."

"No one has ever accused me of being sweet before."

"Perhaps you haven't shown that side of yourself to anyone else the way you have to me?"

"Perhaps not." Until Tom, no man had ever inspired such feelings in her. She couldn't imagine any man ever would again. It was a depressing thought, especially since she knew their time together was quickly running out.

He took her hand very gently in his, cradling it with a tenderness at odds with the fierceness of the kisses they'd shared only moments before. "A few months ago, this would have been enough. Sitting beside you and holding your hand. In London, I'd have given anything for the privilege."

She swallowed. "I remember, one day when I first came to live at Greyfriar's Abbey, I saw Mr. Thornhill and Helena coming up from the beach together. They were holding hands. Except that Helena had removed one of her gloves and Mr. Thornhill had removed one of his. It seemed the most intimate thing. And I thought—"

"What?"

"I don't know. I was glad, I suppose. Glad that they'd found that connection with each other. After what they've been through, they deserve all the happiness in the world."

"Do you think we don't?"

She didn't know what to say. Of course she believed that they deserved happiness. But one couldn't have everything they wanted, could they? Life was a series of choices—of sacrifices. In order to have Tom, she'd have to give up her freedom. The very independence she'd dreamed of for so many years. It was a price she wasn't willing pay. Not for him. Not for anyone.

But she was tempted.

So very, dreadfully tempted.

"I want to ask you something," he said.

Every nerve in her body jangled in warning. It was all she could do to keep her voice steady. "Yes?"

"If Giles agrees to return to England, will you go with him?"

It wasn't the question she'd anticipated. She should have been relieved. And she was. Truly, she was. But along with that relief came disappointment. It settled inside her, a heavy weight lodged somewhere between her heart and her stomach. She endeavored to ignore it. "I've been asking myself that very question for the last four days."

"Have you come to an answer?"

"After a fashion. I think I must go with him part of the way, but…I'm not ready to go back to England. I still need time and I—"

"How far?" The edge was back in his voice. "To Calcutta? To Suez?"

"To Cairo, I think. I'd like to settle there awhile. And it's not so remote that Giles won't mind leaving me. Or so I hope. I haven't discussed that part of the plan with him yet."

"When?"

"I don't know. I—"

"I can't stay here much longer, Jenny."

Her heart lurched.

"I've spent too long away from London. It's past time I got back. If you'd like me to travel with you as far as—"

"Of course I would." Her hand tightened on his. "I'm not ready to say goodbye to you."

His gaze found hers. He was still missing his spectacles. How very different he looked without them. Younger and almost vulnerable. "Do you anticipate that you'll be ready when we reach Cairo?"

"No," she said. "But I won't make a fuss. There'll be no tears. No dreadful scenes like the one in Delhi. You may rely on it."

Tom's mouth hitched in a tight, humorless smile. "How disappointing. I was rather looking forward to a dramatic goodbye."

Tom spent the next two days in a state of perpetual frustration. There were no more opportunities to be alone with Jenny. Giles had seen to that. When they'd returned from their walk together the previous morning, he'd met the pair of them at the door, a look of keen disapproval in his eyes. "We've had to wait breakfast for you," he said.

And then he'd offered his arm to Jenny, escorting her inside with all the authority of an overbearing elder sibling.

Since then, Giles had commanded all of Jenny's time.

It was time that Jenny put to good use.

"Giles has agreed to go home," she said the following evening at dinner. They were seated at the rectangular wooden table in the bungalow's small dining room. A branch of candles stood at its center, silver serving dishes of spiced meats, curry, and rice arrayed around it.

"For a short time," Giles clarified. "Just long enough to sort things out with my sister and my uncle."

Tom refrained from commenting. He wasn't entirely unsympathetic to Giles's plight. The man plainly suffered from some degree of melancholy. However, Tom had seen firsthand the consequences of Giles's actions. The consequences to Lady Helena and even to Jenny.

Could Giles have foreseen that his sister would come to harm? That Jenny would lose her position and be thrown out into the streets? Perhaps not. But he might have anticipated Lady Helena's grief at the loss of him. He might have known how deeply she would suffer. Nevertheless, he'd decided that it was preferable to let her believe him dead.

Tom couldn't muster a great deal of patience with the man in the wake of such a decision.

"We'd be wise to go before the monsoon sets in," Giles said. "Unless the pair of you intend on putting up here until November."

Jenny lowered her glass of wine from her lips. "November? Heavens, no. Mr. Finchley must be back in London before the summer."

"Must he?" Giles fixed Tom with a cool stare. "Are the summer months particularly busy in your line of work?"

Tom looked back at him steadily. "No more than reason."

Jenny frowned at Giles from across the table. "Mr. Finchley has a friend in poor health. He's needed back sooner rather than later."

"How much sooner?"

Tom speared a piece of curried chicken with his fork. "If we leave in two days' time, we can meet the bullock train and be back in Siliguri by midweek. From there, it's less than four hundred miles to Calcutta. We can wire ahead to book passage on a steamship to take us to Port Suez."

Giles's own fork froze halfway to his mouth. "Have it all planned out, do you?"

In fact, Tom had. He'd been talking it over with Ahmad for days, and Ahmad had—in turn—been speaking to the *dak* drivers and the grooms. "Do you have a better idea?"

"None at all. I'm glad to leave the travel arrangements in your capable hands. So long as you understand that Hossein must remain with me at all times. My injury demands it."

"Of course." Tom had observed the way Giles's servant assisted him. Hossein was equal parts valet, cook, companion, and nursemaid. He even cut Giles's meat into bitesize portions to save him the ignominy of asking for assistance at the table.

Tom couldn't imagine what it must be like adjusting to life with only one arm. It wasn't merely the aesthetics of it, though to a gentleman as handsome as Giles, that surely must be a concern. It was the more mundane aspects of the condition that inspired Tom's compassion. The fact that basic tasks—the things one did each day without even thinking, like unbuttoning a button or slicing into a roast—must now seem a struggle.

Doubtless, Giles was still coming to terms with the injury. Tom wondered if it was one of the reasons he hadn't gone home.

"I don't know about Hossein," Jenny said, "but Ahmad and Mira will be glad to leave India. They haven't enjoyed it here as much as I'd hoped they might. It's not at all the way they remember it being when they were children."

Giles glanced up at her from his plate. "They're from Delhi, aren't they? They'd feel differently if they'd lived here."

"Is life so much better in Darjeeling?" Tom asked.

"On the ridge it is. One rarely encounters the tension one feels in the cities."

Jenny helped herself to more curry. "It seems to me that one rarely encounters anything here. It's all trees and mountains and empty fields."

"One of its many benefits." Giles refilled his glass. He looked to Jenny, brows lifted in question, as he held the bottle of wine. She gave him a short nod. He tipped the bottle over her glass, filling it to the brim. "The new location in the valley is less isolated. It will be better for the tea. Less so for my own peace of mind. I'd prefer to remain up here."

"It's not very convenient," Tom said.

"For whom? For visitors to Senchal? That's never been a pressing concern. You're the first I've had since I arrived here. No one has called since the cholera outbreak. They've no reason to."

Tom didn't wonder. "A Khansama at one of the stations told us that the isolation was unhealthy. That many of the soldiers brought to the convalescent depot after the uprising didn't recover."

Giles resumed eating. "I wouldn't know anything about that."

Jenny exchanged a worried look with Tom.

Catering to Giles was taking its toll on her. He wasn't the easiest of gentlemen to interact with. He was subject to moods and prone to sharp words and cold silences.

Was this how he'd been when he was younger? When Jenny had first come to work as Lady Helena's companion? If so, Tom could understand why she'd been so desirous to get away.

"You've lived alone here far too long with only Hossein for company," Jenny said. "It won't be easy to come back into society, but in time—"

"I won't be staying in England for any length of time," Giles replied. "And I've certainly no intention of going about in society."

"You plan to come back here?" Tom asked. "To the ridge?"

"I do. It will be enough to see my sister. To satisfy myself that she's well settled with this husband of hers. As for my uncle..." Giles's fingers tightened on his wineglass. "He and I must have words, obviously."

A long silence hung between the three of them.

When conversation at last resumed, it was nothing of the personal. They spoke of the food and the weather, discussing

India in general terms until the candles burned down and the room drifted into darkness.

Jenny moved to rise. "Shall we go into the parlor for tea? Or would the two of you prefer I leave you to a glass of port?"

Tom and Giles both stood. Tom expected they'd join Jenny. There was no reason to stand on ceremony.

But Giles had other ideas. "Yes, let's share a bottle, by all means, Finchley."

Jenny exchanged another wary glance with Tom. "Well, I'll leave the pair of you to it."

When she'd gone, Giles summoned Hossein to clear the table and bring them a bottle of port and two glasses. "You don't smoke, do you, Finchley?" he asked when the servant had withdrawn.

"I don't." Tom regarded Giles over the sputtering candles. He had no illusions about the man wishing to bond with him over tobacco and port. "Is there something you'd like to say to me?"

"There is." Giles filled both glasses, pushing one across the table to Tom with the tip of his finger. "Miss Holloway appears to be rather fond of you."

"I count her as a friend."

"A *dear* friend, she says."

Had she? The knowledge sent a frisson of warmth through Tom's veins. "We've been traveling together for some time. It's only natural that we've become close."

"I trust that nothing untoward has happened between the two of you?" Giles gave a thin smile. "I'm not blind, Finchley, whatever my failings. I've seen the way you look at each other. It's all very romantic, I'm sure, but I'm afraid I must put a stop to it. You see, despite the intervening years, I still consider Miss Holloway my responsibility."

Tom didn't flinch. He'd spent decades dealing with high-handed men who sought to dictate terms to him. "And I consider that you abdicated that responsibility."

"When I failed to return home?"

"No," Tom said. "When you took advantage of her."

Giles went still. "She told you about that, did she?" He downed a swallow of port. "A youthful impulse. There was no harm done."

"I've read the letter of apology you sent. Clearly you knew you'd crossed a line."

"Are you always so puritanical, Finchley? One would think you'd never stolen a kiss from a pretty girl before. Not every embrace ends at the altar, you know. If it did, the lot of us would be wed at a much younger age—and to females of far less desirable pedigree."

"She was your sister's companion. An employee in your household."

Giles exhaled. "It was a long time ago. And it isn't as if Miss Holloway holds a grudge. If she did, she'd hardly have come all this way to find me, would she?"

"What she's done, she's done for Lady Helena, not for you."

"I see. You've appointed yourself her protector. Very admirable of you, I'm sure, but if you're intending to seek some manner of satisfaction on her behalf—to challenge me to fisticuffs or a duel over her honor—you're well out of luck. Unless, that is, you'd stoop to fight a one-armed man."

"Don't be ridiculous. I've no intention of fighting you." The very idea was ludicrous, as well as completely lacking in imagination. Tom had never been one to rely on brute physical strength to achieve his ends. "But I do expect that there will be no repeat of your misconduct with Miss Holloway. No more affectionate familiarities. No more casual disrespect."

"Or else?"

Tom said nothing. He didn't have to.

"Ah." Giles set his glass back on the table. "In other words, if I meddle with Miss Holloway, you'll treat me to a taste of the hell you visited on the Earl of Warren." He gave a sudden laugh. "And here I thought I was the one who was going to be issuing *you* a warning."

"There's no need," Tom said. "Miss Holloway has nothing to fear from me."

Giles reached for the bottle of port. "Doesn't she?"

Chapter Twenty-Five

Cairo, Egypt
May, 1860

"Shepheard's Hotel looks different than I remember," Jenny remarked as she crossed through the arched lobby at Giles's side.

It was a now familiar refrain. She must have uttered a similar sentiment dozens of times during the course of their journey from Darjeeling to Cairo. The bullock train was different. The *dak* carts were different. The three-week steamship voyage from Calcutta to Suez was different.

And it *had* been different, in the most acutely painful way. There'd been no romance. No hand-holding or stolen kisses. There were none of the private talks she'd had with Tom during the journey to India. No moonlit walks on the spar deck or shared confidences in her cabin.

During the past four weeks they'd had no privacy. Indeed, Jenny didn't think she'd spent a single moment alone with Tom. How could she with Giles there? It wasn't so much that she cared what Giles thought of her conduct, but that he made her visible in a way she hadn't been before. Everything about him and about the party with whom he traveled was worthy of notice. Details of how they looked, what they said, and what they did would no doubt be related in London for the next year or more.

The 6th Earl of Castleton had returned from the dead.

It was an extraordinary event. Even those who had never known him—those on the ship with only a peripheral connection to the aristocracy—had feted him like a conquering hero.

And Jenny was all at once no longer Tom's make-believe half sister. She was Giles's cousin. Not his sister's companion. Not an employee in his household. But a family member worthy of respect.

"My cousin, Miss Holloway," as he'd taken to introducing her.

It had had the desired effect.

As for Tom, he'd still been there to look at and to talk to, as dear to her as ever, but the intimacy between them was gone. It had ended that day in the clearing on Senchal Ridge. They'd left it behind in the mist and fog. After four weeks, the memory of it seemed so much a dream.

Did Tom feel the same?

Jenny couldn't tell. He walked along at her side, clad in a plain gray suit, his hands clasped behind his back. She hadn't taken his arm in a very long while. It was Giles who escorted her now. Everything right and proper and stifling to her very soul.

"It's no wonder it looks different," Tom said. "The last time we were here, we arrived in the dead of night."

"And when we left the next morning, it was dawn. I remember." She smiled at him. "You told me I could sleep all the way to Port Suez."

Tom held her gaze for a heartbeat longer than necessary. His blue eyes were solemn. Was he thinking of their journey to Suez? How he'd held her in his arms as she slept? How they'd kissed each other with such desperation? "You won't be leaving with us in the morning this time," he said.

"No." She tried to keep her voice light. "Unlike the two of you, when dawn breaks tomorrow, I shall remain comfortably abed."

On that score, she was at least partially assured. Shepheard's was nothing if not comfortable. The lobby was testament enough to that with its floors carpeted in soft Oriental rugs and its plush chairs, couches, and inlaid taborets half-hidden by strategically placed palms.

Here and there a porter garbed in magnificent green and gold livery rushed to assist a guest or to murmur instructions to one of the Arab servants—gentlemen who were no less impressively clad in starched white linen with broad red girdles at their waists.

The whole of Shepheard's was an oasis from the heat. Quiet and cool, every private nook and cranny beckoning one to relax and take one's ease.

"Are you still certain you wish to remain here?" Giles asked. "Cairo isn't the ideal city for a lady to—"

"We've discussed this already," she said under her breath. "You know my feelings on the matter."

"Yes, yes, but a female has the prerogative to change her mind."

"My mind is quite made up, thank you."

"Can't you talk her out of it, Finchley?" Giles asked.

Tom didn't answer.

Jenny chewed her lower lip. If she didn't know any better, she'd think he was angry at her. But he wasn't. He couldn't be. It was merely that his distant behavior felt like coldness when compared to the closeness they'd shared only last month.

He accompanied them as far as their rooms—all three adjoining on the third floor. But as the porter unlocked Jenny's door, Tom withdrew.

"I've a few letters to post and a wire to send to Thornhill," he said. "If you'll excuse me?"

He was gone all the rest of the day and even through dinner, leaving the seat reserved for him at their table in Shepheard's dining room conspicuously empty. As night fell, stark reality began to sink in.

Tom wasn't going to say goodbye to her.

"Can't say as I blame him," Giles remarked. "I never did care for them myself. Those protracted farewells with women weeping and waving handkerchiefs at the docks."

Jenny swallowed the last bite of her curry. She might as well have been eating sawdust. "He knows I wouldn't have done that."

Or so she hoped.

Then again, she'd made enough of a spectacle of herself in Delhi to frighten off even the bravest man. The way she'd wept at the thought of him leaving her. She was mortified to think of it now.

Had Tom feared she'd make a similar scene?

If so, she supposed she couldn't blame him for avoiding her.

"Men like Finchley aren't much for gallantry," Giles said. "But he's efficient enough in other respects to compensate. He's seen you have access to your funds? And that all your papers are in order?"

"Yes. Everything is as it should be."

"Excellent. When I come back this way, I'll look in on you, shall I? Helena will want to be satisfied that you're all right."

"By all means. I'm sure in a few months' time I'll welcome the sight of a familiar face."

"A few months." Giles swallowed the remainder of his wine. "I pray my obligations in town will keep me no longer."

Jenny gave him a look of commiseration. The journey had been hard on Giles. He'd tolerated the society only because he must, not because he enjoyed it. Indeed, on the steamship, she'd often seen him looking haggard and gray—as if he couldn't bear another moment of all the noise and incessant company. "You'll be back in Darjeeling before you know it."

"What about you? Do you think to see England again? Or India?"

"I have no set plans."

Giles didn't interrogate her. He'd done enough of that on the ship. "Well, if any woman can make a go of it out here, I daresay it would be you. Just see you don't befriend any more morally suspect solicitors or other unsavory types. Next time it might not turn out so well for you."

"You presume it turned out well this time."

He fixed her with a coolly appraising stare. "You're all in one piece, aren't you?"

Jenny didn't feel as though she was in one piece after her adventure with Tom. Rather the opposite. Her heart had been breaking by degrees ever since they left Darjeeling.

After bidding goodnight to Giles and wishing him safe journey for his morning departure, she retired to her room. Mira wasn't there. She'd gone out with Ahmad to visit the bazaar and then to dinner. The hotel room was shadowed and empty, the heart of it dimly lit by a set of oil lamps with black-and-gold-striped shades.

For the first time in weeks, Jenny felt entirely alone.

Until now, she'd been able to keep reality at bay through constant activity. There'd been no opportunity to dwell on her imminent parting from Tom. She'd thought—or rather, hoped—that they would have time enough yet to say goodbye. That there would be an opportunity to explain how she felt about him—and to articulate more fully why it was she wished to stay.

Tom had plainly had other ideas.

Perhaps he'd thought it would be easier to avoid her? To forego a painful farewell in lieu of a gradual fading away?

Jenny tried to remember the last personal thing he'd said to her, but she couldn't recall it. They hadn't shared a private moment since leaving Darjeeling. How could they have when they were under such constant scrutiny?

She spent the next hour readying herself for bed, unpinning and brushing her hair and changing out of her dinner dress and into her nightgown and wrapper.

Her stomach was in knots, her muscles taut with tension. It wasn't in her nature to sit back and let things happen to her. She wasn't that sort of woman. Would *never* be that sort of woman. Tom must know that by now.

And if he did, he wouldn't be at all surprised if she visited him in his room.

It was a scandalous thought, the likes of which turned the knots in her stomach to rampaging butterflies. Indeed, as she crossed the sitting room to her door, she felt more than a little ill. But there was nothing for it. It was either this or let Tom depart Cairo without saying goodbye. And the latter simply wasn't an option.

She reached for the doorknob, steeling herself for the task ahead.

In that same instant, a soft rap sounded against the door.

Her heart nearly leapt out of her chest. It was an effort to calm its erratic beating. She took a breath and then another. It was past nine. Surely it was only Mira returning from the bazaar.

But it wasn't. Something in her knew it wasn't.

Sure enough, when she cracked open the door, it was to find Tom standing there, his hair rumpled and his leather attaché case in hand.

He looked at her, seeming to take in her unbound hair and prim white dressing gown in one comprehensive glance. "May I come in?"

"Of course." She stood back to allow him entry.

He shut the door behind him and turned the lock. "I apologize for the lateness of the hour. I'd thought to be back by dinner, but everything took longer than I expected."

"Everything? What everything?"

"Shall we sit down?"

She tightened the sash of her dressing gown, feeling a sudden flush of embarrassment to be standing before him in her nightclothes. "If you like."

At the opposite side of the sitting room, two velvet upholstered chairs flanked a taboret. Tom turned them to face the small inlaid table, waiting for her to sit down before taking a seat himself.

He withdrew a sheaf of papers from his attaché case. "No doubt you'll think me high-handed."

She leaned forward. "What are these?"

"The particulars of several houses I looked at today. I haven't let one for you. I wouldn't presume to without your approval. But I've found three suitable options. Each are well within your budget, as well as being safe and—"

She gaped at him. "That's where you've been today? Trying to find a house for me?"

"In large part, yes."

"Why didn't you tell me? I would have come with you."

"For the same reason we haven't been alone together since leaving India. It wouldn't have been proper, the two of us perusing houses together." He turned over another paper. "I won't do any more harm to your reputation. You'll need to be above reproach if you're to remain in good stead with the other British residents of the city. If there's a hint of scandal—"

"How does coming to my hotel room figure into this plan of yours?"

"No one saw me enter."

She pushed a stray lock of curling hair back from her face. "I thought you were avoiding me. I'd just resolved to visit your room when you knocked."

Tom's brows lifted. "Dressed like that?"

"Why not? You've seen me in less."

A faint blush crept up his neck. "Jenny, I—"

"I wish you would have told me where it was you were going today. It would have saved me a great deal of worry. You know I'm always prone to think the worst."

"Even now? Even with me?"

"Especially with you. It's odd really, given the circumstances, but I don't think I could bear it if you thought ill of me."

"You have nothing to worry about on that score. If you don't realize that by now—"

"I realize it. I do. It's only that…we haven't been alone together since Darjeeling. I can feel the distance between us widening every day. Which is as it should be, I know, but… there are times when I find it rather hard."

His gaze sharpened behind the lenses of his spectacles. "Are you having second thoughts about staying?"

"No, indeed. I'm just a little melancholy over saying goodbye to you. It will be easier once I'm settled." She lifted one of the papers. Tom's neat, even handwriting covered the page. The sight of it made her heart ache. "You've been very thorough."

"I've tried to be."

"How did you navigate the city? Ahmad can't have helped. He doesn't speak Arabic. Not that I'm aware."

"I hired a dragoman—a native translator. There are dozens of them hanging about the lobby. I've taken the liberty of engaging one for you." Tom drew her attention to another piece of paper. "His name is Achmet. An older chap. Reliable, as far as I can tell. I negotiated a rate of fifteen piastres a day, which equates to roughly five francs. Well within your budget. He'll be at your disposal for as long as you need him."

She looked up at him, tears stinging at the back of her eyes. "You've thought of everything."

"I couldn't very well leave you here without knowing you'd have a chance at suitable lodging and a decent interpreter."

"Thank you, Tom. I'm in your debt."

"Any solicitor would have done the same for his client."

The impersonal nature of his words chilled her to the bone. If he'd meant them to be reassuring, he'd failed miserably. All she felt was diminished. As if what he'd done had been purely a matter of form. "I don't know about that," she said. "But I thank you for your efforts all the same."

"Not at all." He moved to rise. "Well, I think that's everything."

A jolt of alarm shot through her. "Not quite everything, surely."

Tom went still. "No. Not quite." After a long moment, he reached into the pocket of his trousers and withdrew a small wooden box. He set it on the inlaid table. "This is for you."

An uncertain smile tugged at her mouth. "Something you found at the bazaar?"

"No. Something I've been carrying around with me for months. I bought it that evening in Calcutta when we went to the Chowringhee Road."

Her hands trembled inexplicably as she opened the little box. What she saw inside made her tremble all the more.

It was a ring. A single rose-cut diamond set on a delicately woven band of gold.

Her mouth went dry. "Is this...?"

"At one time I meant it as an engagement ring, but now..." He cleared his throat. "I'd as soon you have it as me carrying it around for the rest of my life."

She lifted it from the box with tentative fingers. The diamond twinkled in the dim light. It was beautiful. Far more beautiful than anything she'd ever conjured in one of her childhood daydreams about handsome princes and romantic proposals. "It's lovely, but...you know I can't accept it."

"Why not? I want nothing from you in return. No promises. I realize this is goodbye."

Jenny's eyes met his. His face was taut, his jaw gone stiff with tension. He looked tired and…anguished. Emotion welled in her throat. "I wanted to explain—"

"What's to explain? You've made your feelings abundantly clear."

"You're angry with me."

"I'm not angry, I'm…" He exhaled a short gust of breath. "I don't know what I am."

"Tom—"

"I suppose I'm feeling sorry for myself. Wishing things were different."

She put the ring back in the box and slowly replaced the lid. "You don't have to go away tomorrow. You could stay here a little while longer—"

"But I can't. My work is in London. Fothergill. My clients. All the people who depend on me. I've built a life there for myself. To leave it now—to drop everything and roam the world with you on a whim—would be nothing short of madness."

"Not if you cared for me more than all the rest of it."

The words were out before she could call them back. She'd have given anything not to have said them.

Tom's expression hardened. "What about you? If you cared for me even a fraction of the way I—"

"That's not fair. Not when you know how much it means to me to have my independence."

"You wouldn't have to give up your independence if you came home."

"That's *exactly* what I'd be giving up. And having done so, I'd be no happier with you in England than you'd be with me, roaming the world on a whim as you called it."

"You could be happy there if you'd let yourself."

He sounded so sure of himself. So certain that he knew what was best for her.

It should have exasperated her, but it didn't. Indeed, the brief flare of irritation she'd felt toward him evaporated as swiftly as it had come. Now all she felt was heartsick and defeated. "We'd be content together for a time, certainly," she conceded. "But what about a year from now? What about all the years to come? I couldn't bear to see the feelings I have for you turn to hatred."

Tom gave her one of his unreadable looks. "Could you hate me, Jenny?"

"I daresay I could hate anyone who took away my freedom. Who made a prisoner of me."

"A prisoner?" He rose from his seat. "Good God. To hear you talk, one would think you'd been subjected to the worst forms of mistreatment."

She stood. "I never claimed so."

He crossed to the center of the room only to turn and face her, his rigid features shadowed in the light of one of the oil lamps. "Do you know, I don't even believe it's the desire for independence that drives you. When it all comes down to it, what you are is afraid. You believe that all men are as unreliable as your father and brothers. As careless of your tender feelings as Giles. You're afraid of being hurt. Afraid some fellow will let you down. But I'm not like them. I've never been like them. If you don't recognize it by now—"

"Of course I recognize it. I esteem you above any gentleman I've ever met, but—"

"You *esteem* me," he scoffed.

"Yes," she retorted sharply. Her hand found its way to her necklace. The memory of how it had felt to stand there, weeping and pleading, as her father plundered her trinket case sent a jolt of nausea through her. "And you're wrong about it being fear that drives me. It's self-preservation. I won't give up my rights over myself to anyone, particularly not to a man who could take away my money and property at the snap of his fingers. Who could rob me of my ability to go where I like when I like. Who could have me confined against my will to a country house in the back of beyond, or worse, committed to an asylum as Helena's uncle tried to do to her."

"Do you believe even for a moment that I'd do any of those things to you?"

"No," she said. "But you could. You *could*. And the law would be entirely on your side." And then what would she do? In past times of trouble, Tom had come to her rescue. But what if Tom became her adversary? What if his feelings faded and all that was left was the ruthless man that Giles had described to her? A man determined to win at all costs? She'd be powerless against him, in law as well as in fact.

"I wouldn't touch your money Jenny. And I'd sure as hell never threaten to have you committed. For God's sake. Not all men are conscienceless monsters."

"And I'm supposed to take it all on faith, am I? To cede control of everything to you." She folded her arms to stop their shaking. "What would you be giving up for me? From where I stand, it seems you're unwilling to change your life at all for my sake."

"It's not the same thing."

"Because you're a man."

"No!" he exclaimed. "Because I'm not going to alter myself any more than I already have. I've had enough in my life of trying to conform to someone else's ideal. Of believing that if only I were richer, smarter, or more handsome, then perhaps I'd be worthy of affection, or God forbid, love. I won't do it anymore. Not with you. If you can't accept me as I am—"

She reached him in two strides and took his hard jaw in her hands. It seemed a vast presumption in the midst of such an argument. Even more so after having gone an entire month without touching him in any way more familiar than the occasional hand on his sleeve.

Tom broke off midsentence on a harsh intake of breath. His eyes were riveted to hers as she stared up at him.

Her voice softened with tenderness. She couldn't bear him to think he wasn't good enough. "You're talking nonsense," she said. "I'm not Mrs. Culpepper or any of those other short-sighted fools from your past. You don't have to change anything about yourself to earn my regard."

His fingers closed gently around her wrists. A glimmer of hope shone in his face. "Jenny…"

"But I can't be the only one to compromise. I can't turn myself into something I'm not just to please you. It's no fairer of you to ask it of me than it would be for me to ask it of you. Surely you must see that?"

The hope flickered and died, leaving his countenance cold. He very deliberately removed her hands from his face. "What I see is that this was a mistake."

Jenny's heart stopped in her breast. "This," she repeated. "Do you mean coming here tonight? Or do you mean us?"

"Both, probably. All of it. All the time we spent together." He moved away from her. The distance was no more than a step, but it felt as wide as a mile. "A proper courtship starts with an understanding. An acknowledgment of shared goals. But you and I…we've done this all backward."

"It was never a courtship."

"No, it wasn't. I shouldn't have suggested that we explore this attraction to each other. It was wrong of me. Deeply wrong."

"How can you say so? Unless you're speaking of morality. Some idea you have that the intimacies we've shared must be confined to a marriage. In which case——"

"I'm not talking about morality. I'm saying that I was fool to believe I could ever be satisfied with half of you. This thing between us, it's all or nothing, Jenny. It's always been all or nothing. I realized it from the moment we kissed that night on the deck of the *Indus*. It scared the devil out of me. I should have known then that I was in over my head. Feelings like these...one can't dip in and out of them as one pleases. They mean too much. To me, anyway."

She blinked rapidly, her eyes stinging worse than ever. "To me as well."

"Then you understand."

"Yes, but...I didn't expect..."

"Nor did I." He gave an eloquent grimace. "If you only knew the tortuous turn my thoughts have taken of late. It's lucky you exacted that promise from me on the train to Marseilles. If you hadn't..."

"What?"

"I've thought of hundreds of ways of manipulating you into coming home. Of trapping you and forcing your hand. Why else do you think I encouraged you to go to Jhansi? I never really expected we'd find Giles alive. The odds seemed too slight. All I wanted was more time with you. I thought——"

"You thought that I'd change my mind."

"Yes." He gave her a bleak look. "That you'd decide I was worth it."

Tears welled in her eyes. "It has nothing to do with your worth. It never has. It has to do with mine. I don't want to spend the rest of my life wondering who I might have been if only I'd had a little time on my own. A chance to exert myself in a manner of my own choosing without reference to the expectations of a father or a brother or an employer. Without that, how could I ever commit myself to anyone? It wouldn't be fair to you or to myself."

He turned his face from her, taking a discreet swipe at his cheek. "I do understand."

Jenny's chest tightened. The thought of him shedding even a single tear over her was enough to splinter her already broken heart into a million pieces.

"I've been thinking of our dilemma the whole of this last month," he said, his deep voice roughened with emotion. "Imagining all the different ways I could fight to win you. It's a rather romantic daydream. Fighting for the woman you care about. But somewhere between Darjeeling and Suez I came to a rather depressing realization. If I fought, I wouldn't be fighting *for* you. I'd be fighting against you. Because staying here—remaining unmarried and independent—is a course you've chosen of your own free will."

"It is." She reminded herself that it was what she wanted. What she'd *always* wanted. To be free and beholden to no one. "But I never meant to hurt you."

"We've hurt each other. If I had it to do over again, I—" He broke off. "But there's no turning back the clock. I can only go forward."

"Back to London."

"It's where I belong." His blue eyes glistened. "I'll be there if you need me. If a problem arises—something with the house or with your letter of credit—you've only to send me a wire."

"I will, I promise. And I'll write to you as well. Unless...
unless you don't wish it."

He swallowed hard. "Perhaps we should give it some time."

"Yes, of course." Her voice quavered. But though a sob
rose in her throat, she wouldn't permit herself to make a scene.
"We should take a while to get our bearings."

He held her gaze. For a long moment it seemed as though
he would say something else—something important—but
when he spoke there was a stark finality to his words. "The
train leaves early. I'd better..."

"Yes, you'd better go."

He gave the hotel room an unseeing glance. "I hate to
leave you on your own. Will Ahmad and Mira—"

"They'll be back soon."

"Good." He collected his attaché case, taking the moment
to give another irritated swipe at his face. His voice deepened. "You'll keep them with you, I trust."

"I will."

"And you won't wander about the city on your own or
take any unnecessary risks?"

"I'll be fine. You can stop worrying about me."

He met her eyes one last time. His mouth hitched in a
brief smile. "Impossible."

She dashed a spill of hot tears from her cheeks with her
hands. But she didn't beg him to stay. She wouldn't. "Goodbye,
Tom."

"Goodbye, Jenny," he said. "I wish you well. Most sincerely."

And with that, he was gone. Gone from her room and
gone from her life.

She sank down on the edge of the bed and wept.

Chapter Twenty-Six

North Devon, England
May, 1860

It took nine days to reach Dover, and another day by train to reach North Devon. Tom and Giles emerged onto the platform at the railway station in Abbott's Holcombe to find Justin Thornhill's elderly steward, Mr. Boothroyd, waiting for them with a carriage and four.

Small, gray-haired, and bespectacled, Boothroyd had once been secretary to Sir Oswald Bannister. He wasn't a sentimental man, but he'd nevertheless done his best to make up for the evil of his former employer. It was he who had arranged for Tom to be articled to Mr. Fothergill. He'd even arranged for apprenticeships for Neville, Justin, and Alex Archer—all to no avail.

The fact that Boothroyd now worked for Justin was yet another aspect of his penance. Tom should have honored him for it. At least the man was trying to right the wrongs of the past. But the sight of Boothroyd did nothing but remind him of things he'd rather forget.

Indeed, in his present mood, Tom would have preferred to have gone straight to London. The sights and sounds of North Devon only served to exacerbate the heavy weight of melancholy he'd been bearing since parting from Jenny in Cairo.

It was the lowest he could remember feeling since he was a boy in the orphanage. The sense of powerlessness—of utter desolation—was so acute that the entirety of the steamship journey from Alexandria to Marseilles had passed in a blur. So too had the rail journey to Calais and the Channel crossing to Dover. Nothing served to rouse Tom from his black mood.

What he needed was work, and lots of it.

But that was going to have to wait a few days longer. For now, duty required that he remain in North Devon.

"Who is this, then?" Giles muttered to him.

Tom performed the necessary introductions, too preoccupied with his own unhappiness to feel any amusement when Boothroyd did all but tug his forelock to the newly resurrected earl.

"It's an honor to welcome you to Devon, my lord," he said, rising from a deep bow. "Lady Helena and Mr. Thornhill would have come to meet you personally, but Mr. Thornhill anticipates an emotional reunion. He thought it best such a scene be reserved for the privacy of the Abbey."

"Wise of him." Giles glanced over his shoulder to address Hossein in brief Hindustani. The manservant had stuck to him like glue throughout their journey. Tom didn't know what Giles would have done without the fellow. He relied on him to an unimaginable degree. "My valet, Hossein," Giles said, turning back to Boothroyd. "He'll attend to my bags."

"Of course, my lord."

They waited while a burly footman from the Abby lashed their trunks to the outside of the carriage with sturdy ropes. When finished, he held the door while Tom, Boothroyd, Giles, and Hossein climbed in.

"Is it far from here?" Giles asked.

"Thirteen miles of good road." Tom withdrew his pocket watch from his waistcoat and checked the time. "We'll be there in time for luncheon."

The weather was cool and brisk off of the sea, with strong northerly winds that buffeted the carriage as they traveled. It was a newer vehicle, glossy black with a green velvet and leather interior. Nothing like the ramshackle carriage Justin had been using when Tom last visited the Abbey.

Jenny had said that Lady Helena had made several improvements there. New paint, paper, and furnishings. Tom couldn't imagine it. The Abbey had always been such a stark place. As cold and unwelcoming as the bleak cliffs that lined the coast from the resort town of Abbott's Holcombe to the small village of King's Abbott.

"Mr. Thornhill only just received your wire from Egypt three days ago," Boothroyd said. "When your wire from Dover came this morning, the house went into an uproar. We were all of us at sixes and sevens, as you can imagine."

Giles gazed out the window at the passing scenery, seemingly unperturbed by the chaos his arrival might have caused. Whatever emotions he felt at the prospect of reuniting with his sister were concealed behind the same cold, aristocratic mask he often wore in times of stress.

Tom leaned back in his seat as Boothroyd continued talking. He was tired, drained of every ounce of energy or will. It made sudden sense to him now what it was that compelled lovelorn gentlemen to drink to excess—to brawl and carouse and generally make pathetic fools of themselves.

Pity he hadn't that to look forward to, at least. A few weeks of drunken oblivion. But Tom didn't do anything to excess, not drinking and certainly not brawling. The only matters in his life on which he'd ever exerted an overabundance of zeal were those with some relation to the law. In every other aspect of his life he'd been careful. Cautious. Never daring to make himself vulnerable.

Until Jenny.

There was nothing careful about his feelings for her. He loved her, fully and too well. If he didn't, he'd have had no compunction about forcing her to come back with him. Instead, he'd let her go. It was the most difficult thing he'd ever done in his life.

Tom didn't regret his decision. It had been the right thing to do. The only thing to do. But that didn't stop him from revisiting their final meeting—reviewing it over and over—torturing himself with the memory of it until his heart was bruised from the constant pummeling.

If he closed his eyes, he could still feel the soft curve of her hands as they framed his face. Could still hear her words, so fierce and tender.

You don't have to change anything about yourself to earn my regard.

But it wouldn't do to dwell on such things. He'd fixated on them enough over the past nine days. It was past time for him to move on. Not to forget her. How could he? But to stop brooding over what might have been and look to his future.

"Will you be staying long with us, Mr. Finchley?" Boothroyd asked.

Tom roused himself to answer. "A day or two at most. I'm needed in London straightaway. I'd like to catch the morning train if possible."

It was the last thing he said until an hour and a half later when the carriage turned onto the narrow cliff road that led up to Greyfriar's Abbey.

"Rather reminds one of the road to Senchal," Giles remarked.

Tom cast a fleeting glance out the window. The wheels of the carriage were mere inches from the edge, stones crumbling and falling beneath them to the foaming surf below. Dangerous as it was, it was nothing like the road to Senchal Ridge. Then, he'd had Jenny by his side. "The Abbey isn't the most accessible of places," he said. "When the rains come, this road often washes out entirely."

"And my sister doesn't mind it?" Giles snorted. "Singular."

Boothroyd hastened to defend his master's home. "Lady Helena is quite content at the Abbey, I assure you, my lord. She and Mr. Thornhill prefer it to residing in London."

"Have they a home in town?" Giles asked.

"They have a house on lease in Half Moon Street," Tom said. "They stayed there for a time during the business with your uncle."

Giles grunted in response before resuming his silent stare out the carriage window.

The cliff road was the only point of access to the Abbey. It ascended along a track just wide enough for a coach and four, curving as it went beneath the branches of trees and shrubs that grew at all angles from the cliff face. It was a good half an hour before they reached even ground. When they did, the coachman urged the horses to a faster pace. The well-sprung carriage rolled smoothly behind them, veering to the left through a sparse woodland before finally slowing as it rounded the curve of the drive.

Greyfriar's Abbey stood in the distance, only a stone wall protecting it from a sheer drop down to the open sea. It had been built on the remains of a twelfth-century monastery, and with its steeply pitched roof, pointed arches, and Gothic tower, it was as bleak and gray as the barren landscape that surrounded it.

The last time Tom had visited, it had been surrounded with heaps of stone—evidence of the repairs Justin had been making to the antiquated structure. Now, however, there were no signs of ongoing construction. The drive was comprised of newly laid stones, and the steps leading to the front entrance were flanked by beds of flowers, rife with blooms of blue, red, and yellow.

Greyfriar's Abbey no longer looked like an abandoned relic. It looked like a home. A rather dramatic home, to be sure, but a home nonetheless.

The carriage came to a halt at the front steps, and the footman leapt down from the box to open the door. Tom climbed out after Boothroyd. The roar of the sea and the incessant squawking of seagulls circling overhead briefly drowned out the sound of the front doors of the Abbey opening. It took a moment for him to realize that Justin and Lady Helena had come out onto the steps.

Ex-army captain Justin Thornhill was a tall man, his lean, broad-shouldered frame towering over Tom's more moderate height. With his black hair, gray eyes, and strongly chiseled features, he might have been handsome if he wasn't so damnably intimidating. The burn scars on his face and neck—souvenirs of the torture he'd suffered while being held prisoner in India—didn't help to soften his appearance.

What helped was the presence of his wife, Lady Helena. She stood at his side, her hand tucked in his, as beautiful and elegant as Justin was piratical. Her wide hazel eyes were riveted to the open door of the carriage.

Giles emerged from the interior of the cab, climbing down the carriage steps with the help of Hossein. At first he didn't seem to register his sister's presence.

And then he raised his head and looked up.

The instant he set eyes on her, his aristocratic mask fell away.

Helena dropped Justin's hand, clutching her skirts as she ran down the steps and threw her arms around her brother's neck.

Tom couldn't hear what she said to him. Whatever it was, it made tears spill from Giles's eyes.

"There, there, love," he murmured, his arm coming around her waist. "I'm home now. I'm home."

Tom climbed the steps to join Justin. He hadn't made any move to interfere with his wife greeting her long-lost brother. He only watched the pair of them, brows lowered in a frown.

"You don't approve," Tom said.

Justin glanced at him. "Where the hell has he been?"

"Hiding in India."

"Hiding from what?"

"Reality, I assume."

Justin's expression darkened. "I could break him in half for what he's put her through."

"Probably not the best idea." Tom paused. "Not yet, anyway."

Lady Helena turned her brother toward the steps. "Giles, may I present my husband, Mr. Justin Thornhill?" She looked up at Justin, tears of joy glistening in her eyes. "Justin? This is my brother, Giles Reynolds, 6th Earl of Castleton."

Justin descended the steps and extended his hand to Giles. "Welcome to Greyfriar's Abbey."

Giles shook Justin's hand. "I believe I owe you a debt of gratitude for looking after my sister."

"Helena is my wife. You owe me nothing."

Lady Helena found Tom's eyes. "How can I ever thank you for what you've done?"

Tom smiled. "It wasn't me. It was all Jenny."

"*Jenny?*" Justin echoed under his breath.

A dull flush heated Tom's neck. "Miss Holloway, I mean." He endeavored to keep his tone businesslike. "This is all her doing. I was merely there in my capacity as her solicitor."

Lady Helena exchanged an unreadable glance with her husband before meeting Tom's eyes once more. "Where is she?"

"In Cairo, if you can believe it." Giles thrust his hand into his waistcoat and withdrew a folded scrap of paper. "She tasked me with giving you this letter."

Tom jerked to attention. *A letter?* When had Jenny given Giles a letter? And, more importantly, what the devil did it say?

Helena cracked open the seal. As she read the missive, a smile brightened her tearstained face. When she'd finished, she folded it back together. After a moment of hesitation, she extended it to Tom. "Would you care to read it?"

He should decline. It would be the gentlemanly thing to do. But he was too hungry for news of Jenny to do anything but take it.

As Giles and Lady Helena made their way up the steps, Giles introducing his sister to Hossein and Thornhill ordering the servants about, Tom trailed behind them, opening Jenny's letter and devouring it in one go.

> *My dearest Helena,*
>
> *Against your wishes, I have decided to remain abroad for a time. But I trust you won't be too unhappy with my decision, for I have sent you a gift in care of Mr. Finchley that I think will please you beyond measure.*
>
> *To that end, you should know who was ultimately responsible for returning your brother to you. Mr. Finchley will doubtless say it was I who found Giles. The truth is, it was my manservant, Ahmad Malik, who discovered the vital clue that led us to Darjeeling and it is to him you should convey a reward—if reward there be.*
>
> *By the by, Mr. Malik has a distinct talent for dressmaking. I do believe, if set up in his own London establishment, he could one day rival Charles Frederick Worth. Do consider it, Helena. I believe Mr. Malik and his cousin, Mira, are worth the investment.*
>
> *As for me, I shall be content here for a while. Write to me when you can and I shall do the same. Until then, I remain your friend and most obedient servant,*
>
> *Jenny*

"Well?" Justin's deep voice startled Tom from his reverie. "What did Miss Holloway write that has you looking so miserable?"

Tom scowled up at him. "Aren't you needed inside?"

"Not immediately. Helena will want some time alone with her brother, and he with her." Justin descended the steps.

"Come down to the stables with me. With any luck, we can roust out Neville."

Tom folded the letter and slipped it into an inner pocket of his coat as he walked alongside Justin down the drive. It curved in a gradually winding slope, leading down past the cliffs.

"Do you wish to talk about it?" Justin asked.

"Not particularly."

"No? You've spent three months traveling with Miss Holloway. Three months alone. Have you nothing to say for yourself on that score?"

"The servants were with us."

"The Indian servants you described in that first letter you wrote to me? I recognize a fig leaf of decorum when I see it."

"I'm in love with her."

"Obviously." Justin cast him a glance. "What are you going to do about it?"

"Nothing."

"That doesn't sound like the Tom Finchley I know."

Tom sighed. "She needs time on her own. A lifetime, possibly. There's nothing I can do about it."

"So...you're just going to give up."

"You don't understand."

"Perhaps I might if you explained it."

"What difference does it make? There's nothing to gain by talking about it. It will only make it worse. I'd as soon forget it than review it again."

"I don't suppose this means you're abandoning that other matter as well? If so, you should know that I've already sent Mr. Treadway to Dorset."

"Your inquiry agent?" Tom had almost forgotten about the man.

"Your inquiry agent now," Justin said. "I wish you better luck of him."

Tom thrust his hands into his pockets. "I'm not concerned with Treadway at the moment." The cold sea air nipped at his face, whipping at his frock coat and rumpling his hair. He took a deep breath. "There is, however, something else I'd like to discuss with you. Something to do with our time in the orphanage."

Justin gave him an alert look. "What about it?"

"Perhaps we should find Neville? He'll want to hear it, too."

"That bad, is it?" Justin's lips compressed. "Very well."

The stone stable block stood ahead. Tom followed Justin inside. It was snug and sweet-smelling, the fragrance of fresh hay, oiled leather, and well-groomed horses permeating the air.

Justin called out to Neville.

"Here, Justin!" Neville's blond head popped up over the side of one of the loose boxes.

During their time in the orphanage, he'd always been considered a good-looking boy, and he'd grown into an equally well-favored man. He was lean and fit—and as muscular as a bull. But though he outstripped Justin by at least an inch in height and a stone in weight, Neville was no brute. He was a gentle man in every sense of the word. Gentler still after his childhood fall from the cliffs. Now he preferred the company of animals to that of people, often spending time in the stables or down at the beach with Thornhill's two mastiffs, Paul and Jonesy.

His face lit up at the sight of Tom. "Tom! Have you come to stay?"

"No. I'm only here for a short visit. Will you come out a moment? There's something I'd like to tell the both of you. Something I should have confessed long ago."

Neville opened the door of the loose box. Paul and Jonesy ran out ahead of him, first barking at Tom and then galloping to their master.

Justin crouched briefly to pet the two hulking black beasts. "You're making me uneasy, Tom."

"That's not my intention." Though it might as well have been. Revelations from the past were never easy to deal with. But Jenny had been right. Tom had borne the burden alone for too long. It was past time he shared it.

Neville dusted off his linen shirt and coarse woolen trousers. "What is it, Tom?"

"It's about Alex Archer."

Justin's expression froze. So did Neville's. They both stared at him, waiting for him to explain himself.

Tom didn't hesitate. As clearly and succinctly as possible, he told them about the day he and Alex had found the treasure. About how Alex had beaten him and broken his nose. And about how Alex had absconded with the treasure some days later, disappearing from Devon, and from all of their lives, forever.

As Tom spoke, Justin paced to the loose box and back again, his large frame taut as a coiled spring. "I've thought him dead these many years," he said at last. "Why the hell didn't you say something?"

"Would it have made any difference?"

"Probably not. But I'd rather have known about it all the same." He raked his fingers through his hair in frustration.

"Damnation, Tom. I thought it was Cheevers who broke your nose."

"Does this mean Alex is alive?" Neville asked.

"I haven't any idea. There were times I thought to look for him, but if he prefers to cut off contact with us, who am I to—"

"You assume it's his choice," Justin said.

Tom gave him a dry look. "What else am I to think? It was always in his nature to be selfish. You know it as well as I do. I'll wager he took that money and ran as far from Abbot's Holcombe as it would take him."

Justin gave a sudden bark of laughter. "Good for him. At least one of us got away unscathed."

Neville's hands tightened on the door of the loose box. His knuckles went white. "Someone was hurting him."

Tom's gaze jerked to his. "*What?*"

"A man at the apothecary's shop. A friend of Mr. Crenshaw."

Justin crossed the stable floor to Neville. "He told you this?" Neville nodded.

A wave of nausea rose up in Tom's stomach. In the months preceding his disappearance, Alex had been appriticed to old Mr. Crenshaw, the Abbot's Holcombe apothecarist. It had been a poor fit from the beginning. But Tom had never thought—had never considered… "Who?" he demanded. "Do you have a name?"

"He didn't say. It was…afterward. He came to my bed and said goodbye. He said he was sorry."

Justin uttered a vicious curse. It was enough to make Neville wince. "Neither of you thought to tell me any of this? I might have done something. Looked for him or—"

"It was *afterward*," Neville said again, a sharp note of insistence in his voice. "I thought it was a dream."

"Afterward," Tom repeated. "You mean after your accident." He gave Neville a fleeting smile of understanding. "Of course you thought it was a dream. Perfectly logical. You were out of your head for a while."

Justin's shoulders sagged. "What a bloody mess."

Neville's face was pale, his hands still clenched on the loose box door. "Are you angry, Justin?"

"Not at you. At myself. I should have realized—"

"How could you?" Tom wondered. "You're not omniscient, Justin. Besides, when it came down to it, you were a boy, no different from any other Parish orphan. We none of us were equipped to handle what happened at that place. It's not a matter of being strong or smart or knowing everything about everything. We had no power. No real power, anyway."

"We have it now," Justin said quietly.

Tom met his eyes. An unspoken understanding passed between them. It was true: Justin Thornhill had been an orphan boy just like the rest of them. He had also been their fearless leader. "What would you like me to do?"

"Find him," Justin said.

Neville nodded. "Find him, Tom."

Tom exhaled. "Well. Having just unearthed a missing earl, how difficult can it be to locate one larcenous former orphan?"

Very difficult, he suspected.

And probably impossible.

Tom arrived back in London the following day. There hadn't been any point in lingering at Greyfriar's Abbey. He was in no mood for festivities, and after speaking with Justin and Neville, it was plain that Tom would be of more use to them at his offices than if he remained in Devon halfheartedly celebrating the Earl of Castleton's return to the bosom of his family.

After depositing his luggage at his rooms, he hailed a hansom to take him to Fleet Street. As he climbed the steps to the front door of his office, he saw a light flickering in the second-floor window.

What the devil?

It was Sunday. Keane would be at church with his family, as was his habit. Keane's clerk was, presumably, occupied in a similar manner. No one else had a key—not even the elderly charwoman who cleaned for them.

Tom unlocked the door and entered, bounding up the stairs to his office to find...

Josiah Fothergill hunched over his desk.

"Ah, Finchley. You've returned at last. Have a look at the wording I've used here and tell me what you think of it." Fothergill extended a paper to Tom, the ink on it still glistening wet.

Tom took it carefully between his gloved fingers. "What are you doing here?"

"Your job. Precisely what it is you should be doing—and *would* be doing had you not followed some auburn-haired female all the way to India. You haven't married the girl, have you? But of course you haven't. If you had, you wouldn't be here of a Sunday morning."

"There's no need for you to be here, either. I have no open cases at the moment."

"No?" Fothergill motioned to the paper. "Read the third paragraph, if you please."

Tom skimmed it. When he'd finished, his gaze jolted back to Fothergill's face. "What is this?"

"Viscount Atwater called on me in Belgrave Square last week. It seems there's some difficulty with the terms he agreed to with the Earl of Warren."

Tom sank down into a chair. Probably the very same chair Jenny had sat in when she called on him in February. It felt like a lifetime ago. "He wants to renegotiate a contract they've both already signed?"

"He wants you to have a talk with Warren. To see if you can convince him to come to more favorable terms. If anyone can do it, you can, my boy. It's past time you resumed your work. I didn't invest all of my knowledge in you so you could shirk your duties whenever a handsome woman chances to flit by."

Tom ignored the barb. "This case is settled. If it hadn't been, I'd never have left London."

"I believed it so as well. But you know Atwater. He's a gentleman of many moods."

"His moods have no bearing on the legal force of that contract."

"The contract notwithstanding, there remain several actions you might take to reshape the outcome of the case to his satisfaction."

Tom was familiar with the sort of actions Fothergill was referencing. He wanted him to apply pressure on Warren, just as Tom had done before. To make every other aspect of Warren's life a legal nightmare until such time as he capitulated to Atwater's demands. "Undoubtedly, but I have no desire to re-litigate the matter."

"Your desire is of little concern. It's your client who—"

"Atwater will never be satisfied. I've long begun to think it isn't the land he wants, but Warren's complete destruction."

Fothergill regarded Tom with an enigmatic stare. His face had grown more cadaver-like in the past three months. He must have lost two stone at least. A reasonable man in his position would have taken to his bed. But Fothergill had never been reasonable—not when it came to his practice.

"It won't be at my hand," Tom said. "Not the destruction of Warren. Not the destruction of anyone who doesn't deserve it."

"You presume to know who deserves what and when?"

"No. But I have a mind to direct my talents to worthier clients—and to setting right injustices more grievous than the bad blood between two aging noblemen intent on getting the better of each other."

"Few in the legal profession have the luxury of representing worthy clients and those who do are invariably underpaid—or not paid at all. Is this really the course you'd choose for yourself, Finchley? I can't think it advisable. Especially not if you intend to marry and start a family."

An image of Jenny Holloway smiling up at him in the clearing on Senchal Ridge sprang fully formed into Tom's mind. His chest tightened on a rush of bitter anguish. "I have no plans to marry, as I'm sure you're well aware."

"Hmm. And what about your natural mother? The shrill female who makes so many demands on your purse."

"What about her?"

"She's called here twice in your absence. Once inflicting herself on poor Keane. And the second time…inflicting herself on me."

Tom's eyes narrowed. "What did you say to her?"

"I sent her off, naturally, in terms she could understand." Fothergill paused before adding, "You're too softhearted with women, my boy."

"She's not just any woman."

"No, indeed." Fothergill set down his quill pen and leaned back in his chair. "She's the low creature who abandoned you as an infant. Who left you in the custody of individuals even lower than herself. As I understand it, she won't stoop to acknowledge you, though she certainly has no qualms about accepting your money. Is this the sort of woman to whom you owe filial loyalty?"

"She's my mother."

"And so you're content to let her get the better of you?"

"Myra Culpepper has never gotten the better of me." Tom's voice was cold. "I know her for exactly who and what she is. What I feel for isn't filial loyalty. It's pity."

"Pity?"

"Tempered by compassion."

"Because you're her son."

"No." Tom was rather amazed Fothergill didn't understand. "I've never been her son. I've been yours. But no longer. Not if it means I must constantly prove myself to you by destroying anyone who stands at odds to one of our clients."

Fothergill's lips thinned. He shuffled the stack of papers on the desk and screwed the cap back on the inkwell. "You have nothing more to prove to me. If you wish to marry your Miss Holloway—"

"It's not about her. It's about my conscience."

"A costly thing, a conscience."

"Perhaps it is," Tom said. "But I've lately found that I can no longer do without one."

Chapter Twenty-Seven

Cairo, Egypt
July, 1860

Jenny stood, as still as a statue, atop the low footstool in her parlor as Ahmad knelt at her feet, pinning the hem of her new riding habit. It was one of his latest creations. An elegantly tailored costume of deep green with an exceedingly tight bodice, close-fitting sleeves, and skirts that spilled down in a sweeping fall of brilliantly cut fabric.

"I thought your skill only ran to fashionable dresses," she said. "But it's the riding habits on which you truly excel. I don't know how you manage to make them look so flattering."

Ahmad glanced up at her. "When I was a boy in Delhi, I was apprenticed to a tailor."

"Making men's clothing?"

"Cutting and sewing the patterns for coats, vests, and trousers. A lady's habit isn't so different."

She admired the velvet cuffs at her wrists. They were complemented by a matching velvet collar. "Lady Helena claims that the best women's riding costumes in London are made by gentlemen tailors. Though I can't say I've ever noticed the difference. Until today, one habit looked very much like another to me."

"If I made riding habits for the ladies of London, everyone would notice them."

Jenny laughed. "No one could accuse you of having false modesty, could they?" She smoothed a hand over her fitted bodice. "Nor why should you? You've a rare talent, Ahmad. Between you and Mira, I suspect I may be well on my way to becoming one of the best-dressed ladies in Cairo."

Ahmad only smiled as he continued his work. When it came to dressmaking, he was incredibly single-minded.

She gazed out the window into her courtyard. The limestone house she'd taken on lease was located near Esbekiya Gardens, in the modern part of the city, where most Europeans tended to dwell. Staffed with a cook, housekeeper, and groundskeeper, it had been one of the houses Tom recommended to her on his last night in Egypt.

Jenny liked to imagine him walking through the rooms, his blue eyes drifting over the carpets and furnishings as he scribbled particulars in his notebook.

She imagined Tom rather too much, truth be told.

After he'd gone, she'd spent nearly two days in bed at Shepheard's Hotel, burying her face in her pillow to hide the sounds of her weeping from Mira. It had taken a herculean effort to haul herself out of bed, to bathe and dress and begin her life.

And it wasn't a bad life. Far from it. She'd made friends in Cairo, both of the Cairene women and the Europeans. She volunteered at the local native hospital and school. She was even learning to drive a donkey cart.

It was independence of a kind she'd never had before.

After a month in residence, she felt more herself—more certain of what she was capable of.

It was only during moments alone that her mind settled on Tom. Memories of him and the time they'd spent together punctuated her days. She missed him dreadfully. It was an ache that never fully went away. She often longed to ask his advice. And many a regretful moment passed when she wished she could turn to him and share the joy she felt, whether at seeing an antiquity in the museum or even at finding some particularly interesting trinket in the bazaar.

Sometimes at night, she lay awake in her room, wondering where he was and what he was doing. Wondering if he'd forgotten her.

He hadn't written yet. Not a single letter.

As for herself, she'd put pen to paper at least a dozen times, but on each occasion, after writing no more than a few sentences, the memory of their last meeting had stopped her.

Perhaps we should give it some time, he'd said.

Time for him to recover from the hurt she'd given him.

Or time for him to forget her and find someone else.

"I'm finished." Ahmad's voice wrenched Jenny from her thoughts.

Her gaze dropped to his. "Already? That didn't take long."

"It's only the hem."

"And the sleeves and waist and bodice." She was marked all over with chalk and fairly riddled with pins. "Do you suppose it will be ready in time?"

"For your visit to the pyramids next week? Yes. For your driving lesson today? No." He got to his feet. "Mira will work on the skirts this afternoon while I finish the jacket."

Jenny clasped Ahmad's hand for balance as she stepped off of the footstool.

Moments later, Mira joined Jenny in her bedroom to assist her in removing the needle-ridden garments.

Mira's health had improved greatly since they'd settled in Cairo. Jenny had seen that she got enough rest and never pushed herself too hard. It was enough for her to occupy herself with her little sewing projects—trimming out the gowns that Ahmad made or helping to alter the seams and hemlines.

"It's much warmer today," Jenny said as Mira helped her into a day dress. "I wonder if Abdullah wouldn't prefer to give me my driving lesson earlier?"

"Shall I go and ask him, madam?"

"No, indeed. I'll dash off a note and have one of the boys take it round. Is Karim in the kitchen?" The cook's young son was forever hovering about begging sweets from his mother.

"I'll fetch him." Mira exited with the habit over her arm, shutting the door behind her.

Jenny sat down at the little inlaid writing desk in the corner and pulled out a slip of paper. The silver nib she used on her quill was usually kept in the same deep drawer. She reached inside, searching for it amongst the notecards, gum sealing wafers, and half-empty bottles of ink.

"Drat," she muttered. Why was it that the thing one was looking for was never where it was supposed to be? She stretched her arm further to the back of the drawer, feeling about with her hand.

Her fingers closed around a small wooden box.

And her heart stopped. Indeed, for one aching moment, she couldn't quite catch her breath.

She knew what it was. There was no reason to torment herself. No reason to take it out of the drawer and look at it. If she had any sense, she'd leave it alone.

But she couldn't leave it alone. Couldn't prevent herself from drawing out the box, opening the lid, and staring at the diamond engagement ring Tom had given her.

Her throat closed on a swell of emotion.

That night in her hotel room at Shepheard's, he hadn't proposed marriage. He hadn't proposed anything. But he'd left the ring when he'd gone. She'd only realized it later when she'd finally finished crying.

Had it been a mere oversight? Or had he meant something by it?

Jenny had no idea. All she knew was that a gentleman didn't give a lady such an item on a whim. He gave it to her because he had feelings for her. And because he hoped that someday she might reciprocate those feelings and consent to be his wife.

Was that what Tom had intended?

After six weeks with not a single letter from him, Jenny had cause to doubt it.

Upon moving into her new house, she'd placed the ring in her writing desk drawer and tried to forget about it. Perhaps she had for a while. And yet, seeing it now, it seemed the most heartless thing to hide it away. As if it were a rejection of Tom and the tender feelings he'd had for her.

But what else was she to do? She couldn't wear it. They weren't engaged. She had no right. And putting it on her finger, even if only for a second to see if it fit, would have far too much meaning.

Jenny touched the fine gold chain at her throat. Images of her mother's medallion danced at the edges of her memory, her stomach trembling with the familiar feeling of nausea.

She wouldn't forget what it felt like to be powerless. And she'd never lose sight of how important it was to maintain her independence.

But love was important, too.

Tom was important.

She unfastened the clasp of her necklace. It slid from her neck, pooling into her hand in a heap of Venetian gold. Her eyes fixed on it for a moment.

And then, with surprisingly steady fingers, she threaded Tom's ring onto the chain.

When she'd finished, she once again fastened it round her neck. The ring dropped to fall in the hollow of her bosom, a light but significant weight hidden beneath her bodice.

It was enough for now.

If there was one thing Jenny disliked about Ahmad and Mira's sartorial creations, it was the unforgiving nature of their silhouettes. A corset cinched within an inch of its life wasn't at all conducive to riding sidesaddle on a donkey as one trotted across the Egyptian desert.

She'd said as much to Ahmad this morning after Mira had helped her into her new riding habit.

In answer, Ahmad had turned Jenny toward the pier glass in her room. "Look at yourself," he'd commanded.

She'd looked. And she'd continued looking for a good long while.

Jenny slowed her donkey to a walk, squinting her eyes against the blazing sun. She didn't think herself a vain woman, but when wearing the riding costume Ahmad designed for her, she wasn't far from believing herself the most fashionable—and beautiful—woman in existence.

"Nearly two months in Egypt and you haven't seen the pyramids?" Mrs. Clancy brought her donkey alongside Jenny's. "I can't understand it."

Jenny smiled. Mrs. Clancy was one of her closest friends in Cairo. A half-Egyptian lady married to a retired British soldier, she lived in the house next door and from the first had taken Jenny under her wing. "I've seen them, of course," Jenny said. The pyramids were visible from several places in the city. "But I haven't visited them."

"Why ever not?"

"There's been no time."

"You spend too many hours at that school."

Jenny shrugged a shoulder. "I enjoy the company of the children."

"If you fancy children, you must have some of your own." Mrs. Clancy's donkey pranced beneath her. "But first we must find you a husband."

Jenny's smile faded. All her married women friends in Cairo were keen to play matchmaker. "No, thank you. I'm quite content on my own."

"Hmm." Mrs. Clancy didn't look convinced.

Ahead, Mr. Clancy waved his arm back and forth to get their attention. The guide they'd hired for the day to take them to Giza rode along at his side. The remaining servants trailed behind Jenny and Mrs. Clancy.

The pyramids were only ten miles from Cairo. To reach them, they and their donkeys had had to cross the Nile by ferryboat—a journey of half an hour. Six miles more, trotting through small villages and across several ploughed fields, brought them to the desert. There, a horde of Bedouins accosted them, offering their services as guides and attendants.

Their own guide hired several of them to accompany them the remaining two miles to the pyramids.

"Shall we gallop?" Mrs. Clancy didn't wait for Jenny's answer before urging her donkey forward.

Jenny gave her own donkey its head. The rotund little fellow stretched out his neck, his hooves pounding over the sand.

Their party finally stopped in the shadow of the Sphinx. Jenny saw it up close for the first time, looming ahead, more magnificent than anything she'd ever beheld. A servant appeared at her side to assist her down from her donkey. She stood on the sand, gazing upward in awe at the enormous limestone statue, as the Clancys, their servants, and the hired Bedouins milled about her.

After a long moment, she fumbled for her reticule, withdrawing her battered *Bradshaw's*. She flipped through the dog-eared pages. Marseilles, Malta, Alexandria, and Suez. Calcutta, Allahabad, Delhi, and Jhansi. And in the back, the page folded carefully, the section on Darjeeling. Everywhere she'd visited with Tom on her grand adventure. Each city marked with little notes made in smudged ink.

Elephant, she'd written on the Allahabad page. And on the page about Darjeeling: *the hill of mist and fog.*

Jenny numbly turned to the section on the pyramids of Giza, her eyes drifting over the paragraph on the Sphinx, but her heart was no longer in it.

Perhaps this was why she hadn't been able to bring herself to visit any monuments since her arrival in Cairo. She'd stayed within the bounds of the city, her activities far more domestic than adventurous.

Because what were adventures without Tom?

Jenny wasn't immune from the wonder that lay before her. The Sphinx was beautiful and majestic. The pyramids were breathtaking. But she had no one special to share them with. No one who belonged only to her and to whom she belonged in return.

She was alone.

It was what she'd always wanted. To be free and independent, accountable to no one but herself. And she was all of those things now, as much as any woman. Free to go where she wanted and do what she wanted. Free to live in the manner of her own choosing.

But Tom wasn't here. He was gone, possibly forever.

And she loved him.

She loved him.

Chapter Twenty-Eight

North Devon, England
August, 1860

Greyfriar's Abbey had a strip of private beach below the cliffs, only accessible by a steep—and rather treacherous—footpath. During his brief stay, Tom had taken to walking there alone. Well, not entirely alone. Justin's dogs, Paul and Jonesy, usually insisted on accompanying him. Their intermittent barks were the only sound outside the roar of the wind and the sea and the screech of circling seagulls.

A lead on Alex Archer had brought Tom back to Devon three days ago. He had anticipated learning something new. Instead, he'd found himself right back where he started.

Finding his former friend was proving to be more difficult than Tom had imagined. Wherever Alex had gone after he broke his apprenticeship, he'd somehow managed to cover his tracks with extraordinary efficiency. He'd simply vanished, leaving behind no trace of himself at all. As if he'd never existed in the first place.

For all Tom had been able to discover, he might as well not have.

There were no orphanage records any longer. No one alive outside of Justin, Neville, and Boothroyd who seemed to remember him.

Even Tom, with his better-than-average memory, wasn't certain whether he could accurately recall what Alex looked like anymore. He'd been tall, like Justin, with raven-black hair. As for his face...would Tom recognize it if he ever saw it again?

He thrust his hands into the pockets of his trousers as he strolled farther down the beach. The wind off of the sea rustled his hair. He was in his shirtsleeves, his black cravat loosened at his neck. Ahead of him, Paul and Jonesy frolicked in the sand, running and jumping at each other as they tussled over a large stick.

The cliffs of Abbot's Holcombe loomed in the distance. As a boy, this had been the extent of his world. From the orphanage and down the coast to Greyfriar's Abbey. He'd wanted nothing more than to have control of that world. To be safe from the whims of fate and the cruelties of men.

His world was bigger now. It stretched across London. Across England. Wherever he went within its boundaries, he could navigate with confidence and authority. It was a variety of power, he supposed, to have such control over one's surroundings.

It was something he hadn't had when he'd been traveling with Jenny.

Had keeping that control meant more to him than she had?

You don't have to go away tomorrow, she'd said. *You could stay here a little while longer.*

But he hadn't stayed. He'd left her there.

Tom rubbed the back of his neck, muttering an oath at his own stupidity.

She was safe, at least. He still had charge of her accounts. And Ahmad sent the occasional wire. According to him, Jenny was settled and happy. She wasn't in any danger. And she certainly wasn't fading away of unrequited love.

Tom wished he could say the same for himself.

Ahead of him, Jonesy sprang to attention. He dropped his stick, raising his great black head to look up at the cliffs beneath the Abbey. And then he gave an enormous baying bark, the likes of which would have done a bloodhound proud. Paul soon joined in the cacophony, the pair of them charging across the beach.

Tom turned to look after them, his face to the sun.

Justin and Lady Helena were gone for the day. Tom hadn't expected them back until dinner.

But it wasn't Justin or Lady Helena. It was someone else. A lady, making her way down the cliff path, her voluminous skirts clutched in her hands.

It was Jenny.

Tom's mouth went dry. For the barest instant, he lost the capability of rational thought. He could only stand there, frozen, as if he'd seen a ghost.

The next thing he knew, he was moving toward her, crossing the distance between them in long, purposeful strides.

She hopped down from the cliff path, brushing off her black jacket bodice and giving her skirts a shake. She looked poised and elegant, her skin golden from the sun. "Good morning."

Tom came to a stop in front of her. The beat of his heart was an agony. He couldn't think for how hard it was pounding. "Good morning."

A smile tugged at the corners of her mouth as she gazed up at him. "You look very well."

He stared down at her. Her thick hair had half-fallen from its pins. Curling tendrils framed her face in a wild auburn tangle.

She was more beautiful than in his memory. More beautiful even than that blasted pencil sketch of her he'd spent so many hours gazing at. Indeed, as she stood before him, she didn't seem quite real. He half expected to feel Neville nudge at his shoulder and tell him to wake up.

But this wasn't a dream.

A dream couldn't have done Jenny justice. Couldn't have created a vision so warm and vibrant and breathtakingly real.

"What are you doing here?" he asked.

"I've come home," she said simply.

His breath stopped. "Have you?"

"For a while. I only arrived in London yesterday. I'd intended to visit you at your office, but Mrs. Jarrow said you were here. She said you had personal business to attend to."

"Ah." Tom belatedly ran a hand over his rumpled hair. He wished he were better prepared to see her. That he'd had time to shave and put on a fresh suit. Not that Jenny seemed to notice. She was looking up at his face, her eyes fixed on his. "I've been searching for Alex Archer," he said. "I told Thornhill and Cross the truth about him. They've asked me to try and find him."

Her mouth curved. "That's wonderful. Have you had any luck?"

"I thought I might have, but it was another dead end. I'd planned to return to London tomorrow."

"Then I'm glad I came today. I wouldn't like to have missed you again."

The wind gusted down the beach, rippling through the sand and stirring the hem of her dark green skirts. Paul and Jonesy trotted off to resume their battle over the stick.

"Where are Helena and Mr. Thornhill?" she asked. "I went up to the Abbey, but Mr. Cross said they'd gone."

"They drove into Abbott's Holcombe with Giles."

Her brows lifted. "Giles is still here?"

"For the moment. He leaves for London at the end of the month. He'd have already gone, but Lady Helena didn't think he was ready to face the full force of society yet, let alone resume his seat in the Lords."

"Is he going to resume his seat?"

"I doubt it. He's still keen on returning to India. He'll likely sail back after the monsoons, sometime in November, I expect."

"I thought he might."

"What about you?" Tom asked. "Have you brought Ahmad and Mira along?"

"I left them in Half Moon Street. They needn't escort me everywhere now I'm in England. Not at my age."

The reference to her aged condition almost made Tom smile. But he didn't feel very much like smiling. His heart was slowly forming into a lead weight in his chest. He hadn't seen her since May. Hadn't kissed her or held her in his arms in months. And here they were, together at last, and talking as politely and civilly as if they were two well-bred strangers.

He'd threatened her with just such a fate on the train to Cairo.

If we ever meet again someday in London or Devon, it shall be as common and indifferent acquaintances.

A petulant thing to have said. Ridiculous, too, because in reality it was impossible to be indifferent to her. Worse than impossible. Indeed, he didn't think he could bear it, being near her and having to pretend that she didn't matter to him.

"Jenny, I——" He broke off. "May I still call you Jenny?"

Her brows knit. "Of course you may. Why shouldn't you?"

"It's been a long while. I didn't like to presume."

"Nearly three months." She folded her arms at her waist and began to walk toward the shoreline. The waves lapped against the sand, covering it in a froth of seafoam. "You never wrote to me."

Tom kept pace at her side. She was close enough that her skirts brushed his legs. Close enough that he could smell the faint fragrance of her perfume. Her warm, feminine presence provoked a storm of emotion within him. "No, I didn't." He paused before admitting, "I wanted to. Rather badly."

"Then why…?"

"You needed time."

"I've had it."

His heart thumped hard. "And?"

"And…here I am."

Tom was silent for a long while. "How long are you staying for?"

"There's a question."

He touched her arm, bringing her to a halt on the wet sand. "Do you have an answer?"

She turned to face him. "Partly. But it isn't complete."

"I don't understand."

"What I mean to say is…what I do next very much depends on you."

He looked at her, unwilling to hope. But hope flickered nonetheless.

Jenny sighed. "I've thought of a hundred things I might say to you since you left me in Cairo. In my imagination, I'm always much more eloquent. But now I'm here…" She gave him a rueful look. "The inadequacy of words."

"You have something you'd like to tell me?" He scarcely recognized the sound of his own voice.

"Yes, though heaven knows I'm going to make a mull of it. You know me, Tom. I'm not comfortable with poetic declarations or grand romantic displays." She took a step toward him. "But if I were…"

Tom's gaze was riveted to hers.

She set both hands on his waistcoat. "If I were…I'd tell you that I can't live without you. I'd say that the mountains of India—even the pyramids of Egypt—are nothing without you by my side. That I'd give it all up to have you back with me. For one moment longer in your arms." Her lips tilted in a faint smile, even as a warm blush swept up her neck and into her face. "That's what I'd say, anyway, if I were a romantic sort of female."

His throat bobbed on a swallow. "What would the unromantic Jenny Holloway say?"

Tears brightened her blue-green eyes. Her voice, when it came, was husky with emotion. "Only that she loves you. And that she's sorry—so dreadfully sorry—that she hurt you."

Jenny waited for Tom to say something. Anything. In truth, he looked rather shaken. Her hands slid up the front of his black woolen waistcoat a fraction of an inch. She felt him inhale an uneven breath.

"I see." He regarded her steadily. His eyes were bluer than she remembered. There was an expression in them that was hard to read. "Does this mean you've changed your mind?"

Her pulse beat a throbbing rhythm at her throat. She suddenly wished she hadn't permitted Mira to lace her corset so tightly this morning. Was it any wonder that fashionable ladies often swooned in situations like these? Between her racing pulse and the rioting butterflies in her stomach, she felt as though she'd soon follow their example.

Had she said too much? Dared too much? She was fraught with sudden uncertainty.

And then, in the loosened folds of his cravat, she saw a glint of sapphire.

Her heart took flight.

"I haven't changed my mind," she said. "Not about you. I've loved you for months."

Heat flared in his gaze. "Have you?"

"Yes," she said. "I believe I fell in love with you on the *Valetta*, somewhere between Marseilles and Malta."

"When you were seasick."

"When you came to my cabin and took such good care of me. I'd never before seen a gentleman fold a pair of stockings." She leaned closer to him, her voice dropping to a whisper. "And I thought…he's perfect. Handsome and intelligent and always capable of doing precisely what's required."

His mouth hitched briefly. "Folding your underthings?"

"And all the rest of it. Kissing me. Listening to me. Being my friend." A rogue tear slipped down her cheek. "My best friend, who I've missed so very much."

Tom raised a hand to gently wipe her face. "I've missed you as well." His voice went gruff. "When I left Cairo, I was in a wretched state."

"I know." More tears spilled.

He brushed them away. "I love you, Jenny. I've loved you since you kissed my cheek on the pier at Dover. These last months without you have been hell. A day hasn't gone by that I haven't wanted to give everything up and go back to you. And I will. If that's what it takes—"

"Don't say such things."

"I mean it. It was wrong of me to leave you there. I should have stayed with you. I should have—"

"You'd have been miserable in Cairo. You're meant to be in London."

"What about you?"

She slid her hands further up his waistcoat. "I'm meant to be with you."

"*Jenny*—"

"I mean it, Tom."

"Before…" He searched her face. "You were so certain that you didn't want to make a life here."

"Yes, well…I've had a great deal of time to consider our situation."

"You've decided that independence isn't as valuable a commodity as you'd originally thought?" His thumb moved gently over the damp curve of her cheek. "My dear girl, forgive my skepticism, but I can't imagine you've changed your mind to that degree—not about something so important to you."

"I haven't. I still want my independence. But I don't believe you'll take it from me."

"I won't. Upon my honor."

She swallowed back another surge of tears. "You were right about my being afraid. I was afraid to trust you. Not because of anything you've done, but because of my father and all the other people who've let me down. I didn't even give us a chance. I sent you away—"

"You weren't the only one who was afraid."

"You?" She blinked. "What did you have to be afraid of?"

"The same things as you, I imagine. Being powerless. Having no control over what happens. Trusting someone you love not to hurt you."

And she had hurt him. The knowledge of it squeezed at her conscience. "I'm so sorry, Tom."

"Hush, love." He smoothed her hair. "You don't have anything to be sorry for. You're here now. That's all that matters to me. The rest we can work on."

"Yes." She took a tremulous breath. "I'm still a little scared to give a man so much power over my life. It would be foolish not to be. But you're not just any man, are you? You're the man I love."

A spasm of emotion crossed over his face.

"Besides," she went on, "it's lately occurred to me that you and I have exhibited an infinite capacity for solving other people's problems. Surely, we can use a fraction of that ingenuity to solve our own. There must be a way we can both have what we want. We've only to set our minds to finding it."

"At this point," Tom said, "all I want is you."

Her fingers tightened on the front of his waistcoat. "That's rather convenient because I feel the precise same way where you're concerned."

Tom bent his head to hers. "Are you sure?"

"Yes." It hadn't been an easy decision. There would be consequences to giving up her freedom. She'd have to adjust. Adapt. But the alternative was no longer an option. A life without Tom would be no life at all. She loved him too much. Needed him too much. "It won't be easy, but…if I have you by my side, I feel I could endure anything."

"You won't have to endure. And you won't have to take it all on faith. There are things that can be done to protect your money. Legal safeguards. I'm still your solicitor. I can draw up documents. Set up a trust. It won't be the same as remaining wholly independent, but it would give you some sense of autonomy."

Her heart swelled. She hadn't thought it was possible to love him more. "And you'd do that for me?"

"Anything it takes," he swore. "If you'll stay with me, I'll make it my life's work to see that you're happy."

"*If*," Jenny repeated. "As though there's any doubt when I've traveled all the way here from Egypt just to see your handsome face."

"It's hardly that."

"Isn't it? To me it's the dearest sight in the whole world."

He stared down into her eyes. His gaze was no longer unreadable. It shone with tenderness and rare vulnerability. "I confess I still can't believe you've come back. I thought you were an apparition standing up there on the path. Something conjured out of my desperate imagination."

"Would you like proof that I'm real? Evidence that I mean it when I say that I love you?"

"Jenny, I—"

"Here, I want to show you something." She took a step back from him to reach inside the neckline of her jacket bodice. After a bit of fumbling, she withdrew the end of her necklace. His diamond ring sparkled there in the sunlight.

Tom went still. "Have you been wearing that this whole time?"

"Since last month. Do you think it too sentimental?"

He touched the ring. "What I think is that it belongs on your finger."

"You must put it on me afterward."

"Afterward?"

She unclasped her necklace and dropped it into his palm. "You did say that we'd done everything backward."

"Ah. So we have." He unthreaded the engagement ring from the chain. "After today, I propose we proceed in a more linear fashion. It will make things easier."

"You *propose*."

Tom smiled. "Yes, that. Forgive the oversight. I suppose I never quite got up the nerve." He took her hand. It trembled slightly in his. "Will you marry me, Jenny?"

"I will. With all my heart."

Tom slipped the ring onto her finger. It caught at her knuckle before sliding snugly into place. "There. A perfect fit."

She held out her hand to admire it. "I don't know how you managed to guess my size with any accuracy."

"Don't you?" His expression softened as he looked at her. "I've memorized everything about you. In the end, I fully expected those memories would be all that I had."

Jenny brought her hand to cradle his cheek. "Because you respected my choice. You were willing to let me go in order to make me happy."

"You make me sound frightfully noble."

"You *were* noble. And I know how much it cost you. I don't think I'll ever forget the way you looked when you left my room that night at Shepheard's. The memory of it has plagued me every day that we've been apart."

"I hope that isn't why you came back."

"What? Guilt, do you mean? No. It was love that brought me back. I don't believe anything else in the world could have persuaded me."

He lowered his forehead to rest against hers. "I do love you, Jenny. More than I've ever loved anyone. It's rather a burden to put on you, being loved so much by a man like me."

"I think I can bear it. The real question is whether you can bear being loved by me. I have it on good authority that I'm a managing female. An eccentric one as well. Our marriage isn't likely to be a pattern card of perfection. Do you suppose you could be happy?"

In answer, Tom bent his head and captured her mouth with his. He kissed her softly, deeply, drawing her close in a fierce embrace.

Jenny brought her arms around his neck, returning his kisses with equal fervor. The waves lapped up around their feet, but she didn't mind it. Tom didn't seem to mind it, either. It was only the sound of Paul and Jonesy's furious barking that finally roused them from their embrace. The two dogs were running up the cliff path back to the house, making the most tremendous racket as they went.

"Well," Jenny said as she caught her breath.

Tom looked down at her, smiling a foolish, lopsided smile. "Well."

"Do you suppose Helena and Mr. Thornhill have returned from the village?"

"They might have done. Would you like to go up and see?"

"Not yet."

"Good." His arms tightened around her. "I'm reluctant to let you go."

"Then don't," she said softly.

He kissed her again. And then again, before lifting his head to look into her eyes. "We'll have to go up eventually. Lady Helena and Thornhill will want to hear our news. No doubt they'll expect us to set a date."

A jolt of alarm brought Jenny back to her senses. "Gracious. I hadn't thought of that. I don't suppose you have a preference?"

"The sooner the better," he said. "I can't be without you any longer. Unless, of course, you'd prefer a large wedding with all of the traditional trimmings—"

"Indeed not. The very idea is enough to put me off my food." She smoothed his waistcoat. "I'd far rather marry at the registrar's office as Mr. Thornhill and Lady Helena did. That way, we needn't wait for weeks on end for the banns to be called."

"An excellent idea. We can return to London for our honeymoon. And then…"

"What?"

He smiled down at her. "The next adventure begins."

An answering smile spread over Jenny's face. "The next adventure." She stood up on the toes of her boots to press another sweet kiss to his lips. "I rather like the sound of that."

$\mathcal{E}$pilogue

London, England
September, 1860

"$\mathcal{I}$ have a wedding gift for you," Tom said.

Jenny's cheek was pillowed on his bare chest, her arm curved round his midsection. She was boneless with exhaustion. "Our wedding was yesterday."

He pressed his lips to her hair. "I know. I meant to give it to you afterward, but we've been rather…distracted."

"Distracted?" A laugh bubbled up in her throat. "That's certainly one way of putting it."

From the moment they'd returned from the registrar's office, they'd been unable to keep their hands off of each other. Kisses in the carriage on the drive to Half Moon Street had led to Tom carrying her over the threshold and—by some miracle—up the stairs to their bedroom.

Jenny had had no mother to tell her what to expect on her wedding night. No elder sister or kindly aunt. But she wasn't wholly ignorant of the marital act.

Even so, she hadn't anticipated that she and Tom's wedding night would commence in the middle of the day. And she hadn't expected to repeat the activity quite so many times, nor with such exciting variation.

Not that she had any complaints.

Tom Finchley was a tender, considerate, and very thorough lover. Even in those moments when he gave himself up to his passions and shuddered in her arms, he always ensured that she was shuddering right along with him.

Jenny hadn't imagined she could feel so close to someone. At once so powerful and so very vulnerable. But she loved him. Trusted him with her whole heart. There was never an instant when she was tempted to hold herself back from expressing it. Nor an instant when she didn't welcome Tom expressing the same.

"Distracted. Deranged. Delirious." His chest rumbled on a husky laugh of his own. "However you choose to describe it."

"I'll have to think of a better word."

"Do that." Tom slowly disentangled himself from her arms. She made a soft sound of protest. "Shall I bring you back a cup of tea?" he asked as he rose from the bed and pulled on his trousers.

"What about my gift?"

"It's still packed away in my luggage." He bent his head and kissed her warmly on the mouth. "I'll be back momentarily Don't move a muscle."

Tom was true to his word. No sooner had she put on her nightgown and sat up in bed, her back propped against a pile of fluffy pillows, than he returned with the tea tray. He set it down on a nearby table.

"What would you like first? Tea or your wedding gift?"

She gave him a look.

Tom grinned. He climbed back in bed to sit next to her. "It's two gifts, really." He put a wrapped package in her lap. "This is the first one."

With all the excitement of a child at Christmas, she swiftly removed the paper and twine. Inside the wrappings was a small lacquer box. She glanced up at Tom in question.

He was watching her intently. "Open it, love."

Something in his gaze put Jenny on her guard. This, she realized, was a gift he'd put a great deal of thought into. Resolving to be thrilled by it no matter what it might be, she lifted the lid and peered inside.

And there, laying atop a bed of velvet, was her mother's emerald medallion.

Her eyes flew to his. "How in the world…?"

"Surprised?"

Tears threatened as memories flooded her mind. But she wasn't going to weep. Not now. This was a moment of joy. "I should say so." She lifted it out of the box. After all these years, the weight of it still felt familiar in her hand. "Good gracious, Tom. How on earth did you find it?"

"Do you really want to know?"

"Of course I do."

"It was Treadway, the inquiry agent Thornhill hired to find Giles. He plainly had no interest in traveling to India, so I had Thornhill send him to Chipping St. Mary instead."

"What?" She blinked up at him. "When?"

"Sometime in April."

"But…we were still abroad in April."

"I know we were. I mentioned the medallion to Thornhill in the letter I posted to him the day we arrived in Calcutta.

After you told me about your father selling it, I knew I had to get it back for you. And since we were already in India to find Giles and since Treadway was doing nothing except making a nuisance of himself, it seemed only logical—"

"Oh, Tom." She embraced him fiercely.

His arms closed around her. "You're pleased, I take it?"

And tears did spring to her eyes then. Not because she was grieved about her mother or her father or the history of the medallion. But because she was grateful. So wonderfully, heart-clenchingly grateful to have married Tom Finchley. To love and be loved by him.

"I'm overjoyed," she said. "Thank you. Thank you. It's the most splendid wedding gift in the world."

Tom held her fast. "You have a second gift," he reminded her. "Not as exciting as the first, I'm afraid."

Jenny drew back from him. In truth, she'd quite forgotten. "You shouldn't have gone to the trouble." And then, with a flash of embarrassment, "I didn't get you anything."

"Nonsense. You're my gift."

A blush warmed her cheeks. "No more than you're mine. Which still puts me woefully in the red as far as gifts are concerned."

"In a moment we shall perform a thorough accounting. Until then…" He placed another wrapped package in her lap. It was larger than the first one. "Open it."

Jenny smiled to herself as she untied the twine. A thorough accounting. That sounded promising. She tore off the paper and pushed it aside.

It was a book. A brand-new copy of *Bradshaw's*.

But not her *Bradshaw's*. Not the *Through Route and Overland Guide to India and Egypt*. This was a different edition.

"*Bradshaw's Illustrated Traveller's Handbook to France*," she read aloud. Her gaze lifted to Tom's. "Are we planning a holiday?"

"Possibly." He paused before explaining, "I've had news about Alex Archer. It's nothing certain. Only the faintest whisper of gossip, but there's reason to believe he might be in France."

"That's wonderful. More than wonderful. But…where in France?"

"As to that, I'm not entirely sure. What it needs is someone to go there. To travel about and ask questions."

Jenny's pulse quickened. "Do you mean us?"

Tom's mouth hitched in a smile. "Why not? It could double as our honeymoon."

She raised her hand to cup his cheek. He hadn't shaved this morning. His jaw was prickly beneath her palm.

There were no words. None she could formulate amidst the emotion building in her chest.

He'd seen what she wanted of life. Independence. Adventure. Love. And he'd given it all to her. There was no way to thank him for it. No way to adequately express how she felt.

So she stretched up and kissed him. Softly, deeply, her lips clinging to his.

One kiss led to another, given and received, until they were both warm and flushed and breathless. "When do we leave?" she asked.

"Soon." Tom eased her back against the pillows. "But not yet."

"No," Jenny agreed. "Not yet."

The End

Research Notes

Where to begin?

The route Jenny and Tom take to get to India is 97 percent accurate, all the way down to the travel times. The *Onyx*, *Valetta*, *Indus*, and *Bentinck* were the actual ships, and the descriptions I gave of their amenities are drawn from historical descriptions of same. Ditto for the names, descriptions, and travel times of trains in France, Egypt, and India. The *dak* cart journey via the *North Western Dak Company* and the bullock train journey in Darjeeling were also accurate, as was the route Jenny takes from Cairo to Giza.

A few random bits of fact: visitors really did chisel pieces off of Cleopatra's Needle in Alexandria; there really was a sinister Khansama in Darjeeling who was reported to have been jailed twice; Senchal really was referred to as the hill of mist and fog; and there really was a convalescent depot there in which some historical reports claim the isolation drove soldiers to suicide.

I could go on, but it may be less time-consuming to focus on the parts that weren't based on fact. In 1860, the year in which *A Modest Independence* is set, there was no direct rail access from Calcutta to Delhi. Instead, travelers would have had to make part of the journey via *dak* cart. I decided to eliminate this obstacle by giving Tom and Jenny a connecting train in Allahabad. In reality, the journey they took across India would have been a lot more painstaking.

Likewise, in a few instances, I featured railway stations in cities in which the station wasn't actually built until later.

Another of my authorial fabrications relates to the mission in Jhansi. Was there a mission there in 1860? I could never verify this to my satisfaction. But missions *did* exist in other cities. The mission I created in Jhansi is based off of research I did on those.

I also made up Mr. Vidyasagar's guest house in Calcutta, the Westbrook Hotel in Delhi (inspired by the Northbrook, which wasn't there until a few years later), and Mr. Bhat's guest house in Jhansi. The other hotels mentioned, such as Shepheard's in Cairo, actually existed.

In addition to my research on travel routes to and across India, I feel I should also note that Mr. Fothergill—and Tom, by extension—was inspired by Mr. Tulkinghorn, the powerful, secretive, and very much feared solicitor in Charles Dickens' *Bleak House*. Specifically, this passage:

> *Mr. Tulkinghorn is not in a common way. He wants no clerks. He is a great reservoir of confidences, not to be so tapped. His clients want HIM; he is all in all.*

Similarly, the decade long case between the Earl of Warren and Viscount Atwater was inspired by *Bleak House*'s Jarndyce and Jarndyce.

Finally, as regards the value of Jenny's modest independence, 5000 pounds in 1860 would equate to nearly 300,000 pounds today. So, not really so modest after all—except to someone as wealthy as Lady Helena.

If you'd like to learn more about the people, places, and events which feature in my novels, please visit the blog portion of my author website at MimiMatthews.com.

And if you'd like to see images of the locations featured in *A Modest Independence*—as well as images of what I imagine the characters to look like—do visit this book's Pinterest board.

Finally, for those of you who want a peek at a *Bradshaw's* guide or would like to have a look at some of the other historical publications I used as research, I've included a partial list of sources at the end of the book.

*A*cknowledgments

*M*y seventeen-year-old Siamese cat Sapphire was with me every moment I wrote the first draft of this story. Often in ill health during the final year of his life, he spent all of his time curled up beside me on a heating pad. On February 1st, the day after I finished the final chapter, he died. His death, though not unsurprising given his age, was a devastating blow. He was with me nearly half my life, through college, law school, work, books, spine surgeries, and house moves. My constant companion in good times and bad. All that to say that, if there is a spirit of love and friendship in any aspect of this story, it came from having Saph in my life. I'm so grateful to have known and loved him.

In addition to Sapphire, I also owe many thanks to all of the humans who helped to bring *A Modest Independence* to life:

To my very patient and sharp-sighted beta readers, Flora, Sarah, Lauren, and Lena; my equally patient and sharp-sighted editor, Deb Nemeth; my cover designer, James Egan; my interior designer, Colleen; to Charlotte for translations; to Adam and Jackie for assistance with Victorian military history; and to my parents for moral support, pet babysitting, and cake.

Last, but certainly not least, I'd like to thank you, my readers. I appreciate your support more than I can express.

About the Author

USA Today bestselling author Mimi Matthews writes both historical non-fiction and traditional historical romances set in Victorian England. Her articles on nineteenth century history have been published on various academic and history sites, including the *Victorian Web* and the *Journal of Victorian Culture,* and are also syndicated weekly at *BUST Magazine*. In her other life, Mimi is an attorney. She resides in California with her family, which includes an Andalusian dressage horse, two Shelties, and a Siamese cat.

To learn more, please visit
www.MimiMatthews.com

OTHER TITLES BY
Mimi Matthews

NON-FICTION

The Pug Who Bit Napoleon
Animal Tales of the 18th and 19th Centuries

A Victorian Lady's Guide to Fashion and Beauty

FICTION

The Lost Letter
A Victorian Romance

The Viscount and the Vicar's Daughter
A Victorian Romance

A Holiday By Gaslight
A Victorian Christmas Novella

The Matrimonial Advertisement
Parish Orphans of Devon, Book 1

Selected Sources

Barber, Captain James. *The Overland Guide-Book*. London: Wm. H. Allen and Co., 1850.

Bengal: Past and Present, Vol. 2. Calcutta: Calcutta General Printing Co., 1908.

Bradshaw's Railway, &c. Through Route and Overland Guide to India, Egypt, and China. London: W. J. Adams, 1861.

"Calcutta." *Household Words, Vol. XVI*. London: Charles Dickens & Evans, 1857.

The Darjeeling Himalayan Railway: Illustrated Guide for Tourists. Calcutta: Messrs. Gillanders, Arbuthnot & Co., 1896.

"Days in North India." *Good Words for 1870*. London: Strahan & Co., 1870.

"Diary of a Journey from Alexandria to Suez." *Sharpe's London Magazine, Vols. I and II*. London: T. B. Sharpe, 1847.

"Egyptian Railways.—The Isthmus Transit." *American Railroad Journal, Vol. XXXVIII*. New York: John H. Schultz, 1865.

"An Englishwoman Among the Himalayas." *Harper's New Monthly Magazine, Vol. LIII.* New York: Harper & Brothers, 1876.

Fane, Henry Edward Hamlyn. *Five Years in India, Vols. I-II.* London: Henry Colburn, 1842.

Firminger, Rev. W. K. *Thacker's Guide to Calcutta.* Calcutta: Thacker, Spink, & Co., 1906.

"A Lady's Railway Journey in India." *Choice Literature: A Monthly Magazine.* New York: John B. Alden, 1884.

Minturn, Robert B., Jr. *From New York to Delhi.* New York: D. Appleton, 1858.

Simms, Frederick Walter. *England to Calcutta, by the Overland Route, in 1845.* London: Harrison and Sons, 1878.

Made in the USA
Middletown, DE
29 January 2020